Treasure
of
Stonewycke

ILLINOIS PRAIBIE DPL

A65500 730303

Books by the Phillips/Pella Writing Team

The Journals of Corrie Belle Hollister

My Father's World
Daughter of Grace
On the Trail of the Truth
A Place in the Sun
Sea to Shining Sea
Into the Long Dark Night
Land of the Brave and the Free

Grayfox (Zack's story)

The Stonewycke Trilogy

The Heather Hills of Stonewycke
Flight from Stonewycke
Lady of Stonewycke

The Stonewycke Legacy

Stranger at Stonewycke
Shadows over Stonewycke
Treasure of Stonewycke

The Highland Collection

Jamie MacLeod: Highland Lass
Robbie Taggart: Highland Sailor

The Russians

The Crown and the Crucible
A House Divided
Travail and Triumph
Heirs of the Motherland

Treasure
of
Stonewycke

Michael Phillips
Judith Pella

ILLINOIS PRAIRIE DISTRICT LIBRARY

110401

BETHANY HOUSE PUBLISHERS
MINNEAPOLIS, MINNESOTA 55438

Cover illustration by Dan Thornberg,
Bethany House Publishers staff artist.

Copyright © 1988
Michael R. Phillips and Judith Pella
All Rights Reserved

Published by Bethany House Publishers
A Division of Bethany Fellowship, Inc.
6820 Auto Club Road, Minneapolis, Minnesota 55438

Printed in the United States of America

Library of Congress Cataloging-in-Publication Data

Phillips, Michael R., 1946–
    Treasure of Stonewycke.

(The Stonewycke legacy ; bk. 3)
    I. Pella, Judith. II. Title.
III. Series: Phillips, Michael R., 1946–   . Stonewycke legacy ; 3.
PS3566.H492T7   1988   813'.54   88–7531
ISBN 0–87123–902–7 (pbk.)

PHI
copy2

Dedication

To those of God's people who are seeking to
impact history and their own posterity, by
building into the generational flow of God's
dealing with man on the earth, according
to Psalm 78:5–7.

"I, the Lord your God, am a jealous God, punishing the sins
of the fathers to the third and fourth generation of those who
hate me, but showing love to a thousand generations. . . .
Know therefore that the Lord your God *is* God; he is the
faithful God, keeping his covenant of love to those who love
him and keep his commands. . . . Tell this to your children,
and let your children tell it to their children, and their children
to the next generation. . . . Let this be written for a future
generation, that a people not yet born may praise the Lord."

—Deuteronomy 5:8, 7:9
Joel 1:3
Psalm 102:18

Fireside

11-17-94 (8.99)

The Authors

The PHILLIPS/PELLA writing team had its beginning in the longstanding friendship of Michael and Judy Phillips with Judith Pella. Michael Phillips, with a number of nonfiction books to his credit, had been writing for several years. During a Bible study at Pella's home he chanced upon a half-completed sheet of paper sticking out of a typewriter. His author's instincts aroused, he inspected it closer, and asked their friend, "Do you write?" A discussion followed, common interests were explored, and it was not long before the Phillips invited Pella to their home for dinner to discuss collaboration on a proposed series of novels. Thus, the best-selling "Stonewycke" books were born, which led in turn to "The Highland Collection."

Judith Pella holds a nursing degree and BA in Social Sciences. Her background as a writer stems from her avid reading and researching in historical, adventure, and geographical venues. Pella, with her two sons, resides in Eureka, California. Michael Phillips, who holds a degree from Humboldt State University and continues his post-graduate studies in history, owns and operates Christian bookstores on the West Coast. He is the editor of the best-selling George MacDonald Classic Reprint Series and is also MacDonald's biographer. The Phillips also live in Eureka with their three sons.

Contents

8

Introduction

From the earliest beginnings of time, God uniquely ordained the family as the primary human organism to transmit His life. The entire structure of ancient Israel was founded upon family. Chief among the commands of Moses to those under his charge was: "Teach these things to your sons and daughters."

The Scriptures make abundantly clear that God's intent when He created the family was that His life be carried down through time, *through the family,* forever—for a thousand generations. Each individual was designed to be nurtured by roots which reached deeply into the soil of the past, giving strength, which then in turn extended into the future.

In Satan's devious cunning, however, he infiltrates and cuts off that umbilical cord of inner life which God implanted within the ongoing and extended family institution. When he is thus allowed to destroy family roots, this many-generational process is undone, and the result is that every successive generation or two, men and women have to discover faith anew. The ongoing vitality and strength of a permanent, life-giving root system is made impotent.

God has given us, however, a responsibility to infuse a heritage into the generations—a heritage involving both the past and the future, a heritage far broader in scope than our own mere lives. God desires permanency from his people, an ongoing fight against Satan's ways, a continual breaking of the chains of evil from the past, even to the third and fourth generation back, and a passing on of the mandate of obedience to God to a thousand generations ahead.

Few apprehend the legacy which has been given us to pass down. We leave the treasure of God's life buried. This parable of Stonewycke is but the universal story which God has been working to infuse within the human chain of generations with every family on the face of the earth. The heritage of God's life within us is a legacy for *all* families, for *all* times.

This is not merely Maggie's story, or Atlanta's, or Joanna's, or Allison's. We *all* must step into it at our own time. Some are born into the bloodline, others (like the fictional Alec and Ian, and the Gentiles of whom Paul speaks) must be grafted in. But the life of God's Spirit moves mightily throughout time, and every man and woman must one day face their *own* place in that life, in that legacy, just as do the characters in the story you are about to read. God takes us where we are—wanderers, orphans, in need of a Father, in search of our true Home—and makes us an integral part of that legacy.

Maggie "became" more than she could have been alone because the stream of God's purpose (of which Stonewycke is a shadow, a type, an illustration) swept over her, drew her into it, and made it *hers*. The legacy is God's life, not Maggie's, but through her obedience was sublimated, and thereby passed on, into future generations.

At every time, in every era, within every human heart, the decision must be faced whether to accept one's place within that legacy. Will we abandon ourselves to God's plan and life for us, or will we ignore the river of the Spirit sweeping over us and let it pass without bringing us up into its inherent life? In every successive generation, every person must face the choices which will determine the impact God's lifeblood will have in his or her own existence, and whether it will move through them into the future, or die. At every turn Satan will try to steal the inheritance which has been given us. Forces will infiltrate our families telling of false priorities, false ambitions, false attitudes which are not God's. But we are commanded and impelled to stand firm, to walk in the calling of the one *true* legacy, and to pass on His heritage to those who come after us in the ongoing flow of generations.

The facts in the story of the Stonewycke Legacy may not be real. But this is a *true* story, in that the truths of God's legacy within His people *are* real. There *is* a treasure, a life, a land, a home, and a heritage that is easy for earthly eyes to lose sight of. As Jesus said, the mysteries of the Kingdom of God are hid, like parables, so that only those with eyes to see and perceive, may truly apprehend them. In so many families, in so many generations, the treasure is buried, hidden, sometimes for centuries. Yet that treasure forms the very strength of God's family, and the ongoing flow of God's life in the world. It is a treasure awaiting discovery by every family, by every man, by every woman, by every child of God in every new generation!

God bless you one and all. It has truly been our joy to experience the life of Stonewycke with you.

Michael Phillips
Judith Pella
% 1707 E St.
Eureka, CA 95501

1 / Mourners

A gray sky hung heavy over the dormant heather. But from the blanket of black umbrellas gathered at the graveyard, it appeared that the misting October drizzle had deterred not a single resident of Port Strathy from bidding their beloved matriarch farewell.

Donald Creary found himself at the front of the throng pressing in around the grave.

He clearly recalled the first time he had laid eyes on Lady Joanna, though he had been but a wee bairn at the time. He'd possessed nerve enough only to steal a glimpse from behind his mother's dress. Yet even then, his childish intuition had sensed she was someone special. She had come with Doc MacNeil to tend his papa's favorite sow. Of course back then she had been only a stranger in town with a foreign sound to her tongue—that was sixty years ago. But young Donald had needed no property deeds or lawyers to tell him that here stood royalty, or close enough to it.

Lady Joanna didn't need to say so either—nor did she. He never knew a humbler soul. The reverence of the Port Strathy folk sprang from deeds, not words. Never had she put on airs, never had she acted the part of head of the region's most important family. Why, her behavior during the Queen Mother's visit fifteen years ago had grown into legend throughout the valley. Joanna had slipped away in the early morning hours while the dear old lady still slept and had driven (herself, with no thought of a chauffeur!) halfway to Culden to take Mrs. Gordon some medicine for her ailing daughter. After helping the widow milk her cow, she had shown back up at the castle just in time for breakfast with mud and who could tell what else all over her frock! The Queen Mother's delight was so great over the story that both women went down into the valley that very afternoon and had tea with Mrs. Gordon in her humble stone cottage.

Memories like that, which were not uncommon, had through the years made Joanna as highly thought of along Scotland's northeastern coast as the Queen Mother herself. Sixty years of selfless love and compassion expressed in her every act of kindness toward the folk of her land had brought out nearly every man, woman, and child in the valley to pay their respects and say their last goodbyes.

The Rev. Macaulay had begun to speak. Donald had to turn his full attention to the voice dulled by the increasing rain and the canopy of umbrellas, not to mention Macaulay's own personal sorrow.

"But I would not have you be ignorant, brethren," he read from First Thessalonians, *"concerning them which are asleep, that ye sorrow not, even as others which have no hope. For if we believe that Jesus died and rose again, even so them also which sleep in Jesus will God bring with him."*

Donald ran a hand over his damp cheek. His tears mingled freely with the Scottish drizzle.

Creary's fond memory of Lady Joanna stemmed not merely from her ministry to Mrs. Gordon, her enthusiasm for helping her husband with his animals, nor the esteem in which she was held at Buckingham Palace. His feelings ran far deeper than that. For it had been Lady Joanna who had helped him get right with the Lord.

The war that had cost him his leg had also left him embittered toward just about everything in life. In the years following he had managed to make things miserable not only for himself but also for his wife and children. Lady Joanna had not failed to visit them every day for months after his homecoming, notwithstanding her own grief after the loss of her son and baby granddaughter. But never an angry word had come out of her mouth toward the so-called fate Donald was so fond of cursing. She had taught him about hope, and gradually led him to a sustaining faith. Because of her, Donald understood Rev. Macaulay's words today.

He stole a glance at the family. Yes, they understood too. He saw the deep grief in their faces. After all, her death had come as a great shock. Four days ago she had been active and vital, hardly showing her eighty-one years. Then, literally, the next day she was gone, suddenly stricken with a cerebral hemorrhage. But despite the sadness in their eyes, he could tell they knew she had passed into a greater life, an even deeper vitality.

"For this we say unto you by the word of the Lord, that we which are alive and remain unto the coming of the Lord shall not prevent them which are asleep."

Donald looked in turn at the faces of Lady Joanna's offspring. All the children had come, just as they had for their father's funeral the year before. No distance would prevent members of this family from saying their final farewells to such loved and revered parents as Lady Joanna and Alec MacNeil.

Lady Margaret MacNeil, now Mrs. Reynolds, had come in yesterday, all the way from her home in Boston. Her brother Ian had been in Greece writing a book when he had been wired the news. He had taken the next plane home.

And of course, there stood Mr. Macintyre and Lady Allison, the undisputed new heiress to Stonewycke now, in the forefront of them all. Donald had to admit that as new overseers of the estate, they would be quite different than Lady Joanna and Doc Alec had been. More cosmopolitan, he supposed, more modern. Doc Alec had remained a country man, notwithstanding that his son-in-law was one of the most influential members of Parliament. And Lady Joanna never lost her simplicity of spirit.

Lady Allison and Mr. Macintyre moved to a faster pace of life. Just last year the Prime Minister himself had come to Stonewycke for a visit! And though Mr. Macintyre's career required that they spend a great deal of time in the south, the sleepy little northern region had become, if not exactly a hub of activity, yet an area well aware of its close links to the centers of power in Britain.

But Lady Allison and Mr. Macintyre were like their predecessors in many ways as well. They loved the land, the people, the heritage, the sense of roots no less than the older folks. That was always clear. They cared, and would do anything for you.

Creary would never forget that night his prize bull had taken sick, and the look of grief in the Doc's eyes when he told him there was nothing he could do. Then, a couple of days later, Donald had been down at the harbor with some of the other men, lamenting the hard times, the lack of money, and he had been especially down on account of his bull. Just then Mr. Macintyre rounded the corner, alone, apparently out for a stroll in Port Strathy, though as usual he was dressed as if he'd only that moment walked out of the Houses of Parliament. He'd approached the small group, greeting each of the men warmly with a shake of the hand and a slap on the back, listening in turn to the tales each had to tell.

But before turning to go back the way he came, he'd unobtrusively handed Donald a small folded envelope which Donald, sensing that it was meant to be private, hastily shoved into his coat pocket.

When Creary was alone an hour later, he sat down, opened the envelope, and read the words: *I hear you'll be needing a new bull, and I always did have an urge to invest in livestock. Buy us the best one you can find and we'll share the profits.* The letter was simply signed *L. M.* Folded up inside the paper were two hundred-pound notes. Donald knew Mr. Macintyre had no more thought of taking half the profits than he would of dismantling Stonewycke. That had merely been his way to insure Donald didn't try to give him back the notes.

Even as one of the former Prime Minister's closest confidants, Mr. Macintyre was still a con man of sorts. There were those in Port Strathy, close friends like Donald Creary and others his generosity had found clever ways to befriend, who saw through the exterior. They knew Logan Macintyre never once forgot he was one of them, never forgot he had started out as nothing more than the estate's mechanic.

In those days he had rubbed elbows with more than a few of the menfolk around the grimy tables at Hamilton's, dealing a pretty fast game of cards. The years might have reformed him in that area, but he always seemed to enjoy mixing with the townspeople, no matter how important he grew in

London society. And he was still not opposed to a con now and then, if by it he could do someone good without making that person feel small.

Yes, it was a different world now—the 1970s! Changes that had been slowly coming for decades had now worked their way fully into the complete fabric of life throughout Britain, from the top to the bottom of the social scale. A nobleman couldn't live off the land anymore, not as an aristocrat whose rents from his tenants kept him living well. Those times were well past. The common man had risen, and now those on top had to struggle to make financial ends meet just like everyone else. No doubt it cost the family a great deal to keep up the old Stonewycke place these days. Doc's veterinary practice and Macintyre's political career were more than mere sidelines. They were necessary to pay the bills. The gentry still played an important role in maintaining tradition, but these men were now just like all the rest of them. They, too, had to work for a living or else go broke trying to maintain an ancient estate that had become a financial albatross.

Creary's eyes strayed to the closed coffin sitting beneath an awning to protect it from the rain.

Life, despite all the changes, had to go on. Lady Joanna never pined for the past, and she had as much cause as anyone. But Lady Joanna understood what was truly important in life. Perhaps that was why her passing was so deeply mourned.

Rev. Macaulay closed the graveside services with the Lord's Prayer. When the last words had died away, the family began to file past the coffin on their way to the waiting cars.

Creary watched a moment, then filed slowly out through the black iron gate with the other silent townspeople. Halfway across the adjacent field he paused to glance back. The rain was coming down more earnestly now. The ancient cemetery with its moss-encrusted gray stones and markers would soon be still once more. As he took in the scene he noticed a stranger pausing beside the coffin.

"Who d'ye suppose that is?" Creary's wife whispered, leaning toward him.

The woman was tall and slim, in her early thirties, and her black cashmere suit was well-tailored and fashionable. Creary couldn't manage a good look at her face, shadowed as it was beneath a floppy-brimmed black hat, but the hair flowing out from under it was the color of a haystack in a field catching the last rays of an amber sunset. It was an unmistakable attribute, even in this dismal weather. She walked with grace and assurance, and you could tell at first glance that she was a woman who knew what she was about. But what could she be doing here? he wondered. He had never seen her before, and he knew every person in Port Strathy.

"I dinna ken," Creary whispered in reply.

"No one o' the family is she?"

"They didna seem to be takin' no notice o' her."

" 'Tis muckle odd," mused Creary's wife.

As they looked, the stranger paused only a moment at the casket and laid on top a lovely red rose she had been carrying. Then, just before walking away in the opposite direction from the family, she appeared to say something. But Creary was too far away to hear.

Indeed, the words she spoke were barely audible, intended for no ears other than those who could hear earthly voices no longer:

"If only I had come sooner. . . ."

2 / Hilary Edwards

Hilary Edwards was the sort who thrived on the activity generated from being part of an organization on the go.

The rhythmic clicking of typewriters beating out their cadence, indifferent to the unbroken ringing of phones and the hum of a dozen different conversations, was to Hilary the one constant of this place. She liked the sound, found it relaxing, as another might the steady breaking of waves on a shore or the unremitting fall of rain upon an attic roof.

Granted, tomorrow was deadline, which made the appealing noises about the place more frantic than usual. If the editors, typesetters, layout and graphics people, and advertising personnel of *The Berkshire Review* were going to loaf, this was not the time for it. Putting out a monthly magazine with a short staff on a thin budget left little time for goldbricking; and if a momentary breath could be inhaled for a couple of days after tomorrow, it would only be succeeded by the immediate renewal of activity brought on by the next month's assignments.

Hilary glanced out the glass walls enclosing her private office and could not resist a smile. She loved the accelerated pace of approaching deadline. It was at just such times that every feature of good journalism had to fit together.

As editor-in-chief, she was proud of her magazine and her staff. This crew in particular was the best she'd had in a long time, and it told—not only in increased circulation, but also in growing acclaim from some of the other literary journals in and about London.

After a brief lapse into such musing, she quickly returned her attention to her typewriter, where the next issue's editorial still reposed half finished.

"East End Redevelopment: Who Really Benefits?" read her caption.

It was a familiar story: old neighborhoods torn down and replaced by high-rise buildings where the rent ended up being three or four times more than the old residents could afford. "It's called 'cleaning up the slums,' " she typed, "but the only ones who *clean up* are the Slum Lords."

Hilary's colleagues had warned her away from the cause. "It's yesterday's news," they insisted. "Who cares anymore—especially among our readership? They want highbrow causes. Who is going to care if a hundred-year-old, rat-infested tenement house is torn down?"

Hilary was not deterred. If they didn't care, then they ought to, and she would make them.

16

So she'd visited the place, taken a room, stayed three days, interviewed people around the neighborhood, and talked to the residents. Certainly *they* cared, even if they were but a handful and hardly the kind of people the rest of the public paid much attention to. Yet these folk, soon to be displaced from their homes, were citizens too—and had a right to be heard. If their representative to Parliament was deaf to their appeals, at least *The Berkshire Review* was not.

After two weeks of investigation, Hilary had uncovered some interesting, even startling facts. Excitedly she'd tackled the story after arriving home from her trip, relishing the discomfort this month's issue of the *Review* was going to cause several highly placed individuals.

The phone on her desk rang. She paused, tucked the receiver under her chin, then returned her fingers to their resting position on the keys of her IBM, as if still hoping—even in the midst of a conversation—that inspiration was suddenly going to strike.

"Hilary Edwards," she said, then paused to listen. "No, I can't come now, Murry," she went on after a moment. "Sure . . . of course I want to see it. But I've got to be over—" She glanced at her watch. "Oh no! I didn't realize it was so late. That press conference starts in fifteen minutes! I have to go. I'm anxious to hear what you've found, but you can update me later."

She hung up the phone, switched off her Selectric, and jumped to her feet. Where had the morning gone? She'd been at the magazine since seven A.M., and had been confident she'd have no problem getting to the interview at Whitehall. But a dozen unexpected things had cropped up. Now she'd barely make it.

As she rushed toward the door, she took a minute to make sure her gray linen suit was in order and that her blue silk blouse was properly tucked in. She quickly freshened her lipstick, gave her nose a powder and her pale amber hair a quick pat. The effect was well spent, but by no means necessary. Hers was the kind of beauty that needed no such assistance. In fact, had she depended too heavily on such devices, she might have detracted from, rather than enhanced, her natural attractiveness.

At thirty-two Hilary Edwards had a fresh, almost girlish look that stood in sharp, though not unpleasant contrast to the high-pressure, cut-throat world of journalism. Well-defined cheekbones, full lips, and luminous blue eyes tended to offset the vulnerability of her pale skin and hair. The combined effect was interesting, occasionally enchanting, and to the unsuspecting, even a bit deceptive. For however girlish her appearance may have been, she had succeeded in her career by her incisive, unrelenting, determined nature. At first glance she may have looked like a college co-ed, but she could hold her own in any company.

From a London working-class family that lived not far from the neighborhood whose cause she now espoused, Hilary was no stranger to hard-fought victories. She attended the university at a time when that ancient, tradition-bound world still belonged primarily to men, working her way through as a waitress, a department store clerk, a governess, and a handful of whatever other menial jobs came along—and managed to graduate near the top of her class.

After that came a string of newspaper jobs, her apprenticeship for what lay ahead. *The Birmingham Guardian, The Manchester Times*, and two obscure London sheets were found on her list of credits when *The London Times* hired her. In that capacity she met Bartholomew Frank, publisher of the flagging *Berkshire Review*. Back then the *Review* had been a scholarly, often stuffy, decent quality but little appreciated magazine, offering high-brow treatises on current events, which drew its limited readership from Britain's intelligentsia.

Frank offered Hilary the position of chief editor and, though the magazine was likely to fold in six months barring a drastic turnaround, she took the job. It was too great a challenge to resist. Neither of them had anything to lose, so Frank gave her *carte blanche*, and she proceeded to revamp the publication. Her inaugural issue showcased an upbeat yet still intelligent style that, while it continued to appeal to the dons and scholars, made a successful bid to capture the interest of a wider range of the public.

She continued to broaden the *Review*'s base, brought in several key people who shared her vision of what the magazine might become, and in a year had doubled the circulation while at the same time fearlessly tackling many controversial topics.

That was five years ago. Today *The Berkshire Review* was making a profit, and she had insured herself a place of respect among her peers.

Hilary grabbed her coat on the way out of her office, then paused at her secretary's desk to leave some last-minute instructions. In three minutes she had descended in the elevator and was outside in the chilly London air of early autumn.

The Strand was particularly busy that noon and it took several minutes to find a cab. She wound up five minutes late for the press conference, but luckily the Members of Parliament who were scheduled as the object of the press's attention had not yet arrived either.

Two or three of her colleagues waved greetings as she took a seat about two-thirds of the way to the front of the crowded room.

"Now we can get started!" one said in a jovial tone, thick with an Irish brogue. "The *real* muscle is here."

"Hardly," laughed Hilary. "The traffic was treacherous. I'm lucky to be here at all," she said, taking a pad and pencil from her purse.

"You'll have to blast the Ministry of Transportation next week, Edwards!"

"Oh, Bert, I'm not that bad," she replied. His only response was a hearty laugh.

Bert O'Malley was a veteran newspaperman with *The Daily Telegraph*. He had won acclaim for his coverage of World War II from the front lines and had been among the vanguard of the press corps at the liberation of Paris. He was tough, boisterous, and generally a nice fellow who smoked cheap cigars and seemed to possess a singular aversion to wearing a properly knotted necktie. Everyone liked him, and Hilary was no exception.

"What do you suppose the Parliament boys are going to pull over on us today?" asked Bert, blowing a puff of cigar smoke in Hilary's face.

She coughed and pointedly fanned the air with her pad. "You mean *try* to pull over on us?" she said.

"That goes without saying, me dear," returned Bert. "No one can put anything over on the press, eh?" He chuckled ironically.

"We had better keep our guard up anyway," said Hilary.

"You're not becoming a cynic, Eddie, me dear!"

"Don't worry, Bert. A cynic distrusts everything and everyone. I reserve my distrust for those most deserving of such scrutiny."

"Do you now?"

"It's been my experience that most cynics find their fulfillment in just being critical. They have nothing to believe in, so they make it their business to tear down everyone else's values and beliefs. To me that's lower than believing a falsehood. Cynicism in and of itself is nothing but emptiness. That's not why I'm in journalism. I do have things I believe in. My motives aren't to tear down, but to get some good things accomplished. At least I hope that's what comes of it. I'm a believer in what I'm doing, Bert."

"Maybe you should be the politician, Eddie!"

"No thanks, I prefer to be just a writer who thinks a little public scrutiny, focused with the aid of the printed page, is the best way to keep our leaders tuned in to the true interests of the people they are supposed to represent."

" 'Power, like a desolating pestilence, pollutes whate'er it touches,' eh, me dear?"

"I wouldn't go that far." She paused thoughtfully. "But let's face it, Bert, too many of our officials have forgotten what it really means to be members of the human race."

"And if anyone can set them straight, it will be you, me girl!"

Bert took two gusty puffs from his cigar, sending a thick cloud of smoke into the air. "Well, let 'em have it, Eddie," he said. "Here they come."

Several expensively dressed men entered from a side door and strode confidently toward the front of the room. As Hilary glanced up, she shifted uncomfortably in her chair, nearly dropping her pad.

"You all right, Eddie?" whispered Bert.

"What?" said Hilary distractedly. "Oh, yes . . . fine. I just didn't expect to see *him* here."

Before Bert could ask what she meant, the room grew quiet and the three new arrivals took seats behind the long front table on which sat microphones and glasses of ice water. All were Labour M.P.'s. John Gelzer and Logan Macintyre represented veteran politicians, both shadow ministers in Harold Wilson's Opposition Labour Party since Wilson's ouster from Number 10 Downing Street by Edward Heath a year earlier. The third man was a relatively new back bencher, Neil Richards.

While they were settling themselves, Hilary quickly thumbed through the notes she had penciled in her pad earlier that morning, an exercise made the more difficult that her hands were suddenly perspiring and cold. Gelzer and Richards had previously agreed to appear before the press following their recent party conference. Macintyre was a new addition, and seeing him unexpectedly walk into the room was the source of Hilary's present discomfort.

She wondered if his presence indicated that the Parliament members thought they were going to need more clout. After all, they represented a current faction arising within Labour that was staunchly bucking the rest of its party's anti-Common Market stance. That summer Heath's Conservative government had launched a blitz of sorts to win the nation's approval for entry into the European Economic Community. Now, in October, Parliament was at last prepared to make the momentous vote.

After some years of vacillation and pressure from the Trade Unions, Wilson was ready to lead his Labour Party in opposing Heath. But there was a solid element in his party, including some influential front benchers, who firmly backed Britain's involvement in the Common Market. A serious split threatened within the party when, during the recent Labour Conference, Wilson and his deputy party leader Roy Jenkins leveled harsh words at one another. Hilary guessed that the three representatives now present, all supporters of the Common Market, were going to try to placate the public, not to mention their leader, Harold Wilson.

Soon a loud hum from an activated microphone filled the room. Richards tapped his mike, nodded toward the sound men, cleared his throat, and spoke.

"I believe we are ready to begin," he said. "Mr. Gelzer will start things off by reading a brief statement."

Gelzer shuffled some papers, straightened his horn-rimmed eye glasses, and then read from one of the sheets in a practiced oratorical tone. He went on for about ten minutes with the usual rhetoric about country, party, and motherhood, closing with a five-minute pitch for the Common Market.

Hilary had to force herself to pay attention, and sighed with relief when he finished. *They would have done much better*, she thought to herself, *to have had Macintyre or even Richards deliver the message*.

The question and answer period proved much more stimulating.

Cauldwell from the *Conservative Daily Express* pressed right to the heart of the issue:

"Can you comment on rumors regarding the possible formation of a new Social Democratic Party?" he asked, pencil ready.

"I can only say," replied Lord Gelzer, "that it is news to me."

"What about reports that Wilson and Jenkins aren't speaking to each other?"

"Surely," sighed Gelzer with great effect, "with so many vital issues before us, there must be more germane topics we can discuss."

Hilary's hand shot up.

"Perhaps you'd like to comment," she called out, "on the fact that the polls still indicate less than half the population favors Great Britain's entry into the EEC."

"You are ignoring the equal number who are in favor of the Common Market," rejoined Gelzer smugly.

Hilary rankled at the glib reply and was about to rebut when Macintyre interceded.

"You are voicing a valid argument, Miss . . . ?"

"Edwards," she replied to his questioning pause. A sudden tight, dry sensation arose in her throat.

"The will of the people, Miss Edwards," he went on, "is vitally important to us. The fact that the percentage you have quoted was substantially lower three months ago is still nothing to hoot about. What do *you* suppose we ought to do when our nation is in such a dilemma?"

He paused, as if expecting her to answer his question. The room was silent.

Hilary returned his gaze for a moment, as if waiting for him to continue. She tried to write off his statement as more rhetoric. But there was a quality in his tone far different from Gelzer's. He was not delivering a pat speech; rather, he seemed to be talking to her as he might if he met her on the street. Still he said nothing.

Finally Hilary shook her head. "I'd rather hear your answer," she said. He smiled.

"I thought you'd never ask," he said lightly, gently dismissing the tension that had begun to build. "And in reality the answer is a simple one—so disarmingly simple that neither the public nor its leaders think of it often enough. When we come upon the horns of a dilemma such as this one, we employ a tactic that perhaps ought to be taken a little more seriously at all times in Parliament—we try honestly to assess what we feel is best for the nation . . . and then we vote our conscience. Hopefully our constituents will pardon us!"

A soft ripple of laughter spread through the room.

Then Macintyre's amused expression turned solemn. "Miss Edwards, I have folks in my district who voted for me simply because they believed I cared. They don't always agree with my politics, but they knew I'd try my best to do right by them. That's how it works in a representative government. Now, here's an issue over which there is a great deal of division. And I personally believe a positive vote, though it means going against my own party's leader, is the best thing for our nation. So I've got to vote for it, because that's what my constituents expect me to do. They don't want a yes man to blindly do their bidding—or the bidding of a party leader. They want a man of principle and conscience. I may not always succeed in that area, nor will I always succeed in pleasing them, but I do always try."

"Is that what you told Mr. Wilson?" asked another reporter.

"Yes, as a matter of fact that is exactly what I told him."

"Is your dismissal from his inner circle, or even from the party, a possibility?"

"Mr. Wilson is a reasonable man," answered Macintyre, "whom I— we all—deeply admire. He understands such principles as loyalty and conscience, and I am confident the Labour Party will rise above our current difficulties."

The grilling went on for another forty-five minutes.

Hilary spent the time listening, for the most part. There were a dozen questions she'd intended to ask, but somehow their urgency diminished. Before she knew it the three members of Parliament were packing up their briefcases and making their exit. She shook the bemused expression from her face in the realization that the session was over.

"Why, Eddie, me dear," said Bert in a tone filled with good-natured taunting, "you disappoint me."

"What did I do?"

" 'Tis what you *didn't* do, me dear!" exclaimed the veteran reporter. "I've come to expect you to go for the throat. But you sat there gentle as a bleedin' lamb!"

"Well, I . . ." she began, trying to make some excuse. She was even faintly disappointed in herself too. But then she realized she had no excuse to make. She wasn't certain about the cause of her docility either.

Hilary bid Bert goodbye and left. There was a less purposeful lilt to her step as she walked out—not exactly hesitant, but definitely thoughtful. Her slower gait seemed to indicate that her thoughts had been diverted, and were now too intense to concern themselves with the triviality of placing one foot in front of the other.

Almost without realizing it she found herself walking to Charing Cross Station. She hadn't intended on taking the tube. Nor had she intended to leave the city. But her feet seemed to know her will better than her mind at the moment. After a couple of transfers, she was soon on a train for Brighton.

3 / Afternoon With a Friend _____

The sky had reflected a hue of autumn gray since morning, but by late afternoon it had turned foreboding. The clouds hung low and the air smelled heavy and ominous with the imminent storm. The dismal pall spreading over the earth somehow suited Hilary's quiet mood, and the air away from the pressures of the city was refreshing—for the moment, at least. Hilary wouldn't want to stay away long. But just now the serene atmosphere of a half-deserted resort town in late fall suited her.

She and her friend Suzanne Heywood strolled along the beachfront, making small talk about the endless rows of two- and three-story houses fronting the shore, poking now and then into a shop whose window had drawn their interest. On their right, a steady stream of waves rushed at the shore, their white-tipped crests offering the only contrast in color between the greenish-gray of the sea and the blackish-gray of the sky. Indeed, where sea and sky met in the distance, the horizon beyond which lay France and the Continent, the green and the black joined in an almost indistinguishable blur of slate.

"This place can be soothing, can't it?" said Hilary, pausing to inhale a breath of the heavy air.

"Sometimes," replied Suzanne. "But not in the summer when it's crawling with tourists."

Hilary laughed.

"That's why I like winters here best," her friend went on. "We great, would-be writers need our peace and quiet, you know."

Hilary smiled but said nothing. That's what she liked about Suzanne— she never took herself too seriously. That was also probably one of the reasons she had sought her out on this day. In Suzanne she had always had a sympathetic ear, someone who understood, someone who would listen.

How can two such different people remain so close? Hilary wondered. They had become friends over ten years ago when both were students at the university. There had been more similarities then, and their affinity did not seem so unusual.

They found their common ground on the field of social and political battle. In the late 1950s they had been at the vanguard of the dawning social awareness that blossomed fully in the next decade. Hilary had been the firebrand, the central figure in every campus debate, the one standing on corners passing out handbills and button-holing passersby to espouse her

23

cause. Suzanne came at protest from another direction. Where Hilary would have been comfortable commanding the troops of their activist band, Suzanne was its poet laureate, the mystic, the esoteric champion of causes more cognitive than practical. If world hunger were at issue, Suzanne would have been more likely to put herself on a starvation diet than join Hilary on a soapbox or march in a rally.

Their different backgrounds had contributed, no doubt, to such divergent approaches. Hilary, from the working class, was bent on changing things in real and visible ways. Suzanne, from a wealthy and affluent family, daughter of a lord, was satisfied to voice her discontent with society using the more abstruse imagery of a poetic and largely quixotic nature. Her most practical act of protest back then had been the disavowal of her noble ties, and with that, her father's money as well.

She had joined Hilary in the latter's stand against the aristocracy, even going so far, for her, as to circulate petitions advocating the dismantling of the ancient tradition. Such a position was short-lived, however, for as Suzanne reached her mid-twenties, she discovered it much easier to take the support her father offered than continue a penniless existence fighting against it. Lord Heywood had long since given up trying to convince her to get her head out of the clouds, and contented himself with providing the means to help her get on with life.

Through the years both young women had changed, and both, curiously, had gravitated toward writing—Hilary attempting to change the world for the better through journalism, Suzanne working on a book-length collection of verse and scattered narrative of vague intent.

But Hilary had learned that Suzanne, for all her flowery flummery about the earth, the sky, Greenpeace, and saving the whales, had a more than decent head on her shoulders. Though Suzanne was still occasionally apt to float in and out between realism and fancy, reminiscent of the months following her pilgrimage to Haight-Ashbury in 1965, Hilary had come to appreciate her depth of sensitivity and her willingness to be still and listen.

Since the death of her father six months ago, Suzanne had been, unknown to Hilary, reflecting on a good many issues more solid and more traditional than either would have thought possible ten years before. The poet in her was at last awakening to see in a new light the world in which she had been raised.

This dreary fall afternoon the burden of talking and listening had been equally divided between the two, but the conversation had focused on lighter topics, mostly filling the gaps since they had last seen each other. Hilary had come to talk with her friend and pour out some of her recent conflicts. But now that she was here, she grew reticent, wondering if she could share her secret even with her best friend.

Hilary paused at one of the shops and nudged Suzanne inside. The Oriental style boutique was clearly attempting to cater to the current fashion craze. Absently Hilary pulled a dress from one of the racks, a coarsely woven sari with an Indian print design.

"Are you thinking of changing your image?" laughed Suzanne.

Hilary gave the dress more cogent attention, then smiled. "It is more you, isn't it?"

Suzanne took the dress and held it up in front of her body. "I rather like it," she said.

Hilary stood back and gave the effect serious scrutiny, musing that she and Suzanne had certainly come toward the mainstream over the years. She had mellowed more obviously than Suzanne, though she defended her acquiescence to the so-called Establishment with the argument that most newspapers were not willing to hire sandal-shod hippies. And through the years she had to admit she had become comfortable with a role she once might have spoken against.

Suzanne, on the other hand, still appeared at a glance to be offbeat in her approach to life. Even at thirty-one, she still bore the progressive look that this dress represented, with straight, long blond hair, often with a flower tucked behind her ear. Her large, intense eyes needed no assistance from makeup to give them depth. She made a point of keeping her exterior self plain, yet such a practice could not hide her lovely features.

"Should I buy it?" asked Suzanne.

"The price is outrageous."

"My contribution to assuaging hunger in India."

"No doubt the profits will just fill the pockets of some fat Indian lord or prince." But even as Hilary spoke the words, she recalled her own current dilemma. The reminder made her all the more unprepared for Suzanne's uncharacteristic response.

"Oh, come on, Hilly," she said as they exited the shop and continued down the walk, "you don't still seriously believe that all the world's ills are because of fat lords and princes?"

"What! Is that you, Suzanne?" exclaimed Hilary. "Standing up for the nobles?"

"Times change," said Suzanne quietly. "I've been thinking a lot lately. You know, post twenties re-evaluation of values and attitudes."

"It sounds serious. What brought all this on?"

"I suppose my father's death. He was a good man, trying to do some good things, and I guess maybe for the first time I'm beginning to see his life and what he stood for in a true light."

"I'm sure your father was very respectable and had admirable qualities," replied Hilary. "But of all people I'd think you would know that the nobility is responsible for so much of what is wrong in the world. That's what we were always fighting for, remember?"

"The environment's getting ripped off and the tuna and seals are being killed just as much in countries where they have no aristocracy at all. The world's problems go deeper than the policies of Parliament."

"But its policies aren't helping matters."

"Politics is a whole different scene. Peace, helping the earth to survive, Hilary, it's an inner thing. When I became a Christian several years ago, nothing much changed. I just kept on with my life as it was. I believed differently, but I didn't live any differently. But as I've grown since then, my outlook has gradually shifted, especially lately. I don't want to blame people like my father anymore for problems we all have a responsibility for."

"Of course, of course. But don't we as Christians have a duty to change society for the better, to bring our values to bear on politics? What can possibly justify how out of touch some of those men are? The House of Lords is hardly a body representative of the people."

"No one ever accused it of being such. That's what the House of Commons is for."

"Hardly a great deal better."

"Give it time, Hilly," Suzanne replied calmly. "Look how far it's come! A hundred years ago women couldn't vote, and there was no such thing as a Labour Party. A woman like you would never have been able to raise herself up so she had a legitimate voice in current affairs. The fact that you do have an impact perhaps speaks for our system rather than against it. There's even talk of a woman Prime Minister someday."

"Interested?" said Hilary. "The way you're going I wouldn't be surprised to see you in the running! I never knew you had such political leanings."

Suzanne laughed. As she did, there was a faint hint in her eyes and in the musical quality of her voice which revealed that perhaps, in her quieter moments, she had given such notions a few fleeting thoughts. But she would admit to nothing.

"You ought to know better than that," she said at length. "Me? I'm the society dropout, don't you know? So my father used to say."

"You don't fool me, Suzanne. You're more in tune than you let on. Why else would you devote so much time to your book?"

"Just poetry, dear."

"Poetry with political undercurrents, if I judge your changing interests correctly. I make an innocent comment about Parliament being out of touch, and you launch into a sermonette about the importance of waiting for change."

"Not a bad solution, in most cases. If a nation or a government is moving in a healthy direction, time usually takes care of many problems without the need for revolt and dissent and bloodshed. The activists like you would raise people to action, while I would rather see people focus on inner realities, and let time heal the wounds of society."

"There you go again, Suzanne! You're impossible," laughed Hilary.

"You are full of contrasts! Ex-hippie lauds praises of Parliamentary system—I can see my next month's article now! But doesn't it bother you that even the House of Commons, even the Labour Party itself, is full of noblemen?"

"I don't have a problem with noblemen. I'm the daughter of one, remember? It's not the system that's bad, just occasionally how we choose to use it."

"But only in rare cases does that system—the House of Commons particularly—ever genuinely represent the man on the street. It's the nobility, I tell you. They've got a lock on everything."

"Always it comes back to the nobility with you," laughed Suzanne good-naturedly. "You've really got a problem with it."

"Not a problem," Hilary shot back defensively. "I just thought I'd find more support from you, that's all."

"Support?" repeated Suzanne inquisitively. "About what?"

"Never mind."

"It's just not that big a deal. There are so many more important battles to fight, Hilly. I wish I could give you a dose of my so-called blue blood so you could see it works just like your own."

Hilary was quiet for a moment. The thought of blue blood running through her veins was not an issue she wanted to face squarely.

"You think I'm prejudiced," she said at length.

"I didn't say that," replied Suzanne. "I simply think you're allowing yourself to see only one side of a very complex question."

Again Hilary did not reply. Then, after a brief silence, she attempted to shake off the melancholy mood that had settled over her. "I underestimated you, Suzanne," she said. "You're no counter-culturalist at all! Underneath the disguise, you're nothing but a political philosopher!"

"You better keep it to yourself. I do have my reputation as a hippie to preserve."

"What would your father think if he heard you now?"

"I've often wondered that."

"I'm sure he would be pleased," said Hilary. "Probably more than I am to hear the words that are coming out of your mouth."

Now it was Suzanne's time to grow introspective. "I often wish I'd begun to think things through sooner. Now that he's gone, it's too late for me to tell him so much I feel."

"You were only doing what you thought best," said Hilary.

"I suppose. But I had such blinders on. All I could see was my own little world. When I moved into that commune in Soho after I got back from San Francisco, I think it really hurt him."

"Didn't he get you out of there?"

"No, he pretty much let me do my own thing. But that scene wasn't for me. Everyone sat around talking about having their own 'space,' writing

ILLINOIS PRAIRIE DISTRICT LIBRARY 110401

weird poetry, singing Hindu songs, and smoking marijuana. They talked about making the earth a different place, but they were all so caught up in their own little private worlds—just as I was. I really did want to make a difference, in my own way, not just sit around and prattle about it while listening to some Maharishi's nonsense. I wanted something I could sink my teeth into, you know?"

"And Carnaby Street?"

"Yeah, my father was involved in that. By then I'd done a flip-flop and came to him asking for the money. And he gave it to me. He'd come to the point where he was content to let my self-expression run its course. Time, you know."

"I never did quite understand why you quit the boutique. It seemed like a good thing."

"In a way, I suppose it was. I made enough money to eat on, trying to convince myself I was being self-supporting and independent from my father. But the Carnaby Street scene was another trip all its own. Just like Soho, only on a different plane. And King's Road. You remember I tried that too?"

"How could I forget!"

"At Carnaby you had all the tourists, and then all the boutique owners trying to be hip and pretend they were marching to the proverbial 'different drummer.' It was so *in* to be weird in '68 and '69. *Sgt. Pepper*, you know— if it seems cool, it must be great. If it looks strange, wear it. If it sounds trippy, like some Tibetan monk may have said it, then embrace it. The little Carnaby Street subculture was in a world of its own, yet all the while chasing after the power of the almighty quid like the bigger businesses round the corner in Piccadilly. No, that wasn't for me either. I've been happy since I moved down to Brighton. I've got my little flat, and I can do my writing without being hassled."

"And carry on the legacy of your father with your budding political and philosophical notions of blending protest with tradition?"

"I suppose so."

"Waiting for the chance to change the world in your own way?"

Suzanne laughed.

"Do I get first peek at the manuscript—exclusive serialization rights for my magazine?"

"When it's ready, you're the first one I'll call. But I know you didn't come all this way to hear me recount my odysseys of the past ten years."

Hilary exhaled a deep sigh. At first she had wanted to talk to Suzanne. At this particular crossroads in her life, she needed the reassuring presence of one who was simply a friend. However, now she wasn't sure they would be able to talk about the things concerning her most without ending up on opposite sides of what was for each an emotionally charged issue.

"It looks as if it's going to rain any minute," she said, as if to steer away from a conversation that had not even begun. "I've got to catch the 5:15 back to London."

"I'm surprised you are here at all," said Suzanne. "Didn't you say tomorrow was your deadline?"

"They can get along without me for a few hours."

Suzanne stopped short and stared with raised eyebrows.

"What's wrong with that?" asked Hilary, defensiveness creeping into her tone.

"It doesn't sound like you."

They continued walking. "Don't worry about the train," said Suzanne. "I'll drive you back."

"You sure?"

"It'll be fun."

"Thanks. A drive through the South Downs is just what I need."

An hour later they passed through the sleepy little village of Arundel and headed north. The drive was unusually quiet. As the silence lingered, there came with it the sense that it was covering up things that needed saying. Suzanne finally ventured to breach it.

"What's troubling you, Hilly?"

"Nothing," replied Hilary, a little too quickly. She knew her answer was too frayed to be sincere. She studied the rolling green countryside out her window for a moment, then sighed.

"It's the same old thing," she said. "You know how we have always fought our country's system of peerage. Well, suddenly it's much more personal to me. The question of the nobility's place in our society is no longer one I can examine from a distance."

"Why's that?"

"I can't tell you—not just now, at least. Maybe it's time for my season of re-evaluation—just like you. But I need more time to sort it all out."

"Sounds serious."

"For me it is."

"You can't have come fifty miles out from town to not talk about it."

"Well . . . I thought I wanted to talk, but I don't anymore," She paused, then added, "I'm sorry. There've been some things on my mind. But it's too complicated . . . and I'm not sure what you'll say now . . . now that you're looking at it from the other side of the fence, so to speak. I know I'm being silly and illogical. I think I just needed to get away from the office, to have a friend beside me."

Again silence descended upon them as the little blue Volkswagen sped its way through the rolling hills and tiny woods which broke up the otherwise open landscape of Sussex. The rain had begun in earnest, and the only sound was the rhythmic thump and swish of the car's windshield wipers.

"Why can't life be simpler, Suzanne?" said Hilary after about five minutes.

"Sometimes it is," she replied, "but the problem is we don't often know what kind of simplicity we want, or need."

"The philosopher again," laughed Hilary.

"Sorry."

"I envy my parents," Hilary went on. "My mother always knew just how her life would be. She spent her youth learning to cook and sew and clean, in preparation for the day she would marry and have children. That was the focus of her whole life—marriage and raising a family. She had no other dreams or expectations. Simple."

"Are you trying to tell me, my dear girl, in your roundabout way, that you're thinking of marriage? Is there a new man in your life, Hilly?"

"No," replied Hilary. "It's just that . . . I've found myself thinking about my own future—not because of a man, but . . . well, what would happen if I met someone, say, who *was* a nobleman. What if, all of a sudden, I found myself on the other side of the fence."

"Is it really so cut and dried, Hilly? I mean, is the division really so sharp?"

"That's what we've been preaching all our lives."

"My father's death has changed my outlook. I spent most of my life rebelling against everything he stood for. Why the dear old man didn't disown me, I'll never know. I deserved it. But he didn't. And now I find that everything that was his is now mine. All these changes have helped me see that he was who he was regardless of his position or title. A *lord* or an *earl* in front of one's name doesn't change intrinsically who a man is, nor does a lady. I thought I'd die the first time someone called me *Lady Heywood* after my father died. But then all at once one day I realized it was the same me. It was only a word, after all."

"So you have no conflict with being a lady?"

"I never trouble myself about it. It never enters my head that I am Lady Heywood. I am who I am, that's all."

"I could never be content as Lady anybody," said Hilary. "My readers trust me to be who I am. I represent something to them. They count on me to speak for the middle classes, for the working people. And whatever readers I have of the so-called elite, they also expect me to address issues that matter in this day and age. To change that, to put a Lady Hilary So-and-So on my byline, would be a sell-out."

"Why all the fuss? Aren't you making much ado about nothing? Or *is* there a man, but you just can't tell me about him? Is that what all this uncertainty is about?"

"No, honestly, it's not a man. Let's just call it an intellectual debate I'm having with myself over the state of our society, and my position in it."

She paused and Suzanne seemed content to let the silence linger. Hilary knew her friend didn't buy her intellectual-debate excuse.

"Why can't people just be themselves, and nothing more?" said Hilary at length, almost as if to herself. "Why couldn't you be just Suzanne Heywood, without the title, without the Lady, without . . . all it represents?"

"But that's what I've been telling you—I am just myself, and nothing more."

"No, Suzanne, there is a difference. I know maybe you don't give much weight to your title. But there are still too many out there who do. I don't care if this is 1971 and some people like you say such things don't matter anymore—they do. There is still segregation in British society, and the line falls right between you and me."

Suzanne chose not to reply further. She knew their friendship was not at stake, and that Hilary's questioning was about something other than that.

Hilary exhaled deeply. "Why do things have to change?" she sighed.

Suzanne's eyebrows arched in surprise. "I thought your goal in life was to change the world."

"The world, yes. Me—no." Hilary hesitated. "I'm not making much sense. Nothing seems to make sense these days."

"Now you're the one running over with philosophical quandaries. But something tells me all you want to do today is pose the questions, not analyze the answers."

"I don't know. You're probably right. I've always been so sure of who I am, what I want out of life. Now everything is muddled. Am I supposed to be a wife or a worker or an aristocrat? Am I supposed to be Hilary Edwards, journalist, daughter of working parents, or . . . something else?" She spoke in a halting voice, then went on after a moment. "How can I be true to my readers when I don't even know what my byline really means? Who I am is important to me, but I don't even know who that is. My mother—" Her voice finally broke and she hid her face in her hands.

"God help me! I don't even know what that means anymore. I don't know—"

She stopped, unable to continue.

Neither spoke for some time.

At last Suzanne said simply, "I'm ready to listen, if it will help."

"I'm not sure I can talk about it yet. It's . . . just too sudden . . . I have to come to terms with it first myself."

"You're not having trouble with your mother, are you?"

An odd look of irony crossed Hilary's face. "If only it were that easy," she said, then fell silent and looked away out the window.

"Well, are you going to make the deadline with that article you were telling me about?" asked Suzanne, trying to lighten the air.

"I don't think I'll even try," replied Hilary. "It will have to wait till next issue." Her lips twisted into an attempt at a smile. "This looks like a perfect evening shaping up for a fire, a pot of tea, and curling up with Lady Hargreave. Tonight I'm going to ignore my typewriter . . . and my thoughts!"

"You're still reading that stuff? What will your professional colleagues think?"

"Sherlock Holmes is now regarded in some circles almost as literature. And Lady Hargreave is every bit as intellectually stimulating. Besides, none of my colleagues are aware of my penchant for murder mysteries."

"I've never read one myself, but they're all the rage down in Brighton."

"You and I should do so well with *our* writing! You really ought to try one, though I suppose a Lady Hargreave mystery hardly fits in with your new avant-garde intellectualism."

Suzanne laughed.

Hilary gazed out at the lush green countryside. The rhythm of the car speeding along the two-lane highway was all too reminiscent of her long train journey of only a week before. If it was not then that her troubles began, that earlier trip had certainly intensified them. She had indeed spoken truly when she said that unexpected change had come upon her, for her world was suddenly upside-down.

Hilary continued to stare blankly out the window at the fields and cottages passing by. Then she drew in a long breath and let it out slowly.

If only she could see what lay beyond the horizon, around the next bend in the road, in the future where she did not know if she dared to go!

4 / A New Era

The tiny dead buds had long since turned brown and begun to fall from the wiry stems which held them. Only a short time earlier these same buds had been the glory of Scotland, crowning its barren hillsides, its mountains, its desolate moors with a majestic robe of royalty. But now, portending the approach of winter, a season which came with unusual fierceness to this rugged northern land, the heather's purple had faded, leaving but tiny husks of death as a memory.

Even on a day when the sun chose to reign over the land in the splendor and warmth of autumn's grandeur, the dying heather spread over the hillsides a solemn coat of unsightly brown. But on a day such as this, when the sun was hidden by an impenetrable blanket of gray stretching for hundreds of miles in all directions, the landscape took on a hopeless complexion of despair.

In the distance, ascending to the crest of a grass-covered knoll, standing out like an island of color amidst the sea of gray-brown dying heather, two middle-aged women walked alone. Just as they reached the top of the small hillock, a chilly gust swept in off the sea, sending the light hair of the one and the dark black hair of the other streaming away from their heads as if to loose it to join the bitter north wind in heralding the end of autumn.

Unconsciously, both women shivered and pulled their coats more tightly about them before starting down the other side. They were seeking a little-used but time-worn trail that would lead them farther away from the North Sea at their backs, inland away from their ancient family home, toward a desolate strip of useless ground. Forgotten now by all but the oldest of the region's natives, the area was known as Braenock Ridge. It was not a pleasant day to stir up memories from the past. But they had put off this encounter, and at last there was no time left. By tomorrow at this time they would again be worlds apart. They had visited their mother's grave one last time together, and now had to arrive at an understanding between them. Both women sensed it, though there were no ready words for the occasion. This was new ground for each. Neither had spoken since leaving the house.

Allison picked at the shriveled sprig of heather in her hand, brushing away the dead fragments of blossom until nothing was left but a slender brown twig. The gray earth, the gray sky, and the dying heather seemed particularly suited to her mood. Her mother was gone, the land was dying, there was no sun, no warmth, no hope, and it seemed as if—after centuries of life— Stonewycke itself was about to breathe its last.

Finally she spoke.

"I'm afraid, May."

Her sister did not reply immediately. She knew her duty for the present was to provide a sensitive listening ear. This was primarily Allison's struggle. May could best serve her by hearing her heart and by understanding her fears. There was no way Lady Margaret MacNeil Reynolds could fully share her elder sister's burden. For tomorrow she would be on a plane back to Boston.

"Everything was so different before Mother died," Allison went on. "I knew someday she would be gone, but I never considered the implications. *Really* considered them, you know—what it would mean . . . to me."

"I understand, dear," said May quietly.

"Oh, May, what am I going to do? Mother's been gone only a week, and already I feel voices from the past calling out to me, loading me with guilt for not measuring up to all the other fabled Stonewycke women. It's 'expected' of me now to assume the mantle, to step into Mother's shoes, just as she did when Lady Margaret died. But, May, I don't know if I can occupy the role all of them did . . . or even if I want to. Times have changed. I've got a life of my own that's not tied to this place. Logan and I are happy in London, and I don't know if—" She stopped.

They walked on. May placed a reassuring hand on Allison's arm. "If it's any consolation, I want you to know that I have no exalted expectations of you. To me you have always been a dear sister, the best sister a woman could wish for. I will love you no less, whatever you decide to do."

"Thank you, May," said Allison, a tear forming in her eye. "You don't know how much that means to me right now. With Mother and Dad gone, and with Ian off to Greece again and Logan called back to London, it really is just you and I. I'd never be able to endure this alone."

Margaret smiled. "But you realize I have to leave tomorrow?"

"I know."

"There are things we have to discuss."

Allison sighed. "I know, May. And I know it rests with me."

"You are the eldest. And you are . . . here. Even London is closer to Stonewycke than either Greece or Boston. Of course Ian and I will support you as best we can, but ultimately—"

"I know, dear May . . . I know. What happens now does have to be my decision. But the thought of leaving the old place desolate, or worse, of letting it out . . . or even selling it! It's just too horrible to think about. Yet Logan and I . . . live in London."

"Have the two of you talked about it?"

"Oh yes. But you know Logan—ever the optimist. He doesn't see what the problem is. 'Lots of people keep two houses up,' he insists. 'Besides,' he says, 'the life of a politician is never secure. You never know when they'll vote you out and you'll need to retreat back to the family farm.' "

"Maybe he's right."

"Logan will never be voted out. The people up here adore him."

"Times change."

"Perhaps. But our home has been in London for so long, I don't know if we'd come back, anyway. Logan and I are city people now—Logan always has been."

"Has any of that changed for you, now that—well, these last several months . . . I mean, now that the past has suddenly turned everything around again for you? Do these recent developments make you think of returning permanently to Scotland?"

"I don't know, May. I had been beginning to feel a security, a peace, as if we might be able to experience some of what we've missed. These last two months have been wonderful—riding again, and I'm learning to paint! Although I must admit the pace seems to be catching up with my years; I haven't been feeling so awfully well lately. Content, but a bit weary."

"I thought you looked a little pale."

"Probably just the strain. Change, even positive change, can be stressful."

"Is there any chance she'd be able to keep the place up after you and Logan return to the city?"

"I don't want to apply pressure—especially not now, not after all we've been through."

"Why don't we postpone a final decision for now, keep the staff on, make sure the castle and grounds are maintained? You and Logan can come up every several months and check on things, and we'll see what happens. That will give you all the chance to see what you want to do now that things are so different."

"I suppose that's the best option, but it sidesteps the real problem— for me, that is. The problem of how I'm supposed to respond to Mother's passing."

May sighed. "I was trying to make it easier for you."

"It's the legacy—that's always been Stonewycke's strength."

May nodded.

"I don't mean to sound like a feminist. And I'm not one either. But we all know that there is something special God has done through the women of Stonewycke."

"An anti-feminist? That hardly sounds like the Allison I remember from years ago."

"I didn't say I was an anti-feminist, May. But I've learned some things about marriage—learned them the hard way. And I finally understand what I don't think the women's lib advocates do. Just because the Stonewycke legacy has come through the women doesn't mean that we don't need the men God has given us. Each of the noble, wonderful men in this family has played an essential role in the ongoing life of Stonewycke. Without them in their God-given roles, this family would not have maintained its strong and holy heritage."

"Many women would deny that we each have God-given roles to fulfill, Allison. Especially in this family, which has for generations supported a strong matriarchy."

"I forget," laughed Allison. "You are an American now. My Victorian views on marriage must go down hard for you. After all, America's where feminism is really in vogue."

May laughed, too. "Allison, you couldn't be a Victorian if you tried! All your life you've been your own person—that is what has prepared you to step into the role Mother has left to you."

"And that's probably also why God knew I needed a strong man like Logan as my husband. He encourages me to be myself, and he shows me the respect of equality as a full partner in our marriage."

"That sounds too good to be real."

"You know it didn't come without sacrifice on both our parts. But now I don't have to worry about equality, because he gives it freely. His authority is no threat because it makes me feel all the more secure as a woman."

"You ought to write a book. Everyone does these days it seems. Olivia Fairgate did—have you heard? Pure feminism, very popular in America."

"I think I did read something about it. But anything I had to say about marriage would be instantly banned by the modernists as too old-fashioned."

"Probably so."

"But all this is beside the point about Stonewycke. Despite the wonderful men God brought into the line—Grandpa Ian and Daddy, and now Logan and your Mr. Reynolds, not to mention dear old Digory—we've always known that the bloodline flowed through us women. And now here I am—fifty-six years old, and I never really stopped to consider that someday the legacy of Atlanta's and Lady Margaret's and Mother's was going to come to rest . . . on me."

"Do you suppose we could talk Ian into giving up his travels and coming back here permanently? Maybe we could shift the birthright onto the men for the next few generations."

Allison laughed at the thought.

"That would be wonderful! But it's no good—it would never work. I tell you I can feel the weight of this matriarchal ancestry sweeping over me from the past. In a way it's got nothing to do with what we may decide to do with the property. We could sell Stonewycke, and I think it would still be there. It's a heritage . . . it's in the blood. I can sense it filling me. And I know there's no escape. Besides . . . Ian has such a wanderlust in every bone of his body, settling him down would be like asking for a winter in Scotland without snow."

"It's already on the way, isn't it?" said May. "I can smell it in the wind."

They walked on for several more steps in silence. By now they had come to the trail and had followed in the direction it led, though its way was often obscured by overgrown weeds and heather. The moor they were crossing was not a pretty one. Scarcely a tree was to be seen, only brown heather, rocks, and a few bristly shrubs.

"What they say," Allison went on at length, "about bloodlines, about generations, about the firstborn—like the patriarchs of the Old Testament. There's really something to it, I think. I'd never really considered it before, not in depth anyway. Of course Mother would say things to me, and I've read the stories of Abraham and Isaac and Jacob and Esau and the genealogies of Jesus, and I realize it's important in God's economy. Yet until this week it was all distant. But I tell you, these last few days have made an impact. I'm seeing that those truths were not reserved just for ancient Bible times but are real today. I scarcely paid it any heed, except in theoretical terms, until recently. But I can feel something happening to me . . ."

"And you're not sure if you like it?"

"I don't know . . ." mused Allison. "Like it? It doesn't seem it's a question of liking it or not. Let's just say I was unprepared for it, and I don't know what to do with it. Maybe I don't feel worthy of wearing such a mantle."

"But you remember hearing Mother talk about her coming to Scotland in 1911—how timid she was."

"But Mother was of the mold, so to speak. I've never been cut out of the same cloth."

"You are of the same cloth—we all are—even though we have our individualities. Who says every line of women in every generation of Stonewycke should be exactly the same?"

"But they all had something—something special."

"So do you, Allison," said May seriously. "Perhaps you aren't able to see it. But I do. And from what I remember being told, you are more like Lady Margaret when she was Maggie than Mother was."

"But what if . . . what if I make wrong choices? What if, after all these years, I can't keep Stonewycke afloat? The financial burdens of the place are steadily growing. Mother did prepare me for that. Logan and I have had charge of the money for years. I can tell you, the outlook isn't good."

"Ian and I will help. That goes without saying."

"But will that be enough? What if I—"

Allison paused, glancing away off in the distance. May knew she was fighting back emotions that were new and frightening to her.

At length she tried to continue, but her voice was husky.

"Oh, May, don't you see? According to the Scriptures, they're all watching—Mother, Lady Margaret, Atlanta, and who knows how many others? They're watching me! And—I'm so afraid . . . that I'll fail them!"

She broke down and sobbed as the last words left her lips.

Gently May took her elder sister in her loving arms and held her. They were silent a long while, the only sounds those of Allison's quiet weeping and the rising wind whistling all about them.

"I'd always just assumed," Allison said after she had regained control of her voice, "because of how things were since the legacy would end with me, that it would pass instead to you. After all, you have a son and daughter. Now everything's changed. But for some bizarre reason I'm still afraid I will be known as the one who let it die—after centuries. May . . . I'm just so frightened. I don't want this thing."

"But what you said is true," soothed May, still holding Allison and stroking her light hair in spite of the wind. "It's not you or I or any single generation. It's bigger than that, bigger than either one of us. Besides, we have no choice in these things. The Lord knows best. It is in His grand design how He orders families. Nothing comes by chance. Everything is to a purpose. We cannot alter that you are the firstborn. I cannot change that. Ian cannot change that. Neither can you change that. It is no accident. The Lord has chosen you—not me, not anyone else—to walk this path, to receive the blessings and to carry the burdens of your position."

May paused and looked intently at her sister. "He has chosen you for His purpose that good may result. He is in control. Stonewycke had passed into the hands of those who had no respect for its heritage sixty years ago. But then the Lord brought Mother here, miraculously restored her in the lineage, healed my namesake Lady Margaret, and gave them long and happy and fruitful lives. These may indeed be new times, and you may he a unique individual all your own. But that does not alter the fact that the Lord's hand is on you. His life is in you, and His loving design is still over Stonewycke and all that lies in its future. You do not have to feel that everything rests upon you. It doesn't, Allison dear. It rests with the Lord, our God. We can trust Him to guide our steps, and to do good. He can do no other."

Slowly Allison released herself from May's arms, stood back, forced a smile, and wiped away the tears with her hand. "You are right, May. Thank you," she said. "Let's walk on a little farther," she added, drawing in a deep breath to steady her shaky voice.

The two women walked on. It was cold, and the wind bit cruelly through their wool coats, but they did not seem to mind. They were, as if by common yet unspoken consent, on a mission—seeking together to retouch ancient familial roots, remembering at this time of earthly loss those who had come before them, and calling to mind memories their ancestors held dear.

Fifteen minutes more they walked. Scarcely a word was spoken. Nothing more needed be said.

At last they reached the crest of a small rise and could see their destination some hundred yards away, where the ground sloped down toward a sort of hollow in the otherwise mostly flat ridge.

"I haven't been here in years," said Allison.

"I don't think I've been out here since that day Mother brought us, remember?"

"How could I forget?" replied Allison, staring ahead.

Before them rose several irregularly shaped stones, piled and leaning against one another in what at first glance seemed like a random aberration of nature. To one who was not acquainted with their history, they would have appeared as nothing but giant boulders in the midst of a dreary Scottish moor. On closer inspection, however, for one who had the perseverance to clear away some of the moss and overgrowth, the stones would begin to take on a decidedly hewn appearance, not unlike some of the more well-known monoliths scattered throughout the British Isles as reminders of peoples long forgotten to the march of time. These stones, however, had been lost to archaeologists and historians for centuries. They possessed a history, but as yet no one had made the discovery that would unlock the secrets of their past. And thus they stood, as they had for more than a century of decades, silent sentinels to a history for the present forgotten, but for the future waiting.

The two women paused, looking toward the stones.

"It was just after Lady Margaret died," said May. "I can hardly believe it was—let's see . . . forty . . . no, thirty-eight years ago. I was only eleven, you were eighteen and just married."

"I remember," smiled Allison. "Mother had been working on her journal all that day—"

"All that day, and the day before, and the day before that!" laughed May. "The moment Great-grandmother died, she seemed almost feverish about it, as if she would forget things she'd been told if she waited so much as a day."

"I'll never forget the walk out here. She was so solemn."

"If what she said is true, I can see why. Remember the tone in her voice when she said: '*This is where it all began*'?"

Allison nodded. "It's hard to believe that seventeen-year-old Maggie— our great-grandmother—and Logan's seventy year old great-great-uncle Digory could have found that treasure and lugged it all the way back home. To think that our ancestors were here, on this very spot, over a hundred years ago."

"I wonder whatever happened to the treasure?"

"When those thugs took it after Logan first came here, we thought it was gone forever. Then we ran across Channing during the war and learned that somehow he'd got his hands on it. Logan's tried to get back on his track several times since, but never with any success."

"Whatever the treasure was, I'm sure it was spent years ago."

"It's never been retrieving the treasure so much as it is the history. It's just too bad for a man like that to make off with something that's part of Stonewycke."

"Channing's no doubt dead by now anyway."

"I'm sure." Allison paused reflectively for a moment. "Well," she said in almost a distracted voice, "it's not the treasure really. It's this place. I just had to come out here again. As difficult as all this is, I suppose something inside me had to try to touch Mother's spirit however I can, and Maggie's, and Atlanta's. If I am destined to be the next in line, then I have to know how they felt about this spot of ground, this valley, this land . . . about Stonewycke and all it represents. I needed to come out here, if, like Mother said, this is where it all began. I really have no choice—I must be faithful to their dreams, their heritage."

"And leave the future in God's hands."

"As hard as that is . . . yes."

"You are now in the first rank of Stonewycke's women. You may not be entirely comfortable with it yet. And it doesn't even matter if you go back to London to live. It's in your voice. I can see Mother's eyes in your face, and hear her voice as you speak. I imagine Maggie's in there someplace, too. The mantle is upon you, dear sister, and you will wear it with honor."

They stood silently gazing upon the stones whose ancient story they did not yet know, then turned around, faced the wind, breathed deeply of its chilly freshness, and started back toward home.

They had not gone far before Allison stopped her sister with her hand. May turned toward her.

"May," said Allison. "Thank you. You are as dear a sister as a woman could wish for. I will miss you now more than ever. Thank you for helping me through this time."

May only nodded.

It was now her turn to feel the tears as they began slowly to fill her eyes. The legacy was in her blood also, and suddenly Boston seemed so very far away.

5 / In a Dark Corner of the City————————

Raul Galvez ducked inside the Cheapside pub several moments too late to prevent a thorough dousing from the sudden cloudburst outside. He jerked off his hat and gave it an angry snap, sending a spray of moisture in the direction of several of the pub's other patrons.

One of the men cursed him loudly and threatened physical violence. Galvez replied with a sufficiently venomous sneer to effectively discourage the cocky fellow. Galvez then pushed his short, muscular frame through the crowded, smoke-filled room.

As he moved, his squinting close-set eyes darted back and forth over the place as if he were looking for someone. But all he saw were foreign pale faces speaking a disagreeable tongue that only served to remind him that he was getting further from home every day. He shoved his way up to the counter, thinking only of taking the edge off his disgust.

"Cerveza!" he ordered in a throaty, unfriendly tone.

"Wot's that, mate?" asked the bartender.

"Beer, estúpido!" retorted Galvez. "And make it strong and dark."

"Comin' right up, but you don't 'ave to get so bloomin' nasty about it," mumbled the man as he turned to fill a glass.

Galvez took the drink without any thanks and, after dropping his money on the counter, stalked away to an empty table. As his chunky body fell into its chair, he continued to scan the noisy room, now focusing most of his attention on the front door through which he had just come. He drained his tall glass and was starting on a second when he paused, the beer halfway to his lips, to take particular note of a man just entering the pub. He was tall, broad-shouldered, and stood as if he'd walked off the set of some cheap Italian western, wearing a cowboy hat, shiny tan boots, and a sport-coat with deep, contrasting leather yokes. He, too, scanned the pub as he entered, but his vigil was rewarded quickly as he locked eyes with Galvez.

"Que paso, amigo!" called the man as he drew near. His inept Spanish was thickly accented with a Texas drawl.

He lowered his lanky but taut frame into the chair opposite Galvez and immediately began waving his hand in the air for service, which he received post-haste.

"Bourbon, honey," he said to the girl waiting tables; "straight up." He threw her a leering wink and reached out his hand playfully toward her. Her reflexes were too quick for him, however, and she was soon out of reach.

"What do you think this is, Mallory," growled Galvez sardonically, "Saturday night after the cattle drive? Why don't you announce our business while you're at it!"

"Aw, shut up, Galvez! What's eating you, anyway?"

"This whole place stinks, that's what!"

"I dunno. I thought it was a pretty classy joint myself." At that moment his bourbon arrived and in his preoccupation with his drink, the Texan forgot his earlier interest in the waitress.

"Bah!" spat Galvez. "We have better cantinas in Patquia. But I am speaking of this whole town. It is cold and wet and dirty. The fog never lifts. Rotten, I tell you! And I'm sick of the place!"

"Yeah, and where you come from it's just dirty, huh, amigo?"

Mallory laughed at his own wit, not at all troubled by Galvez's icy grimace. Then he added with a wink, "The money's okay though, huh?"

"Perhaps the General is paying you more than he is me," groused Galvez.

"Maybe so. . . ." returned Mallory in his easy drawl. "But I been with him a long time—seniority, you know, amigo."

"Well, what dirty work have we got to do now—break into another office building to steal some files on the competition?"

"Nah, no burglarizing. He says it's not business this time. We gotta take the evening train to Oxford."

"Madre de Dios!" exclaimed Galvez. "It goes from bad to worse."

"I thought you couldn't wait to get out of this place."

"At least in London there are señoritas to be found."

"The fence is in Oxford, so that's where we go."

"Who is this fence?"

"I dunno. Some egghead who discovered he makes more bucks moving high-class stolen merchandise than pounding education into a bunch of preppies."

"Why this man? There must be a dozen fences right around—"

" 'Cause he knows his stuff, and that's what the General told us to do, comprendo?"

Galvez twisted his lips in disdain. "Okay, okay! You gringos and your short fuses! Let's go and get it over with."

"We got time. It's two hours before the train leaves." Mallory raised his hand to signal for a refill. "Relax, Galvez. Loosen up. Remember, this is merry ole England."

In a moment the waitress returned with another bourbon, but this time she was not quick enough to avoid Mallory's bony paw.

"Come on, honey," said Mallory, "all this cowboy wants is to have a good ole time."

The girl didn't resist. As distasteful as his attentions might be, giving in for a moment was better than causing trouble. She was used to Mallory's type and would find her opportunity to squirm free soon enough.

Galvez sat back and scowled at the whole scene. He took a long swallow from his glass of beer, all the while thinking that his grimy, poverty-ridden little village was looking better and better.

6 / Back in London

Hilary was back in London from Brighton a little after six-thirty. After making their way through traffic, Suzanne dropped her in front of her office building, and at 6:57 she walked through the doors of *The Berkshire Review*, intending merely to check her mail and go right home for the evening.

Suzanne had pegged her correctly, and her surprise at Hilary's leaving the magazine at the busiest time of the month was well justified. Though she had a competent staff, she was not the type to easily leave the work to others. Delegation was perhaps the most difficult aspect of her job. She always wanted to be fully apprised of every facet of the magazine's progress, from research to copy-editing to typesetting to production to promotion to sales.

As she entered, the earlier frenzy of the office had quieted considerably, but several staff writers were still busily engaged at their typewriters or phones. They threw her friendly greetings, no one appearing particularly concerned that she had been absent the entire afternoon.

Hilary exchanged a few words with her personal secretary Betty, and her hand had just touched the door latch to her office when one of her writers, hurrying through the pressroom, called out to her.

"Perfect timing!" he exclaimed, his compact frame of about Hilary's own height hurrying toward her. "I'm glad I didn't miss you."

"I just got here myself, Murry."

"I know. I saw you come in just as I got off the elevator. Do you have a minute?"

"Of course, come on in," Hilary replied.

Murry opened the door for Hilary, then followed her into the office. The young man was Murry Fitts, an American expatriot who had attended the University of London, and had decided to make his home in England where a promising job awaited him. Now four years out of the university, he was an enthusiastic and skilled writer, as well as a daring investigative reporter. He possessed a reputation for his somewhat flamboyant style and received not a little criticism from his more conservative colleagues for his shoulder-length hair and bushy beard. But he was just the kind of employee that had helped turn *The Berkshire Review* around, and Hilary had never had cause to hold his particular "style" against him. Besides, long hair and other seeming "oddities" were almost the norm in these days of Magical Mystery Tours and "feelin' groovy." Whether you were straight or

44

wore your anti-Establishment prejudice on your sleeve, you were less likely to look twice at long hair and funny clothes than you might have in '64. And to Murry's credit, he made a point of usually wearing a sports jacket and necktie to assuage his more narrow-minded peers. But Hilary wouldn't have cared if he had dressed in a Nehru jacket and beads. He was a solid young man, forthright and sincere, and, in addition to being a friend, was an ace reporter. He and Suzanne had a lot in common, and Hilary wondered why she had not yet gotten around to introducing the two. She made a mental note just before she spoke.

"What is it, Murry?" she asked after they had seated themselves, she behind her desk, and he in one of the other two chairs in the small cubicle which was her office.

"I've got a couple projects I need input on."

He paused, took his notebook from his pocket, flipped back several pages, and began again.

"I haven't had much time, but at this point I'd stake some pretty heavy odds that there might be more to this East End affair than meets the eye."

"Like what?"

"Code violations, unjustified evictions, possibly even collusion with building officials about the redevelopment."

"Do you have anything solid?"

"Not quite. It's just a sense I get. I think it definitely bears further investigation."

"Hmmm," mused Hilary. "Must have been providential that I decided to call off the story for this issue."

"Come on, you're not going to start giving me that stuff again about God leading you! This is the 1970s, Hilary!"

"I've told you before, Murry, and I'll tell you as often as it takes to sink into that liberal, semi-open brain of yours—God does lead His people just as much today as when the Jews were wandering across the desert with Moses. His ways just appear more subtle now, that's all."

"Okay, okay," laughed Murry. "You'll make a believer of me yet! But you're right, I think it would be wise to hold on to your story and see what happens. I want to poke around a bit more."

"What do you have?"

"Probably nothing more than the proverbial gut feeling."

"The reporter's most valuable stock-in-trade," said Hilary.

"Maybe they'll have plausible explanations for everything," Murry went on, "but I have to ask the questions anyway."

"Anything else?"

"You probably heard about the fire out there a few days ago?"

"Vaguely, yes. Is that tied in?"

"Again, who knows? But it's just too coincidental for comfort, so I looked into it—just for fun. The owner of the building stands to profit a cool two hundred thousand pounds from the insurance company." Fitts made his final statement with pointed emphasis.

"Well, keep at it," said Hilary. "What was the other project you needed to talk about?"

"It's the antiquities piece." Murry scratched his head sheepishly. "It's going a bit slow."

"The piece or you, Murry?"

"Well . . ."

"You're one of my best writers, Murry, and I hate to waste you on something you have no interest in. But it is your turn to do the intelligentsia beat, and you know how important it is that we keep open these contacts and do a museum article now and then."

"I know, but history was never my strong point."

Hilary sighed with understanding. "I can't have the others think I'm playing favorites. But if you don't want the St. Ninian's story, I do need someone to cover an item about a woman who claims to have given birth to an alien baby——"

"Spare me! I'll dig through the archives and keep interviewing the old historians in tweed suits!"

Hilary smiled triumphantly. "Who knows? You might even turn up something startling—some hard news. Some of the world's great sleuths wear tweed suits just to throw people off. You never know what might really be behind the horn-rimmed glasses and tweed of those men you interview."

"I'll see what I can find. At least I'll give it my best shot."

A short pause followed and Hilary took the chance to glance at her appointment book.

"You know, Murry," she said after a moment, "I was just thinking again about the East End thing. Maybe we ought to run out there tomorrow. Have a look at the fire locale, talk to a few people."

"Tomorrow's deadline—it's bound to be hectic around here."

"I know, but we want to look into this fire while it's still fresh. A hot story—as it were—waiteth for no man . . . or woman."

"Then I'll get right on it," said Fitts, jamming his notebook back into his pocket and rising.

"Tomorrow, Murry. Tomorrow! And I'll join you. In the meantime, you have my permission to go home first, maybe even get some sleep," laughed Hilary.

Fitts chuckled at himself. "Yeah. Nothing we can do for this issue anyway." He opened the door. "See you in the morning."

"Good night, Murry."

After Murry had closed the door, Hilary sat back and reflected on the events of a full day. It had begun, seemingly, with that Whitehall interview, moved on to Brighton and her thought-provoking conversation with Suzanne, and finally ended with this stimulating interchange with Murry. At least there was no lack of diversion to keep her from sinking too far into morose melancholia. Tomorrow she would be busy wrapping the next issue of the *Review*, going with Murry to investigate the fire . . . and . . . well, there were hundreds of pressing matters to keep her occupied, not including the new and unexpected.

It was 8:15 by the time Hilary arrived at her flat that evening, after stopping by an all-night delicatessen for something to eat.

7 / The Dream

Hilary kicked off her shoes, put on water for tea, then sat down leisurely in her favorite chair to eat her cold cuts on bread with a side dish of vegetables. She was hardly aware of their taste, however, and when she rose to tend to her tea, she went through the motions methodically as if her mind was far away. As indeed it was. She picked up the book beside her and tried to read.

It was no use. Somehow her discussion with Suzanne seemed bent on intruding more forcibly into her thoughts now that she was in the quiet of her living room. It wasn't so much what either of them had *said*; it was the very persistence of the agitating question. As intently as she tried to steer her mind in another direction, whether she liked it or not . . . whether she was prepared to admit it or not . . . eventually she knew she was going to have to confront the nobility issue head-on. Suddenly it was far more pressing even than Suzanne suspected. Their conversation that afternoon had carried overtones that Hilary's friend could in no way suspect.

She tried to shake the fantasies from her mind. She liked her life. She enjoyed her independence. Why this sudden surge of discontent? She wouldn't have to give it up. She could ignore what had happened. Why not merely go on as before? Business as usual. She wasn't obligated to restructure her life just because some stranger happened to think . . .

Was it indeed her visit with Suzanne this afternoon that had triggered this string of thoughts? No. Such anxieties had been pestering her relentlessly for two weeks. She had sought out Suzanne only as someone to talk with about what was already swirling around inside her.

Hilary liked Suzanne. But their longtime friendship could not alter the reality of her friend's aristocratic birth. It was a fact Hilary had always been aware of as one of the given parameters in their relationship. She had been comfortable with it, comfortable in who Suzanne was, and comfortable in the person she herself was.

Until recently. . . .

Now, suddenly, everything was changed. Suddenly she no longer knew who she was, or who she wanted to be. Suddenly all the things she had told Suzanne through the years about the differences in their stations were no longer valid. Suddenly the firm foundations of the world she had learned to rely on were all gone. She felt as one cast adrift . . . without a lifeline . . . without any sense of where the harbor lay.

The eternal philosophical quandary—*Who am I?*—was suddenly a very practical and real concern.

Hilary had always been pretty certain about the person living under her skin—until two weeks ago. And as she sat in her easy chair that evening contemplating her afternoon with Suzanne, she knew that the turmoil in her mind and emotions stemmed from more than any point her friend had raised.

She tried to ignore the other reason, block it from her mind, hide from it, pretend she had imagined it . . . but to no avail.

Since the funeral it had become all the more pressing and insistent. Because since coming back from Scotland, she realized that now everything was up to her.

The decision had been placed directly in her lap. The only other person on earth who knew was now gone. She could ignore the whole episode, pretend it never happened, go on with her life, and try her best to forget it . . . if she chose to.

Hilary rubbed her eyes wearily.

It was ten o'clock, and she had already tackled too many emotional dilemmas that day to face another—especially this one.

Leaving the remnants of her supper and tea on the table, she rose and went to her bedroom.

Yet even after changing her clothes and crawling into bed, she knew her reason for trying to empty her mind and going to bed had more to do with "escape" than sleep. She did not want to think any more about her unexpected visitor, or about the incredible implications of her words, or about the funeral, or about all the turmoil this was bound to cause in her life. Despite the churning of her thoughts, however, to her relief she soon found herself drifting away as sleep overcame her.

Suddenly Hilary awoke with a shuddering gasp. It was the middle of the night. She was drenched with perspiration.

It seemed her eyes had been closed a mere moment, but in reality she had been asleep for two hours. She had been awakened by the horribly real sensation of ear-splitting explosions, and the sounds still clung to the edges of her consciousness as if they had occurred just outside her window rather than in a dream of a remote and distant time.

She found herself shaking with fear, as if she were the little girl of the dream—forlorn . . . helpless . . . alone . . . running madly away from the awful sounds in sheer panic. Running . . . running . . . crying out for help but with no one to hear . . . stumbling over a stone and falling . . . picking herself up and trying to run again . . . across the little bridge . . . away . . . away from the ugly sounds behind her.

Hilary brushed an unsteady hand across her damp brow and groped in the darkness for the lamp switch. She squinted against the light—this time real, and so comforting after the bursts of blinding flashes in her dream. It was after midnight.

By the time she slipped out of bed, she had for the most part regained her composure and was fully awake. She knew she would not be able to return to sleep for a good while; she wasn't even sure she wanted to. Instead, she climbed out of bed and made her way through the darkened rooms to the kitchen. The unsettling midnight disturbance called for the eternal British cure-all—another hot cup of tea.

While the kettle was heating on the stove, Hilary wandered out to her desk in the living room. She sat down, vaguely thinking that she might work on some of her correspondence. *Who am I trying to kid?* she thought after a few minutes of staring blankly ahead. Soon the whining teakettle drew her back to the kitchen.

As she prepared the tea, images of her dream, against her will, began to filter once more into her mind. It was the same dream as always, hardly altered from when she was a child. Years ago it had haunted her more frequently. Once or twice a month she would wake up in the middle of the night screaming and would not be able to sleep again until her mother took her in her arms and rocked her, gently humming hymns into her ear.

It was always the same . . . vague, shadowy, frightening images of light, and loud sounds, and confusion—and always the little girl running to escape, whose tear-streaked face seemed so real she wanted to reach out and dry the dampness on the terrified little cheeks. As the girl ran, farther and farther from the explosions and jumbled confusion that made up the background of the dream, Hilary was not merely watching events as an observer— she *was* the little girl, and felt her panic with every fiber of her being. Every time she woke up trembling.

As Hilary grew older, the dream came with less frequency, making its unwelcome appearance mostly during times of stress. She had not thought of the little girl for at least two years. Usually she had no idea what brought it on. But tonight's episode was a different story. She knew all too well why it had intruded into her dreamy subconscious now.

Her only surprise was that the dream had not come sooner, the night after—two weeks ago—when she had found the unexpected caller waiting in her office.

8 / An Unexpected Visitor _____

There had been a morning interview that day on the other side of the city, so Hilary had not arrived at the office until nearly nine-thirty.

As she thought back, Hilary wondered how different things might have been if she hadn't come in that day at all, or if . . .

Probably no different. The lady had been determined and would not have given up easily.

She remembered seeing the woman seated in her private office with her back to the glass enclosure the moment she walked into the pressroom.

"I didn't know I had an appointment," she said to her secretary.

"You didn't," replied Betty. "She apologized for coming without one, but said it was important. She asked if she could wait."

"Who is it . . . what's it about?"

Betty shrugged. "I don't know. Maybe she heard about your article . . ." Betty's voice trailed off, leaving the thought to finish itself.

"That's probably it."

Hilary looked toward her office and gave the woman closer scrutiny. At first glance she did not appear the type to join a cause. Even as she sat, from her back Hilary could almost detect a kind of inbred nobility in the elderly woman. She doubted she was from the East End, after all. Her very bearing seemed to indicate another world altogether. She appeared to be about eighty, but sat with a poise and grace Hilary would not have associated with age. Her silver gray hair was pulled straight back from her face into a bun at the back of her head. Her carriage certainly would suggest aristocratic blood. Could she be here about the last piece she'd done for the magazine blasting the nobility? No, that had been too long ago, and neither did the woman seem of the sort to make a petty protest.

The woman's face was turned away from the glass, but Hilary saw by the position of her head that she was studying the personal items on the office wall. She seemed to spend some time examining the photo of Hilary with the U.S. Army's "Charlie Company" while she had been a correspondent in Vietnam two years before. Then the woman's eyes shifted in turn to the university diploma, two journalism awards, another photo— this one of Hilary and Suzanne during their student days—and finally lingering on Hilary's pride and joy—an oil portrait of Gladstone. Not only was the famed Prime Minister one of the few politicians Hilary could honestly admire, but the painting had been done while he lived. Only the fact that the artist was somewhat obscure had kept the portrait within her budget.

When Betty quietly cleared her throat Hilary realized she had been staring silently for an inordinately long time.

"Do you want to make a quick getaway?" she asked somewhat coyly.

"Oh no," Hilary chuckled self-consciously. "She looks harmless enough."

But as her hand reached the latch, a sudden wave of adolescent nervousness swept over her. Some sixth sense seemed to be warning Hilary that the encounter which lay ahead was to be no ordinary one. Even then she could not have dreamed how momentous it would really be. She opened the door.

"I see you've noticed my Gladstone," said Hilary as she entered.

The woman turned her eyes from the painting, rose, and smiled. It was a warm, personable gesture, though there was something disquieting in the lady's eyes—a kind of intensity that seemed bent on probing Hilary's depths. She seemed to be trying to integrate the look she had seen in the photographs about the office with Hilary's actual face which was now before her.

"It's quite good," said the woman, her eyes straying once again— almost reluctant to leave their scrutiny of Hilary's features—to the painting. "I haven't heard of the artist, but he has captured a very human quality in the Prime Minister, so rare in most official portraits."

She paused and turned back to Hilary. "Do you collect art, or are you only partial to Gladstone?"

"My budget hardly permits me to collect," smiled Hilary, "but I splurged on this because I think Gladstone was a great man, a true defender of the common man, one of very few politicians with integrity." She stepped toward her visitor and held out her hand. "I'm Hilary Edwards."

The other woman reached out her gloved hand and took Hilary's, pressing it rather firmly for a long moment, trembling slightly.

"I am Lady Joanna MacNeil," she said.

"*Lady* . . . MacNeil," repeated Hilary thoughtfully, "please . . . be seated."

Joanna resumed her seat and Hilary took the chair at her desk.

"I've read your magazine," said Hilary's visitor as if making a casual observation. "You must be a woman with strong political convictions."

"I've never been accused of being a rebel *without* a cause."

"No," Lady MacNeil chuckled softly, "you seem to have no lack of issues to keep you occupied." She paused, as if in thought. "I've never been very politically minded myself," she continued, "but I think there are more men of integrity at Whitehall than we give credit for. I know of at least one."

"One is a rather small minority," countered Hilary congenially, her natural defenses put off their guard by this disarmingly pleasant old woman, yet nevertheless responding to political matters in her habitual manner. "But if there is one, I would like to meet him. Perhaps I should interview him for the magazine."

"Yes . . ." The woman's voice faded off a moment and her eyes grew introspective.

As Hilary observed the change, she had a brief opportunity to study her visitor. The features she noted in the aging Lady MacNeil were fine and delicate. Hilary could tell that in her youth she must have been quite lovely. Her pale skin was creased with many fine lines, and her brown eyes were clear and gentle, but for all her delicacy there was a definite firmness about her chin, a strength, a sense of determination, even forcefulness. Oddly, the look was familiar to Hilary; but as she took an extra moment to analyze it, she was unable to recall where she had seen such an expression before.

The pause lasted a mere moment, and as quickly as it had come, Lady MacNeil's eyes became focused once more.

"But I'm sure you didn't come here to talk politics," said Hilary after the brief silence.

Apparently amused at this notion, the woman chuckled softly, her eyes momentarily growing merry, framed in oft-used crow's feet.

"That is quite true," she replied.

"How may I help you?"

Lady MacNeil grew solemn again and drew in a deep breath, seemingly as much to gather courage as oxygen. "I am here on what might be almost a bizarre quest. I realize I have come without an appointment, though I hope you will understand my reasons for this later. Yet my . . . business may take some time."

"I happen to have some. Please go on."

"For the past several weeks I have been looking for someone," said Lady MacNeil. "As unusual as it may seem for a person of my age, I hired a detective, and I followed what clues I had. And in the end, my search has led me here."

"It must have been a roundabout journey," said Hilary. "If I didn't know better I would think you were from the States, yet your accent is a curious mixture of American *and* Scottish."

Lady MacNeil smiled, oddly again. "That is another story. Perhaps one day I will have the opportunity to tell it to you."

"Who are you looking for, and how do I fit in?"

"With your permission, before I answer your questions, I would like to ask a few of you. Just in case I am on the wrong track, so to speak. We don't want to stir any emotions unnecessarily."

She paused, as Hilary nodded for her to continue.

"Thank you, Miss . . . Miss—Edwards," she said, speaking the name with apparent difficulty. "First of all, I was curious about your name. The nameplate there on your desk reads J. Hilary Edwards. May I ask what the *J* stands for?"

"Joanne—" Hilary answered.

Hardly noticing the sharp breath drawn in by her guest, Hilary went on. "—or Joan. Apparently I had a slight lisp when I was a child, and my parents were never exactly sure."

A clear look of confusion spread over her visitor's face, but nothing was said, and Hilary continued.

"Besides, they preferred my middle name, and I suppose I got used to it."

"I see," replied Lady MacNeil, her brow still creased in thought. "And when were you born?"

Hilary smiled. "I'm afraid that question is not so simple either, but its answer will clear up your confusion about my name as well. You see, I have no idea exactly when I was born. I celebrate my birthday on February 10, the day my parents officially adopted me, but we never knew what the true day should have been. Neither did we know my actual given name for a certainty."

"You were adopted, then?" The lady's voice quivered slightly.

"Yes. I was a war orphan."

"And you know nothing of your real parents?"

"Nothing."

A knot slowly began to form in Hilary's stomach. "I was orphaned under rather unusual circumstances," she went on. "It wasn't so uncommon during wartime, especially in occupied countries. We didn't have so much of it here in Britain, though we did come in for our share during the bombings. I was somehow separated from my parents and was apparently too young to say where I belonged. I was taken to a shelter, but my family was never located. It was assumed they must have been killed. There had been a German raid, bombings, explosions, but somehow I was spared. Eventually I was adopted."

"How—how old were you?"

"About three."

"It must have been difficult for you."

"Children have an incredible capacity to adapt," answered Hilary. "I was at an age before solid memory patterns form. I really don't remember anything of that time—except for a peculiar dream I sometimes have. I suppose I must have cried a lot for missing my real parents, but I have no clear memories. Whatever grief I must have experienced was soon absorbed by a new life, and . . . well, you know how it is with children—they mold to their surroundings."

Lady MacNeil nodded, not without a quick brush of her white handkerchief past one of her eyes.

"So . . . you have no memory of your real parents?"

"None."

"Have you ever wondered . . . ?"

"Every adopted child wonders," said Hilary. "How can you help it?" She paused uneasily, half afraid of where the conversation was leading. "I take it you are leading to something specific?"

Hilary's discomfort brought a certain edge to her voice that she immediately regretted. "I'm sorry to seem impatient," she said. "I suppose I'm not much used to being on this end of an interview."

"It is I who should apologize for being so cryptic." Lady MacNeil paused. "If you'll indulge me a bit more, I'd like to relate a story to you."

"Do go on," replied Hilary, folding her clammy hands as calmly and patiently as she could and resting them on the top of her desk.

"I told you I was on a quest," continued Lady MacNeil, "and the story of how it came about begins during the war with a young couple. Like so many others at that time they were separated, and while he was on the Continent, she remained in London with their child. The bombing had quieted considerably after the Battle of Britain, and they were relatively safe.

"But in late 1942 the Germans stepped up the raids, and this young mother of whom I spoke felt she ought to remove herself to a safer haven. Yet she was torn by a very real need to remain in London. The details of her situation do not really pertain to the story at this point. In the end it was decided that the child and her grandmother would return to their family estate in Scotland while the mother joined them later.

"The irony is that they might have been safer had they remained in London, but only in hindsight are such things visible. For on the way north, the train bearing the child and the grandmother was bombed two hours outside of London. The grandmother had left the child in the care of their nurse while she visited a friend in another car, and it was at that moment, while they were separated, that the explosion occurred."

Hilary closed her eyes.

She had not had the dream for years, yet all at once the very word *explosion* conjured up a host of nightmarish images in her mind's eye. She did not even notice that her hands were gripping each other like opposing clamps of a vise, turning her knuckles white.

"The trivial acts in our lifetimes go largely unnoticed," Lady MacNeil continued; "that is, until some catastrophe changes everything. You cannot feel guilty or ashamed, for you know there was nothing intrinsically wrong in what you may have done. Yet you know the choice will always haunt the deepest recesses of your heart. This is but scratching the surface of the many soul-searching and agonizing memories and regrets the grandmother had to face in the years following. But in the end, neither the grandmother nor the parents ever saw the child again, for the car she was in received a direct hit from the enemy's plane, and there seemed no doubt she had been killed.

"I need not describe their grief. Only their faith in God sustained them in their loss. And only time was able to dull its painful edge, the Lord using their tragedy to draw the young husband and wife closer together than they had ever been previously. They had no more children, for this one birth had been a miracle in itself.

"As the years passed, their lives managed to go on. That one void, their childlessness, could never be filled; but they nonetheless lived full and happy lives, expending the great love in their hearts in service to others."

Lady MacNeil paused. Both she and Hilary, almost in unison, took a deep breath. The time to seek one another's eyes, however, had not yet come.

"Fortunately, the story does not end there," went on Lady MacNeil. "About two years ago, the father of the lost child received a telephone call from someone unknown to him, yet well known to the grandmother, but whom she had not seen in twenty-eight years. When the caller first identified herself as Hannah Whitley, the father had no idea that the name was none other than the nurse who had been with his child on the day of the terrible accident. Indirectly as a result of that call, other people were drawn into the stream of events, which eventually led the grandmother to enlist the help of an investigator, and ultimately fill in many answers she had wondered about for years.

"After the bombing, Hannah Whitley had lived her own private nightmare, unknown to any of the rest of the family. By some miracle she and the child had been thrown clear on the first moments of the explosion, and had survived what appeared to be certain death, wandering dazed, unnoticed, farther and farther from the train. In the bedlam following the blast, all attention was focused on locating the dead and trying to drag survivors free of the wreckage. Apparently the nurse and the child wandered off into the countryside. Miss Whitley had a severe head injury and was no doubt in shock. In her benumbed state her only thought was to get away from the horrible fires and continuing explosions. They walked for some time, finally ending up at a farmhouse several miles away.

"There she abandoned the child, though even she could not say why she did such a thing. Perhaps in her fear and confusion, she thought it was the best course of action. The farmer's wife discovered the child the following morning, sleeping peacefully in a pile of straw, and brought her into the house, cleaned and fed her, but was unable to make out anything from the child's babbling. In due time they took the child to a shelter in the nearest town, where all attempts to locate her family ended in futility. Eventually she was sent to an orphanage in London.

"By some coincidence Hannah made her way to the same town, though she arrived long before the child. There her wanderings of the one kind gave way to new and more fearful internal ones. Her injuries finally took their toll. She collapsed in delirium and was hospitalized. She was later shipped to London for more intensive care and some surgery. Hannah's mind never completely recovered. Nothing could be made of her ravings either before or after going to London. The surgery did not seem to help, and she lapsed into a coma, in which she remained for two years. When she came out of it, her amnesia was so total that it took years for her to begin to reconstruct who she was. It took much longer before she began to remember what had happened that awful day. When finally bits and pieces did return, she was afraid to come forward after so long. She feared she would be blamed by the family for somehow losing the child.

"She might have remained silent to this day, except that, experiencing a suddenly wave of conscience, as I said, two years ago, Hannah made a halfhearted attempt to contact the child's father. She lost her courage almost immediately, however, and never did actually talk to the man, only his secretary. After that, Hannah dropped out of sight again, though it now appears other parties concerned may have run across her somehow. In any case, more recently many long-forgotten links to the past seem beginning to come to light."

"Why—why did she change her mind? Why was she reluctant to come forward?" asked Hilary in a dry, taut voice, relying on her natural journalistic instincts to force her forward where her emotions were afraid to tread.

"I can only guess. But the father had become a rather important man in the government," answered Lady MacNeil, "and I suppose she was intimidated. She was, after all, still suffering from her own measure of guilt in the affair, and to a degree still afraid of what they might think."

"What happened then?"

"The grandmother began her own investigation into the matter."

"And . . . ?"

"And, as I said, her path has led here."

9 / Confirmation

A long, heavy silence hung in the air between the two women.

Hilary glanced around at the glass walls of her office. Outside, the busy pace of her staff continued as usual, though little noise penetrated the soundproof enclosure, making the awkward quiet feel even deeper. This hardly seemed like the right setting for so momentous a meeting.

She let her gaze fall to her hands, still tightly clasped together on top of her desk. As if suddenly aware of the tension that had come over her body, Hilary let her hands fall apart. She rose and walked to a small table that held an electric coffeepot and all the related necessities.

"Would you like a cup of coffee?" she asked in a voice so normal that its sound almost startled her.

"Thank you," answered Lady MacNeil, "that would be nice."

"Cream or sugar?"

"Yes, both."

Hilary poured out two cups, methodically adding cream and sugar to one which she then handed to her guest. Leaving the other black, she picked it up, but remained standing where she was.

"I suppose I need not ask," she said after a brief pause, "if you are the grandmother in your story."

"I am."

"And you think . . . that is, you have come here because—" Hilary stopped, staring into her coffee.

Joanna looked up, her eyes filled with gentle compassion. "I believe . . ." Her voice quivered and her eyes filled with tears; she could not help but call to mind her own fateful luncheon encounter with Ian Duncan so many years ago, when she had been even younger than Hilary. "I believe," she went on, "that you are my granddaughter."

Joanna had unconsciously edged forward in her chair as if she wanted to go to Hilary, but something seemed to hold her back, and Hilary made no move toward the older woman. She remained rooted to the floor where she stood, staring down into her cup, not knowing whether she wanted to run or cry or scream.

Hilary sensed that she must reply. But it had to be a sane, rational response. After all, this must be a mistake. The kind old lady had somehow gotten onto the wrong track, Hilary told herself, grasping after straws to relieve her own inner sense of need. She would have to let Lady MacNeil down gently.

Try as she might, Hilary could get no word out of her mouth.

Finally Joanna's lips twitched up into a soft smile. "I'm afraid I could think of no subtler way of putting it," she said. "I suppose there are no halfway words in which to say such a thing." She paused and sipped her coffee.

"You—" Hilary licked her lips, "—you must have the wrong person."

"My granddaughter's given name was Joanna Hilary."

"A coincidence," Hilary replied weakly.

Joanna said nothing, simply gazing at her with those probing, gentle, liquid eyes.

"I mean," Hilary went on in a frayed, defensive tone, "what more proof have you but a string of—well, coincidences?"

She set down her cup and strode across the room, turning sharply when she reached the far wall. That she was agitated was clear, but her reporter's blood had begun to flow once more now that the shock had subsided a bit. "Surely you can't expect me to accept what you say on such, if you'll excuse my candor, such flimsy evidence. In my business we have a saying: one source, doubtful; two sources, perhaps; three sources, confirmation. You have a name, nothing more." She did not think it necessary at the time to give the details of her dream. "I would need something far more substantial."

"You have no desire to become acquainted with your real family?" Hilary tried for the moment to ignore the wounded tone in Lady MacNeil's voice.

"It's not that," answered Hilary with added sensitivity, remembering her earlier resolve not to hurt the lady. "I just haven't given my real family, as you put it, much thought. I *have* a family I have considered my own for almost thirty years. They love me and I love them. I'm content with my life. And now you are asking me—well, you couldn't possibly understand."

"Perhaps I might, more than you realize."

"How could you? How can you know what it's like to find a grandmother—a family—you never knew existed?"

An odd look flitted across Lady MacNeil's face.

"I know this must be difficult for you," she said at length. "I can think of no way to make it easier. But for my part, you must see that I can't simply walk out and forget the whole thing. It has taken me thirty years to find you."

Hilary sighed, turned away, stared out her window for a moment, then said, "I'm sorry. I suppose I'm not making this easy for you, either. It's just that it comes as quite a shock."

She shook her head, drew a hand through her hair, turned back toward the room and began pacing behind her desk. She hadn't wanted to remember. The dream had been so terrifying, yet even as a child she had somehow known that it was the bridge to her old life. And if her old life had been so hideous, who could blame the child in her for wanting to forget?

In her subconscious childhood pain and confusion, there had always lingered a vague sense that she had been deserted by her parents when she had needed them most. The little girl in the dream had cried so frantically—alone, bewildered, afraid . . . yet no one came to help her. As an adult, Hilary possessed the intellectual capacity to analyze and understand childish misconceptions. Still, it was no easy thing to transfer that logic to the seat of her emotions and unlearn the deepest hurts of life. Though her mind was capable of telling her one thing, her heart did not always readily go along.

Suddenly her hand went unconsciously to her throat.

She had almost forgotten the one small link she had always had to a family . . . to a past life she had begun to think never really existed.

Her eyes darted toward the lady. For a brief instant, Hilary entertained the notion of not mentioning it. It could only complicate the matter.

But why be so deceptive? What was she afraid of? Wasn't seeking the truth the very thing she had dedicated her life to as a journalist?

In almost a sudden defiant response to her silent self-interrogation, she worked her fingers under the collar of her blouse. In another second or two she lifted out a delicate gold chain—one she had bought to replace the original, which had broken when she was ten. On it hung a heart-shaped locket.

The moment it rested between her fingers, there came the sound of a thud and splat as Lady MacNeil's cup slipped from her hand and crashed to the floor. Hilary stared, then hurried to the coffee table, where she grabbed a serviette and stooped down to clean up the spill.

She had not even finished wiping up the coffee when she felt a slim, aged hand reach down to her head as she knelt on the floor, and gently caress her hair. She froze, then slowly turned and lifted her eyes to meet those of the old woman's.

"It's true, then?" Hilary said in a barely audible whisper.

"The locket belonged to my grandmother, Lady Margaret Duncan, and it has been passed down to succeeding generations of women in our family. My daughter, on the day of the train accident, bidding what she thought would be just a short farewell, gave it to her daughter."

Quiet tears flowed from Hilary's eyes.

The fears and confusion of her childhood, and her mature struggling to come to grips with her own identity, had by no means hardened her heart. As she knelt there at the gentle woman's feet, it was almost as if the little girl in the dream had finally been found . . . rescued from the horror of the unknown. The part of her that had always, however subconsciously, felt like a stranger; helpless, and reaching out for something to fill the emptiness only an orphan can know, was now—suddenly and unexpectedly—comforted. Here was her *own* grandmother, a woman who could surely love and protect a lost little child. The tears that ran down her face were the tears she had been waiting thirty years to shed.

At the same time, another piece of Hilary's complex self remained hesitant, fearful of returning the older woman's loving gaze. The mature young woman she had become was real. She was a child no longer. She had adult anxieties and confusions of her own. She could not hide herself in this lady's arms and forget who she was. She already had a family, a life, a job, a future, and she hadn't been looking for any other. She had dealt with her past by putting it behind her. What was she to do with a past she had never known, now that it had come seeking her against her will?

"Hilary," asked Joanna softly, as if she had read her granddaughter's thoughts, "why are you afraid?"

Hilary brushed her fingers across her wet cheeks. "I suppose I'm afraid of change," she said.

She smiled ironically. "I've a friend who is fond of pointing out my vast inconsistency in this area," she went on. " 'Hilary,' she tells me, 'you want to change the world, but you fight personal change ruthlessly.' To tell you the truth, I don't know why I'm like that. All my life I've had this feeling deep inside that I had to make it on my own. An independence, I guess. Maybe it's common to orphans, I don't know. I've never been comfortable unless I was in control of my surroundings, in control of my own destiny, so to speak. And now to find everything so abruptly turned around, so . . . so . . . beyond my control—it's hardly a pleasant feeling. It's going to take some getting used to."

"What makes you think we would expect you to change?"

"I'm not from your world. I'm not even sure I want to be."

Joanna nodded in understanding but was silent for some time.

Hilary pulled herself to her feet, despite shaking knees, and took a seat beside Joanna.

"It's all going to take some getting used to," she finally repeated with a long sigh.

"Would you like to know who your parents are?" Joanna asked. Her tone, though free of expectation, held quiet entreaty.

"Did they send you?"

"They know nothing of my quest."

"I merely assumed that they—"

"I made the decision when I first began this to keep it to myself until I was sure. I spoke briefly with my son-in-law to begin with, but shared with him only some of my concerns with, shall we call it, the situation as it then stood. But I wanted to explore the mystery before saying anything to them. It turned out to be a wise decision, for there have been many dead-ends, and my feeling of hopelessness after each failure has been . . . well, you can imagine. I sometimes began to think I had dreamed up everything, or was remembering events and places and landmarks incorrectly. I am getting on in years. I even wondered if senility was starting to creep in!"

"And now you will tell them?"

"You do not wish me to?"

"Of course," replied Hilary, defensively again. "What kind of person do you think I am?"

She rose, turned her back on Joanna, and began pacing the small room again. After a moment, she turned around slowly, her face clearly reflecting that she was torn between her adult fears and the deep hopes of a little orphan child. "I'm—I'm so sorry," she said. "I didn't mean to sound that way."

"Think nothing of it, child," replied Joanna. "I do understand, as difficult as that may be for you to grasp. I hope someday to have the opportunity to tell you just how deeply I understand what you are going through—and why."

Hilary smiled, tears again beginning to fall. "What are their names?" she asked in a soft, shaky voice.

"My daughter is Allison—Allison Eleanor MacNeil. That is her maiden name, of course . . ."

But Hilary hardly heard her last words. The moment she heard the name a strange sensation swept over and enveloped her. Allison . . . the mother who had borne her, given her life, cradled her, and then wept over her and grieved for years after her supposed death.

" . . . you resemble her, you know," Lady MacNeil was saying when Hilary became again conscious of her voice. ". . . the hair and eyes. I knew I had found you the moment you walked in. It was all I could do to keep from shouting *hallelujah!* and rushing to you!" She gave a little laugh at the thought.

Hilary returned her smile.

"And your father's name is Logan Macintyre . . ." Once again Hilary's consciousness trailed away . . . *Logan*—what a solid, yet unusual name . . . the father whose manly heart must surely have softened and melted at the touch of his baby daughter, who must have smiled down at her as she lay safely in his strong and protective arms.

These were her parents—*her* parents! who had lived these many years with an emptiness just like her own. Surely they had been haunted all their lives since that awful day by nightmares of their own just as she had been. *Macintyre* . . .

Suddenly Hilary recalled Lady MacNeil's earlier statement: *The child's father had become a rather important man in the government* . . .

Of course! No wonder the name sounded familiar! She could have written off the similarity as a mere coincidence but for that comment. Her father a politician! She could almost laugh if the thought weren't so dreadful. The man was indeed high up—a minister in Wilson's Labour government before the Conservatives unseated it last year . . . in the news recently for his opposition to Wilson's Anti-EEC policies . . . bucking his own party's stand against the Conservatives along with Roy Jenkins, the Shadow Deputy Minister. *That* was her father!

The very thought was unbelievable—humorous, in a way, were the shock not so stunning.

She knew something of Macintyre's history. A decorated war hero who had caused a bit of a stir back in 1950 when he ran for his first term in Parliament. His opposition for the seat had tried to make an issue of his low-level criminal record prior to the war in spite of his full exoneration by the Crown. Somehow Macintyre had won the seat. It was said he had been a confidence man before the war. The question was then asked by those skeptical of his victory whether he had simply conned his unwitting northern constituents. If such was indeed true, he must be very good at it, for he had managed to retain his seat these twenty years and rise to the inner circle of power in Whitehall.

What kind of a family have I fallen into? Hilary thought to herself with mingled astonishment and dismay. Her mother of aristocratic blood . . . her father a politician! *What other thunderclaps would this day bring?* she wondered in disbelief.

"I've heard of him," she said aloud, rousing herself from her reverie, but unable to keep the tremor from her voice.

"Your father is a good man," said Joanna, "and your mother is a kind and gentle woman." Her words were not mere motherly sentimentalities, but were filled with conviction.

"He's the politician you thought I should meet?"

"For more reasons than one," smiled Joanna coyly.

"Yes, I see that now."

"I'm aware of how difficult this must be. Some of the stands your magazine has taken in matters political are not unknown to me."

Hilary forced a smile, but said nothing.

"When would you like to meet them?" asked Joanna.

"You must realize," Hilary hedged, "this is really quite a blow to me."

"I do know. Do I take it then that you are perhaps considering *not* telling them?"

"No," sighed Hilary. "They have a right to know. It's just that—"

She hesitated, then struggled to continue. "—it's just that I need some time . . . to think . . . to get used to all this. This will change my—my—whole world . . . the way I've grown accustomed to looking at things. And not only for myself, but my mother—my adoptive mother—she must be told. I'm her only child, so you can imagine the emotional adjustments this will cause for her as well as for myself. She has given more than half her life to me, Lady MacNeil. Your daughter and her husband—I'm sure they loved me dearly, but they had their baby only three years. I realize that where a child is concerned, it is more than a matter of time, that the bloodline counts for a great deal, but you can see—"

"I understand, Miss Edwards," interjected Joanna with more compassionate understanding than her mere words could indicate. "How much time do you think you will need?"

"I—I don't know."

Joanna reached into her handbag and withdrew a small white card which she held out to Hilary.

"This is how you can reach me," she said.

"Thank you," replied Hilary, taking the card. "Then you will wait until I contact you?"

"You have my word, Miss—no, that will never do," she said in a quick aside almost to herself. "You have my word, *Hilary*," she continued, "on one condition: that you *will* tell them in good time."

"I will—I promise."

Joanna rose and held out her hand in a parting gesture. This time, however, as Hilary took it she began to grasp the depth of emotion in the woman's intense gaze—a grandmother looking upon her granddaughter, now a grown woman, for the first time in nearly thirty years. She sensed the anguish her tentative and uncertain response must have caused in the gentle, soft-spoken old woman. In an effort to somehow make up for her own seeming lack of enthusiasm, Hilary laid her free hand over Joanna's, clasping her dainty hand between her own two.

"I'm sorry I have been so . . . ambivalent," said Hilary. "I guess I'm not very good at this kind of interview. But I do thank you—for finding me—for not giving up. I know I will learn to . . . to love my family . . . and to love you, the more I know you all."

Joanna smiled—a kindly, noble smile. Then, as if her stoic restraint had suddenly broken, tears spilled from the corners of her eyes. Before Hilary realized what she was doing, she had dropped her hands and had her arms around the older woman's slim figure, herself weeping quietly. Joanna returned the embrace, lifting up—in the depths of her being—silent prayers of thankful rejoicing to God.

The tender reunion lasted only a few moments. But perhaps the two women would not have fallen apart so soon had they known this was to be their first and last embrace in this world.

Five days later, while Hilary was still struggling with the dilemma of how to proceed, Lady Joanna MacNeil succumbed to a sudden cerebral hemorrhage.

10 / Uncertainties _____

Hilary stirred a teaspoon of sugar into her second cup of tea.

She had wandered from her kitchen and was now reclining on her sofa. She marveled at how she had forgotten not a single detail of her meeting with Joanna MacNeil. Every look, every word was by now printed indelibly in her memory . . . and upon her heart.

She glanced outside. Everything was black. The night was still and quiet. I have to sleep, she thought. Tomorrow will be a big day. Drinking tea was probably the worse thing to be doing, but she couldn't help it. She had to give her thoughts some company, even if it was only from a teapot.

She could not unfocus her mind from that day in her office. It was to be the last time she would behold that loving, gentle face. *How much have I missed?* Hilary asked herself with more than a twinge of sadness. But the greater part of her sorrow sprang from the painful fact that she could have had at least five more days with her grandmother had she not been so vacillating in her response.

Yet it was foolish to lament the delay now. Her need for time had been valid, if selfish. Even now, she wasn't sure she had fully accepted the startling revelation that had walked into her life in the person of Lady Joanna MacNeil.

Impulse had driven her to attend the funeral. She had taken the train to Aberdeen and then rented a car for the final two-hour drive to the sleepy little village of Port Strathy. During that lonely drive, she first began to consider what she would actually do once she reached the place. She had come all this way without really thinking through her motives, giving hardly a thought to what would come once she arrived. Was she on her way to Lady MacNeil's home to claim her long lost family? Was she going as a relative, as a member of the inner family . . . or as an observer? The answer was far from simple.

When she had first heard about Lady MacNeil's death, Hilary had hoped, or feared—she couldn't tell quite which—that her parents would contact her. She assumed that, knowing death was near, the grandmother would have felt compelled to break her word and tell her children that their daughter lived. But it seemed the suddenness of the woman's collapse had precluded that communication.

She now knew that if she did approach them, it would necessarily be "from out of the blue," so to speak. How much easier it would have been with Lady MacNeil at her side! Notwithstanding the show of confidence and aplomb she was able to manifest when talking in a professional setting with important people in London and throughout Britain, this would take a kind of courage with which she was not intimately acquainted. She wished it all didn't depend on her.

For the first time the unthinkable idea of keeping silent began to nag at her. It was certainly a possibility now. No one would ever know. She could go on with her life unchanged. Logan and Allison Macintyre would be no worse off for her silence.

Even as the notion came to her, however, Hilary shook it off. It *wasn't* a possibility. How could she even consider such a thing? Where would her integrity as a truth-seeker be if she turned her back on one of life's most fundamental duties: honor to father and mother? Besides, she had given the lady—her grandmother—her word.

When and how to do what she must eventually do, she didn't know. This was uncharted ground. Was it shyness? Was it fear? Was it uncertainty over how she would be received? Hilary shrank from the very weakness all these questions suggested. Now more than ever she would have to be strong.

Yet as she stood at the woman's graveside, watching the stream of strangers file by—friends, and the people who were now supposed to be her family—any nerve she might have been able to summon quickly vanished. *I must say something to someone*, she thought. Yet as the black-garbed crowd slowly and silently disbursed, leaving her standing there alone in the countryside of an unfamiliar Scottish setting, no one seemed to pay her much notice, and her mouth was far too dry to speak. She *couldn't* just . . . just walk up and . . . and—and what?

It wasn't difficult for Hilary to convince herself of the utter foolhardiness of her marching up to these strangers and declaring herself their missing daughter. At best they would think her a crackpot. At worst, a bold-faced fraud hoping to catch them at their moment of weakness in order to get her clutches on a piece of the dead woman's estate. They would never believe her.

With such a conflicting set of thoughts in her brain, and an even more frenetic jumble of emotions in her heart, Hilary—timid, disappointed, and feeling every inch a coward—let them all pass silently out of sight, then made her own way back to her car, drove to the Inn to pick up her things, and then and began the return drive to Aberdeen, and thence back to London.

If she had hoped to find inner peace in the frenzy and anonymity of the city, she was to be disappointed on that front as well. In a matter of a few short days after her return came the Whitehall interview where Logan Macintyre unexpectedly turned up. Why he didn't seem to recognize her, she never knew. Was it a hidden longing to have her secret discovered without she herself having to boldly step forward that impelled her to confront the M.P.'s as she had, rather than cowering down into her seat in silence, hoping he wouldn't see her? And then on the heels of that came the nightmare that had spurred this late night reflection.

The ancient Greeks would say that the Fates were willing her toward her destiny. She knew better, of course. But the truth of Romans 8:28 was hardly more comforting at this point. It still meant she was being guided by a hand stronger than her own, toward a destiny, a plan, a purpose she couldn't see and over which she had no control. Many years ago, as a teenager, she had entrusted her life to God. As she had matured, she had learned to recognize His guidance in her life. She had even tried to explain the phenomenon to Murry. But never had anything of this magnitude confronted her.

If this were indeed His doing, why hadn't He given her the courage and resolve to do the right thing?

"Lord, what do you want me to do?" she prayed aloud.

The only answer she received was the still quiet of her apartment.

She knew she needed to be more patient where things of the Spirit were concerned. But sitting back and waiting had never been her forte.

"Oh, Lord," she sighed, "I want to be the person you want me to be . . . I'm just not sure who that is." Then she added in barely more than a whisper, "Give me the strength . . . yes, and the boldness to do what you show me."

Hilary glanced around, sighed tiredly, then shivered, realizing for the first time how chilly her flat was at that hour. She looked up at the clock over the television. Two A.M. She pulled a blanket up over her shoulders, not really intending to sleep there on the sofa, yet hardly relishing the idea of even the short walk back to bed. In five minutes she was asleep; her last thoughts before dozing off were a vague determination to spend some time in prayer, and an even vaguer anxiety that her nightmare might return if she fell asleep.

11 / The Parcel

The three-block walk to the Underground station helped clear Hilary's head, still functioning obediently after only four hours' sleep. By the time she reached her office at 7:30 A.M., she was—assisted by the growing effect of three hastily gulped cups of strong coffee—fully alert and ready to meet a vigorous day.

Her morning was consumed with meetings—an hour with the people in graphics, another with the budget department, a lengthy and somewhat heated discussion with the printer over increased rates, and finally several individual conferences with members of the editorial staff. When she returned to her private office at 11:30, it was for the first time since she had hung up her jacket and purse four hours earlier. Betty followed her in with the morning mail, which consisted of a stack of letters and one parcel. She barely had begun to glance through them when Murry Fitts knocked on her door. She looked up, then beckoned him in.

"We still going out to the East End?" he asked, poking his head in. "Maybe have a look at that fire site?"

"I hadn't forgotten," Hilary replied. "I even dressed for it." She waved a hand in front of her to indicate her casual clothing—khaki trousers, peach polo shirt, and brown leather oxfords. "Are you free now?"

"Yes, I kept the afternoon clear."

"Great. Then let's go," said Hilary, jumping up, glad for the diversion of continued activity. "If we get out of here now, we might even be able to grab a bit of lunch."

A short while later they were seated in the back of a black Austin. As the taxi snaked its way through London's congested noon-hour traffic, Murry filled Hilary in on his activities during the hours since they had last met. He had spent the morning poring through the Fire Brigade records and had the bleary eyes to prove it. He had also spoken to a building official regarding the permitting process for the various redevelopment projects in the area.

"Hmm. That is interesting," mused Hilary when Murry took a break in his enthusiastic monologue. The contrast, however, between her indifferent tone and her words was not lost on her companion.

When he was through, Hilary turned her attention to the passing view outside the taxi window. They were approaching their destination, and she marveled that despite all the post-war reconstruction in the area, the East

End had retained its look of dingy squalor. This section of London had received the worst of the Luftwaffe attacks, probably in part because Hitler had hoped that it would incite the poverty-stricken inhabitants to revolt against their government. It had produced quite the opposite effect, however, among the stalwart residents. Most East-enders liked their little corner of London, despite the fact that some labeled it a "slum."

Hilary remembered the friendly neighborhood in Whitechapel where she had grown up. It may not have been pretty, but she had always felt secure there. Beyond her own mum, there were always at least five other motherly matrons looking out for her and the other youngsters roaming the streets. She recalled the kindly missionary lady who would set up her little wooden archway on a street corner where any child with a farthing, and not too tall to pass under the arch, could receive a precious packet of small toys.

And there were the street games invented by children who thought nothing of trash-strewn alleys or wartime rubble as a playground offering as many mysteries and delights as any more rural setting. All of it was set against the musical twang of the bawdy Cockney tongue; unfortunately, years of education had obliterated all but a trace of the dialect from Hilary's speech.

The sense of nostalgia came upon her so suddenly she hardly had time to brace herself against the quickly following surge of renewed inner turmoil. The ties of a girl named Hilary Edwards to her home of so many years went deep, and she wondered if she could ever make room in that same heart for a stranger named Joanna Hilary Macintyre.

Murry's down-to-earth voice broke into her thoughts, rescuing her—for the moment at least—from further having to ponder her fate.

"There it is," he said, pointing ahead to where the burned-out skeleton of an apartment building stood eerily against the gray overcast sky. The premises were all cordoned off well back of the debris.

The cab pulled to a stop across the street. Hilary climbed out and paid the cabbie while Murry gathered up his camera bag and followed. They waited for the cab to pull away, then crossed. Hilary shivered involuntarily.

"You okay?" asked Murry with genuine concern. "You seemed pretty quiet in the cab."

"I'm fine. Just got some things on my mind, that's all. And there's something depressing about a burned-out building. It's such a waste. I've never much liked fires. Come on, let's walk around a bit."

While Murry snapped pictures, Hilary gradually made her way about the perimeter of the building; and by the time Murry caught up with her again, she was deeply involved in an impassioned discussion with two residents of an adjoining tenement.

They did not get back to the office till after five.

"How about grabbing a bite of dinner?" asked Fitts as they walked inside.

"Thanks, Murry, but I . . . ."

She paused, then added, "Yes, that sounds great. I will."

"I've got to drop this film off at the lab, and then make a call or two."

"Don't hurry on my account," laughed Hilary. "I've got a dozen things to check on! But I'll try to have it wrapped up by 6:15 or 6:30. That be okay? I doubt if I'll even have the chance to look at my mail."

"Six-thirty's fine. If we make it, that will be the earliest you've left here within memory!"

In reality they did not get away until 7:10—still a record. But the extra forty minutes had still not gotten Hilary anywhere close to her day's mail. As they drove the four miles to Murry's modest two-bedroom home in his aging Renault, Hilary chose not to mention that part of her reason for accepting his invitation was the thought that it might provide just the sort of escape she needed from her tormented emotions—something she had been trying to accomplish the entire day. She knew she would have to make a decision regarding Lady MacNeil's revelation, and soon. But until something solid presented itself, or at least some appropriate course of action became clear, she had to go on with her own life. And she certainly didn't relish an evening alone in her flat. She had been praying, and an answer would come. But until that time there was no reason to beat herself with anxiety. Or so she told herself. But the only way she could keep the unpleasant thoughts at bay seemed to be with continuous activity.

By the time she arrived back home, it was 10:30 and the previous night's lack of sleep had finally caught up with her. She fell into bed and slept soundly and dreamlessly until morning.

The next day was like the previous one; though the people and topics and situations were different, Hilary managed to pack as much into the day after deadline as she had the day before it.

The Common Market vote had been taken the previous night in Parliament. Though she tended to oppose the move, she was not so much upset by the resounding victory of assent as she was by the morning's television reports of the event, which included several shots and two brief interviews with Logan Macintyre.

Seeing his face had been more disconcerting than any political event! Over and over in her mind kept tumbling the incredible words: "That man is my father!"

The very thought had tied her stomach in knots, all the more so in the knowledge that her silence was doing him a great injustice. She had attempted to counter that realization by rationalizing to herself that she was not that great a catch as a daughter—maybe the Macintyres would just as soon never know.

She knew that could never be true, and it hardly helped pacify her uneasiness about keeping silent. Always Lady MacNeil's face would intrude upon her attempts at pragmatism, and then Hilary would feel more deeply than ever her own deceit at keeping her startling revelation to herself.

She had made a gallant effort to bury herself in her work, in unending calls and interviews, and even attempts to pick up her article where she had left it several days earlier. But by late afternoon she had to admit to herself that the effort had not been successful. She could not hide from it.

She grabbed her coat and left the building—for what destination, she had no idea. She couldn't go home. She turned up the sidewalk and began to walk. Unconsciously she went wherever her feet chanced to lead her. Three hours later she was still walking, still thinking, oblivious to pangs of hunger. She had been the length and breadth of Hyde Park, through Kensington Gardens, then past Buckingham Palace and finally the Houses of Parliament and back to the office. By the time she returned, it was 8:30, and the place was deserted. She had a stack of work she convinced herself she ought to take home. She'd get it, then grab a taxi back to the flat.

Hilary unlocked the door and walked through the darkened and empty pressroom directly to her office. There she switched on her light and stood gazing about. Her desk was a cluttered mess. She had been so caught up in activity lately that she had been neglectful of daily office business. It was clear Betty had done what was possible to keep it orderly, but there were two or three days of unopened mail and correspondence sitting in a stack that seemed at least eight inches high!

The sight made her realize more clearly than ever that she had to get her life back in order.

She opened her briefcase, thumbed through the files on her desk, laying the most pressing articles inside. She could probably make some headway this evening in the quietness of her apartment. She wanted to work yesterday's interview with those people across from the fire into the article. Good thing she didn't require eight hours sleep every night.

She picked up what was at least two days worth of mail and gave it a quick scan through to see what was the most urgent. It was not until she picked up several manila-envelope-sized pieces that she noticed the parcel at the bottom of the stack. Now she remembered; it had come yesterday.

It was nearly as large as a ream of paper, and quite as heavy. It was no ordinary packet, for it appeared to have traveled a great many miles, judging from its battered condition and many official stamps.

Closer inspection revealed no return address, but one of the postmarks had originated in Scotland and she could find none from any farther away. Another postmark read Leeds, dated several days after the one from Aberdeen. Whatever the package was, and wherever it had come from, it had certainly taken a circuitous route in finally winding up at *The Berkshire Review*. The earliest date stamped on the package was from some two and a half weeks earlier.

Hilary pushed aside her other mail and, sensing the rising tide of some unforeseen emotion within her, tore open the brown paper wrapping.

Inside, her hands clutched a box. Slowly she lifted off its lid, and her eyes fell upon what could not have been a more unexpected sight. Hilary found herself gazing upon a thick, handwritten manuscript bearing the name: Joanna Matheson MacNeil.

The title beneath the name simply read *Stonewycke Journal*. Under those profoundly significant words, centered in the page, was a single sentence of scripture from Psalm 102:

Let this be written for a future generation, that a people not yet created may praise the Lord.

Tucked between the first two pages was a small folded sheet of light blue stationery. Hilary picked it up and read:

Dear Hilary,

I believe I can somewhat understand many of your present confusions and hesitancies. It is a difficult upheaval in your life you are faced with, and one, I know, which came to you unsought. Although I would never ask you to relinquish or in any way alter your attachments to your adoptive family, it is a reality we cannot change that you now have another family as well. I hope and pray that in time you will feel some affection for us. Thus it came to me the other day that it might help you to perceive our family better if you could understand some of the heritage that is now yours—should you choose to have us. When we met I told you that I hoped I would one day have the opportunity to tell you my story. It would seem that now, perhaps, that moment has come.

So, after much consideration, I have decided to send you this manuscript. It is a journal I have kept over the years chronicling as much of the history of the Stonewycke heritage and the lives of its people as I have been able to learn myself. As you will see, I too came to this family as a stranger. But as I learned of my predecessors, this heritage took me into itself and made me one with it, as I have no doubt it will do to you as well. This is by no means polished or professional by the standards you are surely accustomed to. But I entreat you to read it, and perhaps through it find your own place within the family that is, for better or worse, a part of you.

With deepest affection,
Joanna MacNeil

With silent tears streaming from her eyes, Hilary sank down into her chair, still grasping the precious letter. The note was dated the day before Lady Joanna's death, and Hilary could not help but sense that these were her last words to her granddaughter as surely as if Hilary had been called to the dear woman's deathbed.

Again a great sadness swept over Hilary. She was struck once more, as she had been the day she learned of the lady's—her own grandmother's—death—with the terrible emptiness of "what might have been."

She looked down at Lady Joanna's journal, and with trembling fingers turned to the first page.

I came to Scotland a stranger, it read, *with no past to speak of, and an uncertain future. My quest was a vague one, and never would I have presumed to think that it would radically change my whole life. For my journey led, indeed, to life—full and complete life in the Spirit of Christ. And with this, God added to me an intensely fulfilling past, and a future brimming with promise. He gave me people to love, and people who loved me. He gave me a family, a heritage that will always demonstrate to me God's unwavering presence with His faithful ones. And this is what gives meaning to the story of the Stonewycke legacy.*

It is so clearly exemplified in the life of dear Maggie Duncan—my own grandmother—who will always be the matriarch of matriarchs. Her pilgrimage of faith perhaps began that day—if such a moment can ever be sharply defined—when as a child of thirteen she went into her beloved stables to find that her father had sold her dear horse, Cinder. Ah, how I remember the day she told me the story of Cinder, how the tears of mingled pain and joy and thankfulness spilled down her old cheeks at the memory which was then almost sixty years old, and how her eyes came alive when she began to reflect aloud on the depth of love and judgment passed to her from her own personal childhood sage, the groom who took care of the family stables. . . .

Suddenly the lights in the pressroom flashed on. Hilary's whole body jerked with a start as if she'd been awakened from a trance. She looked up with a dull expression. The janitor had wheeled his cleaning cart into the big room and, looking up to see Hilary still in her office, he waved a greeting and ambled to her door.

"Workin' late tonight, eh, Miss Edwards?" he said, poking his head into the doorway.

"Yes . . . I suppose so."

"I can wait to do these rooms if you like."

"No," said Hilary, gradually coming to herself. "I only have to gather up a few things; then I'm off. You go on with your work."

"Thank you, miss. If it's all the same to you, I'll do just that."

Hilary watched him shuffle away, then stood, laying the journal in her briefcase on top of the other work. As she snapped the clasp closed, however, she doubted she'd get anything else done tonight. She had tried so hard to fill her life with diversions lately, but this uncanny arrival of the journal—many, many days after it should have gotten to her, served as a powerful and unavoidable reminder that she could not run forever from the destiny that awaited her. The thing she had tried to hide from was now too tangible and present to elude. It was as real as the papers she had just held in her hand, as real as had been the kind, noble countenance—and now, as she recalled the face, she realized it had contained another expression as well, an expression of nothing more, nothing less than a deep and personal love—of Lady Joanna MacNeil, her namesake . . . and her own grandmother.

By the time Hilary had reached her flat, all thought of work had vanished. Her mind and heart—indeed, her entire being—was focused on one sole object—a place called Stonewycke, and the life's blood that had been coursing through the inhabitants of its stone walls for over four hundred years.

Before she nodded off to sleep that night some time after two A.M., Hilary had become familiar with names she would never have dreamed could move her so—names which, in the distinctive and significant hand of Joanna MacNeil, took on character and personality and meaning far beyond the actual words printed on the page. In the very handwriting of her grandmother, they seemed to come to life, filling Hilary with a sense of mingled longing and fullness which her intellect could find no possible way to describe. She felt herself gradually being caught up into something far beyond the confines of her own little world.

Here were Atlanta and Maggie, with whom she suddenly felt intimate, and a rebellious young nobleman they called Ian, and a wise old groom named Digory—her own great uncle by several generations past—who, through the miracle of after-years, had been grafted into the family line to an even more significant degree than his master and nemesis, James Duncan. And most poignant of all to Hilary as she read was the touching story of Joanna's own arrival in Scotland, a stranger in a foreign land, whose uncertain future and perplexity of heart certainly outweighed anything Hilary herself had yet had to face.

As Hilary read and read, she began to see more than a mere recounting of events. She gradually realized that the most vital thread which wove through the fabric of the Stonewycke story was the ever-present hand of God moving in the lives of these people—her own ancestors.

This was *her* family! And it was no ordinary one. God had been active among its people for years. And He was moving still!

12 / Hilary's Resolve

When Hilary awoke at 7:30 in the morning, it was all as fresh in her mind as if only moments and not hours of sleep had intervened.

The events of the previous night had been imprinted forever on her heart—they had penetrated into the very depths of her very soul. No more could she run or hide from the destiny that was pursuing her. No more could she deny who she was or turn her back on this family from which she had sprung.

With the reflections that came with morning's light, she knew as clearly as if she were standing gazing into a clean Highland loch that she must, before anything else, face the two new scions of that family—her own parents, Logan and Allison Macintyre.

Hilary knew what she must do.

Though she dressed with particular care that morning, she did so hastily, and with fingers perspiring and cold. She skipped breakfast. She could not have eaten even if she were willing to spend the extra time on it. What she must do she wanted to do quickly—not just to get it over with, but because she was suddenly eager to do so.

She caught a cab a block from her building in a surprisingly short time, and it was only as the cabby asked, "Where to, mum?" that she realized she did not have any idea where the Macintyres lived. It was a silly detail to have forgotten, especially since she had had more than two weeks to look it up, and even drive by if she had wanted. But she had never wanted to before this moment. And now she didn't want to waste the time trying to find the home address. Therefore she answered the cabby with the single word:

"Whitehall."

This would probably be the best way after all, she reasoned with herself. A man could be so much more stoic and level-headed in matters such as this. So, by approaching her father first, she thought, they might be able to avoid an emotional scene. Though why she was worried about that now she didn't know; her emotions were already such a jumble! But hopefully she'd be able to get through it without making a goose of herself. After she spoke with Mr. Macintyre, he could call his wife and prepare for a later meeting. Yes, this was just the thing.

By the time the taxi pulled up at her destination around 8:50, she once again felt collected and, if not exactly confident, at least prepared for what lay ahead.

She located Logan Macintyre's office in the Parliamentary administrative buildings, walked inside, and stepped into the lift as she had done many times before, as if this were no more than an interview with a politician. But this interview would be more—far more—than that. This would be like no interview she had ever had in her life! Before the lift came to a stop, a dreadful fluttering had crept into her stomach, driving out all traces of the composure she had felt earlier.

She stepped outside and began slowly walking down the corridor, aware that her knees had begun to tremble. As she lifted her hand to turn the latch and open the door and walk into Mr. Macintyre's suite of offices, she found it was shaking.

Hilary paused a moment, took a deep breath as if to regain her equilibrium, but instead her head began to swim airily and she had to grab the door latch all the more firmly. What was wrong? She had never felt such sensations before! The thought occurred to turn and flee, except at that very moment she heard the sound of voices approaching behind her in the corridor. Feeling suddenly foolish standing there leaning against the door, she opened it the rest of the way and walked inside.

It was a small miracle she could even speak. Though at that moment her voice was small and sounded thin and hollow.

"May I help you?" asked the receptionist.

"Yes, I'd like . . . I'd like to see Mr. Macintyre."

"Do you have an appointment?"

"No—no, I don't . . . I came rather . . . suddenly."

"Well, you see, today is Saturday and Mr. Macintyre doesn't usually come in, and besides—"

"Oh—" interrupted Hilary almost in a daze. For the first time the day of the week dawned on her. No wonder it had been so easy to get a cab! She hadn't even noticed the quiet streets.

"Perhaps I can reach him at home," she said, regaining her resolve. She had come too far to be easily turned aside.

"It would be of no avail anyway, miss. As I was about to say, Mr. Macintyre has returned north to Scotland."

"Scotland?" A deflated sense of despair was evident in Hilary's tone.

"Yes, to his home."

"How long will he be gone?"

"It is difficult to say. There has been a recent death in the family, and he had only returned to London long enough to participate in the EEC vote."

"Mrs. Macintyre is in Scotland too?"

"That's right, miss."

Without another word, Hilary turned and exited the office. She felt as though an icy hand had clamped itself over her resolve. What could she do now?

As she wandered out of the building onto the sidewalk, she felt a great emptiness inside. If I came here on a kind of impulse, she thought, it was no mere whim. There was a purpose to it, a purpose I cannot ignore. Despite this momentary setback, her course was set. There could be no turning back now. She must follow wherever it led. She *must* fulfill her promise to Lady Joanna!

Sensing a sudden new resolve, Hilary hailed another taxi. This time she instructed the man to take her home. There, she told him to wait while she went inside. In less than fifteen minutes she emerged carrying a small suitcase and an overnight bag. She raced down the few steps, across the sidewalk, and jumped back inside while the cabby put in her bags.

"Driver," she said, her voice as intense as the light in her eyes, "take me to Euston Station!"

13 / North Toward Destiny

She was nearly to Northampton before the import of her sudden decision finally dawned on Hilary.

She was returning to Scotland, to the land of her heritage.

What an impulsive thing to do, she thought to herself, grab the first train out of London to Edinburgh! But the call of her past had beckoned with compelling urgency, and this was no time to be dictated to by a railway schedule.

As Hilary pondered the implications of her decision, she wondered what it would be like to face her parents. That was the question which burned in her brain more continuously than any other. That would be the one thrilling, terrifying moment. Would they open their arms . . . or wish she'd never come?

Of course, once Lady Joanna made her "discovery" of Hilary's identity, the encounter was inevitable. Why had she fought it so long? The exhilaration she felt at having finally surrendered to the destiny set before her—in spite of the dreadful uncertainty—was invigorating. At long last she allowed her mind to explore the possibilities.

What would these people be like? What would it be like to be a part of their family—*her* family now? She thought of her adoptive mother; what would her reaction be? She imagined Christmas dinner with the daughter of the elegant and aristocratic Lady MacNeil sitting beside Hilary's simple, earthy, working-class mother. She had no doubt the wise and solid Mrs. Edwards would be able to hold her own in such company once she overcame her initial awe.

What would her parents' reaction be? Surely the daughter of such a woman as Lady Joanna could harbor no snobbery or prejudice. Then for the first time it dawned on Hilary that Logan Macintyre came from a working-class background himself. Had he traveled too far from his roots to remember, and to feel with such decent and simple people?

With that a more fearsome thought formed in Hilary's mind.

Would they be able to accept *her*? Not only because of her upbringing, but also because she was now a grown woman, with personality and character and values and attitudes already set? They certainly wouldn't agree with many of her social and political views. It did not necessarily follow that just because she was their daughter, they would automatically *like* her. She might not even like them.

She thought of all the chances she had taken over the years—the pursuit of an education against financial and social odds; taking over the management of *The Berkshire Review* despite its precarious position. Not to mention the many causes she had been quick to espouse—the more unlikely her chances for success, it sometimes seemed, the more determined she was to fight on the side of the apparent underdog. Yes, she had tackled many difficult obstacles in her life, yet this simple act now before her of meeting her parents loomed as by far the most formidable.

At that moment a train steward approached her seat. She pulled herself from her reverie and glanced up.

"Ma'am," he said with a smile, "the dining car will be opened only fifteen more minutes if you wish luncheon."

"Thank you," replied Hilary, her voice distracted and as far away as were her thoughts of food. "I'm fine for now. I'll wait for dinner."

He nodded and moved on down the aisle. Her eyes followed him disinterestedly for a moment. She had to change trains later in the afternoon. Maybe she'd get off and have something to eat in Yorkshire before the night train to Scotland.

Slowly Hilary turned her gaze out the window. The countryside rushed past in a blur of fields and farm houses, country roads and telephone lines. She wondered if this was the same route her grandmother and she had taken that fateful day thirty years ago. For the first time Hilary reflected back on those earlier events as something she had actually been part of. Her dream would seem to indicate that, in her own way, she remembered the terrible holocaust of death and explosion as vividly as did Lady Joanna. Perhaps it might not have been too far from where they now were, and the realization sent a shudder down Hilary's spine.

Had her grandmother on that day been looking out on this same tranquil scene, perhaps anticipating her return home, made even more joyful by the presence of her little granddaughter? What mysterious necessity had kept Allison behind in London, leaving her daughter to go off without her? Wartime had certainly forced the change of many priorities. Yet what could have been so important for a mother to send off a young child on such a long trip at such a precarious time?

Unconsciously Hilary's gaze fell to the box on her lap. Perhaps the answers were in Lady Joanna's manuscript. She lifted the lid and almost reverently took out the bound pages. Last evening, after skimming through various parts at random, Hilary had begun to read through it continuously, wanting to gain the full impact of the story as it unfolded historically. And now, as she sat on the train, she resisted the urge to skip ahead to whatever parts might concern her more directly, and instead opened the pages to where she had left off in the small hours of the previous night.

She had read of Lady Margaret's reminiscences of her childhood, of her love for the Strathy Valley, her love of riding. She had read of old

Digory and his tender, compassionate fondness for the young girl. She had read of Maggie's stormy relationship with her father James, and of the caring, yet almost solemn, unspoken love between Maggie and the fascinating yet mysterious and impenetrable Atlanta—a woman who seemed in many ways to hearken back to the lost peoples, lost times, and faded memories of Scotland's silent past.

She read, too, of that fateful day when Maggie left her home, neither herself nor her mother realizing what poignant grief the memory of that parting would later bring to each. Hilary could feel the emotion even as she read the words her grandmother had written.

Then Atlanta, holding the envelope she had prepared, gave it to her daughter. Lady Margaret would never forget her mother's words on that, the last day they would ever see one another: "Maggie," she said, "I want you to take this with you. You need not open it now; you would scarcely grasp its significance if you did. But I want you to have it, in the event that something should happen to me, or in case you are gone longer than we anticipate. It is the promise not only for your return but for the safety of this land we love. This will always be your home, whatever happens. Do you understand me? It is yours!" Those final words never faded from Maggie's mind and heart even after forty years of exile.

Joanna then went on to recount, according to the memory of Lady Margaret late in her long life, the separation from her beloved young Ian, the voyage to America, the heartache of loss, the trip west, and many memories of that sad but strengthening time which had for so long remained locked in the heart of the aging woman.

Hilary set down the manuscript, closed her eyes, and tried to imagine what it must have been like for Maggie Duncan, only seventeen years old, newly in love, torn between father and mother and lover, to have been wrenched from her home so violently by events beyond her control.

But the significance of that moment had extended far beyond simply a young girl's leaving *home*. If nothing else was clearly evident as she read on in this chronicle of a family's heritage, one thing was certain—Stonewycke was *more* than a mere home. Stonewycke and the parcel of earth surrounding it, and all it had come to represent among the people of the region, had grown to the proportion of something almost sacred, pulsating with life. There was nothing that could be considered hallowed in the land or the castle themselves. It was only as God worked in and through them, and gave meaning to places and events by virtue of His greater workings in the hearts of men and women, that Stonewycke began to throb with what seemed a spirit of its own, which was nothing more nor less than God's Spirit himself.

As she wrote, at times, Joanna would pause in her telling of events to reflect on this strange phenomenon of Stonewycke.

How can a piece of real estate, a mere chunk of ground, an ancient castle take on such meaning in a region's life? Sometimes I fear we of this family have elevated the importance of this place all out of proportion. I have at times wondered if God is pleased. But then I recall that it is God himself who has infused this life into Stonewycke, and that it is none other than His life—in us, in our hearts, not in the land itself—which gives rise to these feelings. And in so doing He has indeed put something special here. I had no idea how—when I first came to Strathy as a timid and insecure outsider—this place would draw me into itself.

Lady Margaret often confessed that she felt this love for the land flowed in her blood as if it were part of her cellular makeup itself. Then a look would come over her, and I could almost imagine that she was Maggie again, not my seventy-five-year-old grandmother who had been through so much—a look would come over her of such innocent happiness. She would say, "It is something like the love one has for a child"— and I knew as she spoke, for her eyes said it, that she was thinking of me. "You love that child with all your soul. Yet at the same time you realize she is a gift from God. And surrendering her to Him, your love is not reduced, but made something even greater."

Then again her years would become visible in the far-off gaze of wisdom and maturity in her eyes, and she would say, "It is only as we grasp our possessions to ourselves, without giving Christ lordship over them, that they become millstones instead of blessings. That's why the heritage of Stonewycke never could really pass to my father. He never knew the true Source of life. That is why I have, for these last twenty years, never ceased praying fervently that those who come after me would never lose sight of God's work in and through this place. That, and not we ourselves, is the life that passes down from generation to generation." And at such times I could not but wish I had known her, really known her earlier. Yet God's ways are for the best.

As Hilary paused in her reading, she sighed deeply. Is not that my own response? she wondered. "If only I had known all this sooner . . . if only I had known her sooner." How perfectly Joanna's reflections on her grandmother Lady Margaret now expressed Hilary's feelings toward Lady Joanna! Now she was following in her grandmother's footsteps, making this pilgrimage back to the land of her birth, having no inkling what future awaited her.

The land, passed down from generation to generation through a line of stalwart women—still it remained, immovable, silent, enduring. Atlanta was gone. Maggie was gone. Now Lady Joanna was gone. But the land remained the one constant in the turbulent history of this Scottish family. Now she was going there.

But no, Hilary thought suddenly. That wasn't true. The land wasn't everything. Lady Joanna had made that clear in what she had written. The land was merely an external manifestation of something deeper. The land, no matter how much it was loved, served only as a stage upon which life was lived and choices were made. It was that life and those choices, as they progressed down through time, adding one upon the other, from son to daughter, from grandmother to granddaughter, which led to Life, or away from it. The ongoing daily choice through the years to live in obedience to God's ways, and to make Stonewycke a citadel to preserve a witness to His goodness—this was the true driving force behind this family.

Lady Joanna's faith was clearly evident. Yet it could be seen as an ongoing expression of the faith of Margaret and Ian Duncan, perhaps even owing a good deal of its vitality to the faithfulness of their prayers. Before them had come Anson Ramsey, of whom only a little was said in the journal, but who seemed a bulwark in the family's fortress of belief in God. There had been ignoble ones, too, who had carried the name Ramsey and Duncan. But as bent as some of them had seemed on assaulting the walls of faith, God seemed always to pull the family up and forward through His obedient ones.

What of her own parents? Hilary wondered. Do they, too, carry the lineage of godliness in their veins? She knew that politically Logan Macintyre was reputed to be a man of integrity and uprightness. Now that she thought about it, hadn't she read a profile on him somewhere about his being a Christian too, occasionally outspoken concerning his beliefs?

Suddenly Hilary thought of her own walk of faith. It was not altogether impossible that she was sitting here as a Christian herself, able to grasp the spiritual significance of Lady Joanna's words, because of something deep within her she had never realized existed. There was certainly nothing in her childhood to have stimulated her toward the Lord and His ways. The belief of her adopted parents was nominal. Her father had been a good man, but he had never attended church or thought about spiritual things. His not uncommon view was that religion was for women. Her mother went halfway regularly to Church of England services, but her motivation came from tradition rather than from any hunger toward God in her heart. If she believed in a personal way, the only indication came at times of stress. There was nothing in Hilary's early home life to have planted the seeds of true personal belief in her heart.

But something had always drawn Hilary toward, and never away from God. Even when she branched out, left home, and entered the highly secular university world, and later the active, modern world of London business, there was always a tug in her heart that spoke of a deeper life. She could not remember a time when she had *not* believed, though over the years that belief matured as she grew—from a vague childlike sense that God cared for her, to the firm adult conviction that the Lord was her intimate friend, guiding the direction of her life.

When those occasional times of doubt and insecurity had come, God had always faithfully provided people to help and support her at the crucial moment.

Was it possible that not only the physical but the spiritual blood from the Ramsey and Duncan lines flowed through her veins? Could it be that the pull of her heart toward God, the hunger she had always felt to make Him her friend and live according to His ways—could those desires be the answer to generations of righteous lives and prayers offered up by her predecessors in this unusual family?

Did God really work that way? she wondered. Could life in the spirit be *passed on*? No, she thought, that could hardly be. Every individual is accountable to God for himself. The choices I make must be mine alone.

Yet . . . there might be some internal predisposition *toward* or *away from* God. What about the blessings and curses of God extending to the third and fourth generation? What about the time-demolishing power of righteous prayer? Was it not a fact in God's kingdom that time was of little consequence, and that prayer was not bound by it?

Had Maggie's and Joanna's prayers reached across time and space and thirty years of separation and . . . touched *her*?

The very thought was too incredible to fathom—that she, all her life, had been, without the slightest awareness, affected in a daily and significant way because of the prayers and spiritual disposition and progenetive strength inherent in the lives of people she had never known!

Hilary sighed again. It was indeed too much to comprehend. Was it possible that during all those years God had been preparing her for this moment? Preparing her for . . .

The half-formed thought trailed away as she let herself be distracted by a scene out the train window. A boy was herding a small flock of sheep over a little grassy knoll, probably heading for the stone byre in the distance. It seemed as if the twentieth century had hardly touched the place. Yet they could not be more than two hundred miles from London.

Then Hilary noted the descending sun. She had been traveling most of the day, so intently reading and deep in thought that she had hardly noticed the passing of miles and hours. She would be in Edinburgh in several hours, and from there it would be north to Aberdeen.

She took off her glasses and rubbed her eyes. When a porter called for dinner, she decided to eat on the train rather than wait. She rose, walked to the dining car, and there enjoyed a meal of broiled perch, squash, and boiled potatoes. She was hungry and did not even mind her talkative table-companion, a retired schoolteacher from York who miraculously managed to keep up a nonstop conversation and still consume a hearty meal.

"Bound for Scotland, you say?" said the woman, dabbing the corners of her mouth with the linen napkin. "Beautiful country, I'm sure, but a bit . . . ah, rustic, is it not? Even nowadays. What did you say was taking you north?"

"Well . . . family, I suppose you would say," answered Hilary with an uncertainty her companion took no note of.

"Funny, you don't have a Scottish accent—though there is a bit of something in your voice that's not entirely London. I've got rather a cunning for this sort of thing. I was in Bangkok last year on a Far East tour and met a couple from America. I guessed right off they were from Pennsylvania, and they were astounded!"

Hilary smiled, and the woman seemed to require no further encouragement to regale her with another half-hour of stories from her travels. Hilary could not help wondering what the touring schoolteacher would think of her story—a classic Dickens tale of a poor East End girl who suddenly discovers herself of noble parentage.

Hilary finally took her leave. When she returned to her own car and walked to her seat, there was the journal, as if it were waiting patiently, allowing her the distraction of dinner but then persistently bidding her return.

Within two hours she had made her northbound connection and was seated again, alone with her thoughts. Outside, the dusk deepened, gradually enveloping the speeding train. Hilary read on.

How clearly I remember that day Dorey invited me to his house—The House, as we were accustomed to calling it—for tea. I was escorted into the banquet hall where the great, long table was all decked out with silver candelabra and bowls of the loveliest of spring flowers, along with the finest china and glassware. And there sat Dorey, looking in some respects so lonely and forlorn, yet, dressed as he was in formal attire, I could immediately see this was no mere gardener. That noble look I had caught in his eyes once or twice now returned full force. . . .

I unfastened my grandmother's gold locket and held it open to him. "This is you, isn't it?" I asked through a knot in my throat. Tears formed in his eyes as he wrapped his fingers around the precious reminder of his youthful love.

"At least there's one thing," he said. "There's you. Perhaps it is true that God is merciful. I thought she was dead. That is what they told me. She, along with the child . . ."

Then the truth began to dawn upon me, though it should have long before this, as it had with Dorey. It was more than I could have dared hope for when I had set foot on that ship in New York harbor as an innocent young girl cast adrift into the world. But I knew in my heart it was true, that here—thousands of miles from what had once been my home—I had found my grandfather!

Quite unexpectedly Hilary found tears rising in her own eyes.

So Lady Joanna *did* know what she herself was experiencing! Joanna, however, had come to Scotland seeking her roots; Hilary, on the other hand, had stumbled unwittingly, even unwillingly, upon them.

How cruel her ambivalence must have seemed to her grandmother! How desperately Hilary wished she could now repent for all that. Of course, it was too late. Though her present journey would perhaps make up for it somewhat, and in some measure fulfill Lady Joanna's final quest, it would never gain back those precious lost days and hours.

Continuing through the manuscript in her grandmother's careful hand, Hilary learned that Joanna had had many years with her grandparents to recapture lost time. It was clear they were rich years too, for Maggie and Dorey were not only noble in the aristocratic sense, but they carried noble hearts in their breasts, abundant with godly wisdom. For a long span of years Stonewycke stood like a light on the hill, spreading beams of goodness and caring throughout the Strathy Valley.

Even during the depression of the thirties, a kind of peace had pervaded the financially suffering valley. With the recounting of those years, Hilary began to read the story of Allison and Logan.

She read on, not without some trepidation. All of a sudden she herself was part of this compelling saga. She could no longer maintain a distance as she found herself swept up in the drama surrounding Logan's past life and his activities during the war. As with so many who had come before him, he too had felt the peace which dwelt at Stonewycke, eventually surrendering his life to the Creator of that peace. Nor could she keep from a strong identification with her mother—strong-willed, arrogant, confused about her place in this noble family—and it was with not a few tears that she read of Allison's finding her peace too, and of the renewed commitment of love in her parents' marriage following what they assumed to be their only daughter's death.

As a seasoned journalist, Hilary was attentive to the honesty of Lady MacNeil's writing. Though every word was filled with tender love, there was no attempt to whitewash individual weaknesses or to paint a glowing but unrealistic picture of the family. Lady Allison MacNeil Macintyre had clearly been no angel in her youth. *That must be where I come by my own strong will,* Hilary mused with a smile. There were even those who had from time to time actually called her arrogant. *Must run in the genes,* thought Hilary. And she was certainly confused about her place in that same family. Maybe her mother would be able to empathize with her struggles in a way no one else could. And now, after reading of her coming to Scotland, Hilary realized how deeply Lady Joanna must truly have grasped her conflicting emotions, much more than she gave her credit for during that first meeting. *If only* . . . Hilary thought, but the rest of the thought was cut short as she reached up to wipe away the lone tear that had begun to fall.

Before long a porter came down the aisle and offered Hilary a pillow. She took it, but any thought of sleep was far away. Nevertheless, as she stuffed it behind her head and leaned back against the window, the alertness of her brain began to flag, succumbing to the effects of being emotionally keyed up all day.

The train droned on, the hours of the evening passing with a kind of dreamy quality—the reality of the journal mingling with snatches of dreams that invaded Hilary's subconscious as she dozed and reawakened over and over.

But always the words of Lady Joanna's *Journal* drew her back without fail. Page after page she read until, coming abruptly to a sheet that did not even seem to complete Lady Joanna's thought, she realized there was no more. With a deep sense of disappointment, almost of loss, and wondering what had happened to the rest, if there *was* more, Hilary placed the book in her lap, then laid her head back and closed her eyes.

14 / The Pan Am Red Eye

The dusk was an hour later to descend over Heathrow than it was upon the express coach that sped north from Edinburgh to Aberdeen. Nevertheless, as he made his way across the concrete walkway to the waiting white plane, the solitary traveler shivered as if night had already fully come.

I'll be glad to get out of this miserable hole! he thought. *Fog and rain and cold . . . I hate the place!*

As well he might, judging from his attire, which seemed almost comically out of place. Amid veteran London flyers who pulled heavy wool overcoats, mufflers, and gloves more tightly about them to fend off the November chill, he made his way clad only in a thin white linen suit and a straw hat, which would have done little to keep an August breeze off his graying blond head, much less a bitter winter's blow. Small wonder he was cold. Rather than cursing the weather, one would think he might have dressed more warmly.

The climate would change soon enough, however. He knew that by the time he reached his destination it would likely be 80° or more. It would, in fact, be summertime, and by noon might even reach 100°. Then it would be his turn to laugh at these ridiculous limey businessmen in their tweed overcoats. How they ever won the war, he would never know.

The thought did not console him, however. Rather, it served as a reminder that when the plane touched down, it would be not midday but three or four in the morning, depending on how long their layover in that African vermin preserve lasted.

No wonder they called this the "Red Eye." Every time he took the idiotic flight, it took him days to recover. How bitterly he resented that they always booked him on such low-budget crossings. Sure, he had to make the commute several times a year, but what would a first-class fare hurt once or twice? If anyone might afford it, his boss could.

Carrying only a small metallic briefcase, which he'd declined to check into the plane's baggage hold—"You guard that case with your life," he had been told; "don't so much as let it out of your sight!"—, the man walked up the portable stairway and into the forward compartment of the jet. Without speaking to the stewardess who greeted him, he made his way toward the rear of the plane and found his seat.

He sat down, placed the briefcase on his lap, fastened his seatbelt, then unsnapped the two latches of the case, lifted the lid, and peered inside.

What all the fuss was about, he could not for the life of him imagine. How those things could have any value whatsoever was beyond him. And why his boss would entrust something of such potential worth to a couple of imbeciles like Mallory and—what was the name of that lunk-head Mexican or Colombian or wherever in blazes he was from? Chavez . . . Gervez . . .? What did it matter? They all looked alike anyway, with their dark skin and black hair. Why didn't he just go up to Oxford himself, meet the man they called "The Professor," and then be about his business? Quick and simple. But no. They had to pass the stuff around at night. As if anybody would care enough to tail him!

No doubt there were reasons. There were *always* reasons. As much as he might complain about it inside, he kept doing his duty, and always would. He was still a good soldier who knew which side his bread was buttered on. So though he might inwardly grouse about the system, he would not buck it, for he had become an intrinsic part of it. There were generals and there were corporals. Generals gave orders; corporals obeyed them. It was how things worked.

So he had made his connection with the Texan and the South American and given them the goods, and then had waited. Three days later, Mallory was back at his hotel, handed him the briefcase, and said, "Here you are, pal. The report's inside. The Professor says it all checks out—whatever that means."

What a fool! If he was a corporal, then Mallory was only a private. And as for Galvez—that was it, Galvez!—why, he wouldn't even qualify as that!

Knowing Mallory, he'd probably tried to figure out what was going on from the Professor's report but couldn't read it.

He took out the single sheet of paper from inside the case. Nothing much was there. A few dates, two or three names and addresses, a description of the goods themselves, and estimated antique value.

Slowly he placed the report back inside and closed the case. He hoped this satisfied him. He didn't relish another visit here anytime soon, though before the entire episode could be brought to a conclusion, he would no doubt have to—

His thoughts were immediately curtailed as the taxiing airplane suddenly accelerated toward takeoff. *Well, at least I'll soon be out of this cold*, he thought. The sight of the tarmac speeding by under them with several abandoned hangars in the distance reminded him of the unexpected pre-flight business that had distracted him an hour earlier. He supposed his boss *did* know what he was doing. As innocent as the whole affair had sounded, somehow he had picked up a tail after all. Well, that was all taken care of now. In another moment he felt the tires leave the runway.

The plane banked around sharply to the left, and was soon climbing to

33,000 feet, on a heading that would take them over Portugal, and then along the western coast of Africa to their refueling stopover. But he would not see anything. It would be dark all the way until just prior to their final touchdown.

15 / The Bluster 'N Blow

As Hilary stepped out of her rented Fiat, she could not help wondering how much this scene had changed from that time sixty years ago when her grandmother Joanna had first beheld it.

It was just past one o'clock in the afternoon. She had found a hotel last night in Aberdeen, on Union Street not far from the station. This morning she had rented a car, and then driven the rest of the way to Port Strathy. Now she stood, breathing deeply of the clean salt air, in front of the Bluster 'N Blow.

The sturdy stone walls, clean and smooth from the constant exposure to the sea spray and northern winds, the high windows that, as she recalled from her stay the night before the funeral, let in so little light, the ancient and worn oak tabletops, the huge stone fireplace—it had no doubt changed little in the past hundred years.

Hilary glanced in the opposite direction, down Port Strathy's main street and chief region of commerce. There had been no automobiles when Joanna had arrived; now a half dozen or ten of varying ages and makes could be seen. Yes, times had changed. Yet here she stood, just as had Joanna so long ago—equally uncertain about how to proceed, with her future before her, wondering what it might possibly hold.

Well, Hilary thought to herself, *this is my story, not Joanna's. It's a different world now, a different Stonewycke. I may as well see what awaits me. . . .*

With these thoughts, and the realization that her own part of whatever story lay ahead would never find its way into Joanna's journal, Hilary turned back toward the inn, and walked inside.

A Mr. Fraser Davies ran the Bluster 'N Blow these days—a likable fellow in his late fifties, soft-spoken and almost genteel in his manner. Hilary knew little about him, however, for she had studiously avoided unnecessary encounters with the local folk during her previous visit. This time she purposed to be a little more friendly.

No one was present in the lobby, if such could be called the rustic entryway, with its oak halltree and single padded bench. Toward one side opened the expansive Common Room filled with tables and benches. Straight ahead a flight of stairs wound to the first floor. She set down her luggage and tapped at the bell on the desk. Before long its sharp note brought a response.

90

Wiping his damp hands on a dishcloth, Mr. Davies strode with easy, unhurried steps in through a door behind the counter, which Hilary assumed led to the kitchen.

"Good afternoon to you, miss," he said. "Can I help you?" His tone carried a definite Scottish burr on its edges, yet there was at the same time a certain refinement in his soft voice. He paused, seeming to study her for a moment, until recognition dawned. "Why, 'tis Miss Edwards, isn't it? I remember you from last month, though I didn't get to see much of you, I'm sorry to say."

"Yes, Mr. Davies. You're right, I'm back," answered Hilary. "And I'd like a room, though I'm afraid I don't have a reservation again."

"Hoots! You won't be needing one this time of year. Don't think I'd know what to do with a reservation if it jumped out at me."

Hilary laughed, but Davies went right on.

"We were a bit busier than usual then on account of the funeral, you know, but a full house of guests is hardly the norm around here. It'll pick up some years at the Yuletide, then not again till spring. But today, Miss Edwards, you may have your pick of any room in the place."

He brought out a thick black ledger-book from underneath the counter. "Just sign here," he said, flipping the pages open.

Hilary saw that there had been only two other guests to stay at the inn since she had last signed. She jotted her signature and address on the next empty line, while Davies sorted through a box of keys.

"Here you go," he said, handing her one on a round brass ring. "Same room as last time, if that suits you."

"That would be fine, Mr. Davies. Thank you."

He hurried out from behind the desk, took her two pieces of luggage, and led the way up the stairs behind him to her room. Hilary was relieved he was not an inquisitive man, or at least too polite to probe about her present business in Port Strathy. He merely opened her door, set her cases down inside, and asked if she would be wanting a late luncheon.

"Yes, that would be nice," answered Hilary. "Perhaps just a bowl of soup and a slice or two of fresh bread, if you have it."

Davies nodded, then left Hilary alone, pulling the door closed behind him.

As Hilary kicked off her shoes and lay back on the clean, soft bed, she could not keep her mind from straying to Lady Joanna's first stay at the Bluster 'N Blow. What a shock it must have been, as shy and retiring as she was then, to have gone back downstairs that first evening of her stay to discover that the conversation among the men concerned none other than herself. How mortifying to find that she was the center of local speculations!

Port Strathy had grown considerably since then, boasting a population of some 1,600 today, compared to the 750 back in 1911 when Joanna had arrived via hay wagon over the hills from Northhaven. Fortunately, thought

Hilary, my own arrival seems to have gone completely unnoticed by everyone except the innkeeper.

Without realizing it, Hilary soon dozed off. When she awoke, she found herself feeling uncharacteristically timorous as she freshened up and prepared to descend the stairs to the Common Room. Had Joanna's ghost visited her while she slept, leaving a dose or two of timidity behind as a reminder of that earlier time? But no knot of gossiping Scotsmen greeted her. Instead, a cheery fire burned in the hearth, warming the room furnished with a half dozen or so old English style dining tables with their high-backed benches. Mr. Davies was the only one present in the room and was blowing the fire to life with a small hand-held leather bellows. He heard Hilary's step and turned to give her a friendly smile.

"Hello, Miss Edwards. I was wondering what became of you." He hung the bellows up on a hook over the hearth.

"I'm afraid I fell asleep," replied Hilary.

"No harm done. The soup's still warm."

"Oh, thank you. It will feel good."

"Nothing like it on a day like today. There's a storm brewing up out there. The temperature's already dropped ten degrees since you arrived."

"I hadn't even noticed. But now that you mention it, I suppose it is a bit chilly."

"You get attuned to such things when you live in a fishing village. Here the weather can make or break a man. You're from London, if I recall?"

"Yes. As you might expect, I've had very little experience with country life."

"I do understand. My own background is certainly not agrarian either."

"I thought I detected a hint of refinement in your voice," said Hilary.

Davies laughed. "A shrewd bit of detective work! But after twenty-five years in Strathy, I am probably in danger of losing all vestiges of my former life. A life, I might add, quite different from this one."

"You intrigue me. I'll have to probe that mystery later. Did you take over the inn from Sandy Cobden?"

"Ay! That I did. You know some of our history, do you?"

"Not as much as I'd like to."

Davies grinned and his brown eyes twinkled eagerly. "Don't be saying such a thing if you're not meaning it, miss!" he chuckled. "I've been known to bore the socks off many an unsuspecting traveler who offered me less of an invitation than that."

"But I *am* interested," said Hilary. "I'm a reporter. I wouldn't be surprised if there's potential here for an interesting story."

"If you don't mind me asking, is that what has brought you to our little town?"

"Not exactly, but I certainly wouldn't ignore a good story if one should come along?"

"Whom do you write for?"

"*The Berkshire Review.*"

"Ay. I've read it. You must be the editor then, now that I put the names together."

Small town innkeepers were hardly the *Review*'s prime market. Yet she should not have expected anything to meet normal specifications in this unique town.

"That's right. I really would love to learn whatever of the Bluster 'N Blow's history you'd care to tell me."

"Let me get your soup, and then I can lecture to your heart's content."

Davies turned and disappeared into the kitchen, returning in a few minutes with a tray bearing a large bowl of steaming potato soup, along with several generous slabs of hearty brown bread. But it was the pot of hot tea served afterward which Hilary enjoyed most, for Davies, with her "kind permission," brought another cup and sat down to join her.

"I don't mind saying," he began, stirring cream and sugar into his tea, "that I love this old inn. That's why I go on and on so about it at the least provocation. It seems to hold the heritage of the town together in a way, almost as much as the castle up on the hill."

"Well, if you don't mind my saying," said Hilary, "though you do a wonderful job of it, you somehow don't fit my expectations of a small village innkeeper."

She paused and sipped her tea. "You remind me instead of a museum curator I once interviewed," she went on. "There's a kind of reverence in your manner, as if this place means more to you than a building to get a glass of ale and rent a bed."

Davies smiled, obviously taking Hilary's observation as a compliment. "You are a very astute judge of character, I must say. The Bluster 'N Blow is much more to me than that. All the more that I nearly did not measure up to its standards, precisely because of my un-innkeeper-like character."

"Do you mean it took a while for the townsfolk to accept you? I take it you had a city background?"

"It wasn't the townsfolk themselves as much as the laird himself, or old Doc Alec, as the people still called him all his life, God rest his soul."

"Oh?" Hilary arched an eyebrow. What could there have been in this gentle-appearing man for her grandfather not to approve of?

"You see, Lady Joanna and Doc Alec were looking for a different sort after Sandy died. More the type you were expecting, I think." He paused for a swallow of tea. "Sandy left no heirs, so it fell to Doc Alec to find someone to run the place. He wanted—how should I put it?—an earthy sort, a humble farm type. Maybe a local man and wife whom the people already knew, whom he could be sure would keep the traditions of the place alive. I was an Assistant Professor at King's College in Aberdeen at the time, and I hardly fit the bill. They were wary of having an intellectual.

They didn't think the local folk would accept me. Fortunately my years on the school debating team served me well, and I was able to convince them to give me a try."

"How did you change their minds?"

"My love of history helped, along with changes in my heart following the war. I suppose the same thing was happening to many returning soldiers. Priorities change, and the meaning of life changes too. For me, I found that the cloistered life of the university no longer had its former appeal. Oh, there are advantages to a life in the city. But the older I grew the more my childhood roots began to beckon me. Having come from a family of innkeepers, I had always harbored a dream of one day retiring from teaching to operate an inn. Well, when I chanced to hear about the status of the Bluster 'N Blow, I asked myself, 'Why not now?' So I took an early retirement from the university, and embarked on a second career. The cream on the cake is that this inn is a veritable heaven for a lover of history such as myself. I believe the MacNeils were finally able to see this love in me, and to see that part of my vision for the inn was to preserve its historical integrity."

Davies paused to refill their cups. "So your curator analogy is actually quite apt."

"Does the estate control all of Port Strathy, then?"

"Of course at one time all the lands, even the environs of the town, were owned by the estate and governed by it," answered Davies, growing more comfortable now that the conversation had shifted from his own history to that of the region. "Over time, however, the control of the various properties was gradually released, probably for economic reasons. Then in 1911, Lady Margaret and Lady Joanna, in a decision that quickly became local legend and endeared the family to everyone in the area even more than before, relinquished a huge portion of the land, granting full ownership to the individual resident crofters."

"But the inn was excluded from this?"

"The Ramsey and Duncan clan never exactly owned the inn. Through the years it has exercised a controlling influence over major transactions and changes in ownership. The family has retained this authority, as I mentioned in my own case, right up to this present day. But the inn is actually owned by its individual operator. The Bluster 'N Blow has always operated on its own charter. Back in 1741 Colin Ramsey deeded the property that was to become the site of the inn to his friend, Archibald Munro, to whom he owed a certain debt of gratitude. But no Ramsey, except the Ladies Margaret and Joanna, ever gave away a chunk of their land without attaching strong conditions. Such was especially true back in the eighteenth century. That was just four years before the '45, you know—significant times in Scotland's history!" He paused, grinning sheepishly at his tendency to stray from the point.

"But as I was saying," he continued, "Colin's motives may have been purely economical, for, besides the land, he invested a large portion of cash in his friend's project. Thus, a provision was written into the title that should the inn pass from the hands of Munro's direct descendants, the estate maintained the power to choose the new owner, or, if expedient, to reclaim the property. The family has exercised that right ever since, but I think Lady Atlanta Duncan was the first to use that prerogative for purely aesthetic purposes. She cared a great deal for the land, not only for its economic yield, but also for the heritage bound up in the land in and of itself. That devotion has passed down through the generations ever since."

"And Lady Joanna wanted to be certain that the character of her beloved valley did not change," said Hilary thoughtfully. Even as she said the words the memory of her grandmother's face rose into her mind from that day they met in her London office.

"Changes cannot be avoided," Davies went on like the historian he was, "and Lady Joanna knew it. She wasn't adverse to change as such; the transfer of the property gave evidence of that. She wanted to see Port Strathy prosper, and in the twentieth century, you can't remain static and prosper too. The coming of new times has brought new economic demands on landowners. But the Bluster 'N Blow is a landmark, though you won't find it in any tour book. And that is what she wanted to preserve—the sense of history. I mean, if the London Bridge can be sold to an American, anything can happen in this day and age."

Davies drained off the last of his tea, then smiled at Hilary. "If you're not completely bored, you might be interested in seeing my pride and joy."

"With pleasure," said Hilary.

They rose, and he led the way to the back wall of the Common Room, which Hilary had not noticed before. Hanging on the wall was a series of finely carved wooden plaques, each boasting engraved gold plates underneath, one plaque honoring all of the various owners of the inn all the way back to Archibald Munro. Below, framed in glass, was a brief written history of each owner with a pen-and-ink drawing of his likeness.

"This is wonderful!" exclaimed Hilary. "And you did all of this?"

"I had a time of it with some of my predecessors, of whom I had only a name and vague hearsay as to their looks and physical features. But I felt from the very beginning that my job here entailed more than simply providing food and beds."

Hilary was still examining the wall as he spoke. "Queenie Rankin . . ." she mused aloud. "Why, she's just as I imagined her!"

"You do know more than the average person about our little corner of the world, Miss Edwards!" Davies was both pleased and curious.

"Yes . . . I suppose that's true," was all Hilary could think to reply.

"But I don't recall ever seeing you here before the funeral."

"No, I . . . that is . . . well—" but she broke off, flustered, and unable to come up with a quick lie.

"I'm sorry, Miss Edwards," Davies said quickly. "I didn't mean to pry. Please forgive me."

"An apology is not necessary, Mr. Davies. I've been plying you with enough questions, you're surely entitled to a few." Then, because she could think of no reason not to, Hilary added, "I met Lady Joanna recently. She showed me a journal she had kept about the history . . . of her family."

"Ah . . . you've seen her journal." He spoke as if that suddenly placed an indelible bond between them. "It's wonderful, is it not? She honored me, though she would never think of it in those terms, by showing me it also. I've done a bit of writing—nothing important, just university papers—and she wanted advice. She also felt it would help me in this endeavor," he added, gesturing toward the wall.

They were silent a few moments and Hilary returned her attention to the wall. At last she saw the final plaque. It was of Davies himself. But the moment her eyes rested upon it, he began to shuffle awkwardly, giving an embarrassed cough or two.

"I know it must seem a bit presumptuous . . ." he began.

"No," said Hilary. "You are part of this now, and always will be. Not only do you deserve a spot on this wall, but it is your duty to take your place alongside the others."

No sooner had she spoken the words than Hilary realized their application to herself as well as the innkeeper. Like Davies, she was also intrinsically being drawn into something greater than herself. It had begun to come into focus on the train, and now the feeling returned even more forcefully. Being here, standing on the very land that had been in the family of her ancestors for so many generations, so many centuries, she saw more clearly than ever the depth of love, the yearning Lady Joanna had held in her heart toward her—not only as a granddaughter returned from the dead, but also as an integral part of the Stonewycke heritage.

And Hilary was also a link to the *future* of that legacy. Perhaps she would not find her way into Joanna's journal, but might she not be able to do something to help keep the tale which had flowed from Joanna's pen alive for future generations? Might there be a role for her to play in the ongoing story of Stonewycke?

Suddenly, even as she chatted distractedly with Mr. Davies, Hilary knew that she had indeed not come here by accident, that she was not being swept into this saga by mere chance. As a knot tightened within her, she knew that the course of her future had suddenly all changed. She knew there could be no halfway measures. As there had been a Lady Atlanta, Lady Margaret, Lady Joanna, and Lady Allison—so too must there one day be a *Lady Hilary* as well.

Feeling all at once detached and unreal, in a shambling way Hilary thanked the innkeeper as politely as possible, and broke off her conversation. Her voice sounded strangled in her own ear, and she could feel her heart pounding hard in her chest. A hot sweat broke out over her forehead and her knees began to shake.

Hilary had never fainted in her life. Even in the violent jungles of Vietnam, she had kept her wits about her. But she had never felt this kind of lightheaded sensation, and before she made a complete fool of herself, she realized she had to get outside and into some fresh air.

16 / Uninvited Thoughts_____

Hilary stepped from the door of the Bluster 'N Blow and inhaled a deep draught of the chilly air.

A storm was indeed brewing. The wind off the North Sea whipped at her face and easily penetrated the thickness of her Shetland wool sweater. It quickly restored her equilibrium and forced a thread of practicality into her distraught mind. But still she could not go back, even for her coat.

Gray waves slammed fiercely against the smooth sand that stretched out in front of her before giving way to the rocky shoal at the far end of the promontory in the distance. Overhead the sky was a solid gray mass with little variation of color, except along the distant horizon where a black bank of sinister looking clouds portended the approaching rain. And judging from the wind, coming relentlessly from offshore, the clouds were heading this way and would arrive some time that night.

This northern coast of Scotland was wild and unpredictable. She vaguely remembered Mr. Davies telling her at the end of their conversation that a storm of hurricane proportions had nearly brought down the entire inn over a hundred years ago. Glancing behind her, the inn seemed as solid as the rocky coast upon which it was built. She peered back at the sea, raging in good earnest now, and then toward the harbor. All the boats were tied securely, but that could hardly keep their masts from bobbing up and down and sideways in a frantic symphony of windy, wavy motion.

She began walking along the shoreline toward the harbor. With the physical exertion came some relief from the cold. Her head felt clear now, and it was refreshing to fight against the elements.

Yes, this was a glorious land. She had thought so when she had come twelve days earlier. She had walked along this same beach then too, when the weather had been calmer. She supposed they even swam here in the summertime. What a land of contrasts! It all looked so different now. Not because of the storm. It looked different to her *inner* eyes—the difference between gazing upon an image in a mirror and finally beholding the real thing. Now this wild, beautiful, gray, green, rugged expanse of coastline meant something to her that it never could have before the journal.

Everything was suddenly changed. Now there were so many others whose presence she felt, others who had walked this same way once, others whose feet had passed over this same sand, others whose very blood was part of her own makeup. How many times had young Lady Margaret walked, or more likely ridden her magnificent black Raven along this very shore? And Joanna, too, had come here for consolation during those dark days before she discovered who she was. And here, probably within sight of where Hilary now stood, she had also met her dear Alec.

Once more—the comparisons seemed so frequent lately—Hilary found herself following in her grandmother's footsteps, and seeking the solitude of the sea. Now it was her turn to find consolation, to wrestle with quandaries too complex for the conscious mind to fathom, to ask questions that seemed to have no answers . . . and perhaps—as her predecessors had learned to do during their times of trouble—also to pray.

The truth of her birth had suddenly been laid bare. Not just who she was; she had known that simple fact for three weeks. Now there was much more to face. Now it was a matter of what it all meant.

She had been prepared to accept Logan and Allison Macintyre as her parents. Once the initial shock of Lady Joanna's revelation had sunk in, there had even come a dawning thrill at the thought of being a member of such a fascinating family. Even while reading Joanna's journal, as many tears as that reading had evoked, she had managed to keep a small part of her heart detached from the implications of it all.

But she had not, until standing there in front of Mr. Davies' special wall, realized what membership in this family would mean . . . to her. For just as the heritage of the Bluster 'N Blow had been passed down, though not by blood, from owner to owner, so too the legacy of Stonewycke was no mere static legend that could be relegated merely to the pages of some dusty and archaic journal. It was a living, breathing, ongoing inheritance that went beyond times, places, wills, houses, and earthly possessions. It was a legacy that pulsated with life from generation to generation—a legacy made real, made alive, made imperative, and made inescapable by the journal and the lives of which it told.

Hilary's mind went back to Joanna's note which had been tucked inside the journal. Her grandmother had hoped that Hilary's reading of the words she had written would help her ". . . find your own place within the family." Now at last she discerned what Lady Joanna had truly meant with those seemingly simple words.

And suddenly—strong, decisive, woman of the world that she was—Hilary found herself afraid.

It was not merely the thought of her becoming a member of the so-called aristocracy. That certainly would involve a shock to her system. But it could be dealt with, ignored even if she wished. Surely times of great soul-searching were bound to come in that regard, but it was not that which troubled her most at this moment.

On her mind instead was her innocent conversation with the innkeeper. It had to do with walls and plaques and histories and landmarks, with this shoreline and town, with boats bobbing in the water and the homey little cottages she had passed on her way into town.

Even more than these things, it had to do with people . . . with four incredible women—those women who had fought and suffered and wept and prayed for this land. And had loved it beyond human understanding.

It had to do with the frightening, terrifying, bewildering realization that she was one of them.

Fear . . . because she was *not* like them.

She did not love this land the way they did. Yes, the coast was grand, the mountains, the rivers, the Highlands more scenic than anywhere in Britain. Its villages were quaint. Its history was colorful and intriguing. But the depth of *feeling*, of personal devotion, was simply not in her. How could it be? She possessed more affection for the grimy tenements of the East End than she felt for this coastal fishing village, however lovely it might be.

Couldn't she become part of the family and forget the rest? Couldn't she simply slip in, as it were, unnoticed, without a fuss? Besides, there were other grandchildren who might feel ill-used, being so abruptly usurped from their position. If her parents were the kind of people she imagined them to be after her meeting with Lady Joanna, they would surely be able to understand that she was not equipped for anything more. She could never stand tall enough to rank alongside the memory of her predecessors as being in the direct line of heirs. In fact, stranger that she was, they might not even want or expect such of her.

Everything practical, everything logical, told her that such reasoning was right. No one would . . . no one could expect it.

Yet all logic was swept immediately away with the overpowering memory of Lady Joanna's face that day in her office. As that face rose before her mind's eye, something deeper than she could hope to explain with mere words stirred to life within Hilary's heart. Could it be only her imagination, or was there indeed more behind the sensitive features of that face than the simple joy of finding her granddaughter?

Hilary kicked at the sand under her feet. She had walked well beyond the harbor and now stopped and looked again toward the sea. The gray of the sky had already changed. The black clouds were halfway toward the shore, continuing to tumble over one another as they grew larger and larger. However, behind them, faint hints of deep orange and purple now smeared along the horizon. Somehow the rays of the setting sun had managed to penetrate the thick cover. It would be a lovely, fierce, short-lived sunset that would give way within the hour to the approaching blackness. In the distance, though she wondered if her eyes were deceiving her, she thought she spied a small sloop trying to make the harbor, in spite of the elements seemingly bent on preventing its success.

Hilary looked back toward the town, the inn, the houses of gray stone that all seemed impervious to the perils of wind and wave and rain. Here she was! This was not London. She was in Port Strathy, at the very gates of Stonewycke itself. A decision must be made. She had been so certain of her course of action on the train, so sure of what she must do. She could not now get cold feet and turn around again! But could she do it . . . did she have the inner strength it would require to stand before that imposing place, to knock on the door, and say . . .

What would she say to them? If only there were some other way!

Hilary sighed. There was no other way. All the questions were really unnecessary. She knew what she must do. She had given her word to Lady Joanna. What became of it, she could not know that. But she would present herself to her parents. That much she knew. She had to . . . she wanted to.

Hilary bowed her head. It was time to do what she had done all too seldom of late.

"Dear Father," she prayed quietly, her voice making barely a sound in the lashing wind, "give me courage to step into the future you have marked out for me. None of this was of my design. I know your hand is in it all. Forgive me for forgetting. I know you must have been preparing each of us for this moment. Help me to be receptive to whatever your will for me is. Help me to follow as you lead."

She exhaled a deep breath, then turned sharply back toward town and began walking crisply forward. It was time to face her destiny.

17 / Unsought Heroism

As Hilary strode through the wind, it was clear evening was descending. Approaching the harbor, she now saw clearly what she had taken for a phantom a few minutes earlier: a small boat was indeed making for the dock. But with every dip into one of the troughs between the waves, it was lost to sight and she feared it would capsize any moment.

Before even thinking why she did so, Hilary broke into a run. Reaching the harbor area, she ran onto the nearest dock, then out toward the end. On either side of her were moored boats of all sizes and shapes, securely tethered, yet making a racket as the incoming waves beat against their sides. Hilary slowed, struggling to keep her feet on the swaying dock.

She could see the little boat clearly now. Its single sail flapped furiously in the gale, and the man sitting astern could barely manage to keep her from tipping, with his right hand on the rudder and his left attempting to keep the sail in position. In front of him, on the floor of the tiny sloop, sat a small girl. She couldn't have been more than seven, and the terror in her face was visible even from the distance where Hilary stood.

On they came, slowly, yet inching ever closer to the outermost railing to which the man might secure his fragile craft. Hilary stood, as one helpless, wanting to help, yet without so much as a rope she might throw them when they got closer. Every wave seemed intent on destroying any hope of survival, but the look on the man's face told of an equal determination to triumph in the struggle.

As he crested a small swell, the man saw Hilary on the dock. The mere sight of another human being, helpless though she was, seemed to fill him with hope, and he wrestled all the more powerfully against the stubborn rudder.

"Come on! You've almost made it!" shouted Hilary. Her voice sounded thin and weak in the midst of the gale.

"We'll try to throw ye a rope!" shouted the man in return. "Hang on to it for dear life!"

He spoke to his daughter, who then crept onto her knees and made her way to the front of the craft, laid hold of a bunched rope, then knelt. Swinging it as mightily as her tiny frame would permit, she let loose the rope in Hilary's direction.

But Hilary did not have the chance to see whether it would have reached her, or whether with it she might have helped attach it to the mooring. For the moment the girl's arm was outspread, a gust of wind took evil hold of the sail. The boat lurched violently, and the seaman's tiny daughter was thrown overboard into the angry sea. All thought of the rope was suddenly gone.

"The lass canna swim!" cried the father in a despairing voice, half rising.

But even before he had the chance to act, Hilary instinctively knew that if he so much as took his hand from the rudder for an instant, he would lose his boat to the sea. Without further thought Hilary plunged into the icy water.

A huge white-tipped wave crashed over her head the moment she regained the surface. Sputtering, she tried to grope her way through the turbulent waves toward where she thought the child had gone under. All about was only water—freezing, churning water. She tried to swim, but her body was tossed about and she was powerless to resist it. Another wave doused her, and as she felt herself sinking beneath it, her feet kicked something solid.

All she could think of was the child, though in her benumbed state she could hardly make her arms and legs obey. She struggled to the surface, took a huge gulp of air, then plunged under in the direction from which she had come. Down she went, with eyes closed, thrashing madly with her arms.

There it was again! Her hands felt something . . . something soft . . . yes! It was the girl!

Wildly Hilary grasped at the invisible form, clutching at the girl's clothing, kicking her own feet, trying to swim back to the surface. But, oh! the cold! Her hands were numb now, so numb she could no longer tell whether she still held the child. All about was darkness. She could see nothing. The wild windy gale began to grow distant in her ears. She squeezed her fingers tightly around . . . around what? She could no longer feel anything. With arms outspread she reached out . . . then she felt the burden go from her grasp. Her fingers relaxed . . . the girl was gone.

In mingled despair and a sense of finally giving in to the powerful elements, her body relaxed. All sound ceased. She could no longer feel the thrashing of the waves over her. The cold was gone now too. A strange peace began to steal over her. Out of the blackness, in the distance she perceived a tiny light. Larger now, it was coming toward her . . . a single light surrounded by blackness. Light . . . and warmth . . . and blackness . . . and then a soft voice, approaching her. And then Hilary knew no more.

When wakefulness began slowly again to invade Hilary's consciousness, it was with a continuation of the same vague sensations. While her eyes were yet closed, she was aware that she lay in a darkened room. As she lifted her eyelids a crack, in what looked to be the distance, but was in reality but a few feet, she saw a light approaching, a flickering light.

Closer it came. From it warmth seemed to be coming. This was just like the dream she had had before falling asleep . . . if she had fallen asleep! Maybe she was dead! A figure stood behind the light! It grew larger. She struggled to rise. A voice spoke. She felt a hand pressing her gently back down where she lay. She looked at the light again. It was something she recognized. It was . . . it was . . .

It was a candle! Of course. She could see it now. A woman stood beside her holding a candle. She was speaking, though she had not heard the actual words until now as they gradually began to sift through her mental fog.

" . . . lie still, dearie. Jist lie back . . ."

The gentle woman's voice soothed her. Slowly she began to take in her surroundings. Beyond the candle in the woman's hand, a soft glow and a deliciously radiant sense of heat was coming from a stone hearth that held a bright but subdued fire. The room in which she lay was a small one; it contained no other furnishings besides the bed, which was of a most peculiar composition but comfortable enough. The ceiling was low, and seemed once to have been painted in something resembling white but had over the years darkened considerably, no doubt from the smoke, not all of which, Hilary's nose now told her, managed to escape up the chimney. She lay, in dry bedclothes, beneath several layers of heavy quilts. The entire result was one of dreamy well-being, though Hilary hadn't a clue where she might be.

Her attendant saw wakefulness coming back into her eyes, and spoke again.

"I hope ye dinna mind bein' here yer lain, miss," she said. " 'Tis the best spot we had where we thocht ye'd be comfortable."

"Yes . . . yes, this is very nice," Hilary managed to reply, though her voice sounded weak.

"Ye see, my man he built this extra room some years back. I hope ye dinna hae objection to a peat fire an' a bed whose mattress be naethin' but the stems o' dried heather. 'Tis the auld Scottish way, I alloo, but folks like us, we grow accustomed to the auld ways."

"It's wonderful," said Hilary, forcing a smile. "I can't remember when I've slept so well."

"Nae doobt!" exclaimed the woman. "Ye gave us quite a scare. 'Tis little wonder ye slept so sound; ye was maist likely deid, or so I thocht, when my man broucht ye here in his ain arms, hangin' limp an' wet ye was. Oh, dearie, my heart warms to see ye lookin' at me oot o' them big blue eyes o' yers!" She leaned over the bed and gave Hilary an unexpected kiss on the cheek.

"But, I don't understand . . ." said Hilary. "Where am I?"

"Ye're in the but-end o' oor tiny hoose," answered the woman with a laugh. "Ye're aboot a mile oot o' Strathy, where my husband broucht ye last night. Brocht ye wi' tales o' heroism t' tell me o' yer leapin' into the sea, an'—"

Suddenly the events of the past evening came back into Hilary's memory.

"And the little girl?" she said in alarm.

"Oor little Kerrie's jist fine. She's sleepin' noo too, in the ben-end, and none the worse fer her spill. An' 'tis you yersel' we've got t' thank fer her very life! But I'm fergettin' my manners. The name's Frances MacKenzie."

She thrust a fleshy hand toward where Hilary lay in the bed.

"Hilary Edwards," replied Hilary as she took it. She felt as though her entire hand were swallowed up in the grasp of the hardy woman's affectionate handshake. "I'm from London."

"Ah, winna my little Kerrie be plumb beside hersel'! The first thing she'll ask is if ye ken Prince Charles."

Hilary laughed.

"She cuts oot his picture frae the magazines, an' can tell ye all aboot when his grandmother stayed in Port Strathy. Though 'tis mysel' who should be tellin' ye that. I was here, ye see, an' 'twas my ain aunt she visited wi' Lady Joanna frae the Hoose. Jist yonder, o'er the valley a couple o' miles. Oh, we didna talk aboot anythin' else fer days an' weeks on end!"

Just then the door opened. In walked a large man whom Hilary immediately recognized. Squinting in the dim light, he spoke softly to his wife.

"Is the lass still sleepin'?" Then as his eyes grew accustomed to the room, he saw that she was awake and looking at him.

"Ah, lass," he said, "I'm right glad to see ye lookin' so fit! Karl MacKenzie, at yer service, mem," he added.

"Oor guest's name is Hilary," said Mrs. MacKenzie. "Hilary Edwards . . . all the way frae London!"

"London, ye say! Weel, that is some way. But I'm jist heartened ye was on the Port Strathy dock last night, mem."

"What happened?" said Hilary. "I can hardly remember—"

"I was a fool, that's what happened!" interrupted MacKenzie in a passionate voice. "A blamed fool fer thinkin' I could take the lass oot fer a ride in the new boat wi' the storm comin' like that!"

He began to stride around the room. "What would o' come o' us if ye hadna come along, lass, I darena think!" he went on, wringing his hands.

"I hardly was much help," offered Hilary.

"Na, mem, 'tisna true! Ye leaped into that water wi' oot thocht fer yer ain safety. When I saw wee Kerrie go ower into the water—"

He stopped abruptly, hiding his face for a moment in his hands.

"Then before I could think what was to be done," he went on, "into the water ye went, divin' an' swimmin' aroun' till ye got yer hands on the wee bairn an' pulled her up an' tried yer best to hand her to me. I managed to get Kerrie back into the boat. An' though I couldna lift ye, I got the rope tied aboot one o' yer arms. In but anither two or three swells I was crashin' in against the edges o' the dock. I had but to get Kerrie oot o' the boat an' pull yersel' in an' then lug ye oot o' the water an' carry ye both t' the truck."

"What about your boat?" asked Hilary in a concerned voice. "Were you able to save it?"

"Hank Shaw was jist comin' outta the inn. He saw ye run oot an' jump in after the bairn. He came as fast as he could, wi' a couple o' men besides. They pulled the boat into the harbor while I was tryin' me best t' get ye back here where my wife could love the life back into ye."

"I'm so grateful," said Hilary with a sigh. "You're both too kind."

"Hoots, Miss Edwards!" exclaimed Mrs. MacKenzie. "Ye saved oor Kerrie's life! What's too kind alongside that?"

"Well, in any case, I should be getting back to the inn."

"Nonsense!" exclaimed Mrs. MacKenzie. "Yer clothes arena yet dry. An' ye already spent the night wi' us. A few more hours willna matter."

"But Mr. Davies will wonder what became of me."

"My man's already been to tell him. An' I winna hear o' yer leavin' wi'oot joining us for midday dinner."

"We'd be honored, Miss Edwards," added her husband. "An' we'd be pleased if ye'd consider makin' this humble room yer home so long as ye hae business in Port Strathy."

Hilary thought for a moment, then smiled up at the sweet couple from where she lay. "It is I who would be honored," she said at last. "I would love to have dinner with you."

"And the room?"

"I don't know how long my business in Port Strathy will last. I have but one urgent matter to attend to, and that I must do, possibly this afternoon. Beyond that, I have no plans. But I will most gratefully consider your offer."

"Thank ye, Miss Edwards," replied Mr. MacKenzie, " 'tis all we can ask o' ye."

"Then I'll ask one more thing of you, if you don't mind," said Hilary.

"Anythin'."

"You must call me Hilary."

The two nodded their smiling agreement, then turned and left her alone. As they exited the room, Hilary closed her eyes, a great contentment stealing over her. Something inside had begun to change, though Hilary herself hardly was aware of it yet. A gap had begun to be bridged, vague and undefined though it might be, in her heart.

The God of her forefathers was slowly drawing her into the life of this valley, softening a corner of her heart toward these simple Scottish folk from whom her ancestors had come.

18 / Allison and Logan

Allison Macintyre, now matriarchal head of the Stonewycke household, carried a silver tray of tea into the family parlor. The warmth emanating from the bright fire in the hearth felt good, especially after making her way through the chilly corridors from the kitchen. Pushing aside a copy of the *Daily Mirror* and two or three magazines, she set the tray on the low table in front of the sofa.

"I see you have given up on the newspaper," she said with a sympathetic smile.

Logan, who had been reclining on the sofa, leaned forward and helped her arrange the tray.

He gave a disdainful glance toward the *Mirror*. "I don't know what is worse," he said, "when they rake Roy and the rest of us over the coals, or when they do it to Harold."

"At least it's over now," Allison replied. She poured steaming tea into two china cups. "The vote is done and everyone can move on to other matters."

"If only it were that simple," sighed her husband.

"It's not?"

"I had a call from Roy this morning. I didn't have a chance to mention it to you yet. You were busy with your painting, and I was out looking over that acreage with Ferguson."

"What did Roy have to say?"

"He said Harold laid out a pretty uncompromising agenda for repairing the so-called party split. Went public with it yesterday. No more maverick voting, no more abstentions. When the debate begins on the separate clauses of the Market legislation, we had better all toe the line. That sort of thing In essence, he expects us to undo all we have risked so much for in the first place. At least that's how it looks to me."

"Surely he knows you better than to think you'd agree?"

"Roy is going along with him, and so are many of the others. I suppose if it hadn't been for Mother's death, Harold would be extracting a decision from me by now too."

Allison handed him a cup and saucer.

"Thank you, Ali," he said, laying his hand over hers and smiling.

She picked up a spoon from the tray to stir her tea. Suddenly it dropped from her hand with a clatter.

"How clumsy of me!" she exclaimed in frustration, clasping her right hand with her left and rubbing it. "I don't know what's wrong with me lately!"

"Here, let me take a look."

"No, no, it's fine. But I've been doing this too much this last week. A couple of my fingers have been numb." She rubbed at her troubled right hand as if trying to stimulate the feeling back into it.

"Why don't we have Connally take a look at it?"

"I'm sure it's nothing but the cold. Still, I don't like it."

"Maybe you're right," said Logan good-naturedly. "Winter is coming on, you know."

"I'm sure that's it," agreed Allison, sounding far from convinced. "It wouldn't be so bad if I had more energy. But I just haven't been myself recently."

"So tell me," Logan went on, making an attempt to cheer up his wife, "how did your day go? I haven't seen you since morning."

"Oh, it's been a pleasant day. We painted some."

"She's turning you into a regular artist!"

"I don't know about that. But after all this time it's nice to have something to share, interests in common. And then did I tell you about Patty Doohan?"

"No, what?"

"She became a grandmother today."

"You don't say! Well, that is grand." Logan paused and suddenly a startled expression came over his face. "Ali, don't tell me that you—"

Allison's merry laugh stopped him. "No . . . no midwifing for me. I paced outside while Dr. Connally delivered the baby. I haven't had much stomach for such affairs since that day the elder Dr. Connally was out of town and my mother pressed me into service."

"Your many other talents more than make up for that singular lack, my dear."

"Thank you, Logan. I've often wished I could follow my mother's footsteps as a compassionate dispenser of healing. How well I remember her being called out in the middle of the night with her little black bag in hand. What a team she and my father made—he tending to the cows and goats and pigs and horses, she to the coughing and feverish children of Strathy. I think the women of the community trusted her for some things over the doctor."

"Well, tell me about the new bairn."

"A sweet little girl, Logan. So tiny, so precious. And dear Patty was every bit as proud as the parents."

Allison brought her cup to her lips, steadying it with her left hand, and drank.

"I did something else today," she went on after a moment. "I decided to get out Mother's journal. I don't know why I hadn't done so before now."

Logan reached out and laid his hand over hers.

"I suppose I have been avoiding it," Allison went on. "And perhaps it was still too soon."

"It was bound to stir up old memories no matter when you read it," said Logan.

"I know," replied Allison. "But I thought, you know, with the way it's all turned out these last two months, the changes, the reunion—I thought maybe it would bring tears of joy rather than sadness."

"So . . . which did it bring?"

"That's the strangest part of all," answered Allison. "I couldn't find the journal. I looked everywhere."

"Hmm, that is peculiar."

"But once I was thinking along those lines, about Mother's posterity and what the future holds, I found it hardly mattered whether I was reading her words or not. Seeing the new baby made me think afresh about what lies ahead. I wonder what the future does hold, Logan? What will become of this place and the legacy it represents? For so long somewhere in the back of my mind, I had struggled to come to terms with the possibility of its ending with us. But now that my hope has blossomed anew all at once, I find myself so conscious of the present-day crumbling of long-established traditions. Oh, I don't want Stonewycke to lose its sense of the past, of history!"

"Those things that are truly precious and worthy of permanence will not crumble, Ali. But perhaps I'm not really the one to talk, since I've never been much of a traditionalist."

Allison let her serious expression soften into a smile and patted Logan's hand. "But you know what things are worthy, and that's what matters. I need to pray for that sense too, especially now. I don't want to put on pressure. We might not *all* have the same expectations for Stonewycke's future."

They fell silent for a few moments, each seeming to contemplate the blaze in the hearth. At length, not wanting this quiet time together to end, Allison spoke. "Would you like more tea?"

"Yes, I would," answered Logan, then added quickly as Allison began to lean forward, "Let me this time." He poured a quick blob of milk into her cup, then added the tea, and finally dropped in one lump of sugar, stirred the mixture, then handed her the cup.

"The past seems calling out to me every day now," said Allison as she watched Logan prepare his own cup in like fashion.

"Wishing *you* had a little granddaughter?" asked Logan.

"I can't deny that a spark of envy did try to intrude. But only for a moment. God gave us full and complete lives, and I am content. Besides, now the story may wind up with a surprise ending. But when I think of Mother and what we shared together during the years I was growing up—''

Tears suddenly surfaced in Allison's eyes and she hurriedly retrieved a handkerchief from her pocket. "I'm glad I keep this handy." She dabbed her eyes and sniffed. "I should never have said anything."

"No, Ali. We decided long ago we wouldn't wall up our memories. There can be no regrets. Remember Lady Maggie's time away from Ian? The Lord always brings things full circle. As he is now doing with us."

He paused, musing to himself.

"That word *wall* just made me think of Maggie's nursery," he went on thoughtfully. "Remember Mother describing how she and Alec cut through the wall?"

"Nothing had been touched, and it was all covered with cobwebs and dust."

"Whenever I think of their adventure exploring this old place, and discovering that lost nursery, I can't help but think of when our own little Joanna was a baby. You know that picture of her I have kept in my office all these years—her sweet little face? Sometimes I can almost still hear her small voice as it was back then, and feel the delicate skin of her cheek when I find myself glancing up at that picture. We can't let ourselves lose such memories, despite all those years of loss. We mustn't allow dust and cobwebs to swallow them. Those intervening years are part of the legacy too, as dear Maggie taught us all."

Allison slid over toward Logan and put her free arm around his shoulder.

"Oh, Logan," she said, "God's greatest blessing to me is *you*! Everything is going to come out right, isn't it?"

"He has not failed us yet, Ali. Though I've long since learned that He doesn't always bring things about in the way we might expect."

19 / Into the Future _____

Hilary decided to walk the mile to Stonewycke.

Perhaps it was in part because of Joanna's similar walk sixty years earlier. If she was to fulfill her own destiny, it seemed somehow fitting that she follow in the footsteps of the grandmother who had set this odyssey in motion.

Also, she needed the time alone. Not so much to think, for her course of action was at last settled in her mind. Rather, she needed time to soak in the surroundings of this place, to tune herself in to them so that when she did reach her destination, she would not feel like such an outsider.

The day with the MacKenzies had been so peaceful, just the tonic her turbulent spirit needed. Little Kerrie had endless questions about London and Prince Charles and the Queen and Buckingham Palace. Mr. MacKenzie quietly hovered about, shyly protective of the young lady whose life he had saved, and whom he credited with the saving of his own daughter's. Mrs. MacKenzie bustled about the three-room little cottage as if the Queen herself was expected for dinner! A smile spread over Hilary's face at the memory of that gathering around the plain pine table three hours ago. The beaming faces of the three MacKenzies, so proud to have her in their midst, the pot of steaming potatoes, the plate of cold oatcakes, the boiled cod. Oh, they were dears! thought Hilary.

It was a fine afternoon as she walked through Port Strathy and on up the hill to the east. The sun was already low at her back, though it was not yet three o'clock. The air could not be called warm, yet there was in it a lingering whisper of the autumn now quickly passing. The storm had moved through rapidly as she slept, leaving behind only scattered patches of gray clouds that were now randomly distributed through the pale blue brightness of the sky. Within an hour the sinking sun would send out shoots of red and orange and pink and purple, lining these same clouds to herald the approach of sunset.

Notwithstanding the sunshine, Hilary wore her coat, knowing she would need it later on. She had returned to the inn from the MacKenzies' to change clothes. It would probably have been more practical to wear slacks and sturdy shoes, since she would be doing a good deal of walking. But instead she wore a brown tweed suit with gored skirt and coral-colored silk blouse, along with low-heeled pumps. Her feet would be sore by day's end, no doubt, but she was meeting her parents after thirty years, and she couldn't help wanting to make a good impression.

She'd toyed with the idea of calling ahead. But then, what would she have said? "Hi, I'm with *The Berkshire Review,* and I wondered if you'd be so kind as to grant me an interview?" She could hardly just blurt out, "I'm your daughter you thought was dead. Could I come for a visit?"

There wasn't going to be an easy way to do it. Walking up to the door unexpected didn't seem altogether "right" either. But this was something that she had to do in person, as awkward as it would be.

To her left the sea spread out to the horizon. The climb was brisk, and she stopped when she reached the top to look back down upon the village, then over Ramsey Head just ahead of her and off the bluff to her left. Then she continued on, leaving the road and turning inland toward the estate. A large iron gate stood open, to one side of which had been placed a large stone of granite, in which were chiseled the words: "Welcome to Stonewycke." Hilary passed inside and continued on, through the wooded grounds of the castle. The wooden bridge over which Joanna had walked had long since been replaced by a sturdy, wide stone bridge able to accommodate automobiles and trucks. Every stone had been hauled to the site by Alec MacNeil and Walter Innes from the quarry on the Fraserburgh Road. The trees had grown older since Joanna's day, but little else had changed. Only the distant sound of machinery, and perhaps a car climbing the hill out of Strathy every ten or fifteen minutes, would reveal that the year was 1971, not 1911.

Hilary drank in the air as she walked, enjoying the sight of every oak, every birch, every mountain ash, as well as the green fields that extended out on both sides of her, up toward higher hills to the east, and downward toward the valley of Strathy to the west. This was such lovely country— so quiet, so peaceful, so green . . . so different than anything she had ever had the chance to enjoy in London.

Well, she thought, whatever lies ahead for me will be found at the end of this long driveway. It can't be much farther.

The insistent ring of the phone sounded from across the room. For the first two rings he tried to ignore it. This was the fourth call of the day, and he hoped it wasn't for him. Logan had gone to the sun-room to read, privately hoping to avoid further interruptions.

Still the phone persisted. Then as the ringing stopped, realizing the housekeeper had no doubt answered it and would have to run up the three flights of stairs after him, Logan was invaded by a dutiful sense of guilt. He laid down his book and went out to meet her halfway.

I probably should have instructed her to take messages, he thought. What good could he be to Allison during this difficult time if his responsibilities in London continued to hound him so? He had let his work separate them once before, and it was not an experience he wanted to repeat.

When he had returned to Stonewycke immediately after the Commons session last week, they had both known he might be forced somewhat to divide his time. It was an involved month; he had many irons in the fire that would not cool just because he went north. And, of course, Allison understood. She was part of his work now. They considered themselves a team. Many of his associates had joked more than once that the Honorable Mrs. Macintyre had through the years garnered at least half his votes for him. Logan was proud of that fact—proud of her.

The housekeeper met him as he came to the first-floor landing. She had only had to climb halfway up the bottom flight of stairs.

"Telephone for ye, sir," she said, showing her gratitude at being spared a longer trek.

"Thank you, Flora; I'll take it in the library."

Logan turned and strode down the corridor to the great double oak doors of the room that had served as Stonewycke's library for over a hundred years. Allison had always insisted that the fragrance of musty, aging books was stimulating, both to the mind and the senses. Personally, he didn't care much for it himself. She often teased him that he would no doubt prefer moving his office out to the room above the stables that had belonged to old Uncle Digory. Could he help it, he would joke back, if an uneducated bloke himself finds the fragrances there more invigorating?

By the time he reached the desk and lifted the receiver, Logan was smiling at the comparison of the library with the stable.

"Hello," he said, "Logan Macintyre speaking."

A brief pause followed.

"Ah, yes, George . . . of course, of course . . . certainly, I know you wouldn't have called otherwise. What is it?"

A lengthy interlude ensued in which Logan nodded, shook his head, and responded verbally at periodic intervals.

"I see . . . yes, good work."

As he was gradually caught up in governmental matters, the smile faded from his face, replaced by a keen glow of enthusiasm, visible not on his lips at all, but rather in his eyes.

"And so you've found five possible violators?" he asked at length, "Which companies are they?"

He nodded his head, then let out a sharp breath. "Trans Global Enterprises? I had no idea our fishing expedition would land such a big catch! But as you say it's still too soon to know. We have to remember we're still in the speculating stages."

After listening for another moment, he added, "I agree, it's a sticky situation, but we have never let money and power intimidate us before . . . yes, of course, discretion must be the byword. No coming on like gang-busters, as they say in America. But there are subtle approaches we can make use of."

He paused while the other spoke, then chuckled.

"Thanks, George. I'll take that as a compliment!"

Another brief pause was followed by an outright laugh.

"I don't know about legendary. But there have always been those to make more of my reputation than reality would justify. In the meantime, we had better do our homework thoroughly. I'd like complete profiles on each company—"

He stopped, clearly interrupted, nodded, then continued. "Good man, George! I should have known you'd already have started. Terrific! I want to be well-armed if this thing proves out and I take it to Ted Heath. . . . When will I be returning . . . ?"

The question required more consideration than he had time for on this long-distance call. Nor was George Ringersfeld the one with whom to discuss what to Logan were complex alternatives. He and Allison had talked and prayed, but both were reluctant to make any definite moves just yet. Neither could deny anticipating their return to the activity of the city. But the peace and tranquillity of Stonewycke, not to mention the sudden turnabout of family considerations, had been more a soothing balm to their spirits on this particular occasion than for many years. Especially with Joanna now gone, they were more strongly torn in the two directions that pulled at their loyalties, as they knew they always would be.

"I don't know, George," Logan said at length. "In a few days, perhaps. Probably a week at the outside. Keep me posted if you turn up anything startling. All right, then . . . thanks for the news . . . goodbye."

Logan hung up the phone, then leaned against the edge of the desk in thought. What a time for this to come up! He should be in London to direct the investigation. Yet he knew he belonged here—for right now, at any rate.

He had begun investigating allegations of illegal practices at the corporate level a year ago during his tenure as Minister of Economic Affairs under Wilson. The change in administrations when Edward Heath's Conservatives had ousted Labour from power had abruptly forestalled his work until the new Prime Minister had suggested to his own Minister that he work with Logan on the problem. Then the furor over the Common Market vote had interrupted progress again, though a month ago renewed murmurings had encouraged him to reopen his investigations. He had never expected that he might have to do battle with a giant like Trans Global.

The fight itself did not worry him. He had taken many an unpopular stance on the Parliamentary floor through the years. He could almost relish the thought of a good clash where the issues of right and wrong were clearly defined. At any other time, he would have welcomed the challenge. But Joanna's death, coupled with the rift in the party and, unavoidably, in his friendship with Wilson, as well as family uncertainties—it had all taken a toll on his emotional reservoir.

A soft knock on the door called a halt to his reverie. Allison opened the door a crack and poked in her head. "We were just going to have some tea downstairs. Would you like to join us, or am I interrupting something?"

"Not at all. I can use a pleasant diversion."

"Troubles?" she asked as she came into the room.

"Just the usual," answered Logan. "I only wish they weren't all happening at once."

"What's the newest?"

"You know that corporate investigation?"

Allison nodded.

"It seems Ringersfeld may have uncovered some shady dealings within our borders, in one of our largest and most respected companies."

"Isn't that more a matter for Scotland Yard, or perhaps Interpol?"

"If it develops into something truly illegal, maybe so. In the meantime I have to decide whether to stir up that kind of fallout. If I do, this particular company is powerful enough to put up a real battle. They could make life miserable for me . . . for us all. It could jeopardize my reputation; they might even move to unseat me. Yet if I don't move on it, you can believe my other convictions are going to be called into question when the press gets hold of it. You know I'm just a stooge for big business and such rot."

"Anyone with an ounce of sense would never believe such a charge!"

"You know the fickle public mind," he said.

She laid her hand lovingly on his shoulder. "You'll do the right thing," she said. "I know you will. You know you've never been one to put your reputation ahead of doing what your convictions tell you."

"Yes," he sighed. "I suppose what I have to do is clear. I only hope we turn up something that will put the odds a little more in our favor. You can't try to uncover the skeletons in the closets of a multi-billion dollar company without some pretty heavy artillery."

"The answers will come, Logan. I don't know where you'll find them, but you will."

He kissed her lightly on the cheek. They linked arms and were just exiting the library when the echoing of the front door chime met their ears from downstairs.

20 / A Long-Awaited Meeting⸺⸺⸺⸺⸺⸺⸺⸺⸺⸺⸺

The high stone walls of the huge gray edifice rose suddenly before Hilary as she rounded a curve in the road.

A tight grove of trees, mostly larches, and the steep incline of the hillside around which the road bent, had obscured it from view on this particular approach. Majestically visible for miles around from nearly any vantage point, the magnificent yet sobering citadel known for centuries as Stonewycke remained, until the last possible moment, hidden to visitors making their approach along this main access road.

What startled Hilary most, however, was not the suddenness of its appearance, but rather the sight itself. This was indeed an ancient castle! All of Joanna's descriptions could not have fully prepared her for what now met her gaze. Rising at least four or five stories in the air, with wings attached spreading on either direction from the main structure, replete with towers, turrets, and various stone-carved ornamentations, the imposing stronghold was certainly something out of *Macbeth* or *Camelot*. She couldn't quite tell, at first glance, whether the castle's grimness or its mystical allure was more dominant. Probably the legends surrounding it were due to a healthy dose of both.

Another iron gate stood before her, this time stretching across the road.

One final wave of reluctance swept through her. But Hilary was determined not to turn back now. She walked forward to the wrought-iron barrier, hesitated merely a moment, reached out, and lifted the latch. The gate opened to her touch. She slipped inside, then closed it behind her. Nothing would divert her from the path she knew was hers to follow.

As she approached the courtyard, Hilary was greeted by the perennial view of the rearing horse in the center of a free-flowing fountain. The splashing water was the only sound to be heard in the tranquil setting. No person was visible on the grounds, no barking dog greeted her as she walked.

She paused a moment to study the regal statue, muscles flexed powerfully across the equine shoulders. The nostrils at the end of the stately head flared, the full mane flying back as if the creature had been caught by Medusa's gaze, captured in full flight rather than carved in stone.

The sight brought to Hilary's mind the horses she had so recently read about in the journal, those marvelous creatures that had been such a vital part of young Maggie's life. At the same time it reminded her how unsuited she was to step into the life this august place represented. Her very attire spoke of how out of place she was for the country life, much less that of a country lady. She had ridden a horse only once in her life!

Nevertheless, after her brief stop, she proceeded around the tiled pool of the fountain and drew near the front doors of the castle—doors containing more inherent grandeur than any she had ever seen.

Swallowing hard, she took a deep breath, then reached up toward the bell.

Logan glanced instinctively at his wristwatch at the sound of the chimes. After four telephone interruptions, a caller at the door, whatever the hour, seemed only appropriate as befitting this day.

"Are you expecting anyone?" he asked as they walked toward the stairs.

"No. I can't imagine who it might be."

As they descended, Flora appeared at the bottom of the stairway.

"Mr. and Mrs. Macintyre," she said, "there's a caller for ye."

"Who is it?" asked Logan.

"A stranger, sir. She said her name is Hilary Edwards."

"Edwards . . ." mused Logan, trying to place the familiar sound of the name. "Is she a reporter?"

"She didna say, sir."

"Thank you, Flora. I'll be right there."

Logan turned toward the front door, while Allison headed back toward the kitchen where she had been preparing the tea herself.

"Beggin' yer pardon," Flora added, "but she asked for the *both* o' ye. Right insistent aboot it, too, I might add."

Allison glanced back toward Logan with a puzzled expression, then turned to follow him. "I suppose the tea will keep for a few minutes."

"She's in the drawing room," Flora added before taking her leave.

Allison took Logan's arm and together they walked toward the drawing room.

"I think I know what this might be about," said Logan. "I'll take care of it quickly. Then maybe we can sit down and talk over that pot of tea. It's time we began thinking about some of the decisions we have to make."

Wondering about the tenacity, not to mention impertinence, of a reporter tracking him all the way to Scotland, Logan opened the doors of the drawing room.

He at once recognized the woman seated on the brocade divan as a journalist he had encountered a time or two, most recently at a press conference prior to the Common Market vote, if he remembered correctly. Now that he thought about the incident, he seemed to recall that she had been rather persistent in her style of questioning. But when she looked up at him, he saw none of such qualities. Instead, he perceived a vulnerability. The instant their eyes met, he knew beyond all doubt that she had not come here to grill him. His posture toward her immediately softened.

"Miss Edwards, I believe," said Logan warmly, extending his hand toward her.

Hilary rose and shook his hand.

"Mr. Macintyre," she said, "thank you for seeing me."

"This is my wife, Allison."

As the two women shook hands, Logan could not take his gaze from the eyes of the newcomer. As she looked into Allison's face, the young woman's blue eyes filled with tears that seemed about to overflow down her cheeks.

"You've come rather a long way for a story, haven't you, Miss Edwards?" asked Logan after a moment.

"Actually," began Hilary, turning back toward him, "I haven't come to get a story at all, but rather to *tell* one." Her voice seemed to gain strength as she spoke. "My mission, if such it could be called, is more of a personal nature. And my name isn't exactly Miss Edwards—that's what I've come to talk to you about."

"You have my curiosity thoroughly aroused," said Logan good-naturedly. "Please go on."

"The story I'm going to tell you you may find difficult—even impossible—to believe. I didn't believe it at first myself."

"Try us. We're good listeners."

"About three weeks ago, I received a visit from your mother," Hilary began. As she spoke she turned toward Allison. At the words a puzzled expression spread over Allison's features.

"She told me of the loss of your daughter during the war," Hilary continued, "and of her own recent search to locate her granddaughter when she suddenly became convinced the girl was alive."

Here Logan and Allison looked at one another in surprise.

"We knew of no such search," said Logan.

"Yes, Lady Joanna told me she had said nothing to either of you."

Hilary paused, struggling with previously unfelt emotions rising from within her.

"Oh, how I wish she were still here!" she said. "But I promised her I would come to you, and . . . as difficult as it is to say such words, I must tell you . . . I must try to explain as best I can the incredible story that Lady Joanna told to me."

Again she stopped. By now Logan's jocular expression had turned deadly serious, as both he and Allison listened in rapt attention.

"Without going into every detail Lady Joanna related to me, I would simply say that . . . oh my, I don't know how to say this! . . . what she told me was—"

Hilary took a deep breath, as if to gather courage.

"—she said that I was . . . that she had searched many avenues and had been led at last to me, and that . . . that I was—her granddaughter . . . that the two of you were my own parents!"

In stunned silence both Logan and Allison stared at Hilary, then toward one another, then back at their guest. The moments before anyone spoke seemed interminably long. In reality the shocked stillness lasted but a second or two.

It was Allison's voice that broke the silence.

"But that's impossible," she said. "Our daughter is in the kitchen waiting for us right now. She's been with us ever since she was located, several months ago. . . ."

It had been a dreary summer in Port Strathy. That day three month's past in mid-August proved no exception.

A heavy rain fell with a stiff wind driving the torrent diagonally, knife-like, into the gray castle walls. Inside, even the fire in the hearth seemed a willing accomplice to the black weather. It had been nearly impossible to light, and twice had burned down to cold dead embers before it could be revived. Even then its gloomy warmth could not begin to penetrate the raw chill pervading the ancient masonry. Now and then the swirling wind took the chimney for its trumpet, sending the smoke back into the house in silent puffs. Then, its gusts once more righting themselves, it sucked the smoke back skyward through suddenly glowing coals and a whistling flue.

Outside, that same northerly gale made sport of the trees, shaking them about as if it would pull them out of the ground and toss them into the sea. Indeed, only in a land like Scotland could such a day come during a season bearing the name summer.

Allison pulled back an edge of the curtain and looked outside. She still held a small hope that her eyes might detect a hint of clearing in the dark, ominous sky. But the storm beat down relentlessly. Only large drops pelting the windowpanes greeted her. It was certainly no day to be afoot.

Fierce, deadly streaks of lightning shot across the evening sky followed by deafening explosions of thunder. One of the wicked bursts of light suddenly illumined a moving vehicle, its headlamps barely discernible in the jagged glare of nature's beam. It came through the open gateway into a courtyard prematurely darkened by the mass of clouds, finally pulling to a stop in front of the fountain.

A visitor *was* expected at Stonewycke, though not for two more days. Allison was expecting no callers today, especially at seven in the evening and in such weather. Why someone would be braving the elements at this hour, Allison could not think.

All at once she felt her heart contract. Their preparations had been focused two days from now. Might there have been some mistake? Could this be the moment instead?

She hurried out into the entryway just as the heavy brass knocker struck the exterior of the door. Allison tried to catch her breath but her heart was racing. Slowing to a steady walk, her hands trembled as she reached out to open the oaken portal.

The instant it swung wide another grotesque stab of lightning slashed across the bleak northern sky. Its ethereal glow framed the caller's face for a brief instant, outlining the hair and shoulders but rendering its features momentarily invisible. Immediately the flash passed, however, leaving in the wet dusk a young woman whose precise age was difficult to determine from the youthful innocence staring out from the face, though Allison quickly recognized that she carried herself with a certain degree of maturity.

Intuitively Allison knew that before her was standing the expected visitor come ahead of time. This could be none other than the object of the telephone call they had received but a week and a half ago. . . .

A clipped, businesslike voice had, after identifying preliminaries, delivered the startling news: "We believe your daughter has been located—"

"But that's impossible; our daughter was killed—"

"Do you know a Hannah Whitley?"

The memory of the rest of that conversation would not be easily erased from Allison's mind, nor of the days that followed. They were days filled with endless legalities and calls and meetings and discussions. Logan's London solicitors had conferred with the man in Glasgow, credentials had been verified, several calls to the United States had been made. In the end all the cold, hard matters of law had been satisfied. When Logan was certain everything was in order, he told the gentleman in Glasgow they were ready to meet the young woman, and the final arrangements were made. He and Allison traveled north to Stonewycke, where they had arrived only two days ago. The plan had been for Logan to pick her up at the Fraserburgh train station on Saturday. Now here she was on Thursday night.

"I hope you don't mind my showing up early and unannounced," said a pleasant voice out of the darkened entryway.

"You must be . . ." But even as she tried to speak, Allison's mouth went suddenly dry, and further words were impossible.

"Yes, I am your daughter." The voice contained a delicate, almost breathless quality, sweet and feminine, mellowed yet further with an intense sincerity.

Allison stood before her speechless for another instant. Imagining this moment over and over in her mind throughout the previous week, she had never pictured herself dumb and paralyzed like a schoolgirl. Finally, with great effort, she shook off the spell. She could not leave the poor girl standing with her back to the rain. Something had to be done.

"Come in . . . please," said Allison in an unnatural voice.

"I just couldn't wait another two days," said the young lady, stepping inside, rain dripping from her umbrella and raincoat. "That hotel in Aberdeen was enough for one night. Yet I did not want our first contact to be by telephone."

"I understand," said Allison, finding her voice again.

Then suddenly the tears came. All week she had held them in check, not wanting to let herself believe the unbelievable. But now—after thirty years . . . her own daughter . . . here . . . standing before her!

The young woman put down her suitcase and stepped toward Allison. "Mother . . ." she said in a voice trembling with emotion.

With the word she thought she would never hear in this life, all reserves at last broke down. Allison moved toward her, and as if of one mind the two women embraced. The tender reunion was marred, if only indistinctly, by the barely noticeable stiffness in the arms that encircled Allison. But how could it be any other way? Though perhaps they shared the same blood, as adults they were still strangers.

When they fell apart, Allison half-laughed as she brushed a quick hand over her eyes.

"It's wonderful to have you at Stonewycke . . . again," she said, smiling. "Come, I'll take you to meet the others."

Allison led the way into the family parlor, where before long they were seated with Logan and Lady Joanna enjoying a fresh pot of tea. While they sipped from delicate china cups and Logan engaged his daughter in quiet conversation, Allison took several moments to study the newly found Joanna Macintyre. Her auburn hair glimmered in the reflection of the fire, now at last blazing in the hearth. It shone somewhere between the fiery auburn of young Maggie's and the richer, more subdued tones of Joanna's when she had first come to Scotland. Lady Joanna herself, her own hair now gray, sat quietly observing as parents and daughter acquainted themselves, and the similarity of hair color was not lost on her.

She was no carbon copy of her predecessors. How could she be? Yet the resemblances were more striking than might have been anticipated. Still, her eyes were much darker and her skin not so pale as Allison's. Of course, they must not forget to reckon Logan's side of the family in the girl's heritage.

Young Joanna, or Jo, as she said she had grown accustomed to being called, demonstrated complete poise and courteous mannerisms. Her movements were gracious, almost feline at times, measured but purposeful. They learned that she had attended the best boarding schools and graduated from Vassar near the top of her class. Her adoptive father, a banker, was British by birth but had moved to the States after the war.

"That explains the accent," said Logan.

"Having grown up in America," Jo replied in an almost apologetic tone, "I'm afraid I have lost too much of my British heritage."

"We're open-minded," laughed Logan, "even toward the Colonists." Then he added in a more serious tone, his eyes deepening with intensity, "We are just glad to have found you." Even as he spoke his eyes clouded over with tears.

Jo rose and walked toward him with that calm assurance and steady gaze of her dark eyes that they would soon come to know well. She took his hands into hers.

"Oh, *Father!*" she said, emphasizing the word, "I never dreamed that finding my real parents would be this wonderful. You can't know what it's like for me. I feel that my life is at last . . . fulfilled."

"Perhaps we *can* know a little of what you feel," Logan replied with a kindly smile that hinted of past pain. "We lost a daughter, too, just as you lost your parents."

The days following that momentous evening were indeed filled with great joy. When the weather permitted, Logan, Allison, and Jo could often be found walking upon the hills and paths of the estate. The parents wanted the daughter to see everything, and to feel the importance of the land as her heritage. Jo took it all in with a deep awe.

"This is more beautiful than I would have been able to imagine!" she exclaimed one day as her eyes, wide with girlish delight, swept the landscape.

"Do you remember anything from before?" asked Allison.

Jo hesitated as she thought. "Just vague images," she answered at last. "I remember the castle, I think. I mean just the look of it from the outside. And the landscape seems like something I've seen before, almost like it was part of a dream."

"You were very young."

"Oh, but I'm here now at last! And it's so clean and pretty everywhere. I'll have to paint it sometime."

"You're an artist?" asked Allison, realizing for the first time that, though she was an eager and attentive listener, Jo modestly spoke little about herself.

"I sometimes feel presumptuous saying it, but, yes, I suppose I am. Though I am still learning."

"You should be proud of your talents. They are from the Lord. Do you sell your paintings?"

"Occasionally."

"But not enough to make a living at?"

"No, hardly that."

"And you've no hankering after the struggling Bohemian lifestyle?" offered Logan with a smile.

Jo laughed—a soft, almost musical laugh that was pleasant to the ear. "I would never have been a starving young artist trying to eke out an existence somewhere. I have my adoptive parents to thank for that. They were very kind and generous to me."

"We have never had an artist in the family," said Allison. "It will be a delight to see this beautiful land captured on canvas. Perhaps you might even pass along some of your talent to your mother. I've always wanted to learn to paint."

"With pleasure!"

During their quiet moments Allison and Logan found themselves mar-veling at the blessing their daughter was proving to be, at how the village children followed her about with admiration, at how freely she seemed to adapt to life at Stonewycke. In just a short time she became a special part of their home and community. When Logan found it necessary to return to London, she seemed completely content to remain in Scotland with Allison, who felt she should remain behind, at least for a while.

Only Lady Joanna seemed reticent toward her namesake. It was difficult at her age, she told Allison, to accept change easily, even when it did come in such a wonderful package. But for the next few weeks Allison's mother kept more to herself than usual, absorbed in her journal, distracted, some-times going out for solitary walks on the grounds. She even went off oddly once to Aberdeen by the Fraserburgh train, and a time or two to Culden to visit a man by the name of Ogilvie, the son of an old friend, she said, who had taken over his father's practice. When she returned her face wore a troubled expression.

Allison tried to ignore Joanna's frequent quiet moods, determined as she was to enjoy this happy time of reunion. And after three months, only the sudden death of Lady Joanna had marred young Jo's homecoming. The unexpected hemorrhage was accompanied by not a few pangs of guilt in Allison's heart. Yet even then, Jo kept a bright countenance. She proved so supportive, so sympathetic, that Allison wondered if she could have faced the loss of her mother without her newly found daughter.

So what was she possibly to think when all of a sudden another young woman turned up on her doorstep claiming to be their lost Joanna Hilary? What, indeed, but that the newcomer was sadly mistaken in her informa-tion.

22 / Altered Plans

Sitting in the guest parlor, Hilary did her best to cope with this sudden nightmare.

Sipping the cup of tea that had been offered her, she graciously nodded attentively as Allison recounted briefly the events leading up to Jo's coming some months before. But inside she was paying little attention. She could not keep her mind from playing over and over that scene with Lady Joanna in her own office. How could the woman have been so convincing if it was nothing but a gigantic mistake? Even as she had spoken to Hilary in London, this other daughter—apparently the real daughter—had been here, at Stonewycke, fully known to her grandmother the whole time. What could it all mean?

It was a mistake, that's what it meant. A huge blunder! Her believing the farfetched story in the first place . . . her coming here! She should have trusted her instincts. She knew in her heart of hearts that she, Hilary Edwards—for that was her name after all—could never be part of all this!

And now here they all were—nice, courteous people that they were, who could deny it?—trying to soothe her frayed emotions. Oh, it was all too awful! She had to get back to the city. That was her real life.

"I know how I would feel had this happened to me," said Jo, who had entered the room and was sitting opposite Hilary. Her voice was so delicate, so sweetly consoling.

All Hilary could do by way of response was to set her china cup down a bit too hard. With an awkward chinking sound, its contents spilled over the edge.

"I really should go," she said, rising.

"You can understand our reaction," said Logan in a calm, reasonable tone, despite the tension etched in his face. "We are every bit as bewildered by this sudden turn of events as you must be. That's why we can only hope that by a thorough explanation of everything, we can somehow sort it out."

"Yes, of course, I understand." Hilary, too, attempted to inject calm and reason into her voice.

"Believe me, we want to get to the bottom of this. But we have already gone to such lengths poring over records and documents and verifying the history of . . . of . . . our daughter here"—as he spoke he motioned toward Jo—"that without concrete proof—"

"I only know that Lady Joanna MacNeil came to me several weeks ago with the most startling revelation I could possibly have imagined."

"Why did you wait so long to come?"

"Why did I wait . . .?" Hilary began to feel control slipping from her voice. "I don't know. It . . . it all took me so by surprise. I wasn't sure I wanted any part of it. The upheaval . . . the change. I tried to come to you once. I came up for the funeral, but in the end I talked myself out of a confrontation."

"Surely, then, you must have realized our daughter had already returned?"

"I spoke to no one. I slipped in at the very end of the service. My mind was so preoccupied I hardly took notice of my surroundings."

"But didn't you—"

"Please," interrupted Hilary, her voice thin and strained. "I had better leave. I am not prepared for a cross-examination. I have no proof—only . . . only the look in a dear old woman's eyes. I've been a fool. You have your daughter."

Hilary turned and fled from the room.

Behind her retreating figure she could hear a clamor of protesting voices, all so sympathetic, wanting to help ease her gently back down into the reality that she was nothing but an adopted working-class woman. But right now she could accept no sympathy, especially from them. She had had to gather courage from within herself to come here in the first place. Now she would have to cope with this unexpected crisis of identity in the solitude of her own soul, and nowhere else.

She ran out into the crisp autumn sunlight, now regretting her decision to walk up to the estate. On foot her getaway would be too slow, and might allow those compassionate people to come after her so they could persist in pitying her foolishness.

She broke into a run, exited the gates, then turned sharply to her right. There was a path somewhere along here, if it still existed. She had read about it in the journal. It didn't lead directly back to town, but at least if anyone did try to follow, they would not think to come in that direction.

She skirted the walls and hedge that surrounded the castle, and after some minutes came to a steep, rocky path that led down into a gorge before finally jogging upward again and out onto a broad pasturelike heath. In summer the grassy expanse would have been lush and green, but now it spread out brown and decaying, awaiting the covering of snow that was not far off.

Hilary slowed her pace to a walk, crossed the barren field, and in about twenty minutes came to a road, one she had not been on before, wide but unpaved. Two or three vehicles passed, each offering her a ride into town. But Hilary could bear no human contact just then.

Walking along the rough, uneven dirt surface, Hilary continued on in the direction in which the sea must lay. She would return to the inn, pay her bill, get in her rented car, and leave this place. How could she have so badly misread all the signs? She was sure God had been leading her to come here. What had gone wrong?

What did it matter anyway? She hadn't really wanted any of this in the first place. To find she was not the daughter of an aristocratic family should be an immense relief. She could now return to her life—the life she had grown to love, the city she loved—and resume being the person she had grown content to be.

Yes . . . she should feel relieved, she said to herself again. This had been unpleasant . . . but it would be better this way.

The road wandered north for about a mile, finally intersecting the coastal road just east of the entrance to the estate that Hilary had taken earlier. She walked down the hill, looking out on the sea, icy blue and calm today, so unlike the stormy expanse that had given her solace yesterday. She needed no solace now, only escape. Before realizing it, she found her feet carrying her down the rocky hillside and across the sand to the water's edge. She couldn't face the inn right now either—she had to be alone.

Perhaps it was only to take one more walk along this magnificent shore. She would never return here. This was not her home. It belonged to another—a sweet, beautiful, lovely young woman rightfully named Joanna. This was her home, her heritage—her Stonewycke. She even *looked* like she belonged here.

She would miss the MacKenzies, thought Hilary. She had wanted to visit them again.

But she couldn't think of all that. If the name Stonewycke forced its way into her thoughts once more, she would crack. Forgetfulness would not come easily. The days, weeks spent in trying to accept the truth about her birth—they might have been put to better use consulting attorneys and researching the authenticity of Lady Joanna's claims. She was a practiced veteran at such things, ferreting out bogus leads from real ones. In the face of the woman's intense sincerity, it had never occurred to her to doubt. Yet what if she had been off in her own little world, and her claims nothing but an ironic game of her aging imagination?

"You are my granddaughter." As Hilary walked, her thoughts drifted back to that day in her office. Lady Joanna's face was still as vivid as it had been that afternoon. Hilary had known the words were true, though every logical, practical reaction inside her had cried out against it.

"How could I have been so wrong?" she silently implored.

The only answer she received was the steady pounding of the waves alternatively slamming against the sand and rocks, then slipping back into the sea. The sight did possess a calming effect. Perhaps it came from the eternal consistency of the sea—surely one of the most awe-inspiring elements in God's majestic creation. She could easily grow to love it, if only . . .

All at once Hilary realized all the changes she had been through over the past days were still with her. Despite her concerted attempts to thrust them from her mind because of how foolish she felt, the images and emotions and tuggings upon her heart conjured up by the journal remained. She could not help still feeling intrinsically a part of the sweeping saga of this incredible family. And, in a way she had never before experienced in London in all her life, she felt somehow a part of the land and its people too. The memory of Frances MacKenzie's large, simple, sparkling-eyed face began to take shape in her mind, and the delicious peace in which she had felt wrapped while lying in her cozy bed of heather. Why, that had been only this morning! One didn't meet faces of compassion and hands of humble service like that very often in London. What did it all mean? What was her part in all this?

Slowly, from some distant place—either deep within her spirit or from outside her, she could not tell which—began to form the incredible thought: *But what if it hadn't been a mistake?* What if that look on Lady Joanna's face signified that she *was* indeed her true granddaughter? What if . . . what if the case of mistaken identity actually rested with the girl still sitting up there in the castle . . . sitting there with *Hilary's* rightful parents?

The thought was too inconceivable! And if it was true, what could she possibly do about it? How could she think of dealing such a blow to the other—what should she call her?—the other claimant? She had already been at Stonewycke almost three months. She was already part of the family. It would be too horrible for her now to discover that she had been part of a mistake. That look of innocence in her eyes—Hilary could never do that to her! To tell her that her whole life and past had been uprooted, but that it had all been a cruel mistake, that the lawyers had somehow mistaken all the evidence.

What am I thinking? Hilary suddenly said to herself. *This is absurd! She is Joanna Macintyre . . . not me. How can I even consider the risk of being made the ultimate fool by going back there and . . .*

The thought did not finish itself. As she played devil's advocate with herself, she had no plan, no barometer to steady her conflicting emotions.

I'm getting away from here! she decided resolutely. *That's the only sane thing to do!*

She continued on down the rugged shoreline, making her way over the occasionally rocky shoal toward the harbor, Port Strathy, and the wide expanse of level beach on the other side of the village. At length she climbed a large rock that sat at the water's edge, scampered up, and perched herself on top, gazing down at the swirling water as it ebbed and flowed beneath her. At last her mind let loose its futile debating and her thoughts turned to prayers.

There was an answer in the midst of all this. Something assured her of that. She just had to make sure she didn't miss it altogether in the muddled

mass of her own confused perplexity. Only as she gave up trying to ration-
alize the whole dilemma out did a peace steal upon her—and out of that
peace the answer would come.

"Guide my thoughts, God," she whispered. "Show me what I'm supposed to do."

Again Lady Joanna's face stole into her mind's eye. This time she saw
an aspect of her countenance she had never seen before—neither the day
of the fateful interview, nor in her memory since. Beyond the assurance,
there had been an imploring in her aged, yet tender, loving eyes. Almost
as if she were asking for Hilary's help!

"You give your word that you will tell them?"

Had there been a desperation in her tone beyond that of a grandmother
who feared her newly found granddaughter might opt to keep her identity
a secret? But why?

Why would the old woman have come seeking a daughter when a
perfectly good one—one who bore such a distinct family resemblance, and
wore such a sweet countenance—sat at home the whole time?

Two hours later Hilary walked back toward the inn. Dusk was settling
over Port Strathy. She had already resigned herself to one more night here.
She would return to the inn, take a bath, then perhaps walk over to the
MacKenzies' cottage and spend the evening with them.

Approaching about a quarter mile from the inn—she could see it gleaming white and inviting on its perch above the cliffs that extended out to the
east—Hilary saw a figure coming toward her. In the gathering darkness of
the late afternoon, she could make out no details except that the form
walked like a man.

In less than a minute, however, they had moved near enough to one
another for recognition. It was Logan Macintyre.

All Hilary's emotional equilibrium began to flutter, and, except for great
determination of will, would have fled entirely. She walked steadily on
until they came close and stopped.

"Hello," said Hilary simply.

"I hope you don't mind my seeking you out like this," said Logan.

"Of course not."

"Davies said he hadn't seen you. But your car was still parked out
front, so I took a chance I might find you somewhere along here."

"Is this where everyone in Port Strathy comes to think?"

"Very nearly." Logan's eyes laughed, but he only let a brief smile
flicker across his serious expression, a smile that Hilary felt rather than
saw. "My wife and I spoke together after you left," he added.

"I'm sorry if I caused—"

"You caused nothing, Hilary—if I may call you that—except a good
deal of confusion. No less for yourself, I'm sure. Please, let's walk." He

gently touched her arm, nudging her into motion.

"Thirty years ago," he began once more, "we lost our daughter. In time we resigned ourselves to never seeing her again. But now all of a sudden we have two perfectly lovely young women, both of whom appear justified in laying claim to that position. If you think you are confused, try to imagine our predicament. It would have been enormously easier had we not read such sincerity in your face. But we could hardly deny it. In addition, there is the little I know of you from London, all of which speaks highly of the honorability of your intent. You are a somewhat well-known woman of growing reputation. Thus, it strikes me that you would have much more to lose than to gain by any attempt to deceive us—which I do not for a moment believe you are trying to do. And believe me, I have some knowledge in such matters." He paused, gazing into the gathering darkness.

"But this only deepens our dilemma. For you see, our daughter—Jo, that is, whom you met—has come to us with the most impeccable of credentials and has already been with us nearly three months. I can hardly believe that the people who initially contacted me about her discovery— men of high repute—could have been so grievously in error. Especially after all the checking that was done. And I cannot help fearing the effects of such a blow to her, now to discover she was uprooted and torn from her life in the United States—for nothing but a dreadful foul-up of some kind in interpreting the evidence and records."

"I'm not sure what you are saying."

"If Lady Joanna did indeed come to see you—"

"She did."

"I tend to believe you, my dear," sighed Logan. "At the time you mentioned, she did travel to London. There was some small row about it here, in fact, for none of us wanted her to go alone—at her age, you know. But she insisted. She was to all appearances in perfect health, so eventually we gave up our protests. She was extremely cryptic about her reasons for the trip, however. But the point remains that she was in London at the time you said."

"I think one question should be asked," said Hilary. "Forgive me for it, but I have to know—was she in her right mind?"

Logan seemed on the verge of a quick response, but he stopped himself and did not speak until after some consideration. At length he said, "If you indeed did speak with Lady Joanna, then you would know the answer to that question."

They fell silent for a moment. Hilary was the first to speak again.

"Yes, you are right. I do know the answer. Because, as it turned out, that one meeting with Lady Joanna is going to have to last me a lifetime, I have not allowed myself to forget a single detail of it. She was a remarkable woman. Perhaps one of the most sane persons I have ever met."

"Then why would you raise the question?"

"Because I'm as desperate for answers as you are, Mr. Macintyre. That would have simplified everything, wouldn't it?"

"I believe we must forget about finding *simple* answers."

They were nearing the path that led up to the inn. Logan paused at its foot momentarily and Hilary took the brief lapse in their conversation to study him. It was difficult to reconcile this mature man with silvery hair and moustache with the rakish con man and daring undercover spy of Joanna's journal. But then maybe not, when you looked deeply into his eyes, outlined with distinctive crow's feet now, often deeply introspective. Even in the failing light Hilary imagined hints of wry amusement, even a little mischief. All the features that had made him handsome in his youth had combined now, at age sixty, to give him a markedly distinguished air, mellowed with a sensitivity that had not come except through suffering and hard-fought spiritual victories.

Hilary could not deny the uneasy fluttering within her heart. For against all analysis, she realized this man might be her father! If so, she knew she would be honored to be called his daughter. He was a far deeper and more sincere man than she imagined when she first stood to interview him a week and a half earlier.

But he had begun to speak, and she jerked her wandering mind back to matters at hand.

"In answer to your question, Hilary," he was saying, "I have an interesting, perhaps unusual, suggestion to make. I have spoken to my wife, and we would both like for you to stay with us while we sort this all out."

Hilary gaped silently at Logan. *Interesting* was far too mild a description of the idea!

"I . . . I couldn't," she finally stammered. "It would be—too awkward. I couldn't do that to your dau—to Jo."

"So you will return to London then, and just forget the whole matter?" Logan asked pointedly.

"I don't know. That would be best for everyone, wouldn't it?"

"Then perhaps that answers all our questions. For if you sincerely believed Lady Joanna's claim, then I doubt you'd give it up so easily."

"It almost sounds as if you are *looking* for a challenge, Mr. Macintyre."

Logan sighed. For a brief moment the creases on his youthful face deepened, and he looked old. "I sincerely wish we weren't having to face these baffling questions, Hilary," he said. "But now that they have been raised, we cannot merely turn our backs. Allison and I can never rest until they are resolved." He paused and leveled his gaze steadily at her. "Regardless of what you decide to do, I cannot let this go."

"But you were so sure before."

"Perhaps we still would be if it wasn't for Lady Joanna's part in all this—of which we knew nothing until today."

"She has that much influence, even though she is gone?"

"If you come to know us at all, Hilary, you will soon learn that in this family the women are accorded much respect. For several generations they have been endowed with great wisdom and godliness. The men who have come into the family, such as myself and my father-in-law Alec, we have learned to recognize and honor that wisdom, and never to take it lightly."

"Like the mantle being passed down from one woman to the next."

Logan's head shot around, his eyes suddenly appraising her as if trying to detect if there could possibly be a hint of mockery in her words. But when he saw none, he simply nodded and remarked, "That is an odd thing to say."

"Lady Joanna wrote something to that effect in her journal."

"Her journal?"

"Yes. She sent it to me. Actually, that is what prompted me finally to approach you."

"She *sent* you her journal?" He was obviously stunned by the disclosure. "No wonder it was missing," he said aloud, but as if thinking to himself. Then he turned his gaze from Hilary and focused on the wide sea beyond them.

Logan began walking again. Hilary had to half-jog to catch up. But he said nothing until they had negotiated the short but steep climb up the bluff. When they reached the top, he continued along the flat path for a few brisk paces, then stopped and turned suddenly.

"I believe," he said with decision, "that it is imperative you accept my invitation."

"It would be too strained."

"I might think you were afraid of something, but you hardly strike me as a person who frightens easily."

It was now Hilary's turn to fall silent and momentarily introspective. Perhaps she *was* afraid. Yet her inborn nature had always compelled her to confront her anxieties rather than hiding from them. The same internal force that had urged her to make her first trek to Stonewycke now prevailed upon her to heed this man's words. Neither could she just return to London and forget. The haunting image of Lady Joanna and the stirring words of the journal would never leave her.

"You are right on both counts, Mr. Macintyre," she said, turning to him. "And because I see no other solution, I will accept your invitation."

He nodded, pleased, but remaining grave and thoughtful. They continued on to the inn, where Hilary paid her account, picked up her things, and departed with Logan.

23 / The Oxford Connection_____

A furtive figure dashed out of the shadows, lumbered across the deserted street, darted into an adjacent alley, then stopped.

Clearly unused to the effort, his panting was the only sound to be heard. After a few moments he resumed his flight, crossed the next intersection, and continued at as fast a pace—something between a hurried walk and a labored jog—as he could manage for two blocks. His loose frame gave every appearance of rebelling against the sustained exertion. Sweat had already matted his hair, which was a little too thin on top, a little too long on the back of his neck, and was dripping from his high forehead and down his heavily jowled cheeks. Under the shabby wool overcoat, his shirt was already drenched under the arms.

Halting again, he tried to still his aching lungs, listening all the time for the footsteps he was sure were following. There were none to be heard, but he knew the man was out there—somewhere . . . waiting . . . for him!

He had to get back to his flat! There he would be safe—at least until he could decide what to do.

As he moved once more out of hiding and down the cobbled street, terror was visible in his eyes. He knew the stakes of this game. When he had given up his tenure for more lucrative pursuits, he'd known there were risks. And though he'd met many shady and dangerous characters along the way, and managed to hold his own with them, inside he was still a scholar at heart. He would never be altogether like the men he did business with. That's why he'd adopted the practice of protecting himself by always having information on his colleagues at his ready disposal. *Know your adversaries—and your allies* had long been his code. *You never knew when they might turn out to be one and the same.*

Protect your flank. It was the only way to survive. That's why he'd hired his old gumshoe friend Stonecroft to watch out for him, keep his eyes on his clients, tail them if necessary, learn what he could of their background, who was working for whom, where was the money coming from, motives. Call it insurance.

Maybe it was too much for an art broker to take upon himself. The thought made him realize anew how bitterly he resented being known as nothing but a common fence by some of his seedier clients. He had left the university in order to involve himself more directly in his true first love—*objets d'art*. And through the years he had built up a clientele that included some of the richest men in the world. His name would never show up in a *National Geographic* article. But if people in the know wanted information about what was "available," what was hot and what was not, or how to acquire a given piece and how much it was likely to run on the black market, they knew he was the man to ask. In fact, he had been interviewed a time or two, though his name had never appeared in print.

At least one Sheik's gallery in Arabia, a collection of Egyptian relics in Amsterdam, and a truly historic display of priceless firearms in Sweden had been put together almost entirely with his help. He was not adverse to an occasional plebeian assignment of moving a cache of stolen rifles, or perhaps jewels—drug-related jobs, however, he refused to touch. It kept his bank account at the comfortable level of liquidity he liked.

But it was the sophisticated and rare objects of artistic magnificence and even perhaps what he might call historical value, which gave him the greatest satisfaction. It had given him the chance to lay his eyes and hands on beautiful treasures he would otherwise never have been able to see. At the same time, he managed to build up a rather nice collection of his own. And he felt a bit of pride at the fact that a time or two his own former colleagues at the university had contacted him with a thorny historic art puzzler they hadn't been able to decipher.

He hadn't acquired the handle *Professor* only as a nickname designating his one-time profession. He still ran his business, as he chose to think of it, in a studious manner. If he was going to charge his clients the fees he did—he never liked to think of them as crooks on the one side and black market buyers on the other—he had to know everything he could about them, and about the merchandise they brought him to move or asked him to locate. It kept him in the know . . . and out of trouble. No sudden surprises. He liked it that way.

Now all of a sudden Stonecroft was dead. And it wouldn't be hard to trace him back and link them together. Everyone on the streets of Oxford knew the Professor and Stonecroft were close friends. Though he had been part of this world long enough to know how to blend into the intelligentsia around here, Stonecroft stood out like a sore thumb. There'd never been much reason to hide it before, and their relationship went back fifteen years, before either had gotten involved in this business. But now, suddenly, his connection to Stonecroft had become a lethal liability.

His friend was dead! He could still hardly believe it! No wonder he hadn't been able to locate him for the past forty-eight hours. Now *he* was likely to be next! He had to get back home. He had to sit down, behind double-locked doors, and think! Perhaps have one last pleasurable gaze over his treasures.

This kind of thing wasn't supposed to happen at Oxford. This was supposed to be a quiet little town. That's why he'd remained here.

He'd known those two bumbling idiots Tex and Mex were flunky underlings the moment they'd contacted him. "Your contact's a Mr. Smythe at the Shrewsbury office of Trans Global," the Texan had said in his annoying drawl. "Anything comes up, Mac, and you need to get in touch with us, you just call them up and ask for Mr. Smythe with a *y*. You gotta say it like that, 'Let me talk to Mr. Smythe with a *y*,' and they'll know what you mean. You got that, Mac?"

What a positively irritating chap! Why they'd sent a mismatched pair like that, he could never understand. He couldn't imagine a respected company like Trans Global employing such nincompoops. Sure, a company of Trans Global's repute might have a division in its operation financing an archaeological dig someplace. It would be good PR for them. And they might well come to him to evaluate their find. But surely the people involved would be of a higher caliber than those two buffoons!

That's why he'd put Stonecroft right on them. He had to know who was really behind this thing. If Trans Global, then who in Trans Global . . . and why? It was obvious from the first that the assignment was far bigger than the little tokens they'd brought him to evaluate. But he never dreamed who his friend would turn up.

Stonecroft had called from London two afternoons ago with the startling news that Tex and Mex had turned the goods back over to none other than Pingel.

Pingel! He hadn't heard of him for years. This truly was turning into an international operation! And if he was involved, unless there had been some dramatic upscale change in Pingel's loyalties, it meant that none other than the General was behind it all, funding and directing the strings of whatever was going on.

He'd never dealt with the man directly. And he didn't want to start now. But his reputation in the nefarious circles in which the Professor often had to circulate was vast.

The General connected to Trans Global Enterprises, one of Europe's most prestigious firms . . . it was incredible! Just last month he had read that the Prime Minister had cited the chairman and directors of Trans Global as particularly to be commended for their valiant fight against pollution, calling Trans Global "a company that sets a standard for integrity in this changing industrial age, of which the nation is proud." Edward Heath did not dish out such compliments lightly.

This was not only unbelievable . . . it was a dangerous piece of information to possess! If Interpol got wind the General was involved with Trans Global, it would seriously damage the company's prestige. Especially if— but no, that was too fantastic a notion even to consider . . . that the General was actually running Trans Global behind the scenes!

The General was not the sort of man you tangled with. The minute he'd hung up the phone he'd known what he must do. He had to get out of this transaction altogether. The General was known for dusting off people who crossed him. Pingel was the man who usually enforced that policy.

Even before he'd had the chance to figure out how he was going to do it—a man like the General didn't like cowards either, or fences who reneged on deals—Stonecroft had called again, this time from Heathrow. He was watching him right now, he said. He'd learned his destination from a ticket agent he'd slipped a few quid. The name of the city confirmed everything! Hardly surprising, said Stonecroft. It's where all those guys went. He'd see him safely onto the plane, then hustle back to Oxford with a full report.

That was the last time he'd heard from his friend.

Now suddenly, just minutes ago, he'd learned that his body had turned up at the airport, out behind a pile of carts near a deserted hangar.

The moment he'd heard, a cold terror had seized him. The only question that still remained was whether Pingel had gotten on the plane. Probably by now the General himself knew the Professor had put Stonecroft onto his men. The General wouldn't like that.

He had to get home, and then to safety. Maybe to Dublin, Scotland . . . even the Continent. Pingel had never taken that flight. He was here . . . somewhere. He knew it.

He could feel his presence . . . stalking him!

I've got to get out of here . . . away from Oxford! thought the Professor one more time to himself. Then he flew out of his temporary hiding place. He did not stop again until he was safely inside his flat, doors securely locked behind him.

Nervously he made his way to every window to make sure all the shades were pulled. Then he cautiously turned on but one small lamp, and at last, all precautions taken, collapsed on his bed in exhaustion.

Timidly Hilary opened the door of her room.

For so long she had been used to being in charge. She had had to make her way in life by a determined self-reliance that did not cower in the face of opposition. When she walked through the doors of *The Berkshire Review*, eyes turned toward her in expectation. She was the center of focus, the one who set the magazine's momentum.

Now here she was feeling like a thirteen-year-old suddenly thrust into a new boarding school where she was a stranger amid long-time friends. She was reluctant to so much as walk downstairs alone. She had never felt so out of place in her life.

She stepped out into the corridor, glanced in both directions, then turned to her left. That much at least she was certain of, though it would take some time to familiarize herself with the maze of hallways, rooms, courtyards, parlors, and staircases that comprised the great castle of Stonewycke. She had been fortunate enough to sleep past breakfast, though Logan had come to her room in midmorning and had taken her out and shown her around. They had seen none of the rest of the family. Allison, he said, had remained in bed too, with a severe headache. She would join them for lunch later in the dining room. Now, Hilary only hoped she could remember his directions of an hour and a half earlier.

Her footsteps echoed ominously as she walked. Around any corner she half expected to encounter Lady Macbeth or some Dickensian ghost from a past generation.

At least she did not feel entirely alone in this respect. It seemed that Allison and Logan Macintyre, as little as she had seen of them, seemed a bit out of place as well. Perhaps it was only because they were so much a part of the contemporary world. At the same time, Logan had appeared completely at ease this morning as he showed her several ancient paintings in various corridors, and a five-hundred-year-old vase probably worth tens of thousands of pounds. He seemed comfortable in both worlds, the old and the new, maintaining a kind of casualness toward the house, mingled with not a little respect as well. Actually, the only one who seemed entirely in keeping with the surroundings was Jo, who, with her demure refinement, looked more the part of a Victorian heroine than a Baltimore debutante.

Hilary reached the first-floor landing, hesitated a moment to check her bearings, then started down to the ground floor. There she turned to the right, walked past the family parlor, and arrived at last at the door of the dining room.

Well, she thought, *this is it. Time to make my first "appearance" with the family.*

She reached out, turned the latch, pushed open the door, and walked inside.

"Ah, Hilary," said Logan cheerfully as he rose and walked toward her with a smile. "I see you've found your way."

"Your directions were very clear," she replied.

"Well, I know the hazards of being a stranger in this place," he went on. "I'm not too old to remember my first days here, and I can tell you it was an intimidating experience, even for a streetwise youngster like I was."

Hilary quickly took in her surroundings. Besides Logan, only Jo was in the room, seated at Logan's left hand. She smiled warmly in acknowledgment of Hilary's arrival, but neither spoke to the other.

"Please, Hilary, sit down," said Logan. "My wife will be here soon. She felt better an hour ago and decided to take her morning walk."

Hilary moved around the table to a chair opposite Jo's. "Come now, Mr. Macintyre," she said lightly as she seated herself, "I can hardly picture you intimidated, even by a centuries-old castle."

Logan laughed, but before he had a chance to respond, Jo spoke up. "Just wait till you know my father better, Hilary," she said. "He's full of surprises."

An uncomfortable silence filled the next moment.

Logan cleared his throat. "And that, I'm afraid," he said as his face turned serious, "pinpoints, as it were, our present awkwardness." He took a deep breath before going on. "I don't know how to make this pleasant, for either of you," he paused, glancing in turn toward each of the women. "But the fact of the matter is clear enough: my wife and I had but one daughter. And now, after all these years, it seems suddenly we have two! We're going to do all we can to resolve this confusion as quickly and painlessly as we can. We're going to have everything checked and rechecked. I've already contacted your solicitors in Glasgow"—here he turned and looked in Jo's direction, then glanced around toward Hilary— "and we're going to have to do what we can to trace Lady Joanna's last weeks to see if we can verify what she apparently turned up."

A puzzled expression flitted across Jo's face, but it passed quickly and she said nothing.

"But," he went on, "as much as I am concerned for each of you, the point remains that somewhere a most distressing mistake has been made. I just hope in the end we will all be mature enough to handle the outcome in a Godly manner."

"Are you certain I ought to remain here?" asked Hilary, finally voicing the question that had been haunting her all day. "It might be easier for you all if I just stayed at the inn, or even perhaps if you just notified me in London once it is resolved."

"We had this same conversation last night, as I recall," answered Logan. "Believe me, Hilary, we *do* want you here." As he emphasized the word, Hilary thought she detected a hint of sternness, a side of himself Logan Macintyre had not shown her before. "Besides," he added more jovially, "there is no reason we cannot be hospitable. However this turns out, think of yourself as our guest. After all," he added with the old gleam in his eye, "you and I both have to return to London and, if not exactly work together, at least coexist on opposite sides of the press-Parliament debate. For that reason alone we ought to be friends!"

"You are very persuasive," said Hilary.

"Come, both of you," he said as he rose and took a coffeepot from the sideboard, "let's have a cup of coffee while we wait for Allison. I can't imagine what's keeping her."

"Hilary," said Logan as he filled their cups with coffee, "I was wondering one more thing about your conversation with my mother-in-law. This morning you told me—"

But the sudden look that passed over Hilary's face arrested him in midthought. "What is it?" he asked.

"I'd completely forgotten!" replied Hilary in an animated expression. "I can't imagine why it slipped my mind. But when you mentioned Lady Joanna again, it all came back!"

"What came back?"

"The locket . . . she and I talked about the locket!"

"What locket?" asked Jo.

"A locket I've had since before I can remember," said Hilary. "The instant Lady Joanna saw it, the strangest look came into her eyes. She said . . ."

As Hilary took a breath, the silence in the room was deep.

". . . she said it used to belong to her, and that she'd passed it down to your wife."

"By Jove!" exclaimed Logan as his hand crashed down onto the table to the resounding sound of tinkling china and silver. "That could be the solution to this whole thing! Do you still have it?"

"Yes, yes!"

"Where? Are you wearing it?"

"It's in my room. I don't think I ever took it out of my overnight case." She laid her linen serviette on the table. "I'll get it right away."

"By all means!" said Logan enthusiastically. "We'll have Allison in here to take a look and once and for all—"

Before he could finish, the sound of a commotion outside in the hallway met their ears.

"What in blazes?" said Logan as he hurried to the door and out into the corridor. Hilary and Jo followed him.

A knot of household employees was making their way toward the dining room from the direction of the kitchen. The cook and housekeeper hovered about, while Jake the stableman walked up, carrying Allison in his arms. Logan rushed forward, concern evident throughout his features.

"I'm all right," said Allison as he approached. "I took a bad fall and Jake insisted on carrying me."

"Bad canna be the word for it, sir," said Jake. "My leddy's lucky to be alive. Ye must fetch the doctor here sure. It wouldna surprise me if her ankle be broke."

"Posh, Jake!" insisted Allison. "I'm fine, I tell you. Set me down."

Begrudgingly Jake complied. Allison took Logan's arm.

"Will one of you please tell me what happened?" said Logan, his stern voice now showing through clearly.

"I slipped on the footbridge," said Allison.

"Slipped ye didna, my leddy," argued Jake. "The bridge gave way, an' 'tis only the grace o' God that ye're no lyin' at the bottom o' the creek right noo."

"I was out there just yesterday," said Allison, "and it was perfectly sound."

"Ye go oot there every day," insisted Jake, "and I doobt ye'd be fallin'—"

"Are you sure you're all right?" asked Logan.

"Yes, it will be fine," Allison replied. "But I've interrupted luncheon."

"Don't worry about that; we hadn't even begun."

"I shall go call the doctor," said Jo.

She turned and hurried away, while Jake ambled off in the direction from which he had come, muttering something indistinct about not being able to keep pace with the deterioration of a place this size, while the cook and housekeeper made their way back toward the kitchen with heads together buzzing.

Logan led Allison, limping, into the dining room, where he gently set her down upon the settee.

"Perhaps a drink of water, my dear?" said Logan. Allison nodded and took the glass he offered. Only after a long swallow did Allison first seem to notice Hilary where she stood about ten feet away. She smiled up at her.

"Hilary," she said, "I haven't had the chance to see you since you came back with Logan last night. Welcome—once again—to Stonewycke."

"Thank you," she replied.

Hilary had taken in the whole scene like the reporter she was, as if her eye had been the lens of a camera, objectively observing the passage of events, followed by the reactions of the principal characters involved. She could hardly help the unconscious attempt to locate the proper angle for an article. It would no doubt fall into the category of human interest, focusing perhaps on the love she had read in Logan's eyes, or the genuine concern and devotion of the employees for their mistress. Colorfully intriguing was Jake's gruff insistence that seemed to imply some sinister motive afoot, quickly dismissed by the more level-headed master of the house, leaving the disgruntled handyman walking off alone with no one to grouse at but himself.

"But how could I forget!" said Logan, coming to himself. "Hilary may have solved the entire mystery in one fell swoop, my dear," said Logan to his wife. "She was just telling us that she has a locket . . . *the* locket, according to your mother, that used to be yours."

Before the impact of Logan's words fully reached Allison's mind, the door opened and Jo walked quickly in.

"Dr. Connally is on his way," she said. "I'm sorry I was so long. How are you feeling, Mother?"

"Oh, I'm fine," replied Allison. "Now, go on with what you were saying about the locket."

"She has it here," said Logan. "Please," he went on, turning toward Hilary, "go get it . . . right now."

Hilary obeyed, and left the room.

When she returned ten minutes later, her step was slow and her face told what words hardly needed to say.

"I . . . I can't imagine what happened. But the locket's not there."

25 / Mustering a Force of One

The loud ringing of a phone split the midnight air.

Muttering a curse, the occupant of the room struggled into wakefulness and fumbled for the receiver. The moment he heard the voice on the other end of the line, his body snapped almost as if to attention and sat up on the edge of the bed. All drowsiness instantly vanished.

"It's *you!*" he said. "I didn't expect . . . no problem . . . no, I was just, er, lying down . . . time difference? It's, let me see, two-thirty in the morning. . . ."

He was silent for some time as the voice on the other end spoke, nodding his assent occasionally, a grave expression on his face.

"Hmm," he said at length. "Yes, that should work . . . a clever way to introduce myself . . . they would have no way of knowing . . . right, couldn't check . . . yes, I'll use that. . . ."

Silence again. Another several nods.

" . . . I understand . . . I'll get up there as soon as I can . . . getting into the house, that might be difficult, but . . . no, no, rest easy. We'll handle it . . . what could go wrong? . . .

In response, the voice of the caller shouted a series of threats which the man softened somewhat by removing the receiver from his ear and holding it back about three inches. Then, without his speaking another word, the line went dead, and he hung up the phone.

Well, he thought, this is an interesting twist to the schedule. "Get up there immediately," his boss had said. "An unexpected setback . . . a complication . . . an unknown person entering the scenario."

He'd have to cancel his plans to go hunting with the earl. But then, this assignment would not be without its potential compensating rewards. And his caller was not a man to be refused.

Now, if only he could get back to sleep. There were preparations to be made, and tomorrow would be a full day.

26 / Small Talk in the Parlor _____

The remainder of Hilary's first day had gone by uneventfully. She'd spent every free minute searching her room for the locket, but it was nowhere to be found. Logan drove her down to the Bluster 'N Blow, but neither did a thorough turning over of the room she had occupied reveal a trace of it.

Jo was away a good deal of the day, so Hilary felt somewhat a greater freedom to walk about the house and grounds, visiting with the staff. She and Allison had enjoyed a talk together—admittedly light, but without the strain of their first meeting the previous afternoon. Dinner had been a rather stiff, yet endurable affair—the conversation stilted, no doubt, on account of Hilary's *faux pas* over the locket.

The next morning she had arisen early and walked to town and on to the MacKenzies', where she enjoyed a visit and a simple lunch. Now here it was the afternoon of her second day at Stonewycke, and time was beginning to hang heavy on Hilary's hands. About three o'clock she wandered in to the family parlor. A fire burned cheerily in the hearth and the room was warm. Logan sat to one side reading a newspaper, with a pen and notebook on his lap with which he was jotting down notes from time to time. Kitty-cornered from him across the room Jo sat, a piece of needlework idle in her hands, staring vacantly into the fire. As Hilary entered, Logan glanced up with an inquiring expression, as if to say, *Well . . . have you found the locket yet?* Jo did not move.

The furnishings in the parlor were modern and comfortable, the color scheme bright and upbeat, and there were no ancient vases to be troublesome to the occasional absent-minded guest. A television sat in one corner and a low coffee table held stacks of magazines and newspapers. A great variety was represented, including every single London daily. It was clear Logan made a point of keeping abreast of current events and editorials and the shifting tides of public opinion. *The Berkshire Review* was among the offerings on the table, and Hilary could not help feeling a twinge of pride that an important man like Logan Macintyre would choose to read her magazine. She restrained an urge to pick it up and thumb through it, notwithstanding that it was last month's issue and she already knew every article backward and forward from supervising them all through the different stages of production. Seeing the magazine did serve as a reminder that she ought to check in with the office. She had reported in when she

143

left the inn. They were managing well, which was a good thing since they just might have to get the next issue out without her services at all. But she should call every couple of days regardless.

She picked up yesterday's *Daily Telegraph*, sat down on the sofa opposite Logan, and began to leaf through it.

"Did you have a nice visit with Frances and Karl?" Logan asked.

"Yes, very pleasant."

"They're good folks, the sort that make this little valley so special."

"I can tell. So hospitable. They keep trying to get me to come back down and stay with them, in their little but-end room, as they call it."

Logan laughed. "That is like them!"

"She's always talking about the people 'up on the hill.' She seemed especially fond of Lady Joanna."

"Oh yes! Mother always had a special place in her heart for Frances MacKenzie. As do I. She shares my mother's name, so I've been rather fond of her."

"She said it was her aunt the Queen Mother visited with Lady Joanna."

"That's right," chuckled Logan. "Frances is fond of that story—tells it every chance she gets! She was old MacDuff's granddaughter. Mac-Duff—he was the chap—"

"Yes, I know,'" said Hilary. "I read all about it, remember?"

"That's right, of course. In any case, I think Joanna's love for Frances stemmed more from the soft spot she always had in her memory for her grandfather, who first brought her into Port Strathy."

The door opened and Flora's face appeared. "Ye've a telephone call frae Lonnon, sir," she said.

"Thank you, Flora," said Logan, rising. "You ladies will excuse me. I'll be back in a few minutes. In the meantime, it'll be a chance for you to get better acquainted."

He left the room and silence fell, broken only imperceptibly by the thin crackling of the fire. Hilary feigned interest in her newspaper, trying to think of some appropriate question to ask. It was the first time she and Jo had been alone together.

It was Jo who spoke first, however, rising and sauntering slowly toward the fire. "It's so cold outside! Cook said the back-door thermometer read 23 degrees this morning. She said it will snow soon."

"That will be a nice change," offered Hilary.

"It will be like home for me," Jo sighed dreamily. "I'm from Baltimore, you know. In Maryland. I've been dearly hoping for a white Christmas."

"You should have no worries here in Scotland—even Bing Crosby would be pleased."

Jo laughed softly, and Hilary noted how much the sound resembled tiny bells that seemed in perfect harmony with thoughts of Christmas.

"Do you miss your home?" asked Hilary after a short pause.

"Sometimes, I suppose. Britain is so different in many respects. But I have no real home back in the States any longer."

"Your adoptive family no longer lives there?"

"My parents—my *adoptive* parents, that is—were killed in an auto crash three years ago."

"I'm so sorry . . . I didn't realize."

"There was no way you could have known," replied Jo.

She sat down in an upholstered chair adjacent to the sofa and folded her hands in the lap of her navy cashmere dress. Her lips twitched into a tentative smile as if she were debating some problem in her mind involving the present conversation. Then, apparently deciding to go ahead, she spoke again.

"Hilary," she said with feeling, "it was such a special thing for me that the Macintyres came back into my life when they did. I had been so devastated by my parents' deaths and was so very much alone. It's bad enough to be orphaned once, but twice! I really didn't think I would be able to survive it."

Hilary could think of no appropriate response, so said nothing. A brief silence fell.

"Do you mind my asking you something?" Jo asked after a moment's pause.

Hilary shook her head.

"I'm only curious, so please don't read any other meaning in this, but I heard you say that you spent some time debating whether you would even approach the Macintyres. I wondered what changed your mind?"

"I made a promise to Lady Joanna."

"You knew her quite well then?"

"We only met once."

"Hmm . . . I see."

"Even though she died before I fulfilled it, I knew in the end that I must be true to what I pledged to her."

Hilary paused before continuing. There was another reason she had come. Suddenly she felt a strange hesitation about mentioning it. But just as quickly as it had come over her, she shook it off and went on. "I think it was mostly the journal that convinced me that this whole thing went beyond my personal likes and dislikes and hangups."

"The journal?"

"You don't know about Lady Joanna's journal?"

Jo seemed to consider her response a moment, then slowly shook her head.

"For years she has kept a record of all the events in the life of the family. It begins with Margaret Duncan's life, and is brought up to the time just prior to Lady Joanna's death."

"A history of the family?" asked Jo. "Births, marriages, deaths—that sort of thing?"

"That, but much more too."

"More, you say. Like what?"

"I don't even know how to describe it. A chronicle of . . . of life—emotional, spiritual, as well as historical. It's so much deeper than a mere factual recounting of events. Lady Joanna's impressions come through on every page. It conveys such wisdom, such truth about . . . oh, I don't know, so many things . . . Lord and Lady Duncan, others who touched their lives, how the family was sustained through the years."

"Then she must have written about us—my arrival, her visit with you?"

"That's the peculiar thing. There's no mention made of any of that. Knowing how Lady Joanna wrote down what she thought about everything, I can hardly believe she would omit something so crucial. It's like the last three months were removed from it altogether."

"Removed?"

"The journal ends abruptly, in mid-sentence, actually. It's very odd. But she was getting up in years. Perhaps they were just misplaced."

"Do you still have it?"

"Oh yes. And after misplacing the locket, I've made double sure I don't lose the journal. I've got it safe and sound."

"Would it be an imposition if I asked if I might have a look at it?" Jo's tone was hesitant, demurring, yet a trace of tension could be read in it also.

"I don't know," Hilary began to answer haltingly. "It seems perhaps we ought to ask Mr. Macintyre if he thinks we ought—"

Before she had a chance to complete the sentence, Logan returned and walked briskly back into the room.

Appearing relieved, Hilary said no more, glancing down at the paper that still sat in her lap.

"Well, what have you ladies been talking about?" asked Logan lightly, masking his obvious interest in that very thing. He did not like to have left them so long alone.

"Nothing much," answered Jo. "Just girlish parlor talk, you know."

Logan was at that moment looking toward Hilary, and did not see the momentary flash of defeat that flitted through Jo's eyes, bellying the calm nonchalance of her words.

She sauntered toward the chair she had previously occupied, disinterestedly picked up her needlepoint, and then a moment or two later left the room.

Logan resumed his seat, scanned the notes he had written earlier, quickly jotted down the gist of his phone call for future reference, then laid his papers aside and attempted to engage Hilary in easy conversation.

She did not appear interested, however, and remained quiet. Though her apparent reaction to her talk with Jo concerned him, Logan did not press her. In a few moments he rose again, excused himself, and left the room, this time with a determined look of mingled uneasiness and decision etched on his face.

27 / A Visit to the Stable

The rustic old loft over the stables had not changed much in fifty years. In fact, it had probably hardly changed in the more than one hundred years since its most revered occupant lived there.

The steps were relatively new, at least by comparison, and remained in good repair. Logan had built them himself in 1931. They were good, solid steps and barely creaked as he now ascended them.

When Logan reached the door, he had to brush away cobwebs from above the entry, a reminder that it had been too long since he had come to his dear uncle Digory's humble home. The door creaked when he pushed it open, straining upon its rusty iron hinges. But that scarcely lessened the awe the place held for Logan, for it was a reminder that a hundred years before, Digory too had shoved open this same door every day—though not to the sound of creaks, for he was known to keep his equipment well oiled. Inside, everything was just as he had found it that first time, though a bit cleaner perhaps. A small shaft of the late afternoon light pierced the corner of the single small window high up on the western wall. It wasn't much, but enough to illuminate the small room and even smaller alcove.

Logan ambled idly about for a few minutes, brushing down a cobweb or two, running his hand along the sparse furnishings, absorbing the ambiance of quiet peace this room would always hold for him. He did not come here nearly often enough, he told himself. Though since it was usually times of uncertainty or crisis that drove him here, perhaps he ought not to rebuke himself too harshly.

The last time had been more than a year ago when he had been seeking direction for his career. Wilson's long and successful Labour government had been surprisingly voted out, and for a time Logan seriously thought he ought to take that fact as a personal mandate indicating that it was time for his own retirement from public office. He had tried to tell himself he was getting too old to jump back into the fray of running for Parliament again, with all the strain it entailed.

But after time in prayer in the stable loft, he had realized his reaction was due to bitterness, not age. In six years the Labour Party had brought economic health—at least the strong beginnings of such—to Great Britain, yet the election of 1970 had turned into a rejection of the party. It was difficult not to take the rejection personally, for he had played a key role in the formulation of many of the party's policies. But once he recognized the bitterness for what it was, he had been able to ask God sincerely for a change to occur in his heart. With the answer to that prayer came renewed enthusiasm for his job, and renewed faith in and love for his constituents. When he had told Allison of his decision to re-seek his seat in Commons, she had sighed with relief.

"I hadn't wanted to push you before," she said. "It had to be your decision. But I wondered when you would see through that excuse of being too old. Why, sometimes I think it's the political battles that keep you young, Logan! You love the 'fray' as much as any part of the job."

How well she knew him!

Logan was not the sort whose job consumed every aspect of his life. Yet he had to admit that his job was an important part of what kept him going. He loved what he did, and felt he was making a contribution as a Christian to society and to his fellow man.

His position had come as a gift from God, a true answer to the prayers of a returning veteran, coming home from a war that contained many dark hours for those in the thick of it. He had desperately needed direction to his life back then, for even if his faith and his marriage had been substantially healed, he could not keep from fearing stumbling into the pitfalls that had been the catalyst of his personal deterioration before the war.

The first few years had been tenuous, at best. Though he and Allison were at last able to trust one another fully, Logan found himself still lacking in marketable skills. Arnie Kramer had secured him a position in public relations in his father's shipping company. Logan enjoyed the work well enough, yet not to the extent that he was able to envision it as his life's vocation. But the hard-learned lessons of his war years served him well and he stuck with the job for four years. As a result of his tenacity, in the course of his assignments he became associated with members of the Trade Commission and thus first tasted the outer spheres of political life. He knew immediately this was something he liked!

Arnie had been the first one to jokingly mention his running for public office. Logan had scoffed at the notion. But Arnie wouldn't let it go, and began to bring it up with increasing frequency, and with deeper and deeper sincerity—with at least as much seriousness as the old windbag could muster.

"Logan," he exclaimed one day, "everyone knows that politicians are nothing but legalized con men! You'd be a natural at it, old boy."

To Arnie, Logan merely laughed. But inside the suggestion took root. He struggled with the possibility for a long while. He no longer cared to submit to his "natural" instincts, whatever they might be. A wise priest had once told him: "Certain things are truly natural because they come from God. Others are not natural because they originate in our so-called 'natural' man."

He had prayed a long while, over the course of many months, right here in Digory's old room, before he gradually became certain that God did indeed desire him to embark on this new career. And after that first election, which had been a battle worthy of the name, he first understood what Jean Pierre had meant when he spoke of giving oneself wholly to what one is called to do. Becoming a member of Parliament had indeed provided direction in his life. And more, it gave meaning—something he had not found in any of his previous *natural* endeavors.

Yes, Logan had come to this stable loft in the wake of many crises, and to face many difficult decisions. And thus he had come today, even if it had been a year since the last time. The problem facing him this day was unlike anything he had ever confronted, and was a question filled with many complications.

A heavy oppression had grown upon him these last two days since Hilary's arrival. It only made his confusion of late greater. He knew the source of the pressure—it came from the host of unpleasant questions that had been bombarding him. It was not hard, therefore, to associate the oppression with Hilary herself and her arrival.

But when he went deep down inside himself, he had to admit that it had begun even prior to her coming. He had not been able to pinpoint it. Then she had come, and his disquietude took on wider dimensions. Yet somehow he viewed Hilary more as a victim than an instigator. Still, her presence in and of itself raised even more questions. It had come to a head just moments ago in the parlor. Seeing the two young women together, alone, both of them in a frightfully awkward position toward one another— at that moment he had known he had to do something—and soon.

But what? Ultimately, it all seemed to come back to Lady Joanna.

Why had she gone to see Hilary? And without mentioning a whisper of her intent to anyone? It seemed too far-fetched a story for Hilary to have fabricated. And how else could she have gotten hold of the journal? Joanna had admittedly become quieter than usual about two weeks after Jo's arrival. But if she'd had questions, why had she kept them to herself? If only he knew what she had known, whom she'd talked to, what she'd learned and where, maybe some of his own questions would have come into focus. But it was too late to find such things out. She was gone, and her secrets with her.

He and Allison had hoped that by inviting Hilary to Stonewycke, their own instincts and discernment would have the chance to get at the truth; that somehow seeing the two women together for an extended period of time might reveal which one was truly their daughter. But each bore distinctive family characteristics, and after this afternoon he realized he had to take some greater form of decisive action.

He was sure the whole mix-up would in the end be explained by some clerical blunder—either by Jo's Glasgow lawyers and investigators, or by Lady Joanna in her oddly-timed quest that had landed her in Hilary's London office. On one side or the other, there had to be an easily explained error.

Yet another terrible suspicion nagged relentlessly at him. And down inside perhaps this was the crux of his recent anxieties. It was so unthinkable he had not even mentioned it to Allison. But if he was going to get to the bottom of this it had to be considered. Was it possible that one of these women could purposely be attempting to deceive them?

The very thought made him tremble. For if it were true, then the level of such duplicity was incredible. Logan was well known for his ability to read a man's face—one of his attributes as an ex-gambler that served him well. But in this present dilemma he could not venture so much as a wild guess who the impostor might be. If there was indeed hypocrisy, there must be evil genius behind it. Which was why he could not bring himself to believe such a thing. It was too fantastic for even him to swallow.

Perhaps his talent for probing the depths to discern hidden motives did not extend to *women's* faces. Or was he just too personally involved to be properly objective?

He did not dwell on that train of thought for long. He remained convinced that somewhere an enormous mistake had been committed. But in any case—foul-up or fraud, innocence or deceit—he had to do what he could, and take what precautions lay open to him.

He walked into the alcove where the table and chair Digory had used still sat. He eased himself down into the chair, propping his elbows on the table, then bowed his head in prayer.

28 / Help From a Friend

When Logan descended the steps from the old loft some thirty minutes later, at least some of the peace he had been seeking had come to him. While he didn't have a complete answer to his dilemma, he did know what action he must take next.

He breathed deeply of the homely, wholesome, earthy animal smells around him. Though he didn't ride, he was glad they still kept a few horses. It was part of Stonewycke's heritage. This would always be Digory's stable, he supposed, though many grooms, mechanics, and handymen had come and gone since his great-great-uncle's time. Logan reminded himself that Digory's peace had not come because the stable was a quiet place where the anxieties of the world seemed far away. His peace came from a higher Source, and so did Logan's. Because he felt God had spoken to him just now, he walked with a lighter gait and a ray of hope in his eyes.

Logan briskly crossed the back grounds and gardens, entering the house by way of the kitchen. The cook was slicing two cold steamed chickens for a late tea; dinner that day had been served at one in the afternoon; Hilary had been with the MacKenzies at the time. The cook threw Logan a cursory greeting, mumbling something about the impossibility of preparing a *proper* menu with unexpected guests appearing every other day, and with the grocery order being late.

Logan chuckled to himself. Three months ago she had been complaining about how quiet the place had become. *I might not be able to give her warning about our next guest either,* he thought. *Not just yet, anyway.*

He mounted the stairs to the first floor, turned purposefully down the hall, and came to the library. He opened the door, stepped inside, and glanced about carefully before closing the doors behind him. Certain that he would not be disturbed, he went to the phone on the desk and picked up the receiver.

"Long distance," he said when the operator came on.

He gave her the number, then waited while the connection was made.

In a few minutes another feminine voice answered. He identified with whom he wanted to speak.

"May I say who is calling?" she asked in an efficient receptionist's tone.

"Logan Macintyre."

"One moment, please."

There followed a brief pause. Then she came back on the line. "He's just finishing with an appointment. Can you hold a moment?"

"Yes," answered Logan, "I'll wait."

He took the interval to move around the desk to the chair, where he sat down and took some papers from a drawer that needed attending to. He had barely looked at the first one when he heard a masculine voice in his ear.

"Logan, what a pleasant surprise!" it said. "I'm sorry for having to make you wait."

"I know the rigors of a public life," laughed Logan. "Always busy. But I would appreciate it if I could steal a few minutes of your time."

"Of course!"

"This one's personal."

"Go on. What can I do for you?"

"I have rather an unusual problem," Logan replied. He laughed again. "Actually, that's an enormous understatement, as you'll see. It's an extremely delicate matter, and I need some outside input."

"From me?"

"I need someone I can trust, my friend," said Logan earnestly. "So on that count you are my top choice. But I need your keen analytical mind as well. Along with your other, shall we say, non-erudite pursuits—about which you are so bloody closemouthed that even a friend such as myself can't uncover what you are up to!—don't you have a chum in Scotland Yard to whom you've lent your wisdom upon occasion?"

Now it was his friend's turn to laugh. "You make me sound like a genuine mystery man! All from one unguarded comment I made four years ago. I tell you, Logan, you're imagining the whole thing. I'm just what I appear to be, nothing but an innocent—"

"I know, I know!" interrupted Logan. "Always the same answer! And you've got the credentials to back up what you say. But someday, believe me, I'm going to find out what the deuce you are up to!"

"A pointless sleuthing exercise where the object is nothing more than the boring chap he appears to be."

"I don't believe that for a moment. But tell me, isn't what I said about your having a friend at the Yard true?"

"Yes, but my only contributions have been for the sake of mental calisthenics. He's made me privy to a few of their cases, and sometimes by sheer luck, he solves one when I happen to be around. It is a rather stimulating breather from my boring routine, if nothing else."

"Quite, quite! As is this snow job you insist on shoveling my way. Well, perhaps I can propose another 'breather' for you, if you are interested."

"Proceed. You have my curiosity aroused."

Logan briefly outlined his situation, then went on to explain what he hoped his friend might do for him.

"I'm afraid," said Logan, "that I have become incapable of being objective. I must be missing something—perhaps the very thing Lady Joanna saw but kept so silent about. Thus, I thought it might be helpful if someone neutral could observe the situation. An outsider, so to speak, sifting through the evidence, helping me to see what perhaps my own eyes are unable to."

"There's no fault with the credentials?"

"No, none on either side. Everything on the complete up and up. I've had everything double, even triple checked. I verified that Lady Joanna did indeed visit the offices of *The Berkshire Review* at the specified time. And the Edwards girl does indeed possess the journal; the only way she could have obtained it is directly from Joanna. If there is deception involved in any way on her end, it would extend all the way back to my mother-in-law's being fed spurious information. Yet if that is the case, I can hardly believe the girl herself knows about it. She seems to have been genuinely moved by her encounter with Lady Joanna. All indications point toward complete innocence."

"And the other—what did you say her name was?"

"Jo, after Joanna. That was our daughter's name."

"Yes . . . and what about her?"

"Nothing much to say. Everything checks out. She seems innocent enough, too. Allison's been quite taken with her."

"Hmm," mused Logan's friend, "you do indeed have a puzzle on your hands. Have you consulted the police?"

"Heavens no," replied Logan. "No crime has been committed, for one thing. It has to be a muff somewhere down the line. But even more than that—and this is the crux of the matter, after all—one of those women is apparently my own daughter. That alone necessitates treading somewhat lightly."

"I see . . . and you would like me to—"

"Just get to know them, even just socially at first, see what your instincts tell you about the two of them."

"That should be an enjoyable exercise! Tell me, what do they look like?"

"Both beautiful," replied Logan laughing. "But you would need to come up north for a few days. I know your schedule is—"

"Nonsense! A vacation will be a welcome diversion. I need to get away!"

"So you'll do it?"

"I'll have to clear a few things up, but I'm sure I can manage it. At this point, I'm too curious not to."

"There is one last thing I ought to mention," said Logan. "It might be best if we kept a low profile on your reasons for being here. No need to cause undue tensions. The women will be more open if they are unaware of our connection, and you've never met my wife. So I think it would be best if your coming was made to appear purely accidental, and if you and I keep our past association in the background."

"Yes . . . I see what you mean. Any suggestions?"

"You are a clever fellow. You'll figure something out."

"Surprise you, eh?"

"Right! I can't tell you how much I appreciate this, old chap!"

"Then don't. Wait to see if our efforts bear fruit."

After solidifying a few more arrangements, Logan bid his friend good-bye and replaced the phone in its cradle. He laced his fingers together behind his head and leaned back in his chair.

For some reason he felt relieved. Probably because he had finally taken some action, done something concrete. A solution seemed much closer now than it had several hours ago.

Hilary had not slept well since her arrival at Stonewycke.

Part of her temporary insomnia was definitely due to the tension surrounding her visit. It was augmented by the intense quiet of the place once darkness descended. She could hear it now—the sounds of absolute stillness . . . nothing. No night wind was blowing. They were too far from the sea to detect any sound from the shore. The horses in the stable were still. Everyone in the house was in bed. The tranquillity was not broken by so much as the occasional chirping of a cricket, for the cold had driven the creatures into hiding.

Hilary was accustomed to being lulled asleep to the constant accompaniment of sirens, blasting horns, and the screeching brakes of London's taxi system. Her city-acclimated mind could not allow the peacefulness of the country to penetrate beyond her surface senses.

But when she crawled into bed an hour ago, she thought she would have little trouble drifting off to sleep. For the first time in days she felt some release from the burden of confusion that had been weighing her down. For that she could thank Allison.

Shortly after dinner, following two more rather tedious days at the castle, during which time the temperature had dropped even further, Hilary had ventured up to Lady Macintyre's room. Allison was still recuperating from her fall, though she had been out and about some today. The doctor had been in, and upon examining the swelling and discolored ankle had remanded her to bed for a minimum of twenty-four hours, prescribing elevation and ice. Jo had been most diligent in tending Allison and bringing in cold packs ever since. She had, in fact, been in almost constant attendance upon Allison, which was the primary reason Hilary had waited so long to visit the patient. But at the first break in Jo's ministrations, she took the opportunity to pay her own respects.

"I would have come sooner," explained Hilary, "but I didn't want to get in the way. I do hope you're feeling better."

"Much, thank you," replied Allison. "But I have absolutely no patience with being laid up. I'm more frustrated than anything. I'm no good at all with the helpless woman role."

"I understand that," said Hilary. "Activity is certainly part of my profession."

"That's right, you're a career woman."

"I suppose that's as appropriate a term as any."

"I'm sure all my activity drives everyone crazy at times. My poor mother, as tolerant as she could be, was often scandalized at my outspoken participation in Logan's campaigns and work. But it just doesn't pay to try to be something one is not."

She paused and shifted her position in bed. "Please, sit down a minute."

"Don't let me wear you out."

"Don't worry about that. I feel fine. Better, in fact, than I have for two weeks—if it just weren't for my ankle. But I haven't had a chance to talk with you since your arrival. Perhaps the Lord brought about this accident to force me to be still a while."

Hilary pulled a chair to the bedside and sat down.

"I must admit," Allison was saying, "that something inside me has been avoiding this conversation. I had no idea what I would say. In fact, I still don't. The whole situation is filled with so many emotions, many that I have yet to identify within myself. I want to get to know you. But at the same time I have to admit to some fear, for I've become very attached to Jo these last two months. She's become, well . . . if not a daughter to me, then certainly like one. Now suddenly . . . your coming—it's all very befuddling. I feel like pulling back from everything, from both of you, but I know that won't solve anything, either."

"I understand," replied Hilary. "I would like nothing better than to run back to my own secure little world. Believe me, I resisted coming back that night Logan met me at the inn. The only reason I decided to stay was that I had already invested so much of myself in my decision to come to Stonewycke in the first place. I couldn't walk away from it. Besides, after my initial hesitation, I have come to believe quite strongly in everything Lady Joanna told me."

"Logan says you have read my mother's journal."

"Yes, and that journal, and the portrait she paints of your family through the years, played a significant part in my decision."

"It does seem peculiar that she sent it to you. . . ." Allison seemed to muse over the thought before continuing.

"I asked her several times if Jo could read it," she went on. "She agreed whenever I brought it up, but it was always, 'Let me finish this one section,' or, 'I'd like to polish up a few paragraphs first.' So she never got around to it. She died so suddenly."

"She possessed great wisdom, and a wonderful way of expressing herself. The people she wrote about, even you and Mr. Macintyre, are all very real on the pages. I feel as if I know you all."

"She is the one who comes through more than anyone else."

"I wish I'd been able to know her better."

A short silence followed, each reflecting on the confusing turn of events. Finally Allison asked, "Hilary, do you mind my asking about your beliefs . . . your spiritual values? Are you a Christian?''

Hilary smiled. "I suppose you always hope someone won't find that question necessary, that the way you visibly live will be answer enough. But yes, I am. I have been walking with the Lord since I was a teenager, though every year it seems the growth works its way a little deeper.''

Hilary paused, wondering how far to open herself to this near stranger who just might be her mother. At length she plunged ahead. "I suppose that accounts for a good deal of my present confusion. I prayed and was sure God was directing me here. Now it seems perhaps I was wrong.''

"Are you certain of that?''

"No. I'm not certain of anything anymore. But if God was leading me here, I cannot help wondering why things have turned out as they have.''

"Nothing has 'turned out' yet at all. We are all confused. Nevertheless, if there is a single principle that shouts out of my mother's journal above all else, it's the simple truth that God can take the bleakest of circumstances and, for those who are walking in His way, transform them wonderfully so that good results. I am sure God brought you here for a reason.''

What a boon those words had been to Hilary—exactly what she needed to hear. They enabled her to shift the weight of the present confusion into God's infinitely more capable hands. Everything that had come about must indeed be part of some design greater than her small mind could fathom. She was here at this very moment for a purpose. Perhaps that was why sleep had eluded her this night, for an anticipation was gradually creeping over her since her conversation with Allison. For the first time since her arrival, she found herself eager for what God had in store. Moreover, she was not so willing to turn tail and run as she had been when she first discovered Jo's presence.

If God had brought her here, then He *would* direct her path and make the way into her future clear.

30 / Snowy Rendezvous

Hilary rolled over in her bed, squeezed her eyes shut, and tried to force sleep to overtake her.

But it would not come. Many years ago she had learned the futility of fighting a temporary bout of insomnia. During such times it was generally her habit to get up and do one of two things: spend time in prayer, or seek out her typewriter. In either case, the night hours always proved profitable.

But on this particular occasion, as she had already spent a good forty-five minutes in prayer, and as her typewriter was four hundred miles away in London, she had to settle for the third option: a cup of tea—hot enough to be relaxing, weak enough not to send sleep even further away.

She rose from her bed, wondering if she dared roam about the house at nearly midnight, much less rummage through an unfamiliar kitchen. But the worst that could happen might be a scolding from the cook, who, Hilary could already tell, possessed strong territorial feelings toward her domain.

Hilary crossed the room to retrieve her robe from a chair. As she glanced out the window, suddenly all thoughts of tea faded from her mind. It was snowing!

She rushed forward and pressed her face to the windowpane. The white flakes must have been falling for some time, for already one or two inches covered the ground, casting over the countryside an eerie luminescent glow. The boughs of tall firs were just beginning to bend under the weight, and the absence of wind allowed the slender piles of whiteness to grow high upon the branches before falling silently upon the powdery blanket below.

"No wonder it was so quiet outside!" exclaimed Hilary.

With a childlike sparkle in her blue eyes, she threw down the robe in her hand, slipped out of her nightgown, and quickly stepped into her slacks, pulled a sweater over her head, put on her shoes, and grabbed her heavy overcoat as she headed out the door and into the stillness of the corridor.

She could scarcely remember the last time she had been out in a fresh snowfall. The bustle of London usually turned what scant snow did fall there into brown slush before nine in the morning. But she had always enjoyed the snow. Even as she hurried down the staircase, another night came to her mind when she had been about ten years old. The night had been a similar one to this, although she had slept well. In the middle of the night she had awakened suddenly, almost as if some inner voice had told her something extraordinary, beautiful, magical was at that moment taking place in the forbidden midnight hours. The instant she had seen the white gleaming cover spread out over the streets, reflecting the glow of a pale moon peering through a break in the cloud cover, she knew she must venture forth.

Creeping from her parents' flat and down the single flight of stairs, grimacing at the loud creak as she landed on the next to last step, opening the door as noiselessly as she was able, soon she was outside.

Notwithstanding the presence of the moon, snow was still falling, and huge lightly textured flakes brushed against her face, upturned in awe. What a glorious moment that had been for the city-bred youngster, made all the more wondrous in the realization, as she first looked down toward her feet, that neither milkman nor bus nor workers returning home from factory graveyard shifts had yet marred the perfect, velvety mantle.

Funny how things come back to memory, she thought. The uncanny silence, the ghostly illumination. It had been these sensations, more than the sight of the snow itself, which had triggered the memory. It had been many years since that night had come into her mind. As a child she had determined to keep her adventure to herself. But then the terrible cold that resulted two days later forced a confession of her errancy to her worried mother. Mrs. Edwards had smiled gently, and in her eyes could be detected a certain camaraderie which seemed to say that she, too, held memories of one or two childhood journeys such as Hilary's.

"Well, tonight I'll not catch cold," said Hilary to herself as she opened the great front doors and stepped outside.

Her face was met, not with a blast, but yet with the impact of the cold. Huge flakes fell unhindered from the midnight sky—soft, noiseless, gentle.

Hilary held out her hands in unabandoned delight, letting the mystical crystals glide through her fingers. She started down the steps, and was all at once overcome with the curious sensation that she had been there before, standing on those very steps, standing just as she was now, looking out into the sky, with snowflakes fluttering all about. For the briefest of instants, snatches of a dreamlike childhood passed through her mind, with images altogether distinct from the more lucid memories of London. Then came the picture of a small girl again, standing in the snow, with just a trace of high-pitched giggling floating, as if audibly, in the air about her.

Just as quickly as the obscure images had come, they were gone, leaving behind only the sad melancholy of something very precious being lost. Trying to shake the feeling, Hilary continued down the steps and began to cross the courtyard.

She smiled as she went, looking behind her at the footprints she left, feeling the thrill of being the only one in on nature's delightful secret. She made a wide circle around the fountain, then wandered aimlessly toward the gate across the entry road some hundred feet away.

Suddenly she stopped. There again was the faint sound. Maybe it hadn't been merely a dream of childhood! Though now there was no giggling, only the faint muffled sounds of voices drifting toward her across the snow. She was not alone in the pre-dawn world after all! Peering ahead, barely visible in the midst of the white earth, Hilary spied two figures. They stood just off the roadway, beyond the gate, in a grove of silver birch. If they hoped for the cover they might afford, the barren, leafless trees offered none. Only one of the figures was identifiable.

Jo stood facing the castle, whispering with emphatic gestures, apparently in heated dialogue with a man whose back was toward Hilary. The usual impassive serenity of Jo's face was flawed with tension to accompany her motions. Even in the night, Hilary thought she could see her dark eyes flashing.

Instinctively Hilary stepped to one side of the gate, wondering what she should do. Before she had the chance to contemplate long on the question, however, the couple embraced, then stepped apart.

Hilary knew she could not get back into the house without being seen, and her footprints would give her away in an instant. She stepped farther into the shadow of the gate, knowing even as she did so that the last thing she could do was hide.

The dilemma of an encounter was forestalled, however, and then Hilary realized why there had been no footprints but her own in front of the house. When the man disappeared back along the driveway, Jo turned and walked through the trees, where a breach in the hedge at the side of the house admitted her to the garden area. There she crossed the relatively short space to the kitchen door, adding a new set of footprints to the ones she had made earlier, and was soon inside.

Breathing a sigh of relief, Hilary waited another five minutes where she was, then walked back across the courtyard—by now feeling the effects of the cold—into the house again, and back up the stairs.

Long after she had climbed once more into the warmth of her own bed, Hilary asked herself for the twentieth time what the strange meeting could signify. If Jo had a lover, why the secrecy? Surely Logan and Allison would not deny a romantic interest to a thirty-two-year-old woman. If not romance, then what other reason could have driven her out in the snow in the middle of the night to meet a man?

She had no way of answering her question, however, and eventually fell into a deep sleep, whose only interruption was a silly dream about two snowmen crossing a large field of ripening grain together. The larger of the two began to melt, causing the smaller great dread. Before long there was but one snow figure left, a child of a snowman, made with two balls of snow rather than three. When she arrived at a village after walking a long distance, there were no other snowmen to be found. And when all the people asked her name, the little snowgirl couldn't remember. When asked where her mother was, all the little snowgirl could answer was, "I don't know where I'm supposed to be."

When Hilary awoke the following morning, she felt oddly refreshed. Never would she have guessed that her night had been interrupted by snowfalls, secret trysts, and wandering snowmen.

At breakfast everyone seemed to have been similarly affected by a positive wave of good cheer that had come with the snow. Jo entered the dining room, glowing and full of enthusiasm. "It snowed in the night! Isn't it grand?"

"Indeed!" agreed Logan heartily as he dished up his plate from the trays and bowls on the sideboard.

"I should like to take one of the horses out for a ride today," Jo continued. "The day is too gorgeous not to be out in it."

"This terrain's difficult for a horse even in the best of conditions," said Logan. "It might be a bit tricky. Have you ever ridden in the snow?"

"You know I'm quite an adequate horsewoman."

"So you've shown yourself, I admit."

"Why don't you join me, Father?"

Logan laughed. "Surely you know by now that the extent of my association with horses lies in the area of wagering, not riding—and even in that regard I've grown a trifle rusty these days."

"And you've no desire to learn the equestrian side of life at the track?"

"None whatsoever."

"And you call yourself the progenitor of the Ramsey-Duncan strain?"

"I call myself nothing but a humble Macintyre, sprung from the common, yet noble blood of grooms. Don't you know," he added with a wink in Allison's direction, "it's the women who wear the pants in this family?"

"I'd not be adverse to joining you if it weren't for this silly ankle," Allison put in. "But I'll not stay indoors on such a day," she went on with some defiance in her tone, and a coy, sidelong glance at Logan. "I think I shall try my hand at painting a winter scene. I'm feeling good, and I haven't painted in days!"

"I didn't know you were an artist," said Hilary, settling down at the table with a plate bearing half a stewed tomato, a couple of smoked kippers, a piece of toast, and a soft-boiled egg.

"I am merely a student," replied Allison. "Jo is the real artist among us, and she has encouraged me to take it up as a hobby."

"Don't let her fool you," said Jo. "She has quite a talent for it." She

162

paused, then brightened suddenly. "I've a splendid idea! Mother, I'll get you all set up with your paints. Then, Hilary, you can join me for my ride. You haven't yet had a proper chance to see the countryside."

"I'm not much experienced with horses either," said Hilary. She would have been closer the mark had she said she'd only been on a horse one other time in her life, and that was fifteen years ago. But she let her statement stand.

"Say you'll come," prodded Jo. "It will be the perfect opportunity for us to get to know one another better."

Hilary suppressed the urge to say that what she was really interested in was knowing Allison and Logan better. But again she kept quiet, and in an hour thus found herself dressed in riding habit borrowed from Allison, browsing through the horses in the stables. Jake followed after her, pointing out the merits and idiosyncrasies of the half dozen beasts. She finally settled upon a sedate-looking chestnut which Jake then led from its stall and saddled. In the meantime, Jo had chosen her favorite, a spritely dapple gray mare.

The two women mounted. Side by side they provided an interesting contrast. The chestnut, which in the sunlight showed a fair smattering of gray in her coat, hung her head low and, to Hilary's great relief, seemed barely capable of more than a slow trot. Hilary, however, sat bolt upright, looking confident, the reins held expertly in her hands, exactly as Jake had placed them. It was not the first time in her life as a reporter she had had to feign expertise where none existed. She'd snagged many a good news story that way. She knew how to watch and listen, and pick up appropriate clues from others. Why she did so now she couldn't quite explain, except that perhaps she was growing weary of being the odd person out at Stonewycke.

She had no delusions that she would fool Jo with her act once they began to move. It was obvious Jo knew her way around horses from the masterful way she sat the gray. There, atop the powerful mount, Hilary thought she detected an almost imperceptible change in the look of her face. Was it something in the tilt of her chin, or the glint of her dark eyes? It seemed that the animal energy of the gray mare was being conducted through the saddle and up into the rider. Demure and passive the effect would not be called. Untamed, stormy, perhaps. A hint of wild challenge, a daring, supreme self-reliance.

Before Hilary had time to evaluate this hidden person, Jo jabbed her heels into the gray's sides and was off at a trot. Hilary followed as best she could.

Jo led the way at a spirited pace. They headed west for a short distance; then Jo turned sharply toward the south. The night's snowfall had deposited several inches of white covering, but many patches of brown earth showed through, and dormant shrubbery and boulders otherwise spotted the landscape. The pale morning sky, more than half filled with thick gray clouds in front of a backdrop of white, gave every indication that it would not be long before snow dominated the entire countryside.

They continued on for about half an hour, following a rough, narrow trail that surely saw little general use. The air grew colder, and the wind, which had been but a chilly breeze lower down near the sea, turned icy and whipped fiercely at the two riders and their steeds. The chestnut's flanks heaved with the added exertion, but Hilary dared not slow for fear of falling too far behind. Eventually the ground leveled off, and to Hilary's relief she saw that fifty yards ahead Jo had reined the gray to a stop. Hilary trotted up next to her.

"I thought we might need a rest," said Jo, brushing a strand of hair from her face.

She might just as well have said *you*. But Hilary swallowed her pride, gratefully nodded her head, and dismounted. The solid ground had never felt so good. She rubbed the chestnut's white face.

"You are a nice beastie," she said, "but I think even you will agree that we were not made for each other."

Jo swung easily off her mount. "I rode nearly every day in Baltimore," she said, striding over to where Hilary stood. "My adoptive father had a fine stable, even a few thoroughbreds."

"All my father owned was a mangy yellow cat," laughed Hilary. "But she was a good mouser, and that was a valuable possession in Whitechapel."

"Whitechapel?"

"Where I grew up . . . London—the East End."

"Ah."

"I have a feeling that you and I had quite different upbringings. Whitechapel is far removed from all this, believe me." Hilary swept her hand through the air to indicate their surroundings. "In more ways than one."

"It will grow on you."

"But surely you must hope it doesn't." Hilary purposely kept her tone light.

"I hate to think we are rivals," Jo replied.

"But we are, aren't we?" asked Hilary, the interviewer in her surfacing.

"You may look upon it that way. But I feel no sense of competition. I know my credentials are irrefutable. I only feel bad for the mistake that will ultimately be uncovered in Lady Joanna's investigation. It's only a matter of time, I'm afraid." For a brief instant her eyes narrowed and sent out a dark flash. Almost immediately that icy glance was replaced with the gentle breeze of a smile. "I am sorry, Hilary. I really am. I so wish you could be spared the pain."

Hilary walked on in silence, leading her equine companion with the reins in her hand.

"You should see this place in late summer," said Jo, when she caught Hilary again and came up beside her. "It's a sea of purple. When I first arrived, I was just mad to get it on canvas."

"Might I see some of your work sometime?" asked Hilary in her most sincere attempt at friendliness.

"Of course, if you are really interested," Jo answered with apparent shyness, unable at the same time to mask her pleasure. "Look, there's a rock rose bush. Two months ago I painted a gorgeous late bloom right there. Now it's just a tangle of thorns."

"What's that over there?" asked Hilary, pointing toward a huge pile of stones about a quarter mile distant.

"Oh, nothing much. I think they said it was the ruin of an ancient village of some prehistoric people."

"The Picts," said Hilary. "So that's it," she added, almost to herself. Suddenly mesmerized, she began walking toward it.

"Wouldn't you rather ride?"

"Not at the moment," Hilary called back.

"Go on then. I'll bring the horses."

Hilary continued walking as if she were stepping out of the year 1971 and into an ancient fairy tale. Before her stood the ruin where a thousand years ago, maybe more, a marauding band of Viking warriors had slaughtered an entire Pict community—man, woman, and child. Or so the legend went according to Joanna's journal. But the pillaging Scandinavians had not found the treasure they were seeking. That was left for one George Falkirk to unearth a millennium later, only to lose it again in a sordid tangle of murder and deception. Here is where it began—Falkirk's murder, Ian's imprisonment, and Maggie's tragic exile from her homeland. Here too a carefree London con man had been swept into the drama of the Ramsey-Duncan clan, nearly losing his life in his own personal search for the missing treasure.

Yes, so much originated here, perhaps even in my own history, thought Hilary. For so long she hadn't wanted to accept this change in her fortunes. Then once she had come to accept it, suddenly she was having to compete for it.

Jo's intrusive voice was almost a relief. "We ought to be getting back. It may begin to snow again."

Reluctantly Hilary mounted the chestnut. The horse seemed suddenly skittish, more reticent about the arrangement than earlier. The animal snorted and stamped one foot in a most irritable manner. Already the distance between the chestnut and the gray had widened. Not understanding the finer points of a horse's temperamental psyche, Hilary gave her mount a little kick with her heels in an attempt to catch up. The horse broke into a trot and Hilary struggled to hang on. The first time she bounced in the saddle, however, coming down squarely upon the animal's back, the mild-mannered chestnut whinnied and reared like a wild stallion, then suddenly shot off in a frenzied run. An experienced rider might have been able to bring the creature quickly under control. But all Hilary knew to do was hang on and hope she wasn't thrown off onto the rocky ground.

The animal tore past Jo, who gasped in surprise. Immediately she urged her gray into a gallop as she sought to overtake her companion. But the chestnut seemed determined to make it a worthy race. Suddenly she was running like a two-year-old thoroughbred rather than the old nag she was. She took no thought for the icy, rock-strewn terrain under her hooves, but plowed ahead, wildly splattering snow and dirt up behind her churning feet. In unmitigated terror Hilary clutched the reins and horn of the saddle, only wondering how much longer she could stay on the horse's back and into which ditch she was going to fall, battered and bruised and broken, and most likely dead!

Behind her Jo trailed on the gray, but did not appear to be gaining ground. Ahead, less than thirty yards away, the ground slopped off into the precipitous descent they had labored to ascend only a few minutes earlier. Once the animal crossed the edge of the ridge there would be no stopping, for the sheer momentum of the descent.

Suddenly in the blur of her panic, Hilary saw a horse galloping toward her. But it wasn't the gray!

She tried to scream for help, as if her distress might not be clearly evident, but no sound would come from her throat.

She flew past the rider. They tumbled past the precipice and now bolted more steeply downward!

The sound of hoofbeats from behind distracted her attention. She tried to glance back, but could only make out fuzzy images of animal flesh and snow. The rider had wheeled his own steed around the moment Hilary had torn past and was now charging after her, and gaining ground.

In another moment, out of the corner of her eye Hilary saw a hand reaching for the chestnut's bridle. Side by side the two horses galloped! Then first she felt a change in the pace. At last her horse was slowing!

It was some time before they came to a complete stop. Even as they did so, notwithstanding its exhaustion and heaving flanks, the chestnut continued to snort and paw the ground. All Hilary could think about was getting off the crazed animal, and in her haste she cared not in the least how clumsy or awkward her dismount appeared! She threw herself down, but even before her feet touched the ground her rescuer was at her side offering a strong arm.

"Thank you," was all the gratitude she could manage, still shaking from head to foot and barely able to stand.

"Come," he said. "I see a rock over here where you can sit."

Beginning to catch her breath, Hilary took his offered arm. "I can't imagine what I'd have done if you hadn't come along," she panted. "I must have looked pretty foolish!"

He led her to the rock, where she sat down and continued to breathe deeply.

"On the contrary," he replied. "Foolish you did not look. Panic-stricken . . . yes! But beautiful on your runaway mount, if I might be so bold as to add."

Hilary laughed. It felt good. She hadn't laughed in days. "Panic-stricken I certainly was! And I'll forgive your forward compliment, under the circumstances."

Now it was the stranger's turn to laugh.

As he did Hilary first took note of her rescuer's accent, and she forgot her own brush with disaster long enough to give him closer scrutiny. He could not have more perfectly epitomized the stereotype of the tall, dark, and handsome hero. Accustomed to looking past the surface for deeper qualities of character, in another setting Hilary's first response toward such a good-looking man might have been suspicion. Yet given what had just taken place, she forgave him his dashing appearance; perhaps he might have the character to match, she thought. His dark brown hair was smooth and well-groomed even after the harrowing ride. Dark green eyes glinted like emeralds in the winter sunlight, and the tanned skin of his well-proportioned face could scarcely have acquired such golden tones anywhere but on a southern summer beach. A neat black pencil-thin moustache, above ivory-white teeth always poised on the edge of a smile, completed the face, lending to the foreign mystique of his Germanic accent.

"May I introduce myself, Fraulein?" he said. Bowing ever so slightly, he went on. "I am Viscount Emil von Burchardt, at your service!"

"I am very glad to meet you. I'm Hilary Edwards." She held out her hand, which he took and, bowing again, kissed gallantly. "But it is I who should be at your service."

He chuckled softly. "Ah, you modern women are so delightful."

At that moment Jo rode up and dismounted. She glanced at the stranger and smiled.

Feeling much steadier, Hilary stood to make introductions. "Herr von Burchardt—"

"Please, please. You must call me Emil all the women I rescue do!"

Hilary laughed and continued. "Then, Emil, I'd like you to meet Joanna . . . Macintyre." Hesitating over the last name, but knowing no alternative, she forced herself to use it. "Jo, this is Viscount von Burchardt."

"Emil, if you will, Fraulein," said the Viscount, bowing once more and kissing Jo's hand. "I had no idea the north of Scotland would display such beautiful women."

"And where might you be from, Emil?" asked Jo sweetly.

"I am of the Austrian von Burchardts; you have perhaps heard of us?"

"No, I'm sorry. But then I am from America and I'm afraid we don't keep much abreast of the European aristocracy."

"Ah, yes. You Americans have such a penchant for throwing out traditions."

"Only some of them. But I do want to thank you for your timely intercession today. I was afraid to press my own horse harder for fear of finding myself in a similar predicament."

"What brings you to Scotland, Emil?" Hilary asked.

"I decided to put in and let my yacht weather in your fair harbor of Port Strathy," von Burchardt replied. "I have been touring the British coast for some months. But today a great yearning for solid ground overcame me, and besides yachting, my second favorite sport is horseback riding."

"It's fortunate for me your legs tired of the sea," said Hilary.

"But I do not want to detain you ladies longer in this cold air. Please, may I accompany you safely home?"

"Thank you very much," replied Hilary.

"May we thank you even further, Herr von Burchardt, by inviting you to lunch?" asked Jo.

"I would be honored!"

They returned to their horses. The chestnut showed further signs of agitation. Von Burchardt insisted that Hilary ride with him; he had just the kind of saddle that would make it comfortable, he said. Hilary consented with a smile. In the meantime, Jo had a quick look at the chestnut's hooves, commenting that she thought the animal might have taken a stone. She took its reins and followed behind the Viscount and Hilary, who talked amiably the whole way back to Stonewycke.

Hilary was much relieved to deposit the horse into Jake's care. As the three riders walked to the house, Jake led their animals away, speaking soothingly to his charges and patting them as he removed their saddles and dug out a handful of oats that he let them eat from his open hand.

As he lifted the chestnut's saddle he paused, his wrinkled brow knit in concern. "What be this, lassie?" he mumbled tenderly, rubbing his hand over a sore on the animal's back. Examining the spot closely, he picked out several sharp thorns. "Noo, whaur did ye get these? Sma wonder ye went a wee bit off yer chump when she landed on ye."

He carefully cleaned the tiny wound, rubbed in some salve, then led the weary chestnut back to her stall.

The Viscount von Burchardt proved himself a charming guest.

He was witty, an adept conversationalist, knowledgeable in whatever direction the discussion went, well traveled with an abundance of stories to tell, yet at the same time perfectly gracious in drawing out discourse from others, in which he seemed to display a profound interest. Logan expressed great fascination with his yachting exploits, asking him question after question. When the viscount would answer, Logan leaned back with a smile which seemed to contain more meaning than its owner would let on, and replied, "You don't say!"

Von Burchardt was vague about his recent itinerary, but when pressed by Logan, who said he hadn't recalled seeing a yacht in the harbor yesterday when he was in town, the viscount merely laughed, saying, "Well, you know us continental gadabouts—we never like to be too tied down, and I only just arrived this morning." Smiling oddly again, Logan let the matter drop.

Allison was the only one who did not seem to be taken in by his charm. Throughout lunch she was grumpy, complaining of a headache that had come upon her during her morning's session with her paints. She found the viscount's mannerisms annoying, and finally excused herself and left the room on unsteady legs.

Logan jumped up to follow her, caught her in the corridor, lent a steadying hand, and now her to their bedroom, where he sat her down on the edge of the bed.

"What can I do for you, my dear?" he asked tenderly.

"Nothing, nothing at all!" Allison snapped. "Just go back to your idiotic guest Bergmark, or whatever his name is, and leave me alone!"

"Can I make you more comfortable?" said Logan, maintaining his cheery countenance and fluffing up the pillows under her.

"No, no . . . I'm fine. It's just . . . that stupid painting! I couldn't get anything to come out—"

She stopped and suddenly burst into tears.

Logan sat down beside her and tenderly wrapped her in his arms.

" . . . my hand wouldn't go right, and I couldn't keep from mixing colors where they didn't belong," she sobbed, "and my fingers wouldn't stop shaking. The moment I took the brush from Jo's hand this morning I began to feel sick again. Oh, Logan, I hate it! Just when I was starting to feel good again. I so wanted to paint that little stream trickling through the snow, and now I've ruined that canvas and the painting's a mess . . . and look—I've still got paint on my fingers—"

She held out her hands imploringly like a little child, her eyes red from crying.

Gently Logan stroked her hair, speaking softly into her ear. Gradually she calmed, and he laid her down on the bed. In a few moments she was fast asleep. Logan remained at her side a few minutes longer, his hand resting gently on her back, his mouth speaking barely audible prayers on behalf of his troubled wife to the Father of them both, who was watching all, and understood.

Meanwhile, Hilary and Jo were doing their best to keep up the dialogue with their guest, hardly difficult when the guest was a man like Burchardt. By this time he had bent his charms fully upon the two attractive women—with a definite emphasis, it seemed, in Hilary's direction. For her part, Hilary found him pleasant enough, certainly handsome and courteous. She wondered, however, if he might be just a bit too polished. She did not try to analyze the viscount or his motives too deeply. For the moment she opted to put her reporting instincts in the background so that she might simply enjoy the diversion his presence offered. She took him at face value, and for the present that seemed sufficient.

They were just finishing a light dessert of sliced apples and cheese, with oatcakes and butter, when Logan reentered the room.

"I apologize for the interruption," he said.

"How is Mother?" asked Jo, her voice laden with concern.

For the briefest instant, Logan's eyes seemed to recoil with her presumptive use of the appellation. But almost before it had come, the look was gone, and he answered without comment.

"She's sleeping now."

"Oh, I'm so glad. Whatever is the matter?"

"The same thing as last week—nausea, headache, irritability. I think she's frustrated with the painting."

"I really should take some more time with her," said Jo in a concerned voice. "She was doing so well, I thought she would rather experiment on her own."

"Perhaps," replied Logan thoughtfully, "but I'm wondering if she shouldn't give it up altogether. It doesn't seem to be doing anything but upsetting her. Who knows, maybe she's allergic to the paints. She began having these headaches almost the very day you began with her."

The same dark flash passed quickly through Jo's eyes, but when she spoke her voice remained one of expressed concern. "Some people do have such a reaction to the oils," she said. "That's why I usually take Mother out-of-doors when we paint. She was outside this morning, in fact."

"Yes, I suppose you're right," said Logan noncommittally. "But now—come," he went on in a sudden shift of tone, "let's take our guest on a tour of the house!"

"A splendid idea!" remarked von Burchardt with enthusiasm.

"I have, let me see," said Logan glancing at his watch, "until two o'clock when I must meet with the factor. That gives us about an hour. If we move quickly, that should do fine."

He led the viscount out, commenting to him lightly and confidentially as they walked, and the two young women followed.

They had not gone far along the wide corridor when Jo moved up alongside Logan, slipping her hand through his arm, and smiling up at him. On the other side, Hilary quickened her pace until she drew even with von Burchardt.

"Ah, Fraulein Edwards—"

"Hilary, remember!"

The viscount laughed. "Touche!" he said. "I was about to comment to Mr. Macintyre that this maze of corridors and stairways is enough to confuse even the most skilled of cartographers. Judging from the outside, I would never fathom the intricacies contained within these walls."

"I am only just learning the way around myself," replied Hilary. "I have been here less than a week."

"Yes, your—er, Mr. Macintyre, I should say, was just telling me something of this intriguing dilemma facing you all. I must say I have never before run across quite so—"

But at that moment he was interrupted by the sound of Logan's voice.

"If we turned down that hall," he said, "we would come to the East Wing of the castle. It has been out of general use since before Lady Margaret Duncan's time. It's in a serious state of disrepair now and is locked off because of the hazard it presents. We are, however, engaged in the process of restoring it, whenever the townspeople are short of work. We will make a good deal of progress this winter, but it is a slow process. We have never been able to afford a wholesale reconstruction, so we do what we can every year and try to keep ahead of Mother Nature's tendency to tear away at old places such as this."

"When was it last used?" asked Hilary.

"In the old days it was occupied for the billeting of the clan army; legend has it that Bonnie Prince Charlie hid out here after the disastrous battle of Culloden Moor. More recently, James Duncan, Lady Margaret's father, kept a private office there. But that was the last attempted use of the place, for a portion of the roof caved in about fifty years ago, discouraging further use. It is that roof, in fact, which we hope to shore up sufficiently this winter to keep the spring rains out."

Down another corridor, Jo took the lead, motioning them into a large room with high ceiling.

"We call this the heirloom room," she said. She waved her hand about

the room, indicating the many glass cases that held precious family me-
morabilia and clan relics. Positioned about the floor were several manne-
quins displaying various of the patriarchs' Highland garb. "Lady Joanna
prepared this room herself," Jo went on, "expressly for the benefit of the
visitors that come to the house, both from the village and as a result of
Father's position in London. There are a few valuable objects here, but
their chief worth lies in their historical significance. There is a tatted handkerchief with a primrose design, given to Margaret by Lucy Krueger, and
several of Lady Atlanta's stitcheries. In fact, over here"—she motioned
them toward a particular case—"is one that is reputed to be her very first
stitchery, done when she was ten years old." Jo beamed with pride.

"My, but you certainly are well-versed on Stonewycke's history," Hilary found herself commenting.

"I am so fascinated with it all," replied Jo in her glowing and innocent
voice. "I hang on Mother's every word and am constantly nagging her to
tell me more."

When no one spoke further, she resumed the dangling thread of the
tour. "In this case here is a more recent find—architects' prints dating to
the sixteenth century when Stonewycke was first constructed. They bear
Sir James Hamilton's authenticated signature. He was King James V of
Scotland's own architect and personally supervised the building of Stonewycke."

She paused a moment to allow her audience to fan out through the
room. Logan disengaged himself from her arm, and wandered aimlessly
toward the far wall, focusing more on his own thoughts than on any of the
items in the room, with every one of which he was intimately familiar.

An odd mix of emotions rose in Hilary as she moved about—a strange
mingling of detachment and reverence as she studied all the treasures in
the room. Part of her felt like a member of a tour group walking through
one of the great mansions of Surrey, viewing mere historical relics—
antiquities from a time as far removed as ancient Rome or Babylonia. Yet
in another corner of her heart, perhaps even her soul, a strange stirring was
bubbling into life. She wondered if Jo felt the same way, that same sense
of involvement, of personally *belonging* to this history. Maybe it all
stemmed from nothing more than having read the journal. But no analysis
could still the palpitating of her heart when she actually beheld with her
own eyes Atlanta's stitchery and Maggie's handkerchief.

They departed the heirloom room and continued on. Walking on ahead,
Logan had grown uncharacteristically quiet, seeming distractedly to have
left von Burchardt alone to the ladies.

As Logan rounded a corner ahead of them, to her right Hilary glanced
inside a door that stood partially ajar. It appeared to be a large open hall,
but they passed by so quickly she could see few details.

"What was that room?" she asked as they continued to walk.

"That was the gallery," Jo replied.

"Might we stop for a moment?"

"I'd love nothing more than to show it to you," said Jo, "but it would take quite a while to do it justice, and I think we have already monopolized far too much of Emil's time. It is almost two o'clock."

"I would not want to stand in the way of the lady's wish," said von Burchardt grandly.

Jo's eyebrow shot up almost imperceptibly; then she turned toward Hilary and smiled. "Let's wait until we can do it properly, Hilary. It is a very special place, and I know you'll want to be able to appreciate every painting fully." Jo's steps did not slow as she spoke.

They followed Logan around the corner, and in a minute or two came to a stairway which they descended, soon arriving at the guest parlor. Jo swung the door wide open, the perfect hostess, and allowed her guests to enter. Logan was inside.

"I have already seen to the preparation of tea," he said. "Make yourself comfortable, Herr von Burchardt. Jo," he said, turning toward her, "would you mind helping Flora with it? She's in the kitchen."

Hesitating only momentarily, she turned and fluttered away. As soon as the door had closed, Logan said, "I hope you don't mind if I excuse myself. It has been a pleasure having you." He extended his hand to the viscount.

"I appreciate your hospitality!"

"I hope I have the opportunity to see you again," said Logan. "But for the present I must leave you in the company of my two—lovely friends."

As Logan exited, von Burchardt took up a position standing by the marble mantel. Hilary seated herself on the rose-colored brocade divan.

She was about to ask about his family when he first broke the silence with apparently the same idea in mind.

"I am still rather confused about you two ladies," he said. "Mr. Macintyre's attempt to explain it all left me quite confounded. But perhaps I am prying."

"I think it is an honest curiosity," said Hilary. "I would be surprised if you *weren't* puzzled by it. I am still rather baffled myself."

"But you both have documents to prove your relations to the Macintyres?"

"Actually, I have no such documents."

"But you have other, shall we say, evidence?"

"I don't know. That might even be too strong a term. I really have nothing at all now that the locket is missing."

The viscount's face clouded over momentarily, but he apparently thought better of pursuing that line.

"How does one sort out such a mix-up?"

"I believe Mr. Macintyre is looking into it all."

"Incredible!"

At that moment Jo returned carrying a tray of refreshments. She set them on the low table in front of the divan and began pouring out tea, quite naturally assuming the role of hostess in the absence of either Logan or Allison.

Taking his tea and settling into a chair opposite the divan, von Burchardt spoke. "I was just commenting on what an interesting dilemma you both have found yourselves in."

"Very unfortunate," replied Jo, sitting down next to Hilary. She laid her hand on Hilary's as if to comfort her.

Hilary cringed involuntarily at the chilly touch of Jo's fingers. She glanced into her eyes as if to assure herself she would still find warmth in the other's smile. It was there, but somehow did not reassure Hilary. It was the warmth of October, not of June.

"Where will you be off to when you depart Port Strathy?" asked Hilary of von Burchardt, attempting to sound upbeat and move the conversation away from their family situation.

"Wherever a fair wind blows, Fraulein," laughed the viscount. "But seriously, my journeyings are drawing to a close. After a stop in Aberdeen, we shall make as straight a route as possible for Bremerhaven. I gave my family my word I would be home for Christmas."

"Your wife and children?"

"No, no," replied von Burchardt with an amused chuckle. "My parents and two brothers. I have no wife at present, and certainly no children. I'm afraid I've never been the sort to settle down. There is too much of the wide world to see."

"I've always been rather a homebody myself," said Jo.

"And you," he said, turning toward Hilary, "perhaps in the spring you would join me on my yacht? Have you been to Buenos Aires?"

Before Hilary had a chance to respond, Jo's cup suddenly rattled in its saucer.

"Oh, clumsy me!" she exclaimed, brushing away the spill from her riding habit. Hilary whisked a serviette from the refreshment tray and tried to help her blot up the stain.

"I'd better take care of this right away," said Jo, rising, "or it will never come out."

Von Burchardt stood also. "It is time for me to be on my way as well. There are some repairs to my boat I must oversee."

"You are welcome to visit us any time for as long as you are in Port Strathy," said Jo, momentarily forgetting her mishap.

"Thank you very much. It will prove a most pleasant diversion, I am sure." He took Jo's hand, bowed slightly, and kissed it. Then he turned toward Hilary. As she stood he took her hand also, but she noted that he seemed to linger a bit longer than was necessary as his lips brushed her hand.

"Auf Wiedersehen, my dear ladies," he said.

"Let me walk you to the door, Emil," said Jo. "I have to go that way myself."

Hilary watched as they took their leave, then sat back down and finished her tea, pondering the intriguing interchanges of the afternoon.

Emil von Burchardt . . . a captivating fellow! she thought. *Full of mystery, and—who could deny it?—romance.*

She could not restrain a slight smile at the notion of falling in love with a courageous horseman who had rescued her from disaster.

Good thing I am no romantic, thought Hilary. *I've got to keep a level head on my shoulders. Besides, I have too many other complications in my life right now to add the confusion of love to it. Not to mention the man's noble blood! Even if I'm going to turn out to have blue blood in my veins, that certainly doesn't mean I have to fall in love with a nobleman, too!*

She stood and began gathering up the tea things, thinking how appropriate it was that Jo should play the part of the hostess while she acted the servant.

33 / Stadium Appointment

These Britons did love their football—though ex-patriate American Murry Fitts would never get used to calling soccer football. It had its exciting moments, he had to admit, though the game itself could never compare to watching the passionate crowds thronging the stands. The stoic English gave all for their game.

Much as Murry would have liked to concentrate on the rousing action on the turf below, he had come here on other business. The call he had received this morning had been tantalizing as only a journalist could appreciate.

"Meet me this afternoon if you want the biggest story of your career . . ." had come the enigmatic voice on the other end of the line.

What reporter could pass up a hook like that?

He'd met the caller once before, only a few days ago, one of the blokes he had interviewed at Oxford for his antiquities article. That's where the sensational call began to lose some of its credibility. Why else would he be calling except as a follow-up to their earlier conversation, and what could be so earth-shattering about a bunch of clay shards or ancient swords?

Now the fellow was fifteen minutes late and Murry was beginning to wonder if he'd been stood up. Glancing down at his watch again, he was trying to decide how much longer to give him when a nervous man passed in front of him.

"I say, is that seat next to you taken?" he asked.

"Yes, it is," replied Murry.

"Are you quite certain?" persisted the man, looking squarely at Murry, then sitting down in it nevertheless.

All at once recognition dawned. If the man's canvas sport hat and dark glasses were intended as a disguise, they had been quite effective. The noise of the crowd made it nearly impossible to be heard. A nice setup, Murry mused. Even if someone was sitting three feet away, he could never tell what we're talking about.

"I'm sorry to be late," the man was saying. "Had to be sure I wasn't followed—as much for your sake as mine."

"What's this all about, Professor?" asked Murry. "Surely not archaeological finds or ruins of ancient cities?"

"No, no!" cut in the Professor sharply, as if he had no time for tedious explanations. "It has nothing to do with any of that. This is, as you reporters say, hard news. This involves crime in the highest corporate echelons."

"Why don't you go to Scotland Yard?"

"Because there are certain . . . aspects of my life the Yard might call into question. I don't want to end up in prison myself."

"You, Professor?" said Murry, with a semi-gleam in his eye.

"I don't have time for your foolish banter," snapped the other, shifting nervously in his seat. "Do you want the story or don't you?"

"What's in it for you?"

"I hope it will save my life."

"Explain. Why have you come to me?"

"I came to you because you were convenient. I had just seen you. I knew how to reach you. I could go elsewhere, but it would take time. That much I will say. But I will explain nothing until I have your answer."

Now it was Murry's turn to shuffle uncomfortably. He wanted no part of an attempt merely to air some personal grievance. Yet if this guy were on the level, with a legitimate story of such magnitude, perhaps involving the underworld, then it might well be of the importance he claimed. It would also mean his fears were on the level too, and that if Murry listened he might be implicating himself in the danger as well. At length he sucked in a deep breath.

"Okay, let me have it," he said resolutely. "What kind of reporter would I be if I weren't willing to take a risk? But I reserve the right to bug out if it gets too heavy."

"Fair enough."

The Professor glanced surreptitiously about before beginning again. "I can't give you many details or facts because I don't have them all myself. But if you look in the right places, you will find all you need. The other day I found out something, and now my life is not worth a farthing. I know running is useless; he will find me no matter what rock I hide under. Nevertheless, once this interview is over, I am gone. It will be pointless to try to look for me. My only hope is to get to him before he gets to me. That's where you come in."

"You're talking about killing someone?" asked Murry incredulously, half rising. "You've got the wrong guy to help you there, pal!"

The Professor laughed humorlessly. "No one could get close enough — I doubt the entire Queen's army could get near him—to kill him. The only way to *get* to him is to expose him. Bring the structure he represents down on top of him. An exposé of the highest order, do you understand? That's why I need a reporter."

"You want me to get the goods on him, then make it public, is that it?"

"Right on target! But you must hurry. I cannot stay out of his clutches interminably."

"So who is the bloke?" asked Murry.

"Have you ever heard of *the General?*"

"What general?"

"*The* General," snapped the Oxford man irritably.

Murry shook his head.

"He keeps hidden, extremely low profile," the Professor went on. "No one really knows who he is. It's probable a fourth or a fifth of the world's big underground racket deals—gun smuggling, narcotics—pass through him at some stage. He controls multiple billions of dollars in underworld activities. That's a conservative estimate."

"And he fronts it all with a legitimate operation?" queried Murry.

"Putting it mildly," mused the Professor almost to himself. "His legal enterprises are clean beyond reproach. Very respected, very profitable. And until a short time ago no one knew of the connection. As far as I'm aware, I may be the only one at this moment who does."

"What connection?"

"The connection between—are you ready for this?—the General and . . . Trans Global Enterprises!"

Murry let out a long, incredulous whistle.

"*The* Trans Global?"

"The very same!"

"How did you find out?"

"That's not important. Let's just say they hired me for a job and I found out more than I was supposed to. And lost a friend in the process."

"That's a rather remarkable accusation," said Murry. "T.G.E. is right up there with Lockheed and Dow and all the other multi-national corporations. You're talking about tangling with some powerful boys."

"Do you want to back out? I can find someone else."

Slowly Murry shook his head. "But how can I touch them, knowing as little as we do?"

"Sometimes it takes a David to bring down a Goliath," replied the Professor.

"That's easy to say when you're not the David and don't intend to stick around for the battle."

"If I could help you, I would. But now it is I who must keep a low profile—an extended vacation, as it were. Far away. Besides, you Americans are better at this sort of thing than we are."

"What do you expect me to do now?" asked Murry.

"You're the investigator. Investigate! You must have friends. Sources, don't you call them? I tell you, Interpol has a file on the General as thick as your wrist. I don't know what you should do. If you turn over enough of Trans Global's rocks, under one of them you're going to find a scorpion. But watch out—his sting is lethal."

"Do I thank you or curse you for this perilous assignment?"

"Time will tell. Now I must go," the Professor said hurriedly, already rising. "I've already been here too long, I fear. If you pull this off and I live to tell about it, I'll repay you for your efforts."

"I'm not doing it for you, Professor."

"Ah yes, that American independence and forthrightness again! Well, I hope you get a bloody good story out of it—the Pulitzer Prize and all those other accolades you writers so admire!"

With those parting words, the Professor turned and squeezed his way along the aisle and soon faded out of sight in the mob of spectators.

Murry sat back in his seat and exhaled a long sigh, hardly aware of the noise or the game. *What have I fallen into?* he wondered.

Pulitzer Prize, indeed! He silently remonstrated himself. *I'll be lucky if I just get out of this without ending up at the bottom of the Thames in a cement overcoat.*

But imagine. What if it *could* be pulled off? If Hilary were in town, he'd talk to her right away. But she wasn't, and—danger be hanged!

He smiled to himself, and knew immediately he was caught!

34 / Another Arrival

Snow fell again during the night. Though she slept soundly, when she rose the following morning, however, Hilary felt unrefreshed. It had been five days since she had come to Stonewycke, and there were as yet no signs of a resolution.

As she dressed, she determined it was time to speak to Logan in a more straightforward manner. Murry was doing a good job filling in for her, but the *Review* remained her responsibility. I can't keep my life on hold forever, she thought as she tugged her sweater over her head, for what is beginning to seem nothing more than an illusion—if for no other reason than that I am so frightfully short of clothes! She hadn't planned to stay more than a day or two and, at that, her packing had been hasty.

Breakfast offered no break from the mundane schedule. The Macintyres were unusually taciturn, and Allison appeared more pale than usual, with dark rings encircling her eyes. Hilary wondered aloud about the ankle, but Logan said it was on the mend.

Throughout the meal it seemed all were content left to the privacy of their own thoughts. The clanking echo of silver against china became nearly as unbearable as Jo's usual banter about the table.

Hoping to nab Logan immediately after the meal, Hilary was foiled when he was called away to the telephone and did not return. Dispassionately she agreed to join Allison and Jo in the solarium, which, since Jo's coming, had been converted into a small studio. But after they took up where they had left off the previous afternoon on a still life, Hilary grew restless.

"Would you like to try your hand?" asked Jo cheerily. "I'll set you up with a canvas and palate."

"I don't think so," she declined.

"It's fun, Hilary," urged Allison, "although I think I get more paint on my hands than the canvas." Her voice sounded hollow as she spoke. She did not look well.

"But you remember what I've told you—artistry doesn't worry about neatness," laughed Jo. "Come now, Hilary, how about it?"

Hilary shook her head and excused herself. The only way she could paint pictures was with words.

She set out for the library, hoping Logan might be there. When she walked in she saw him sitting at his desk in one corner poring over several documents. He smiled when he looked up, but it quickly faded once he saw her solemn expression.

"What is it, Hilary?" he asked with sincerity. "Is something wrong?"

"How can you ask such a question?" she snapped, all the frustrations of the day gathering in her sharp tone. "Everything is quite wrong, and I see no change in sight. I can't stay here forever. I have a magazine to run. This whole thing is beginning to look hopeless."

"I understand," he replied sympathetically.

"Do you? My whole life has been turned upside-down, and I have no idea what I'm supposed to do to right it."

"I do understand, Hilary," he said again. "Though it may be hard for you to believe just now. And it may not help knowing this, but there are others whose lives are also in a state of confusion over this." The rebuke in his tone was gentle, fatherly, even kind.

Hilary was silent a moment. She knew he was right.

"I'm sorry," she said at length in a calmer tone. "I didn't mean to be so blunt. I just don't cope very well with being in limbo like this."

"Nor do any of us," sighed Logan. "We each have our own ways of hiding the frustration, the uncertainty. But I think we are all feeling the strain."

Hilary nodded with a sigh, then turned away to glance over the books on a nearby bookshelf. The titles on the spines, however, did not even register to her brain as her eyes scanned them, for her thoughts were far away.

"Perhaps it would help for you to be assured that I am taking action," Logan went on, trying to sound upbeat. "I have some excellent men in London on it at this very moment. I have taken other steps also. But I realize you do have responsibilities. I cannot force you to stay here."

"Please don't take me wrong," said Hilary, turning back to face him. "It's not that I don't appreciate your dilemma, or the efforts you are making. I realize the delicacy of the situation, especially for someone in your position. But . . . perhaps it might even help if I returned to London. It would ease the pressure on everyone around here. Jo and Allison could do their painting without having me underfoot, and you . . . well, at least you wouldn't have to worry about entertaining me. Maybe I could even put some of my own resources to work to help sort this out."

A cloud passed over Logan's face. Now it was his turn to avert his gaze momentarily, looking down at the papers on his desk. Somehow the thought of Allison and Jo spending even more time alone together painting did not reassure him. But he could not voice his reservations aloud. *What we need is a diversion*, he thought to himself. *An event. A ball . . . an open house . . . a live concert—something to get the focus off the problem.* He looked back up and sought Hilary's eyes.

"Do what you feel you must," he said finally. "But if you could find it within yourself to give it a couple more days . . ." He hesitated. "I would like you to stay," he went on earnestly. "Consider it, if you will, a personal favor to me. If nothing has been resolved . . . then at least we will have done what we could."

Still reluctant, it was a long pause before Hilary answered. "I suppose another day or two won't hurt," she said finally.

"Thank you," he said. His tone carried in it the sound of relief. His eyes held hers for a long moment; then he went on in a lighter, friendly voice. "Please feel at complete liberty to use our phones as often as you need. I know you have business concerns. And if you wish, you are perfectly welcome to call upon the resources you mentioned even while you are here." A restrained smile played at the corners of his lips. "You might well do better than my West End lawyers!"

"Thank you very much. I'm sorry to have grown surly."

"The tension is telling on us all. Everyone could no doubt use a break." He mused upon his words for a moment. "Yes," he continued, "I will definitely have to give that some serious consideration."

That afternoon, while they sat enjoying an informal tea in the family parlor, Flora entered with the announcement that a caller was at the front door.

"I'll see to it," said Logan, rising.

In less than five minutes he returned, followed by a younger man.

"Ladies," he said, "may I present Ashley Jameson." Then turning to his wife, he explained further, "A colleague of Ian's at the university, Allison." Then to Jameson, he added, "This is my wife, Allison. And these are our two houseguests, Hilary Edwards from London, and Joanna Braithwaite from Baltimore."

Jameson nodded politely to each, then smiled wanly, directing himself toward Allison. "It seems I have made rather a fool of myself," he said. "Do forgive me for intruding on you thus. I appear to have gotten my dates rather badly confused."

"Apparently Ian made arrangements to meet him here," explained Logan.

"I was just telling your husband at the door that Ian and I had planned a bit of collaboration on that book of his. I had no idea he was back in Greece."

"Ian was to come here?" said Allison with noticeable enthusiasm, ". . . again? He was home only three weeks ago for the funeral."

"Well, that's no doubt where the confusion comes in. I spoke with him then and there must have been a mix-up somehow. He always told me when we were working together at Oxford, 'If you're ever in the north of Scotland, you simply must go by the estate,' and now it appears as though I put that rather general invitation together with mistaking the time and place of our supposed meeting, and so I show up at your door unannounced, looking like the absent-minded professor Ian always calls me!"

"An honest mistake," laughed Logan. "No harm done, I assure you."

"I tried to carry around a pocket date-book for a while. But I was forever losing it until it scarcely seemed worth the effort. My secretary tries valiantly to keep me on track. But there is only so much even that worthy soul can do." He chuckled, and though he appeared genuinely embarrassed at his *faux pas*, he also seemed at ease enough with himself to take it in stride.

"Won't you join us for tea?" said Jo, stepping forward into the hostess role.

"I don't want to impose further."

"No more talk of imposition," said Allison. "Any friend of Ian's, you know. I'll tell Flora to get a room ready immediately. You must spend the night with us at the very least. Even a day or two."

"Oh, I couldn't put you out like that. You already have guests—"

"Nonsense!" interrupted Logan. "You can't possibly think of starting back to Aberdeen. It's four o'clock in the afternoon, and nearly dark, with snow on the roads."

"We insist," added Allison.

"That's most kind of you," pondered Jameson, thinking how much easier this would make his job. "It is certainly more than I had counted on . . . or deserve under the circumstances."

"Any friend of Ian's is always welcome in our home," said Logan.

"In that case . . . thank you very much."

Logan pulled a chair forward and Jameson sat down between Logan and Hilary. Jo rose quickly from her own seat to pour him a cup of tea from the pot, eyeing him carefully. Her scrutiny did not pass unnoticed by Hilary. She made her own observations more inconspicuously.

The newcomer looked to be about thirty-five, and Hilary hardly needed to be told of his scholarly background. He had academia written all over him. Already she had observed that he carried his tall slender frame carelessly, with an ease which indicated that his thoughts moved on too bookish a plane to worry about mundane pursuits like walking or dressing. His tweed jacket and corduroy trousers were hardly the most fashionable; indeed, the whole effect of his wardrobe gave the impression that dressing each morning was probably an afterthought. At the same time, however, there was a precision about the man that almost belied the bemused and distractable image he tried to put forward. It could be seen best in his sharp, probing gray-green eyes, which at times, Hilary noticed, reflecting an innately wry sense of humor. He spoke in an easy tone too, Oxfordian and refined.

"So what do you do, Ashley?" asked Logan, once the visitor held his tea in his hand.

"Actually, Ian helped me through during some of my rugged earlier years, and now I teach where he left off when he abandoned the university to write his book. Ancient classics . . . Grecian history, that sort of thing."

"What is it you and Ian work on together?"

"Ancient Greece, mostly. He's more the archaeologist, I the linguist."

Jameson's modesty obscured the more notable fact—which subsequent conversation and Logan's probing questions revealed—that he already had three acclaimed translations of Greek classics to his credit, and his name as a collaborator with Ian on a book jacket would do nothing but enhance the book's prestige. Though Logan fairly had to drag any personal information from him, it also came out that Ian, who had been for the last several years involved in biblical archaeology, had in the course of his research turned up some interesting finds in Greece which he felt could benefit Jameson's work as well. For a number of reasons, therefore, their guest concluded, they had remained in close touch with respect to their mutual projects.

"Actually," he said, "I was looking forward to a bit of a busman's holiday. Ian has always said you have marvelous country up here. I've never been north of Aberdeen, but the brief glimpses I've had so far would certainly seem to confirm his words."

"It will all still be here next week, or the week after that, or whenever you and Ian do manage to get together," laughed Logan.

"Unfortunately, I won't," replied Jameson. "I have to be off to a conference in a few days. That's why I was so certain Ian had said this week."

"Well, we'll just have to do our best to entertain you," said Logan, "and give you that holiday you're after. We've had so many other guests lately, besides Jo and Hilary—what was the name of that chap yesterday?" he asked, turning toward the others.

"You mean von Burchardt?" answered Jo.

"Yes, Burchardt! An interesting fellow! Anyway, one more guest will be no problem. The more the merrier, don't they say?"

"Well then, under the circumstances, I accept your hospitality," said Jameson with a smile.

35 / Suspicions Aroused

When Hilary dozed off later that same night in her room, she was fully clothed, and an open book still rested in her hands.

She awoke an hour later with a shudder. Her old childhood dream had just begun to intrude upon the outer edges of her subconscious. But her sudden waking prevented its closer and more terrifying approach. She nevertheless felt the heavy discomfort of one who has been roused too soon from a nap. Her mouth was dry and tasted foul, her neck ached from the awkward position in which she had been sitting, and she was chilled to the bone.

All at once her body snapped straight up in the chair. Was that a sound she heard out in the corridor?

Perhaps it had not been the dream that had awakened her at all, but some noise within the castle walls! A door closing . . . the drop of some object on the stone floor.

Intently she strained to hear. She heard nothing more. Rising from her chair, she walked quietly toward her door, placed her hand on the latch, then opened it a crack, doing her best to prevent the hinges from betraying her. Wider she opened the door, then slowly leaned her head out, glancing up and down the hallway in both directions.

At the end of the corridor a retreating figure glided along, then rounded a corner and was out of sight!

Hilary's view had been so brief in the darkened passageway that she couldn't begin to identify the late-night walker. Without two moment's hesitation, she was in the hall. Leaving her door ajar so it wouldn't slam shut and give away her presence, she moved swiftly in the direction of her unknown visitor.

Her room was the only one occupied in this particular part of the house—whoever it was must have known that. Jo was in another wing. It could have been she . . . but why? And if she had intended on paying Hilary a visit at this late hour, why then had she turned back? Perhaps she had been trying to come upon Hilary unawares, and her plan had been foiled by whatever noise it was she had inadvertently made. Or had someone else created the disturbance and frightened her away? It couldn't be Allison; she had gone to bed feeling sick late in the afternoon. She doubted Logan would sneak around in his own house. One of the employees? She didn't know in what room they'd put Ian's friend.

Carefully Hilary approached the end of the hallway, stopped, then peered round the edge of the wall. She could see nothing, but in the distance a faint sound, as if from shuffling footsteps, reached her ears. The figure, whoever it was, was either making for the main stairway or another part of the house. She would never catch the person now without making a disturbance herself.

Slowly she turned and walked back to her room. Once inside she closed the door behind her, locked it securely, then found herself drawn to the window by the glimmer of moonlight coming in from outside.

The snow had ceased falling, and a full moon reflected off the white blanket covering the ground, causing the night outside to look almost like a Scottish summer's gloamin'. The window of her room faced west onto a wide stretch of well-maintained yard, which in late spring and summer would boast a lush, manicured green lawn. On this night, however, a thick soft covering of white stretched from the castle walls to the great hedge that surrounded the castle grounds proper. Hilary recalled Allison telling her it was this section of the grounds which boasted a fine rose garden every spring. It was out there, no doubt, where Lady Joanna had first seen old Dorey and had wrongly taken him for the gardener. Allison hadn't detailed the story to her, but it wasn't necessary; Hilary recalled every moment of the legendary interaction from Joanna's journal.

Before she realized it, Hilary found herself caught up again in memories and images from the past. Sitting at the window with a blanket over her knees, she glanced once more through the precious journal that she had recovered from its hiding place among her things. Alternately reading portions here and there, then lifting her eyes to gaze outside into the peaceful night, she let her thoughts roam back in time.

Of all the intriguing members of the Duncan clan, the enigmatic Dorey, or Theodore Ian Duncan, seemed the most difficult to understand. As she read of his suffering the familiar aristocratic, second-son syndrome, Hilary ruefully thought how this was just one more reason for doing away with the stifling institution. Ian's father didn't even pretend to care for his younger son. A wild and frenzied lifestyle had resulted, until a soft ray of hope, in the person of a Scottish lass by the name of Maggie, shone upon the lad's troubled life. But the irony of the whole drama that followed stemmed from an age-old mythical fatalism: poor Ian proved both the catalyst and the victim of woes which, in certain measure, he brought upon himself.

How I would have liked to know him! thought Hilary, setting down the manuscript and looking out again on the tranquil winter scene below. What an interesting man he must have been in his later years, after he had come to know both himself and God, and had been reunited with his dear Maggie! What a contrast between his youthful boisterous and shallow personality, and the humble demurring introspection of his later years. What wisdom must have worked its way into his character as a result of that transformation! And to have such a man for a great-great-grandfather. . . .

Suddenly Hilary became aware of the folly of her wandering train of thoughts. She could no longer assume he was her ancestor!

In the last few days since her arrival at Stonewycke, Hilary had made great efforts to distance herself from all the ties that she had previously allowed to form within her as a result of reading the journal. This was the first time in days she had given over to serious speculation of the personalities of the family and her potential relation to it.

"I can't think of all this now!" she said to herself. Tomorrow the call could well come from London informing Mr. Macintyre that the entire substance of Lady Joanna's visit had been a mistake, that she had, for whatever reasons, gotten her facts and her interpretation of them badly confused, and had drawn Hilary into this little episode, though in reality she had no possible connection to Stonewycke or the Macintyres.

Hilary wanted to keep a level, practical head about her. She simply could not allow her emotions to give way.

Exhaling a bewildered and frustrated sigh, she began once more to consider the possibility of sleep.

Then without warning, again all her senses sprang to life! This time she was not struggling to disengage herself from sleep. She knew exactly what she saw.

A figure was walking across the snow-covered lawn below! She shot a quick glance at her bedside clock; it was 11:30. Though she had not been able to catch a good look at the furtive hallway visitor of a few minutes ago, something in the walk told her this was the same person. It was certainly not Jo, she could now see, but a man.

Immediately in her memory arose the vision of another night—only two nights ago—when she had seen Jo and an unknown stranger outside the gate together. Could this be the same man? The height seemed about right, though her view of Jo's companion had been dark and incomplete.

Whoever this was, what was he doing out at such an hour? What had he been doing in her hallway? Had he mistaken her room for Jo's, and was now correcting his error? The walk was familiar . . . could it . . . yes! It reminded her of the viscount!

Something about him had puzzled her from the first. He seemed too suave, too—

But before she had time to finish her conjecture, all at once the man down on the snow stopped, then turned, glancing directly up at her window!

Instinctively Hilary pulled away and ducked into a shadowed recess, hoping the small light in her room would not betray her face. It had almost been as if he had known she were there, and was looking for her. But whatever the cause of his sudden turn and probing of the night for her eyes, at least she now knew the identity of this night prowler. For in the split second following his turn before she had backed completely out of sight, the reflected moonlight had shown full on his face, and there could be no mistaking the man. It was not the Austrian.

It was the professor from Oxford, Ashley Jameson!

What could this new houseguest possibly be doing meandering about the house in the dead of night?

After a moment she sneaked another glance out the window with one eye peering round the edge of the window frame. Jameson was nowhere to be seen, but his footsteps in the snow made a clear track to the door toward which he had been heading.

Slowly she put away the journal and climbed into bed, the paradoxes and questions of the night's happenings plaguing her until sleep at last swept her away.

Throughout the following morning she could not shake a heaviness that seemed bent on weighing her down. If she had been uneasy around Jo before, now everything was magnified ten times. Every look, every chance word spoken, especially from the mouth of Jameson, seemed to hold multiple meanings. Added to this, to further blur Hilary's perspective, was a call about eleven o'clock by the Viscount von Burchardt. Applying his charm both toward Jo and herself, in no time he had wrangled himself another invitation to luncheon, to which he heartily agreed.

"One o'clock, then!" said Logan, once the arrangements had been confirmed. For the past half hour they had been gathered in one of the West Wing parlors. "Now I have to see my factor, Moryson, about some things." He laughed. "I get up here so rarely that when I do, he tries to get me as much as he can so all his questions and problems can get cleared up. I'll be back before long."

Hilary, too, excused herself. The viscount cornered Jo and plied her with his charm—an exercise to which she did not seem adverse—and meanwhile the mysterious Oxford don wandered outside alone. Allison had still not made an appearance all day.

Hilary went straight to the library, where Logan had directed her when she had asked him about making a call. With the others occupied, she hoped there she would not be disturbed.

She dialed the number and felt oddly relieved as she did so. It felt good to take some action, even if it was nothing more than making a simple phone call.

"Hello, Murry," she said when the magazine switchboard put her through to her associate. "How is everything?"

"Smooth as glass," he said, then chuckled. "Betty told me to say that no matter what, she doesn't want you to worry about anything."

"What's wrong?"

"Nothing, really. Only the usual snags." He paused, and she could tell even across hundreds of miles of phone line that his next statement would not be pleasant. "Well," he went on, "there is talk of a printer's strike—but I have already lined up some scabs."

"Scabs?"

"Finks . . . strike-breakers, you know."

"Is it serious?"

"Right now they're just blowing off hot air. The contracts aren't up for renewal for a couple of weeks."

"It sounds as if you have everything under control." She smiled to herself. Suddenly in the face of her personal concerns, even the news of an impending strike did not sound terribly earth-shattering.

"By the way," added Murry, "I've got to thank you for that antiquities assignment."

"Oh . . . ?"

"Hanging around Oxford's been very stimulating."

"You met a new girl?"

"Don't I wish! But no, I was speaking of a great new story my Oxford source put me onto."

"What is it?"

"Too early even to tell you about. Let's just say it's either going to be a bomb or a bombshell!"

"Well, then, since you're hanging around Oxford, I have a bit of a favor to ask of you."

"Name it."

"Do you still keep in touch with that fellow from Scotland Yard?"

"Once in a while. I have to keep my contacts greased, you know."

"Could you ask him to run a name through the Yard's computers?"

"Sure," answered Murry, "but what does that have to do with Oxford? Say, what's going on up there, anyway?"

"I can't go into it now, Murry. I'm not even sure I know." She then gave him Jameson's name and what little she knew of him. "You might check around next time you're out at Oxford, a little street research to go along with the official report."

"I'm not sure I'll be going back soon. My guy's flown the coop for a while. Insists his life's in danger."

"That *is* interesting. Your guy *leaves* Oxford just as my guy arrives in Scotland from Oxford!"

"Coincidence?"

"I don't know. Find out for me, Murry, will you?"

"I'll do what I can."

"And, throw the name Emil von Burchardt into that police computer while you're at it. He's an Austrian viscount."

"You *are* meeting some interesting chaps up there!"

"Let's put it this way—the one *says* he's an Oxford professor, and the other *claims* to be a viscount. And when you call, Murry, don't leave me any messages. Talk directly with me.''

"Gotcha. It might take a couple of days."

"Put a priority on it. Thanks, Murry!"

Hilary slowly put the receiver down.

She sat back in her chair, reflecting briefly on what she had asked Murry to do and wondering if her suspicions were totally unfounded. Deciding that his efforts would be worthwhile regardless, even if she only discovered through them that everyone was on the up and up, Hilary rose and walked toward the library door.

As she opened the door toward her, Hilary's entire mental focus remained intent on what she had just done. As she swung into the hallway, she found her loose hand taken and then pulled upward in a familiar grasp.

36 / Hidden Complexities

"Ah, Fraulein Edwards . . . what a pleasure it is to see you again!" said Viscount von Burchardt, kissing her hand.

"Emil!" replied Hilary, "I did not know you were so nearby."

"I'm afraid I startled you. Forgive me. Actually, I was on my way to see you. I had a feeling you might be in the library."

"I thought you and Jo were deeply engrossed in something."

"A mere facade, I assure you. I was watching you out of the corner of my eye."

"Should I be flattered?" said Hilary, regaining her poise.

"Take it any way you wish," replied von Burchardt. "But I would be less than truthful if I told you anything but that I returned today particularly in hopes of finding you alone."

"For whatever reason?" asked Hilary coyly.

"Surely you don't mean to suggest that I am the first man to seek you out?" said Emil, a gleam of mischief in his eye.

"The first viscount," countered Hilary.

"So then," said von Burchardt, offering his arm and starting down the hall as Hilary took it, though lightly, and followed, "tell me more about this intriguing situation here. You and Jo, both vying for the loyalties and fortunes of the Macintyre domain, is that it?"

"A bit crudely put. And perhaps that captures the gist of it. But I would not say we are 'vying' for anything. The truth about our relative status within the family is merely unknown. It's really quite simple."

"Simple, quoth she," said Emil with a grin. "Don't you know that simplicity is but a surface manifestation of hidden complexities?"

"Shakespeare?"

"I'm afraid not. Von Burchardt, actually."

Now it was Hilary's turn to laugh. This man was too straightforward to be other than he seemed!

"You laugh as if in scorn," he added lightly. "You do not agree?"

"About simplicity hiding complexity? I don't know. What do you say to trying out your theory on Jo? What do you know of her?"

"Your temporary *sister*, as it were?" said Emil. "I know nothing about her."

"I thought, perhaps, that you knew her from somewhere else?" probed Hilary with pretended innocence. As she spoke she gazed deeply into the viscount's eyes.

"Me? I've never been here before in my life! But now let's take *you*, Hilary," he said. "You seem soft-spoken enough. Perfectly without motive. Yet something tells me there is much more to you than meets the eye at first glance."

"Merely an illusion," she answered off-handedly.

"I doubt that sincerely. No, you are more intricate a young woman than you would like people to think. I've watched you as you sit back and observe the rest of us, sizing up the other players in this knotty little scenario. You do not say much, Hilary—unlike Jo, who is constantly talking in that carefree voice of hers. But you are always thinking. I can see it in your eyes. And how dearly I would love to know what is going on inside that brain of yours."

Hilary's only response was a half-smile, which said that now she had to give consideration to his remarks.

"You see! There you are again—trying to size me up on the basis of what I've just said! There's no denying it! I am right about you!"

"Perhaps, Herr von Burchardt," replied Hilary, still smiling. "But if what you say is true, you would be one of the last persons I would tell what was going on inside my brain. After all, I know nothing whatsoever about you."

"Except that I saved you from a nasty spill off your horse."

"Yes, of course. And that is no small thing. I am grateful. But that still tells me nothing about *you*—who you *really* are."

"Ah, but that is the beauty of it! I am nothing more than I seem!"

"An Austrian viscount touring the coast of Scotland?"

"Precisely."

"And how are the repairs coming to your yacht?" asked Hilary.

"Repairs?"

"You mentioned having to weather here in Port Strathy on account of some repairs."

"Ah, the repairs—of course! Quite well . . . almost completed. Shipshape of a crew I have!"

"And you've never met Mr. Macintyre either?" queried Hilary.

"Never. Why would you ask? I told you, my coming here is purely happenstance," replied von Burchardt.

By now they had reached the parlor where they had previously been. As no one was there, and as the sun had come out over the winter's landscape, they slowly made their way to one of the outside doors.

"So tell me," said the viscount, seeking again to divert the attention off himself, "how did you come to be here? I find the whole thing terribly fascinating. You were visited by Macintyre's mother-in-law in London, was that it? And I understand there is a journal someplace which sheds light on all this."

Hilary nodded noncommittally, wondering where he had heard about

Joanna's journal. Wracking her brain to recall whether it had been part of any conversation to which he'd been privy, in the distance all at once they saw Logan enter the grounds through a gate in the hedge.

"Ah . . . our host!" exclaimed von Burchardt. "Will you excuse me? He promised to let me have a look at the horses!"

"Of course," replied Hilary.

"We will have to continue this discussion later," said the viscount, walking away. "I must know more of what is inside that beautiful head of yours . . . and what brought you here."

37 / Of Ovid and Aristocrats _____

Throughout luncheon von Burchardt, strategically placed between the two, managed to keep up a steady and inquisitive conversation with both Jo and Hilary. On the opposite side of the table, Professor Jameson observed the proceedings with what was now an amused twinkle, now a look of concern in his eye, following the flow of dialogue from one, then to the other. He and Logan lapsed occasionally into discourse of their own, but it seemed stilted and was broken by long silences. They both appeared content to let the viscount carry the ball, and gained what entertainment was possible from his probing. The Austrian appeared intent on unraveling the mystery of "the two daughters," as he termed it, on the basis of asking question after question, then carefully scrutinizing the faces as they responded.

When the meal was nearly over, the door opened and Allison made an appearance. Logan jumped up from his chair and went to meet her.

"You look much less pale, my dear," he said. "How are you feeling?"

"Better . . . much better. At least I was able to pull myself out of that horrid bed for a while."

"Won't you join us, Frau Macintyre," said von Burchardt, rising and going to meet her.

"Thank you, but nothing to eat for me. I just didn't want to be a completely negligent hostess."

When they had finished eating, Hilary excused herself, Jameson went outside, Jo said she was going to the drawing room, the viscount, continuing to make himself engaging, went with her, and Logan followed, with Allison on his arm, at some distance.

The sun had come out, and, notwithstanding the cold, the day was an inviting one, made all the more so by the thin layer of snow that covered the land, though paths and roads were by now appearing through it. Hilary, determined not to remain cooped up in her room the entire afternoon, went upstairs and changed into the warmest clothes she could find—a white wool Norwegian sweater, blue jeans, a royal blue down parka she'd borrowed from Allison, thick wool socks, and leather boots—and then made immediately for the main front door of the house. It would be good to get out, she thought. The landscape was so lovely, and even the cold would feel good on her face. She needed something invigorating to snap her back into life.

She had hardly taken two steps after closing the door behind her, when around the wall walked the professor, nearly knocking her over.

"Why, Mr. Jameson!" she exclaimed.

"Hello, Miss Edwards," he replied in the easy tone that seemed characteristic of him. "I'm afraid I wasn't paying much attention. I didn't expect to find anyone else out braving the elements."

"I couldn't resist the sun shining on the snow."

"Well, I was myself just off for a bit of a stroll about the grounds. Perhaps you would like to join me?"

Hilary hesitated but momentarily, then nodded an affirmative smile, and the two headed around toward the garden in the direction Jameson had been walking. He was dressed in a heavy plaid wool coat, casual corduroy trousers, and heavy walking boots.

He led across the snow-covered lawn, then struck out across the footbridge on which Allison had fallen a few days earlier, and which Jake had since repaired.

"Careful here," he said, "these wooden planks might be rather slippery."

Hilary negotiated the bridge easily, and within ten minutes they had left the castle's immediate grounds and were making their way across the wide, untouched landscape—expansive common, dotted with bracken, rocks, and what would have been browning grass except for the snow—east of the house.

"How long have you been here, Miss Edwards?" Jameson asked casually after some minutes of silence—noticeable, though not awkward.

"Only a few days."

"Has it been enjoyable for you?"

"That's not exactly the word I would have chosen to describe it," replied Hilary. "It's beautiful . . . peaceful of course. But the circumstances are awkward."

"Yes . . . I can see they must be."

"Tell me, Mr. Jameson," said Hilary, turning the conversation around and assuming the initiative, "I would have thought you'd be back on your way south by now, busy man that you must be, since your plans have fallen through."

"The Macintyres invited me to stay on—just for a day or two more. And since I haven't had a holiday in some time. . . ."

He let his tone finish the sentence.

"That is the only reason?"

"Yes . . . why? What do you mean?"

"I thought perhaps . . . I don't know what put the notion into my head exactly," said Hilary, trying to sound her most innocent, "but somehow I had the idea that you might have known Jo prior to coming here."

"What . . . Jo? No, I've never seen her before yesterday," he replied quickly, sending an uncertain glance in Hilary's direction. "Why would you think that?"

"I don't know. Just my reporter's inquisitive mind, I suppose," replied Hilary with a laugh.

"An *over*-inquisitive mind, I would say."

"That's the only kind of mind a writer can have—that is, if he's worth his salt as a writer. You should know that. You're an author, though; perhaps it's different when you're writing history." She paused, waiting for him to take up from her lead. But he seemed willing to let the subject drop.

"Would you agree?" she asked.

"About what?"

"Writing . . . history writing being different from other kinds, requiring less inquiry."

"*Less* inquiry, Miss Edwards? Heavens no! Good history requires more inquiry than any other kind of writing."

"Is history the only writing you've ever done?" she asked.

Again, the question seemed to throw him momentarily.

"Why . . . yes . . . er, history is, of course . . . it's my field."

"So you've never thought of trying your hand at something else, a contemporary article . . . the here and now, rather than ancient Greece?"

"No . . . that is to say, I'm not sure I quite understand you. As I said, my field is history, and that is what I write about."

Hilary let the subject drop. It was leading her nowhere, although Jameson did seem flustered by her questions. There was more to him than met the eye, and she was determined to uncover it. He too, like the viscount, was full of questions.

"But, Miss Edwards," he went on before Hilary could decide what tack to take next, "I find myself puzzled by one thing. If this Lady Joanna—Macintyre's mother-in-law, I believe it was—if she came to you, identified herself as your grandmother, gave you her family locket, entrusted you with her precious journal, apparently had documents to show the legal connection . . . in the face of all that, why is there this apparent doubt in the minds of the Macintyres as to the veracity of your position?"

"You know about the locket?" Hilary's tone was sharp, and she looked intently into Jameson's face.

"It must have been Macintyre who told me about it, and the journal."

"Then he must also have told you that the locket has apparently been lost . . ."

A grave look passed over Jameson's face.

" . . . or if not lost, then misplaced. In any case, it's not in my room. And Lady Joanna's dead, so no one knows of the 'legal connections,' as you put it. There were no documents. Yes, there is the journal, but the ending pages of it are missing. If they reveal anything about the search she made and her reasons for undertaking it after Jo had already arrived, that knowledge is lost to the rest of us."

"Has there been a search initiated for the locket or the missing pages?"

"Not a formal one, to my knowledge," replied Hilary. For a moment she considered bringing up the late visitor to her wing of the house the previous night, but then thought better of it. "As to the missing pages," she went on, "no one's ever *seen* them. There's no evidence to suggest that there *are* pages definitely missing. When I said that, I was perhaps saying more than I should have. I only assume she must have written more than she sent me."

Jameson nodded, in apparent thought. "That *is* interesting," he mused. "If we could just find that part of the journal," he added in a mumbling tone almost to himself.

"Now *you* seem the one with the over-inquisitive mind," said Hilary playfully, but with design behind her light tone. "Are you sure you only write history? If I didn't know better, I might think you were a mystery buff."

"What's that! A mystery buff? Ridiculous!" replied Jameson, flustered. "I tell you I'm nothing but a dull Greek historian."

"I don't believe that for a minute! There is more to you than you want to let on, Mr. Jameson. Or perhaps I should call you *Dr*. Jameson! Is that what your colleagues call you?"

"No, no, please. *Mr*. will be fine."

"Then you must call me Hilary. No offense to history as a field of study, but I loathe the archaic modes of expression."

"I take it you must be quite the progressive woman, then . . . Hilary."

"Progressive? Perhaps. I don't think of myself as a modernist, but on the other hand I don't think my Creator expects me to wear black and walk dutifully ten paces behind a man, demurring to his every whim."

"God, you say?" said Jameson thoughtfully. "What is it you think God *does* expect from you?"

"He gave me a good head on my shoulders, and some wits, and I think He expects me to use them," she answered firmly. "Which is what I am trying to do as, if you'll pardon the expression, a career woman. Beyond that, I think His highest expectation is that I love and serve Him without getting so muddled with the inconsequential."

"You sound like someone whose faith means a great deal to you."

"That's because it does."

He gave her a quick, sidelong glance, which she pretended not to notice. However, she could not help but wonder at the cause for his apparent astonishment.

"That's very interesting," he said, after pausing to give the statement deeper consideration. "A rare enough thing in today's world."

They walked for a few paces in silence.

"Look!" said Hilary suddenly, pointing ahead. "Isn't that a wheatear?"

All Jameson could see besides snow and shrubbery was a small bird perched upon a low branch sticking up out of the snow.

"That bird over there?" he asked.

"Yes. It's really rather late in the year for it—most of the others must surely have migrated by now."

"I see you are an ornithologist as well," commented Jameson.

"Not really. I once covered an ornithology convention. Not very stimulating, I must admit, but I learned a few things in spite of myself."

They had stopped in their walking and Hilary continued to gaze at the little bird with interest. "There's nothing like an outdoor hike on a cold day for invigorating the senses and making fascinating discoveries," she said.

"Walking is the one form of exercise I highly endorse," agreed Jameson. "I try to walk several miles a day."

"Even at night?" The words escaped Hilary's lips before she even knew it, though the question sounded casual.

"If I find no other time," he replied, faltering ever so slightly—as if he had sensed her motive in the question, or as if he was thinking of hiding something.

"I saw you out last night," said Hilary, plunging ahead.

"It is—walking, you know—an excellent antidote to insomnia." There was a trace of something in his tone, Hilary thought, a slight inflection that sounded too glib for truth.

"You have trouble sleeping?"

"Occasionally. And so must you if you were also up at that hour."

"I have ever since I arrived here. Does prowling through the hallways cure insomnia just like the outside air?"

"My, but you are suspicious!" he replied with a laugh. Was it a nervous laugh or an innocent one? Hilary couldn't tell. "*Prowling*, Hilary? Come now, I was merely walking off the effects of my journey, hoping not to disturb anyone. So I purposely avoided any contact with those who were trying to sleep."

A very plausible explanation, thought Hilary to herself. Who can tell, maybe it is even the truth. They began walking again.

It was the professor who first spoke.

"Logan tells me you were reluctant to come in the first place, even after speaking with Lady Joanna?"

Hilary looked askance at Jameson. Everyone around here seemed filled with questions!

"Lady Joanna's revelations came as a great shock to me," she replied finally. "I simply could not imagine myself part of such a—well, *this* kind of family."

"*This* kind of family. . . ?"

"Aristocrats, you know. I had the commonest of upbringings."

"Rags to riches—what's wrong with that?"

"Nothing, I suppose, for fairy tales. But I happen to think the nobility is archaic. There's *my* two pence worth of your history! Perhaps a noble institution for two hundred years ago. Outmoded and even dangerous today."

"Pretty strong words."

"I believe them."

"So you couldn't face the fact that maybe you were an aristocrat yourself?"

"Imagine the shock."

"I get your point," he replied, an amused smile hidden from view.

"And not just plain aristocrats, mind you. This family lives in a 400-year-old castle, entertains the Queen Mother, and occupies a seat in the Shadow Cabinet!"

"But as I understand it, Logan is the one member of the family who is of common stock." He cleared his throat dryly, as if he had made a point. "So if you turn out to be a member of this family, you will be only *half* an aristocrat."

"That's quite enough, thank you."

"You do have a serious problem about this, don't you? For a seemingly open, Christian, modern young woman, I must admit that surprises me. I admittedly do not know you very well, Hilary, but it smacks of prejudice."

"A class-conscious society, my dear Mr. Jameson, is doomed to extinction in this age. And Britain is one of the great class-bound societies of the world, though we refuse to admit it."

"That almost hints of Marxism." His tone was not argumentative, at least much less so than Hilary's. But he sounded as if he enjoyed the prospect of a debate.

"I would never go that far," replied Hilary. "But you must admit that when the masses are repressed, it's only a matter of time before the fabric of society bursts apart at the seams."

"We have survived as a nation longer than just about any other on earth."

"Yes, but just look at Victorian England," said Hilary, "when British power was at its apex throughout the world. The squalor of the majority of the population was reprehensible—all while the nobility amassed huge wealth."

"But when did British world dominance begin to collapse?" he asked, then went on to answer his own question, still in a casual tone. This was no argument to him, merely an exercise in logic. "In the twentieth century, coming on the heels of sweeping social reform, enfranchisement, and the welfare state."

"You blame that on the lower classes!"

"Not at all." He smiled. "But I think you would blame the nobility for just the opposite reaction."

"Whose fault is it, then?"

"Must blame be apportioned at all?" queried Jameson rhetorically. "If so, perhaps it ought to be taken to a higher plane—that of spiritual need, of the depravity of man."

"Spoken like one who also possesses spiritual convictions. But even accepting what you say, there is still something intrinsically wrong with a system that says one person is higher than another on some arbitrary scale of worth simply by chance of birth."

"'*Nam genus et proavose et quæ non fecimus ipsi, Vix ea nostra voco,*'" was Ashley's reply.

"I don't understand a word of Latin," groaned Hilary ruefully, "but I have the feeling my argument has just been doomed."

"Hardly," chuckled Jameson. He seemed to be thoroughly enjoying Hilary's discomfiture. "You see, even Ovid agreed with you: '*Birth and ancestry, and that which we have not ourselves achieved, we can scarcely call our own.*' And I wouldn't say that I don't agree also. But it would be a mistake to thoughtlessly throw it out altogether. They tried that in France, and the Reign of Terror was the answer. The nobility may have been corrupt, but Robespierre was nothing but a terrorist. It has nothing to do with *class*, Hilary. It has instead to do with the state of a man's *heart*."

"I see your point," she answered reluctantly. "But what benefit then does the aristocracy have at all?"

"Perhaps it has more to do with aesthetics than politics. Think of the nobility as a thread in the larger fabric of society. Don't judge right or wrong, but rather consider what would happen if you pulled out that thread suddenly. The warp and woof of the cloth itself would be noticeably weakened, as it would if any other thread were removed. What would happen to society if suddenly there were no laborers, or if you took away the educational system, or if Parliament suddenly ceased to exist? The nobility is the same—it's an intrinsic part of what makes society function—with its good points and its bad points, like every other aspect of civilization."

"You seem to have thought this through very carefully."

"History does have its contemporary application. But in another way, it's all just a matter of simple logic."

"I don't know—you sound like something more than an impartial proponent of the aristocratic order."

"Perhaps I am a bit of a traditionalist. I suppose I have even been accused of being stuffy by some. That's what comes of being hidden away in a place like Oxford."

Something in his tone seemed to indicate this admission of stuffiness was a smoke screen. That there was more to this man, there could be no doubt. Hilary hated to admit it, but she rather liked his style. He was so confident and self-assured, but with such an absence of pretense, that he could not help but be intriguing. Still, she reminded herself, she could not drop her guard.

Hilary's reverie was interrupted as Jameson spoke again, maneuvering the conversation back to its original point.

"I think I now begin to understand the answer to my original question about your reluctance in coming to Stonewycke," he said. "But then, what did finally change your mind?"

Hilary thought for a moment. That was not easy to say. She still wasn't sure herself. "I suppose," she answered at length, "that I found myself having to confront my own *prejudice*, as you so pointedly put it. Part of me still feels as I always have about the nobility. But then another piece of me way down inside, the part of me that *does* want to be open, says, 'Maybe you haven't thought through the whole story yet, Hilary!' Perhaps it's my conscience. But whatever it is, that little voice has been growing stronger recently. And one day, as I was wrestling with what Lady Joanna said, and with what I knew of Logan Macintyre from my professional dealings with him, that little voice stood up and shouted, 'Go to Scotland!' "

"I see . . . very interesting."

They had by now come back to the castle grounds and were just approaching the little footbridge.

They walked back toward the front door to the house. Theirs were still the only footprints across the snow on the lawn. After a few more moments of light conversation, they opened the door.

"Ah, Jameson . . . Fraulein Edwards!" exclaimed von Burchardt as they walked in. "We were hoping to meet up with you!"

Behind him stood Logan and Jo, bundling up with overcoats and scarves. "We were just heading out," said Logan. "If the two of you are game, we thought we'd drive to town and have a look at Emil's yacht."

"Sounds like an interesting proposal," replied Jameson, "although I must admit my feet are nearly frozen. We've just been out for a tromp through the fields to the east of the castle—beautiful enough, but covered with snow!"

"Yes, please," shivered Hilary, hardly noticing the cold until she was now back inside. "Do let us warm up a few minutes first!"

"I'll go and tell Flora to have some hot tea waiting for us when we return," said Logan. He left while the others continued with readying and warming. In a few moments he returned from the direction of the kitchen.

"And Mrs. Macintyre?" asked Jameson. "Will she be joining us?"

"I'm afraid not. She went back to her room to lie down. Well . . . shall we?" he said, indicating the door with his hand.

Five minutes later the five were seated in Logan's gray Mercedes, Jameson, his long legs pulled up in front of him, seated between Hilary and Jo in the backseat, von Burchardt keeping Logan company in the front. Snow still covered the estate driveway, broken only by the tracks made earlier by the viscount as he walked up the hill from town, and Logan inched along carefully. When they reached the highway, however, the road was clear down into the village. Logan parked in front of the Bluster 'N Blow, and the small party made their way toward the harbor. It was obvious immediately which boat was von Burchardt's.

Pure white, sleek, some eighty feet in length, the yacht boasted the daintiest of little portholes just above the level of the water indicating cabins below, and an upper deck, mostly open, around which a three-foot high rope railing stretched. About two-thirds of the way toward the bow rose the enclosed control room, surrounded on all sides by spacious windows from which the crew could maintain a 360-degree lookout.

"I say, Burchardt!" exclaimed Logan. "Good show! She's positively stunning—easily the most magnificent craft ever to grace our little harbor!"

"Coming from you, sir, I take that as the profoundest of compliments!" replied the viscount graciously. "Come, I'll take you all aboard."

He led the way, offering Hilary his hand, which she took to step up onto the deck. Jo followed, assisted by Jameson, and finally Logan stepped aboard.

"Oh!" squealed Jo with delight, "it's a shame we can't take her out!"

"What kind of repairs are you making?" asked Logan.

"Oh, nothing much really," replied von Burchardt. "In fact, the crew is mostly finished, and I gave them the day off."

"It looks shipshape enough," said Jameson. "Why, I don't see any evidence of work at all."

"Tut, tut, Professor," said the viscount. "Merely internal difficulties. Nothing visible to the novice."

"Then you won't mind if I have a look around?"

"Not at all! Make yourself at home!"

Meanwhile, Logan had wandered toward the control room, while Hilary peered down the narrow stairs which led below deck.

"Would you like to see the cabins?" asked von Burchardt, offering Hilary his hand. "But hold on tightly, these steps are steep."

They made their way slowly downstairs, followed by Jo. Jameson, in the meantime, meandered toward the stern of the craft, then made his way to the back railing and stooped down and peered over the edge. Walking toward it from the dock he had noted the yacht's registration sticker and identifying numbers. Now he examined them more closely. When he stood up a moment later, ruminating to himself, he mumbled something inaudible and rubbed his hand across his face in puzzlement. Spying Logan fore, he walked briskly toward him, but was interrupted by the three others as they emerged from below.

"Find anything interesting, Mr. Macintyre?" asked the viscount as he deposited the two ladies back on the deck.

"I'm not much of a sailor, I admit, Burchardt," answered Logan. "But you certainly seem to have nothing but state of the art equipment."

"Where was she outfitted?" asked Jameson.

"Bremerhaven."

"Everything?"

"Mostly. It is my home port. Actually I bought the vessel in Trieste."

"Ever take her further south . . . the south Atlantic . . . coast of Africa?"

"No, no," laughed von Burchardt. "I'm no world traveller!"

Jameson nodded knowingly, but said nothing.

"We don't want to let that tea get too cold," said Logan. "Before we go, von Burchardt, won't you explain your instrumentation? There are a good many I've never seen."

"With pleasure!" replied the viscount with a broad smile. "Won't you join us, ladies . . . Jameson?" he added, leading the way back toward the front cabin.

Fifteen minutes later the small party piled out of Logan's car in front of the castle.

"Well, that was certainly a pleasant diversion," said Logan. "Thank you, Burchardt, for the whirlwind tour!"

"Perhaps if the weather turns for a bit, I might take you out, say a run up to the Orkneys for a day or two?"

"You are staying around then?"

"Oh, not much longer, but making plans that are too definite always makes me feel tied down. I merely have to return to the Continent before Christmas."

When they were seated in the drawing room and Flora had served tea along with some oatcakes and a tray of shortbread, Jameson picked up the thread of conversation.

"So you're headed back toward Germany then, Herr von Burchardt?" he asked.

The viscount nodded as he sipped at the hot tea. "And then by train down to Vienna," he added. "But tell me, Macintyre," he went quickly on, "I'm intrigued by this whole situation of your mother-in-law's journal. Seems that such a document would shed a great deal of light upon your present dilemma, especially if she documented her contacts and associations, which, as I understand it, turned up different, shall we say, 'evidence' than your own?"

"You're right, I daresay," replied Logan. "But the journal itself, the main part of it, that is, which Hilary received from Lady Joanna and still has in her possession"—as he said the words all eyes involuntarily glanced in Hilary's direction then back to Logan—"is not of particular significance."

A questioning look on the viscount's face invited further explanation.

"Perhaps you would like to explain what I mean, Hilary. You have read it more recently."

"Most of what Lady Joanna recorded was family history, detailed lives of her ancestors and a recounting of her own life and coming to Scotland," said Hilary. "There is no mention of recent events."

"That's because the ending is missing," put in Jo. "Can you believe it? Isn't it mysterious?"

"Missing pages!" von Burchardt exclaimed. "And you've no idea where they might be?"

He seemed to direct the question to Hilary, but then turned back and focused his innocently inquisitive gaze toward Logan.

"Such a pity," he added quickly, "that such a precious family heirloom should be lost or left incomplete."

All at once Logan realized he had given the ending to Joanna's journal no more than passing consideration. Suddenly the truth dawned upon him that she well may have documented her final thoughts and travels in a most revealing way.

"Might we have a look at what you do have, Hilary?" said Logan.

Hesitating awkwardly, Hilary replied, "I really would rather not, right now. This just doesn't seem like . . . the proper time."

Slightly annoyed at her rebuff of his request, Logan nevertheless kept his reaction to himself, thought for a moment, then rose. "Excuse me," he said, "I'm going to dash up and see how Allison is feeling."

He returned in only two or three minutes, Allison with him.

"I have asked Allison about the journal," began Logan as they entered the room, "but she has no more idea about the pages than the rest of us."

"They could be anywhere," said Allison. "But I have never known Mother to be careless, especially where her journal was concerned. Whatever she did with the final entries, I'm sure it was well-thought out."

"There would be hundreds of places around here where she might have hidden them," said Jo.

"Hidden them?" repeated Logan. "I wonder if we're getting a bit carried away. It may be but an oversight of some kind." His voice was wary.

"Perhaps we might have a look about the place, split into groups . . . we would want to start with the most likely places frequented by Lady Joanna," said the viscount enthusiastically.

"I appreciate your concern," replied Logan coolly, "but this is a matter for my wife and me to resolve. Hilary was right, this isn't the proper time."

"Of course! Please forgive me," said von Burchardt. "I've rather gotten carried away with myself, haven't I?" He chuckled softly. "I suppose I cannot resist a good mystery."

Jo seemed disappointed at the chilly turn of the conversation away from the pages. Hilary was relieved. Logan's forehead showed unexpressed thought and concern. Allison looked tired, and Jameson was saying nothing.

"So, do you read mysteries too, Emil?" asked Hilary after a few moments had passed, "or merely try to solve them?"

He laughed. "I'm a doer not a reader," he replied.

"And you think the two mutually exclusive?" asked Jameson, rising slightly out of his chair. This sounded like the beginning of a discussion more to his liking.

From there the conversation strayed innocuously off into a discussion of Sherlock Holmes, Agatha Christie, and the newest British creator of mystery, Lady Hargreave.

When Hilary ascended to her room later that evening, she found she was very tired. It had been a full day, and the time outside, probably the cold, had sapped her energy. Reflecting upon the day's events, what remained most vividly in her mind were the two conversations she had had with the two visitors, Ashley Jameson and Emil von Burchardt. Both were fascinating men, although as different as the very worlds they represented—Emil with his polished savoir-faire and striking good looks, Jameson with his unassuming refinement and casual manner. Both were capable of catching one off guard—the viscount with the direct, cheerful, upbeat approach, the professor by the many subtleties which seemed to quietly radiate out of his character.

Why compare them at all? Hilary asked herself. If for no other reason than they both seemed up to something. Why would they show up at the same time, and then hang around incessantly, always asking questions? Something felt peculiar, and she was right in the middle of it!

She sat down on the edge of her bed, thought for a moment, then rose and went to the suitcase, stuffed under the bed, where she still kept the journal. She pulled out the case, reached to the bottom, and pulled out Joanna's manuscript. She had been meaning to give the book to Allison, but somehow had continued to avoid doing so, even at the risk of appearing possessive of it. She knew her insistence on keeping it seemed peculiar to others in the family, yet somehow she felt it important she not relinquish it just yet. There remained much to resolve, and—who could tell? She might yet be called upon to play an important role in the unfolding of events.

The missing pages . . . Joanna's final words—they seemed to be the key. But where could they be? Again Hilary thumbed to the last page of the manuscript. Nothing had changed. Again she began to read, realizing as she did that she had never *really* read Joanna's final entry, never really perceived what Joanna was trying to say. As she continued her eyes widened. Yet Lady Joanna's words, if anything, served only to deepen the mystery:

August 27, 1971—Today and for the last several days it has been stormy like I have seldom seen on this north coast. Perhaps that explains my mood. I usually love these wild Highland blasts. But not today. I am chilled to the bone, and we cannot even keep a fire in the hearth. But what I feel goes beyond mere climatic conditions. It is a heaviness that has come over me, almost a sense of foreboding, as if some evil presence were incarnate in the storm itself. It is a feeling I have had only on rare occasions in my life, and the memories are too unpleasant to recall. Suffice it to say that I recognize the feeling and to this day am repelled by it.

I am not one to give heed to such ethereal notions, but can it be that the Lord is trying to tell me something? Warning me? Perhaps the hour of my death is near. With that in mind I have spent the last hour in prayer, and though no specific answer has come, I do sense a peace invading my heavy spirit, as though the evil may be present in the storm, but His almighty presence IS in and throughout the storm. Indeed, He made the storm and rules over it yet, and even now is preparing His messenger to combat the forces that would destroy what He has built. A Scripture continues to come to my mind which I know is from Him, but I do not yet understand its significance: "The angel of the Lord encampeth round about them that fear him, and delivereth them." Perhaps I do not need to understand just now—it is enough to know that He is indeed with me, and that He will lead me to—

And there the final entry of the journal broke off.

Unexpectedly tears welled up in Hilary's eyes. "Oh, Grandmother!" she whispered to herself, not even considering that it might not be so. She felt Lady Joanna's spirit with her, and remembered the lady's loving embrace. She had *felt* the love emanating from the dear lady! But was that enough to make her Hilary's grandmother?

Again she glanced at the date of the passage. *I wonder what might have happened that day to put her in such a dark mood?* Hilary asked herself. I should question Mrs. Macintyre about it.

She laid the journal back on top of the other things in the open suitcase on the floor, then sat down in the chair next to the window. Tonight there was no light, and although it was still relatively early, only nine o'clock, outside it was pitch black. The moon was still several hours away.

She was so tired—she had to get to bed. Yet she was too keyed up to sleep. The castle seemed unnaturally quiet, as if some mischief were abroad, awaiting the stroke of midnight to unveil itself. She could not keep from imagining noises, first outside, then above her, as though someone were walking softly in a room directly overhead, and then in the hallway outside her door.

With each imagined sound, she strained to hear more and each time was met with only a deeper silence.

For a long time she was undisturbed, and gradually drowsiness began to overtake her. Indeed, the unknown guest in a small sitting room—not above her room directly, but on the next floor and across the hall—was making no more stealthy noise in his stocking feet. The Viscount von Burchardt, whom everyone had bid goodbye about six o'clock, at that moment lay reclining on a sofa, having been let back into the house at a side entrance by his secret accomplice, awaiting the deeper slumber of the occupants of the castle that he might be about the real business for which he had been summoned to Port Strathy.

All remained still. Hilary had just lapsed into semiconsciousness when suddenly a loud knock sounded on the solid wood door of her room.

With a jolt she sat up in her chair, the fear of sudden waking upon her face.

"Pardon me, Miss Edwards, for disturbing you so late . . ." came the voice when Hilary opened the door.

In disbelief she found herself staring at Ashley Jameson.

" . . . but I couldn't sleep, and I wondered if you would care to join me for a cup of tea?"

"But it's . . . it's . . ."

Still disoriented, Hilary glanced down and tried to focus the hands of her watch.

"It's nearly ten o'clock. I apologize again. I only thought—but if it's not convenient—"

"No, it's not that," Hilary interrupted. "You startled me, that's all." Coming to herself, she added, "Yes, I'd enjoy some tea. Just let me put on a sweater."

In another minute she was back in the hallway, closed her door, and they walked toward the main stairway, speaking softly as they went, as if their very presence in the quiet corridors indicated some sinister intent.

The hallway was chilly and dark except for dim nightlights at each end. As they padded down the deserted passage, Hilary began to have second thoughts about her decision. To her knowledge she was the only one quartered in this particular wing. Jo's room was around several corners. Logan and Allison occupied the master bedroom not far from Atlanta's dayroom. She did not know where Jameson's room was or from which direction he had approached. As they passed closed doors she felt an eerie sensation, as if from the darkness at any moment might spring wild images of wraiths. Hilary was flooded with relief when they turned the corner of the lengthy passageway and saw the stairway at hand. She glanced down in the direction toward Jo's room, but all was quiet and the lights were out.

Neither spoke as they flitted down the staircase, as if by common consent they knew the night air did not want to be disturbed. Jameson led the way to the kitchen, and upon entering Hilary saw that the lights had already been switched on and a teakettle was already on the stove.

"I see you are already prepared," she said.

"I hoped you would join me," he replied, "but I must confess I had my heart set on some tea regardless."

The room was furnished with modern conveniences—two refrigerators, an electric stove, a long wide tile counter with two spacious sinks at either end, and several other appliances. The cook still burned a wood fire in the brick hearth, however, now chiefly for heat, though at one time that same hearth had been used for huge pots of water and boiling oatmeal and potatoes. At the moment the fire was banked for the night, but still emitted a pleasurably warm radiance.

Hilary found a teapot and the tea. Jameson tended the water, and in about ten minutes they were seated at the rustic thick pine table, each with a warm cup in hand.

"So I take it you were not suffering from insomnia tonight, Miss Edwards?" he began.

"It started out so," she answered. "I had just drifted off when you knocked on the door. However, it would appear the affliction still plagues you?"

He smiled in that easy, unaffected smile she did not yet know how to interpret. "So it would appear."

As Hilary sipped the strong black brew, she determined to find out once and for all what this fellow was about, even if it meant she had to relinquish some of her own privacy and aloofness to do so. She had to sort out these people and their motives. Chances are she would learn nothing conclusive from Murry, in which case she was on her own. This story, if there was a story to come out of her sojourn to Stonewycke, would be hers and hers alone to write.

"I enjoyed our conversation of earlier," she said. "I have missed that level of mental stimulation since coming here. Some of what you said forced me to think."

"I'm surprised you haven't cornered Logan—I should say, Mr. Macintyre. I would think with your political interests and leanings, and his position, you could strike up quite a rousing discussion with him." He smiled wryly.

"The situation hasn't quite been conducive to that sort of dialogue." She paused and shook her head thoughtfully, almost regretfully. "I would have liked that though, to really talk to him."

"Perhaps you may still have the opportunity." He stirred cream and sugar into his tea.

"I'm beginning to doubt it. I don't think it will be long before I pack up and return to London."

"You sound disappointed."

"Crazy, isn't it? For someone who didn't want to come here in the first place, you'd think I'd be glad to go." She raised her cup to her lips. "There is something about this . . . place. The quiet, the stillness, the openness of the landscape . . . and the people. You should meet this lovely family I've become acquainted with down in the valley!"

"Perhaps you can introduce me."

"Maybe one day we can do that," said Hilary almost wistfully. "But as I was saying, there is something about this place that grows on you, gets under your skin. Part of me doesn't want to leave. It has nothing to do with whether I'm a member of this family or not. It's . . . it's something bigger than that! At the same time, there is something about this family too . . ."

"Yes, it is a truly incredible family."

"I thought you had only just met them." Suddenly Hilary was on the alert again.

"But naturally I have heard things—through Ian, you know."

"Yes, I'd forgotten. Have you known him long?"

"We've been associated at the university for years. He was my professor when I was a student."

"When was that?"

"I first came to Oxford in 1955. I completed my post-graduate work in 1962."

Hilary made a mental note of the dates. She'd have Murry do some double-checking next time she spoke with him.

"Then it must be quite a thrill now to collaborate with your former mentor," she said, as if she were baiting him.

"An honor, to be exact." The look of admiration in Jameson's eyes seemed genuine enough. "The man is highly renowned in his field. I don't know how much of your . . . what should I call it, your 'potential' family, you know about. But Lady Allison's brother Ian is responsible for several important archaeological finds."

Hilary again found herself aware of the prestige of this clan. In addition to a famous politician, it appeared the noble blood had produced a noted scholar as well. Hardly a surprise, though, she thought. Every one of them, if Joanna's journal was a correct mirror of character, seemed to have been bestowed with some inexplicable measure of . . . what was it? Godliness, character, integrity . . . ? What *was* the ingredient that set apart the people she had read about? She had sometimes felt as if she were reading the lives of a family of Old Testament patriarchs . . . or matriarchs, in many cases. Lady Joanna would no doubt have attributed it to the blessings of God, the result of prayers directed heavenward on behalf of future generations. Hilary could not help wondering what more she would continue to discover.

The voice of her companion interrupted her momentary reverie. "What are you thinking?" he said. "The oddest look just came over your face."

"Oh, forgive me." She gave a light, though hollow chuckle. "I was thinking again about this family. As you said, they grow more and more remarkable."

"But surely you have noticed how down-to-earth they are."

"That doesn't alter what they are."

"On the contrary," he rejoined, "I believe it *is* what they are. The other—the position, the titles, the notoriety, the public spotlight—that's all peripheral to what these people really are. I do believe they could walk away from all that and not change an iota."

"Yes, I suppose I have seen that," she remarked quietly, thoughtfully. "Mr. Macintyre is a different sort of politician than most I encounter. There is a reality to him even I find refreshing. But you must understand that I grew up on the East End in nothing much better than a tenement. My father worked hard for a living—twelve, fourteen hours a day—to put bread on the table and a little besides—for me. I was an oddity on my street when I went away to the university. True, in recent years I've rubbed shoulders with some important people, and traveled to places my parents would never have dreamed going. But it doesn't matter a great deal where I was actually born. I don't even know that. Whether it was here, or in London, the roots of my being, the person I have become, still spring from simple folk. That's my point of reference to life. I can't change that. I don't think I even want to."

"But what if those London experiences aren't your roots? What if you were transplanted there? Don't you want to know from what stock the taproot of your life truly comes, independent of the sort of tree you may have been grafted onto before you can even remember?"

Hilary was silent a while. "You have a very good point, Mr. Jameson," she finally said.

"Ashley . . . please."

"Nevertheless, that was very deftly put. You do have a way with logic, I must say. I suppose I didn't want to examine that taproot in my own life at first. I was content with who I was and didn't want to discover that in reality I was someone different."

"Doesn't truth dictate that you have to find out?"

"Truth, Ashley?"

"Yes. If something is true, aren't we bound to find out, to learn whether it is, and to order our lives by it?"

"Bound by whom, by what?"

"By . . . integrity . . . by truth itself! To refuse to seek after, and know, and live by truth would be complete and total inconsistency. To me truth must be the guiding principle no matter what your other philosophical leanings."

"Strong words."

"But true words. Truth is the foundation stone for life, for rational thought, even for emotions. To deny truth, in even a small area of your life, is to deny your own personhood, and thus become a nonbeing. Truth—seeking first to know it, and then to live by what you have discovered—is the essence of life. There's no such thing as what you said earlier—ignoring who you really are so you can keep being someone you're not. Don't you see? That's nonpersonhood, nonbeing. The opposite of truth isn't false-hood, as the theologians and philosophers would have said a century ago. Neither is it different truth for you and me, as the modern theologian and philosopher quacks would say today. No, the opposite of truth is emptiness, nonbeing . . . ceasing altogether to have meaning."

"You are very convincing. What you say makes sense. I see I have not thought this through nearly enough." She paused; an odd flicker passed through her eyes, then she added, "I do want to live by truth, Ashley, however it may appear to the contrary."

"I believe you."

"If my taproot, as you say, comes from elsewhere than I had anticipated, even from such an unlikely source as the nobility of northern Scotland, then I will have to deal with that. You are quite right, it is not a fact I have the option of ignoring."

"Perhaps you won't have to make that decision. It may well turn out that Jo is the daughter, anyway, leaving you content with your East End upbringing."

Hilary peered over the rim of her raised cup at this peculiar professor. Was he mocking her with this sudden twist to a serious discussion? Or was he—consistent with what he had just been saying—merely speaking the truth without malice or motive?

From his passive expression, she couldn't tell.

But she did suddenly realize one thing. She had intended on grilling him for information, yet somehow he had turned the tables and she had been the one on the receiving end. The same thing had happened this morning.

She really shouldn't talk so freely—at least not until she had figured out just what he was up to.

"Yes, you're right," she said at length; "my worry may all be much ado about nothing, as they say."

After ten more minutes of inconsequential conversation, Hilary yawned and declared herself ready for bed.

"I think I might have another cup, myself," replied Jameson. "But I'd be happy to walk you back to your room."

"Oh no, don't bother," said Hilary, rising. "I can find my way. What harm could be afoot on a peaceful night like this when everyone else in the place is asleep?"

"No doubt you're right," he laughed. "Thank you for joining me. Good night."

On her way upstairs, Hilary reflected on their talk. He was on the mark, of course. She might not be Logan and Allison's daughter after all. As emotion-charged as had been her time with Lady Joanna, and notwithstanding the locket and the journal, the lady's visit could have been nothing but a misguided mistake. If so, it would not be long before her life would get back to normal. She would continue on as Hilary Edwards. Then she would have to face no major changes, no emotional upheavals in coming to grips with her identity—just as she had wanted in the first place.

Yet even as she tried to convince herself that maybe such a turn would be for the best, she realized that now she wasn't so sure she wanted it that way anymore.

She entered her room and sat down on the bed, still deep in thought. She really ought to return the journal. There had been so much discussion surrounding it, everyone had wanted to see it, she should give it safely back into Allison and Logan's hands.

Hilary stood again, walked around to the other side of the bed, knelt down beside the suitcase, and almost without conscious thought reached for the journal.

It was not there!

A quick panic seized her. Hastily she rummaged her hand through the few items on top of which she had set the manuscript, but Joanna's pages were not in the suitcase!

She jumped up and frantically scurried about the small room until she suddenly spied the manuscript lying on top of the dressing table. She grabbed it up with both hands and held it to her breast, exhaling a long sigh of relief.

With the journal still clasped to her, she sat down in her chair as one suddenly delivered from a nightmare, leaned back, and closed her eyes. The locket was bad enough; she could not lose this journal! It was too precious, and as if to assure herself once more of its reality, Hilary opened her eyes and gazed once more on the handwritten signature on the cover, and the words she had grown so familiar with: *Stonewycke Journal.*

She sat for some minutes, quietly rocking, still holding the book to her, reflecting on her visit with Lady Joanna. But as the initial alarm subsided and she was thinking more clearly, she began to question just what the journal was doing on the table. Hadn't she placed it in the suitcase on the floor just before Ashley had knocked on her door?

Yes, she was sure of it! But then that could only mean—

Was it possible someone had been in her room?

The idea seemed incredible, yet as Hilary stood and began to walk slowly about, there was one of the drawers not quite closed. She never left drawers like that. Alarm coming over her again, she rushed to the wardrobe in which she had placed her few clothes.

Everything seemed in order. Yet they did appear shoved more to one side than she remembered. Had someone been through her very clothes, actually snooping through her pockets? She shivered with the thought.

Retracing her steps, she returned to the dresser, opening one drawer at a time, now bringing all her reporter's instincts to bear on a thorough examination of each, struggling to recall precisely where every item had been placed when last she had used each drawer. As she methodically made her way from one drawer to the next, a resolute look of confirmation gradually came over her.

Yes, there could be no doubt. Someone definitely had been in her room! Everything had been carefully put back in order, but not until it had been ransacked first. Someone had been looking for something, and then tried to make the room look just as it had been.

Had it not been for the misplaced journal, Hilary would never have known!

Who could it have been? The thought plagued her, although the choices were extremely limited. The viscount had left the house hours ago, and she was with Ashley. That left only Logan, Allison, and Jo . . . or one of the maids, or Jake. No one seemed a very likely suspect. If they had wanted to read the journal, why hadn't they simply asked?

But no, she thought suddenly. If it had been the journal the interloper was seeking, then why had he left it? And why had the rest of the room been disturbed when the journal was clearly visible?

Whoever it was had clearly been after something else! What could it possibly be?

But even with the question, immediately Hilary knew the answer.

Of course . . . the missing pages! The ending to Lady Joanna's manuscript!

No doubt the intruder had glanced quickly through the journal itself first to see if she had been telling the truth about the ending. Then, not finding any substantive information there, he had laid it down and quickly gone through the remainder of the room, forgetting to replace the manuscript in the suitcase.

Suddenly for the first time came the question: How had her unwelcome guest known she would be gone from her room?

And in the same moment came the frightening thought that perhaps the culprit had merely waited, somewhere close by but out of sight, until an accomplice succeeded in getting her out of the way for twenty or thirty minutes! Perhaps with an invitation to tea!

So—perhaps those around her were not as transparent as they seemed!

Sitting down again, the journal still clutched in her hands, Hilary resolved anew to be on her guard.

Professor Ashley Jameson waited ten minutes after Hilary left the kitchen.

He rose slowly, cleaned up the few tea things, then exited himself. He moved quietly along the darkened corridors, came to the main staircase, which he ascended, being careful not to make a sound. But instead of continuing up to the third floor where his room was located, he paused and turned to his right. He passed stealthily through two long hallways, around a corner, and came finally to two large oak doors at the end of the hallway.

Here he paused, glancing both ways, then pulled out a large old-fashioned iron key. He inserted it into the lock and turned the latch. The door opened with only the hint of a creak, and Jameson walked inside.

It was pitch dark. He groped about carefully for several moments before his hands found the lamp he had been seeking, nearly knocking it over before his fingers were able to switch it on.

The light flooding the chamber revealed a spacious sitting room, decidedly distinct in its French provincial decor from the heavier, Elizabethan furnishings in the rest of the castle. In daytime hours the room must have been light and airy with abundant sunlight streaming in through the French doors that opened onto an outdoor veranda. But the damp, chilly atmosphere of the place indicated that it had probably not been opened up in months, perhaps years.

Well, he thought to himself, there may or may not be anything in *her* room—I will have to find that out later. He still had to look through the library more thoroughly, as well as in the other places Allison's mother would have been likely to frequent. But here possibly he would find something to at least point him in the right direction.

Whether Jameson realized the historical significance of the room he had just entered was doubtful. For he had just entered Lady Atlanta Duncan's own personal sitting room.

He walked directly to the French provincial desk situated near the French doors, sat down at the chair still there, and immediately went to work.

The next morning Hilary was late coming down for breakfast. When she arrived in the dining room she found it empty, although platters and covered bowls still sat on the sideboard. Ambling to them, she lifted a lid or two, but found the contents lukewarm and unappealing. Suddenly she wasn't very hungry anyway.

Trying to decide whether to have a cup of coffee at least, she turned to see the cook walk in.

"'Tis all cold by noo," she said in a slightly remonstrative tone. "But I can be warmin' it up for ye, dearie."

"Thank you, no. I don't think I'm going to have anything after all."

"'Tisna guid t' be goin' wi'oot yer breakfast, ye ken."

"I'll be fine. But where is everyone, Mrs. Gibson?"

"Here an' aboot. I heard talk o' a drive to toon later."

Opting to go without coffee, Hilary wandered out, just in time to see Logan walk by.

"Good morning, Hilary!" he said cheerfully. "Did you sleep well?"

"Yes, thank you. Once I got to sleep."

"Mice in the walls?" he asked with a laugh.

"Actually, more like persons unknown in the halls," she replied.

"Oh?"

"I think I had an uninvited visitor in my room last night."

"You think?"

"While I was gone from my room for a few minutes."

Logan grew grave. "I'm sorry to hear that." He paused, appearing deep in thought, then said, "Who else knows of this?"

"No one," Hilary replied. "I've seen no one since. I only just now came down." As she spoke, her journalistic instincts scrutinized Logan's eyes—after all, he was one of the persons who would have had a strong motive for unearthing the end of Joanna's journal.

"I'm on my way to the library, Hilary," he went on. "Won't you walk with me?"

She nodded, and they continued down the corridor. For some time neither spoke. Then at last Logan began.

"I've wanted to talk with you, Hilary," he said. "I realize the awkwardness of this situation, and there are times I repent of having twisted your arm to come. I worry that I may have done you an injustice."

"No harm has come to me yet," said Hilary lightly.

"Nevertheless, I feel bad that we—perhaps I should say *I*, for my wife is quite unlike herself these past few days—have been so lacking in hospitality and have left you more or less to fend for yourself. It has not been intentional, I assure you. But with Allison's sickness, which continues to grow worse and baffles the doctor, and with these other guests, not to mention ongoing business I have to tend to, I'm afraid I've just been rather swamped. I'm on my way to return a call to London right now."

"I understand. I know you're busy."

"In any case, please accept my apologies. It was my hope we could get to know one another better. Unfortunately that has not exactly happened. And there is of course the uncertainty of it all as well, which I had hoped my inquiries would have cleared up long before now. But alas, that has not happened either, and we appear no further toward a solution than before."

"I take it then that *you* did not send someone to my room?" Hilary said with a laugh, intended to sound humorous while still getting at the truth.

"That's a good one!" chuckled Logan. "But if I'd have wanted to find something, I'd have just come and asked you."

She knew he was right. That is exactly what a straightforward man like Logan Macintyre would have done. How could she doubt him?

"How is Mrs. Macintyre?" asked Hilary in a new vein.

"Not good," he replied with a serious expression. "She is up today, and even talking about driving to town with Jo. But she is pale, and I am worried. I can't imagine what is the problem."

"Her ankle?"

"No, no, it can't be something that small. She's had little injuries of that kind before, but nothing to knock her so out of sorts."

From what Hilary had read in the journal, Allison Macintyre did not seem the sickly sort. On the contrary, she came across as having inherited a full dose of the family spunk. Perhaps the fall had taken more of a toll than anyone including her husband—realized.

"Well, here we are at the library," said Logan, "if you'll excuse me. But we'll talk again . . . and soon. I promise to make your stay here more pleasant than it has been. In the meantime, please make yourself at home. Go anywhere you like. Not only do I want to know you better, I want you to know Stonewycke."

With that he disappeared inside.

Hilary continued on, wandering aimlessly through the deserted corridors. It came into her mind to have a look inside the portrait gallery past which they had gone the other day. She stopped, tried to get her bearings, and then set off in the direction of what she hoped was the East Wing. That should get me close to the gallery, she thought. In fact, maybe I'll have a peek at some of the mysteriously unused rooms down in that section, too. Everywhere she turned this ancient castle held fascination!

Before she reached the East Wing or the gallery, however, Hilary found herself standing before the door of the heirloom room. She opened the door and walked inside.

The first sensation to come over her was the intense quiet, not unlike the awesome hush of a great cathedral. There was a sense in which she was indeed walking upon hallowed ground, if not spiritually then in the familial sense. Many of the same feelings she had had during her previous brief visit welled up within her, though now Hilary was alone and had the chance to let the feelings in her heart have fuller sway.

Slowly she walked about, retracing her steps from before, now giving her full attention to each item she saw—clan tartans, young Maggie's seventeenth birthday dress, ancient swords and *skean-dhus* and firearms, and a lovely music box given as a birthday gift to Maggie by her father.

Immediately the music box arrested Hilary's attention, drawing her eyes to the mantel where it sat. In another moment the tiny wooden box, so ornately carved, the gift from James Duncan to his daughter Maggie, was resting delicately in the palm of Hilary's hand. This same box had traveled to America with that young Maggie when she had been forced to flee from her father's wrath.

Carefully Hilary lifted the lid. Instantly the strains of Brahms' Lullaby, faint yet clear and bell-like, undiminished with age, filled the air of the large room.

Hilary stood as one enraptured by the sound, transported in her mind back through time, as if she were that little girl one hundred and twenty years earlier. When the tune ran down, she wound up the box again and listened once more to the familiar melody.

Suddenly a voice broke the stillness of the huge room. "Oh, there you are!"

But Hilary did not hear the words. Jolted so unexpectedly from her reverie, her startled jump sent the music box out of her hand. The next moment she was on her knees beside the poor thing, which had landed with a discordant crack, and was examining its broken leg.

Behind her Allison rushed forward.

"Dear Lord!" she cried as she lurched forward and sank to her knees also. A strangled sob broke from her lips. "What have you done!" she cried. Tears streamed from her eyes, and her shoulders shook with anguished sobs.

"I'm so sorry," said a stunned Hilary, shattered by the sudden disaster. Glancing about, she found the broken piece, picked it up, and as if in mute appeal for mercy for her heinous deed, held it out to Allison.

Allison snatched it from her hand as if she were rescuing it from the clutches of the Evil One himself.

"You!" she shrieked. "You broke it! You destroyed my music box!" Her voice trembled with pent-up passions as if they had been simmering for days. "It's your fault! You destroyed everything! Why did you have to come here! Everything was all right until you came!"

"Allison, stop!" The voice was Logan's, coming from the doorway where he had just entered. He rushed inside, followed by Ashley.

Both women looked up at the intrusion of the sharp voice.

Logan rushed forward and laid a strong arm around Allison's shoulders, gently urging her up. "Allison," he said softly, "what's come over you?" Though filled with beseeching, his voice was gentle.

"She's ruined everything, Logan!" sobbed Allison. "We were happy before!"

"I'm so sorry," was all Hilary could manage to say through her own tears of stinging pain. Then she turned and fled the room.

Feeling utterly helpless for one of the few times in his life, Logan glanced back toward Ashley as one paralyzed.

"You stay here," said Jameson in response to Logan's unspoken entreaty. "I'll see what I can do." With that he turned and followed Hilary from the room.

Turning back to his distraught wife, Logan sought to comfort her. She was always so strong and in possession of herself, he hardly knew what to say. He had never seen her like this.

"Ali, dear," he said softly.

"Oh, look at it, Logan! Look at it . . . after all these years. Maggie will never forgive me! I tried so hard to keep it safe . . ."

"Ali," said Logan, "it can be fixed." He lifted the lid. Much to his relief, the tune played just as before. "With a bit of glue, this leg will mend like new. No one will ever be able to tell."

"No, no! It will never be like it was!"

Logan realized the broken music box was only part of the problem. But what *was* the problem? What was happening to his Allison?

Tenderly he brushed back the tears on her cheeks. "Ali," he said, almost whispering, "it's all going to come out right in the end . . . and very soon. We must just be patient a while longer; then it will be just the way it used to be—"

"No, Logan! It will never be the same again! I know it!" But now her voice sounded faint and hollow, losing its fight. "I'm afraid, Logan . . . afraid . . ."

She collapsed, weeping like a child, into his arms. In another moment she was asleep—whether from exhaustion or a fainting spell, he could not tell.

He lifted her like a baby and left the room. When he had deposited her safely into bed, he hastened to the phone to call Dr. Connally. He knew what would be the doctor's reply, but he couldn't stand by and do nothing.

As he went, Logan thought to himself how pale Allison's face was, and how cold her body felt.

41 / Duplicity or Veracity? _____

Ashley found Hilary in her room. She had hoisted her suitcase and another bag onto the bed and was frantically throwing her belongings into them.

"You're leaving?" he said quietly.

She spun around, her eyes filled with mingled anger, hurt, and confusion. "What else can I do?" she replied heatedly. "I don't belong here— I never did!"

"I didn't take you for a quitter."

"What do you know?" she retorted sharply. "You've only just met me."

"I suppose it is presumptuous of me to say such a thing, though I still believe it's true."

"Well, it doesn't matter anyway. I've given it plenty of time, and things are only getting worse." She sighed, her anger easing slightly. "They already have the daughter they wanted."

"Do you really believe that?"

The question took Hilary off guard. It was not the question itself, but rather the tone in which he had spoken it. There was a probing hardness to his voice, with just enough emphasis on the *really* to make Hilary wonder about its intent.

She regarded him seriously for a moment. Suddenly it dawned on her that she didn't know his intent. She continued to fix her gaze upon him, her mind ruminating on all the possibilities that had occurred to her during the past few days, but arriving at an endless string of questions in the end. The outburst that finally escaped her lips, however, was altogether unexpected.

"What business is it of yours, anyway?" she asked.

He faltered, momentarily taken aback, then groped for words with which to answer. "Perhaps none," he said, "but I care about—"

"Truth?" she shot back. "Is that what you were going to say? Ha! Truth indeed!"

"I meant those things I said before."

"Oh yes! Truth and integrity . . . ordering our lives consistently by those principles—bosh! And you're telling me that's what life means to you?"

"I never said I lived truth perfectly," he replied calmly. "But that takes nothing away from the fact that such is my desire, and such I attempt to do to the extent I am capable."

"I see! And is that why you always seem to appear just at the most appropriate times, to start grilling me with questions?"

The interview was going much differently than he had planned. He took a deep breath, considering the best way to respond, but Hilary hardly gave him the chance.

"And while we're on the subject, Mr. Ashley Jameson, supposed Oxford professor, I would just like to know what you're doing here in the first place."

"I made no secret of that. I was here to meet—"

"To meet Ian! Of course! Who just happened—conveniently and coincidentally—not to be here and to be off where he couldn't be reached."

"I'm sure if Mr. Macintyre had any doubts, he could easily—"

"But there are no doubts about you, are there? Mr. smooth, polished, studious, soft-spoken Jameson whom everyone adores! Well, I would still like to know how you managed to appear just at the right moment! And while we're on the subject of your mysterious presence, what were you doing snooping around so late last night, wandering around the place? I suppose you just *happened* to want some tea, and then just *happened* upon my room!"

"It was all just as I said, Hilary," replied Jameson, his voice still calm, but a deep look of concern filling his eyes. "Yes, I did simply want a cup of tea, and thought I would enjoy your company, notwithstanding the hour."

As he spoke, he scrutinized her face, as if inwardly assessing what he saw, weighing the fluid features of her emotion-filled eyes, the flare of her nostrils, the slight lift of her right eyebrow, the curvature of her forehead, the angle of her chin, the intonation of her words—all given form and a thousand nuances of subtle expression by the shape and ever-changing movements of her mouth and lips.

Just as he spoke the words "notwithstanding the hour," a sudden look as of revelation filled his countenance. With an inward gasp, he caught his breath.

Hilary, however, remained too caught up in her own tirade of frustrated emotions that she saw none of what passed across his face.

"How convenient! How convenient!" she fired back. "Get me out of the room and down to the kitchen so someone else could search my room undisturbed!"

"What?" he said.

"I suppose you knew nothing of it!"

"Nothing, I assure you."

"No doubt, no doubt! The fact remains that *someone* ransacked my room while we were in the kitchen last night!"

A grave expression came over Ashley's face. Things were taking a serious turn. He hoped he could patch it up with Hilary later, but right now there was one more piece of confirming testimony he needed—even if it would be equally subjective to the one he'd just received. And then, once he was sure in his own mind, it was time to let his accessory in this little game fully in on what he had discovered.

"I truly am dismayed to learn of this, Hilary," he said. "But for right now, I think it best I leave you alone. It would be fruitless of me to say anything further."

He turned and left the room. Hilary watched him go, then turned back inside, her emotions calming in the wake of her outburst. She glanced over her things strewn about on the bed, then sat down and sighed. *What should I do?* she wondered. *What should I do?*

Thirty minutes later Hilary still sat on the edge of the bed, still pondering her fate, though by now beginning to recriminate with herself for the vicious verbal thrashing she had given Ashley. After all, he had not really been the object of her frustrations at all; rather, she had been angry at herself over the accident with the music box . . . angry with herself for coming here in the first place. Something down inside her had responded favorably to Ashley from the very beginning. The fact remained that she believed him when he spoke to her of truth. His bearing, the tone of his voice, told her that he was speaking from his heart. And Hilary prided herself on being able to read people accurately. She had not risen in the journalistic ranks by being a pushover. She knew people. She was no easy mark for a huckster. In fact, she possessed not a little of the audacity of a street con herself, and had more than once plied such trait to her advantage.

Everything in her experience with people told her that this Ashley Jameson was either everything he claimed, consistent on the surface as he appeared to be, indeed, probably just as he said, a lover and seeker after truth—he was either all this, or else he was the most bold-faced, skillful liar she had ever met, a hypocrite beyond compare, who was able to look deep into her eyes and hoodwink her utterly.

The thought almost frightened her. But there were no other options. He must be one or the other.

She rose and walked slowly away from the bed, chiding herself for being so hard on him. He was just trying to help, she thought.

As she approached the window, Hilary looked out on the lawn below. She could hardly believe her eyes!

There were Ashley and Jo, walking slowly toward the back of the castle, close together, lost in what to all appearances was a lively discussion!

He is a liar, after all! she cried, half audibly. How could she have been so easily duped? *Why, he's nothing but a spy for Jo!*

Hilary spun around and ran from the room. She flew along the hall, down the stairs, and out the front door. Before she realized where she was going, she had left the gates of Stonewycke behind her and was walking hurriedly along the estate driveway toward town.

As Hilary came around one of the sharp bends in the driveway, paying little attention to her surroundings, in front of her she spied Emil von Burchardt walking briskly toward her.

"Ah, Hilary!" he exclaimed in the greeting she had already come to associate with him. "A pleasant morning to you!"

She smiled, forcing down her vexation with Ashley, and approached him. "This is a pleasant surprise," the viscount went on. "As a matter of fact, I was just on my way to the castle for a visit, hoping to see you, I might add, but I did not anticipate so immediate a granting of my wishes as to meet you while I was still on the approach!"

"I was out for a walk," said Hilary lamely.

As von Burchardt reached her, they stopped and shook hands. His look took her face in for a moment or two, then spread over with concern.

"But you look upset, Hilary! Or perhaps just flushed from the walk? May I be so bold as to ask if there is anything wrong?"

"No, nothing! Thank you," answered Hilary, rather too quickly. "Yes, I'm sure it is the morning exercise. I've been walking fast," she added, puffing as if in confirmation of her words.

"I can see that," said the viscount, still seeming to peruse her. "Well, would you care to accompany me back to the castle?"

Hesitating only momentarily, Hilary replied, "Why, yes, thank you," turning as if in resolution. She took his arm and began walking back the way she had come, as if secretly hoping to encounter Ashley that she might make a show of her own independence and disinterest in him.

Beaming with his good fortune, von Burchardt strutted forward with the aplomb of a peacock in full feather, crowing to himself for the fine piece of work he had done in winning over this lovely chickadee. In less than five minutes they passed the gates and entered the courtyard, chatting amiably. Hilary's reactions were perhaps a bit too animated and her laugh a little too loud to suit von Burchardt's half of the dialogue. When she saw that they were alone on the grounds, however, her tone and exhilaration abated slightly.

"So tell me, Hilary," said von Burchardt, "have there been any changes in your fortunes?"

"Only that I am planning to leave soon."

"Oh?"

"There have been no changes, so I think it's time for me to beat a retreat. It was probably a mistake to come in the first place."

"Hmm. Now that is an interesting turn," said the viscount, his matter-of-fact tone revealing far less interest in the disclosure than he was feeling inside. "Then perhaps I might interest you in that cruise aboard my yacht, after all."

"What, Emil? No attempt to talk me into staying?" rejoined Hilary, cocking one eyebrow as she glanced in his direction.

"Why should I do that?" he replied jovially. "It's your life, not mine."

"I suppose I expected it because that's all I get from the other two men around here—exhortations to stay till it is resolved."

"You mean Mr. Macintyre and that Jameson fellow?"

Hilary nodded.

"Ah well, as I say, it's your life to do with what you will. It seems to me that everything would be rather neatly tied up, so to speak. You and I could sail off for a couple weeks. I could deliver you back to London. And we could leave these people here with their problems. What do you say?"

"I don't know. I didn't say I had made up my mind yet."

"A little of the fight left in you?" he asked, throwing her a glance meant to be merry but full of meaning. "Protect your interests, eh?"

"I don't think it's that. I just have to be sure, that's all."

By this time they had walked around by the side of the castle. Hilary had been paying little attention to the direction their steps took, and all at once they found themselves abreast of a small iron gate toward the distant back of the house. Through its bars they could see a little-used garden that neither had visited before. Hilary paused before the gate, then suddenly reached up into a broken piece of rock in the stone wall to which it was fastened, where, in a crevice, her fingers clutched an old and rusted key.

"I see you have become quite familiar with the estate," commented von Burchardt.

"No," said Hilary in a bemused tone. "Actually, I have never been to this place."

"Quite a lucky stroke then, finding the key."

Hilary glanced down at the key in her hand, just as an unsought image flickered through her brain, lasting but an instant:

Standing before a gate, which appeared to be this very one, a little girl grasped the hand of an older woman. Then the child wriggled free from the larger hand which held hers, and began jumping up and down in front of the iron bars, reaching up toward the broken stone in the wall. But even her outstretched arm fell far short.

"Grandma! Grandma! Key! See garden!"

As quickly as it had come the phantasm faded. The faces of the two figures had been turned away from her, and Hilary had been able to discern no details of either person or dress or mannerism. Yet something within her shivered with a recognition of the older woman which she felt rather than saw. The apparition had been but a fleeting snatch of something whose purpose or origin she could neither ascertain nor guess. She turned her perplexed countenance toward von Burchardt.

"I must have read about it in Lady Joanna's journal," she said, then jammed the key into the lock. "Shall we go in and have a look about?" As she spoke Hilary's attention was fixed on the insertion of the key into the old gate. She therefore did not see her companion's reaction to her momentarily lapse. He had read more of the truth in her eyes than she would have guessed possible. For the Viscount von Burchardt—like Hilary herself—was no mean judge of character, and was especially well-versed in reading between the lines of the feminine psyche in all its mystifying complexity. When he saw what passed through Hilary's eyes, over von Burchardt's face spread a look of resolve. He knew the time to act was drawing near.

Hilary found the lock troublesome and stubborn, and it took several attempts to persuade its ancient workings to give way. When it finally surrendered, von Burchardt opened the gate, and then followed as Hilary entered. Both were silent for some time in the hushed atmosphere of overgrown willows and birch trees, under whose wings spread out in all directions lawns and hedges, and bordered flowerbeds.

In the very center stood a gnarled and hoary birch—its great, twisted roots scoring the earth for many feet in all directions, making the ground uneven and rough in its vicinity. In the winter, with its branches barren, the tree took on a mournful air; but Hilary tried to imagine it in summer, covered with greenery, presiding over the lush vegetation on the ground beneath it, with flowers gracing the beds rather than black earth. Even in the garden's present desolation, Hilary could sense that the place was pregnant with unseen life.

Had there indeed been mention of such a garden in the journal? There must have been, she thought, for she felt she already knew the spot so well, though something inside told her it had once been even more unkempt than it was now. How mysterious and wild it must have once been! she thought.

At each end of the enclosed space sat two stone benches, heavily weathered, one displaying a prominent crack. Hilary walked slowly to the far end, the viscount following her silently, and sat down. He joined her.

"It's like entering another world," he said.

"I think that if I were a young girl growing up here," said Hilary dreamily, "I would come and sit on this bench every day and gaze at that grand birch, maybe even try to climb it, and dream to my heart's content."

"What would you dream?" asked von Burchardt.

"I don't know. When I was a girl I used to fantasize being swept away by dashing young men and sailing away to exotic lands." She smiled, suddenly feeling silly. "I was quite the romantic in my youth."

He laughed. "And now, look at you!" he said. "Here you sit with—well, as to being dashing, I will make no comment! But as to the exotic lands, you have only to say the word, and my vessel waits to spirit you away!"

Now it was Hilary's turn to laugh. "*In my youth*, I dreamed of such things."

"But no more?"

"Such fancies hardly befit a hard-headed magazine editor."

"Come now, Hilary. You do not seem the hard-headed type."

"You've not seen me crack the whip the day before deadline! But you might be right. Perhaps I am still a romantic after all, though I hope by this time in my life it's tempered with some good sense. And how about you, Emil? You strike me as too much a man of the world to have escaped the clutches of some ravishing beauty this long."

"We marry late in my family—something to do with being fully apprised of the field."

"And that's what your travels are for, to scout the 'field' of eligible heiresses throughout Europe?"

"I hate to balk at family tradition," he replied with a slight laugh.

"Well, you seem to have landed on your feet here," said Hilary. "You have two of us to choose from!"

He laughed, nervously, she thought.

For a time neither spoke, a palatable silence enveloping them as the peculiar magic of the garden weaved its enchantment. Here one could escape the modern age without so much as leaving the grounds. Emil had commented on its being like another world—it was that, and so much more. Everywhere her gaze fell Hilary sensed history overflowing her, in much the same way she had when reading the journal—personal history, real history . . . the reality of being in a place that was part of her very being . . . her roots—like the roots of the huge tree in front of her.

Again, as she reflected within the quietness of her own soul, von Burchardt quietly scrutinized her, and again read more of what was passing through her spirit than he let on. *It is indeed time to act*, he thought. *The moment has come.*

"Come," he said, rising. "Let me take you to town. The yacht is ready to sail, the weather is favorable. If you won't agree to let me take you back to London, then at least join me for the afternoon."

Hilary remained seated. "I hate to leave this place," she said at length, as if she had not heard him. "I feel as if I am under a spell."

"Yes . . . I feel it too. But come," he added, reaching out and taking her hand, "I won't take no for an answer."

Hilary exhaled a long breath and looked up at him with one last lingering hesitation in her eyes. Then she recalled what had driven her out-of-doors in the first place—the incident with Allison and her irritation with Ashley's chicanery. At least Emil was what he seemed, she thought—no more nor no less.

"All right," she said finally. "You're on."

It was about two in the afternoon when Ashley entered the sitting room. "Has anyone seen Miss Edwards?" he asked. "I must see her."

The only ones present were Jo and Logan. Jo did not look up, and Logan replied that he had only a moment earlier come in from outside and had not seen her. He asked if he had tried her room, to which Jameson nodded in the affirmative, adding that he had been throughout the house and no one had seen a trace of her.

"Has Herr von Burchardt called today?" he asked, divining a measure of what he feared might be the truth.

Logan had not seen him. Jo said she thought he had planned on dropping by today, but she had seen nothing of him yet.

Ashley thanked them and left the room.

Within a few minutes, before he had had time to reason out his actions logically, he was sitting behind the wheel of his car and driving toward Port Strathy. Something told him danger was afoot threatening to thwart his mission.

Aboard the viscount's yacht, everything had been made ready to cast off.

Von Burchardt had retrieved his crew from the Bluster N' Blow and from Hamilton's. They had gone through the preliminaries of a thorough voyage, even though the Captain, as they called the viscount, repeatedly stressed the fact that they were only going out for an hour or two, a little shake-down cruise. While they made their preparations, von Burchardt gave Hilary a more extensive tour of the vessel. They were both standing before the controls at the bridge, waiting for the first mate to cast off, the engine idling in readiness, when Jameson's car pulled up at the dock and Ashley jumped out. He quickly ran out on the platform.

"Ahoy," he called up. "Miss Edwards . . . I must see you!"

Still irked from the events of the morning, Hilary looked down, debated within herself whether to ignore him or accede to his request, then turned to the viscount and said, "I'll only be a minute. Don't leave without me."

"I wouldn't think of it. Just make sure he doesn't twist your arm for an invitation and wind up joining us."

Hilary laughed. "Don't worry! I wouldn't think of it! If he goes, I stay!"

She left von Burchardt standing at the helm, carefully climbed down the steep stairway to the main deck, crossed it, then addressed Ashley from where she stood.

"Yes, what is it?"

"Please, I must speak with you."

"So, here I am. Talk."

"I mean down here . . . privately."

"What is it that's so important that it can't wait till we return? I'll be back to the house in a couple of hours."

"Are you sure of that?"

"We're only going out for an hour, then back in."

"And you're certain the viscount doesn't have anything more extensive in mind?"

"Don't be ridiculous! At least *he* plays it straight with me."

"I won't bother to ask you what you mean by that. The point remains that I simply must see you in private immediately."

"Well, if you can't say what you have to say to me here and now, then it will have to wait."

She turned and began walking away.

"Miss Edwards . . . *Hilary!*" he called after her in an imperative voice. "You are wanted at the house. I'm afraid it can't wait two hours!"

She stopped and turned to face him.

"Wanted? For what?"

"That I cannot tell you. But you simply must come with me."

"Who wants me?"

"Mr. . . . Mr. Macintyre," replied Ashley, his voice shaky.

Convinced at last, Hilary hesitated only another moment, then said, "I'll go tell Emil and be right down."

"Please, Miss Edwards," Ashley enjoined, "say nothing to him. He must not come up to the castle . . . not today."

"Why not?" asked Hilary, her irritation returning.

"Again, I'm afraid I cannot tell you. But I implore you to climb down and come with me at once."

Hilary sighed, obviously not pleased with this turn of events, and even more displeased with Ashley himself, but then waving up at the viscount where he stood watching the proceedings, called out, "I'll be back as soon as I can," and then walked down the short gangway to where Ashley stood on the dock. Quickly he began whisking her away, to Hilary's extreme annoyance, before von Burchardt, who had immediately run off the bridge and down to the deck to protest this interruption to his plans, could get close enough to make his displeasure known.

Ashley opened the passenger door of his car for Hilary, but did not wait to close it himself. While she was still climbing in, he ran around to his own side, watching out of the corner of his eye as von Burchardt followed down the gangway and onto the dock after them. Scarcely had Hilary pulled her door shut before his BMW had spun around and was heading past the Bluster 'N Blow, leaving a red-faced Burchardt standing in a cloud of dust silently cursing the professor's untimely interference.

Inside the automobile the tension between the abductor and abductee was thick enough to cut. Not until Ashley had crested the hill overlooking Port Strathy to one side and Ramsey Head on the other did he abate his speed. Then he pulled off to the side of the road and stopped the car.

"What is this?" asked Hilary in a piqued tone.

"I'm afraid we have to have a little talk before we get back to Stonewycke."

"What about the urgent message Mr. Macintyre has for me?" she asked, growing more exasperated with this man by the moment.

"That's what we have to talk about. I'm afraid Mr. Macintyre didn't send me after you at all."

"What! You lied to me!"

"I apologize. I'm afraid I've never been too good at thinking on my feet. I had to do something to get you away from there, and before I realized what I was doing, out it had come."

"How dare you!" snapped Hilary, reaching for the door latch.

Ashley reached across and held her hand firm.

"I simply must not allow you to go back down there."

"What right do you have—after all that talk about truth? It's all just hogwash to you! I can't believe a word you say!"

"I'm sorry you feel that way. I hope someday I can show you otherwise."

"Let me out of here! I will not sit here and listen to you insult my intelligence, or the intentions of my friend Emil. Either you let me go my own way or I'll—"

"I will not let you go back to that man," said Ashley. "I'm sorry if you think me cruel or unreasonable. But I have my reasons."

He started the car before she had a chance to protest further, ground it into gear, and sped up the road. In the passenger seat, Hilary sat with face red, silent but inwardly fuming. She would get out of this idiotic place the instant she was packed, she said to herself, and never set foot here again!

When they reached the turnoff into the Stonewycke estate, Ashley accelerated right past. He didn't know exactly what he was going to do, but of one thing he was sure: if Hilary had the chance, in her present mood she would run right back to von Burchardt.

"Where are we going?" she asked with venom in her tone.

"I'm not sure," replied Ashley. "Somewhere you can cool off . . . and where I can think."

Thirty minutes later they drove into Fraserburgh. Though the drive of less than twenty miles had been silent and uneventful, by the time they reached the town of some ten thousand, Hilary had calmed considerably, and Ashley thought he might get her safely back to the estate without risk of her running away. He drove to the middle of the small village and stopped.

"Why don't you have a bit of a look about?" he said, trying to sound friendly. "I've got to make a phone call. There are several rather nice shops within walking distance."

"How do you know? I thought you had never been to this part of the country."

"I'm very well read," he said, a small mischievous smile playing at the corners of his mouth.

She said nothing in reply, merely grunted and folded her arms across her chest.

"You may as well make the most of this," he prompted. "It may not be Carnaby Street or Piccadilly, but who knows, you might find something you like."

Hilary opened the door with an exaggerated *humph* and stepped out.

"I'll meet you back here in an hour," said Ashley. His sentence was punctuated with a forceful closing of Hilary's door as she walked off in the opposite direction without another word.

The smile Ashley had been restraining with great difficulty now escaped and spread across his lips. "Well, Professor," he muttered to himself, "you've got yourself in the middle of a fine pickle now!" But the hour by herself should help settle her ruffled emotions and injured pride, he hoped—not to mention giving him time to consider how best to handle this delicate situation once they arrived back at Stonewycke. After all, he had abducted the Macintyre's guest for no more reason than that his instinct told him trouble was brewing. If an issue were made of it, he could find himself hard pressed to explain his behavior.

An hour later he was parked back alongside the same curb when Hilary walked up the sidewalk toward him, carrying a package. He jumped out and ran around to open the door for her, which attention she accepted with a nod as she climbed into the passenger seat.

"I see you found something, after all," said Ashley cheerfully as they drove away.

"Nothing much," said Hilary with a deadpan expression. "A dress."

"Well, let's have a look."

"What interest could you possibly have in a woman's dress?"

"Actually the fashion industry is quite fascinating. Believe it or not, I've even been to a fashion show."

The incongruity of a stuffy university professor sitting watching a parade of models sauntering by displaying the latest in outlandish French design caught Hilary so off guard that a smile escaped her lips.

"You, Professor?"

"Are you shocked?"

"Let's just say . . . amused."

"So . . . do I see your new purchase or not?"

"All right, you win," consented Hilary with a sigh, opening the box that sat on her lap. "I'm still angry, you understand. What you did was inexcusable, and you have not heard the end of it. But I'll show you the dress."

"A truce, then?"

"For the time being."

Jameson smiled to himself. *The detour to Fraserburgh has been a capital stroke*, he thought to himself, *even if I didn't exactly plan it!*

Hilary pulled out the dress and held it up as best she could, unable to avoid the fact that buying it *had* made her feel better. The man was insufferable, but that was no reason she should not make the best of the situation.

She had never worn this particular color before—a subdued and subtle mixture of purple, gray, violet, and pink. She had always leaned more toward muted, earthy tones. But the moment she had held this dress—whose label identified the shade as "Heather in Bloom"—in front of her and gazed into the mirror, she had been surprised by the effect.

"It's beautiful!" said Ashley, glancing over from his driver's seat. "Positively stunning!"

"The clerk kept trying to push off a cream-colored frock on me," said Hilary, inwardly pleased with his enthusiastic response, yet trying to hide it. "But I loved this immediately."

"I can see why. You will look smashing in it . . . just lovely."

"Thank you," replied Hilary with a half smile. "But don't think you can win me back over with compliments. I have not forgotten what you did."

"I was not trying to win you over. I *do* like the dress."

"Fine. Just so long as you know I'm still angry with you."

"Understood." *This young woman is really too much*, thought Ashley with an inward chuckle. *I'll never be able to live this down!*

But if Ashley's *intended* indiscretions were not enough, he soon found himself facing a most unintended one. About three-fourths of the way back, when they could not have been more than five or six miles from the estate, all at once without warning the BMW's engine began to cough and sputter. Ashley slowed and down-shifted but the automobile did not respond. His gaze fell on the instrument panel and he immediately pulled off the road.

"What's wrong?" asked Hilary.

"I am afraid," he said with a forlorn sigh, "that I have committed the classic blunder."

"What do you mean?"

"It appears we are out of petrol." He attempted a light chuckle, but his humor fell on deaf ears.

"I really can't believe this," said Hilary. "I should think a man of your intelligence would plan his kidnappings more carefully."

"I will be sure to do so in the future. But this is my first time."

"So . . . what do you propose we do?"

"I see nothing for it but to get out and walk."

"Walk? It's freezing out there!"

"It will soon be freezing in here, too. The distance can't be too far. We can make it. If you'd prefer, I'll go myself, and send someone back for you."

"Never mind." Hilary opened her door and stepped out. "How do I know you wouldn't just leave me here to rot?" She started on her way down the road.

Ashley climbed out, locked the car with Hilary's purchase inside, then jogged to catch up with her.

"I thought we had a truce," he said somewhat breathlessly when he reached her.

"I changed my mind." She hurried on ahead of him.

I am a patient man, thought Ashley to himself, hurrying to keep pace with the insufferable woman. But he was no villain, and had just about had his fill of these barbs.

They walked on in silence. The cold and the wet snow began to make its mark felt on Hilary's pace after three or four minutes, and soon they were once more walking side by side. Another ten minutes passed in silence as frosty as the ground upon which they were walking. They had covered perhaps a mile when finally Ashley spoke.

"I am terribly sorry about all this," he said. "I suppose half of what you think about me is justified. But what I did today, no matter how it appears, was for your own good."

"You deprived me of a delightful sail. I am freezing. I have frostbite in my toes, and my shoes are ruined. And you say all this is for my own good!"

"I fear that your delightful sail, as you call it, would have proved something a little more ill-fated. I do not trust that man's—"

"What right do you have to pass judgment on another?" she said, stopping and focusing full on him. In her eyes was the look he had expected. "Moreover," she added, "who are you to dictate my preferences?"

"So you think von Burchardt had only sailing in mind?"

Hilary chuckled. "You were attempting to protect my honor?"

"You are a grown woman," Ashley replied, "quite capable of doing that for yourself. I simply thought—"

His words were cut short by the loud roar of a vehicle approaching behind them. As they turned they saw a truck, possibly of late forties vintage, braking to a stop. Its battered body showed every rough, backroad mile indicated on its odometer.

"Mr. Mackenzie!" Hilary exclaimed as the driver stepped out. "You are heaven sent!"

"What a coincidence meetin' up wi' the twa o' ye oot here," he said.

"I'm afraid we ran out of gas back there," said Ashley, extending his hand. "I'm Ashley Jameson."

"Karl Mackenzie, at yer service. So 'twas yer fine new car I seen back aboot a mile?"

"I'm afraid so."

"Weel, ye'll be needin' a ride, so aboard wi' ye."

"It seems I am always cold and wet when we meet," said Hilary, climbing in.

Mackenzie laughed. "Nice excuse to have ye for a cup o' hot tea." He threw the truck into gear and the ancient vehicle lurched into dubious motion. Neither Ashley nor Hilary, however, were in any mood to disparage their good fortune. "The wifie will be so pleased to see ye again, mem! Ye will join us for a bit tea before we rescue yer auto?"

"We'd be honored, Mr. Mackenzie," replied Ashley. "You're most kind."

Thirty minutes later the two wayward travelers found themselves seated on the floor of the Mackenzie's cozy cottage, bare feet propped up toward the fire to gain the best advantage of the warm hearth. Struggle as she might, under the circumstances Hilary found animosities difficult to maintain, notwithstanding what Ashley had done. Frances Mackenzie's broad, friendly smile and hugging welcome as if Hilary had been her own daughter did not help Hilary to nurse her grudges either. Soon pleasant conversation began to flow among them, covering a wide range of topics, though conspicuously avoiding any mention of the house on the hill.

"What do you grow here, Mr. Mackenzie?" asked Ashley.

"Oh, whatever I can make my wee plot o' land produce. Potatoes, wheat, oats, sometimes barley."

"And you raise livestock?"

"Na that much. A half-dozen nowt—"

"Nowt?"

"Cattle. An' two or three pigs, a handful o' chicks. My byre's nae so big."

Ashley questioned his host further, and before long they were deep in a discussion of spring planting, the fickle Scottish weather, and the delights and hazards of fishing off the north coast. Little Kerrie hovered about, awaiting every pause in the dialogue to question this new representative of the wide world about her favorite crown Prince.

"I think yer shoes an' socks'll be aboot dry when I return," said Mr. Mackenzie at length, standing up. "I'll jist be off to town to fetch ye some petrol."

"I'll join you," said Ashley, jumping up off the floor.

"Ye'll do nae such thing, yoong man," expostulated Mrs. Mackenzie. "Ye'll sit right where ye are an' drink another cup o' tea."

"I'm well able to handle a bit cannie o' gas," said Mackenzie. "So ye jist heed my woman, an' I'll be back 'round shortly."

He left the room and Mrs. Mackenzie walked back into the kitchen to set more tea brewing, Kerrie following her. Ashley and Hilary were left alone.

Ashley sighed. "They're marvelous folks," he said. "I can't help thinking that this is what it's really all about."

"What what's about?" said Hilary in a relaxed tone, her previous anger by now forgotten.

"Life, I suppose." He paused, reflecting on his words before continuing. "I don't know. You meet so many people. And the pace of the twentieth century in places like London, even Oxford to a degree, is so fast, so impersonal. Everyone caught up in his own life without much regard for what's going on about him. But then you step into a place like this . . ." He stared at the bright tongues of flame licking at the slabs of dried peat in the hearth. "My first reaction is that it's from another world, another century. Yet . . . I cannot help but think that *this* is the *real* world and all that—out there—is the illusion. I have my Greeks, and I love them. I have learned a great deal about character from them. Yet the study of Classical Greece, the bankers and investments of London, the political decisions around which the world revolves—none of it could get along, none of it would have meaning without people like the Mackenzies."

"Lady Joanna was constantly saying that very thing in her journal," said Hilary. "The people are what makes the land what it is. They are its

life, she said. Had I not met the Mackenzies, I probably would not understand what she meant. I still don't fully know what she meant, because she
spent so much longer here than I have. But perhaps I will learn."

"The place is growing on you?"

"How can it not? Stonewycke is no longer just an estate, a castle. Now
everything about the whole region has more meaning—the Mackenzies,
Mr. Davies over at the inn, even this weather, the wild sea, the desolate
moors. I am beginning to feel a little of what Lady Joanna wrote about, I
suppose." She paused. "I will be sad to leave," she added.

"And you think it will come to that?"

"Someone will have to go."

A brief silence fell before Ashley replied.

"I sense, Hilary, that you belong here," he said. His voice was deeply
earnest.

"A city girl like me? I wonder."

"It has nothing to do with that," said Ashley. "It has to do with something deeper. The Macintyres, Logan and Allison, probably have to live in
London. Perhaps they prefer it, I don't know. Yet they *belong* here no less.
They are an intrinsic part of it, and it is part of them. I'm sure it's bound
up in birth and ancestry. But it's more than that too. They *love* Stonewycke
and its people and all it represents. I think what I sense is that same deep
love growing within you."

Hilary grew restive and cast Ashley a long serious glance.

He was making it very difficult to maintain her anger, justified as she
still considered it. Was all this just his clever way of soothing over his true
intent? She couldn't tell. His words fell pleasantly on her ear. Yet she didn't
really know what he intended. Perhaps she would have to watch herself
more carefully—around both von Burchardt and Jameson.

They arrived back at the estate about an hour later. Hilary spent the
rest of the afternoon in her room.

Dinner that evening was rather a tense affair. Hilary sat in relative
silence. Though her ire against Ashley had subsided, she was still confused
and wary. Ashley seemed more introspective than usual and said little.
Allison was present, looking pale and worn. She ate hardly at all, and did
her best to make an apology to Hilary over her outburst in the heirloom
room. But her words seemed so detached and feeble that with Hilary's
remaining caution preventing any genuine warmth from showing itself, the
whole display came off as forced and unreal.

Midway through the meal, Logan stood to make a surprise announcement, which he hoped would clear the air, put the events of that morning
behind them, and enliven the gloomy atmosphere that seemed to have
descended upon the place.

"I've been thinking it is time for a bit of a change of pace around here.

It is no secret that we have all been under varying degrees of stress, and I believe such is sufficient reason for us to lay aside our mourning of Lady Joanna's passing for a few hours—I'm certain she herself would give us her blessing. Therefore, I have decided that Stonewycke shall host a small 'soiree' for our friends, neighbors, townspeople, and perhaps a few of my political associates—a thorough mix, just like a creamy Scottish trifle. What do you all say? We'll have some music, kick up our heels a wee bit. Of course we'd insist on you remaining with us until then, Jameson. How about it?"

"Splendid idea!" replied Ashley. "I'd be delighted."

"Allison, dear, what do you say? I'll have Flora, and maybe Jo and Hilary, help take care of all the arrangements. You won't have to do a thing but be your charming self. Mrs. Gibson can ask some of the village ladies to help with the food and drink."

Allison seemed to have some difficulty focusing on him. Then her quivering lips bent into an attempt at a smile.

"Good! Good!" Logan grinned, rubbing his hands together. How much of his buoyancy was an act intended on bolstering his wife's suffering only he himself knew.

"I'll send Jake around town and to some of the farms first thing tomorrow," Logan went on as if running through a preparations list in his mind. "I'll call some of my own cronies in the area. Moryson can drive over to Culden and down to Huntly—I'll want the Gordons and Blacks to be here if they can. Professor Jameson, perhaps you'll be kind enough to help us set up the large hall, furniture out of the way for dancing, tables set up for refreshments, that sort of thing?"

"Certainly—my pleasure."

"You'll invite the Mackenzies?" asked Hilary.

"Of course!" replied Logan. "And what about that von Burchardt fellow?" he added. "He seems to have rather taken a liking to you, hasn't he, Hilary?"

"I hadn't really noticed," she answered, flushing slightly.

"As a matter of fact, he was here earlier asking for you, but apparently you were out with the professor here." He motioned toward Ashley. "Seemed almost frantic to see you. But after cooling his heels in the drawing room for half an hour, he finally left. You entertained him a while, Jo. Did he say anything about what he wanted?"

"Uh . . . no, nothing," Jo replied, taken off her guard by the question. "Just small talk, that's all. No, he said nothing."

"Yes, well . . . in any case, we ought to try to contact him on his yacht. Anyone planning a trip into town?"

Before Hilary could volunteer, Jo answered, "I have to go down to one of the shops tomorrow morning. I'll see if I can find him and invite him."

"Fine! Now, there's a great deal to do, and we'll all have to pitch in.

So let's get a good night's sleep. Tomorrow will be a big day. There are many preparations we have to make. I propose, if we can get everything in order soon enough, that we don't delay. Let's have our—let's see, what shall we call it? Our 'Goodbye-to-Fall-Welcome-to-Winter' party two evenings from tonight, on Friday."

Friday came.

All day the usually quiet castle was a beehive of activity, cars and vans and delivery trucks arriving at regular intervals, the telephone ringing almost constantly. It had been no small matter to notify and then prepare for over fifty guests in such a short time. But Logan had been determined to divert attention off their own personal concerns, and hard work seemed to be the answer.

As the day wore on and as things shaped up, he could not help being pleased. Every time he walked by the kitchen, where the cook was superintending a makeshift crew of six of her friends from the village, Logan chuckled to hear her complaints about the impossibility of the task, "When ye're no gi'en enocht hoors in the day t' make what ye'd conseeder *proper* preparations."

Yet whenever he saw her in the hall, tiny beads of perspiration on her forehead, he gave her a pat on the back and a "Well done, Mrs. Gibson! We'll make it on time!" And by midafternoon the faithful woman was beginning to take on a lively glow as the fruit of her labors began to appear in the form of completed trays and dishes of food ready to be carted into the hall.

In the big hall itself, all furniture had been removed except for the long rows of tables to one side, which would display Mrs. Gibson's wares, and some forty or fifty folding wooden chairs set up around the perimeter of the room for the guests not inclined to dance.

About two o'clock, a small band arrived and began setting up their equipment. There was not a great deal to be done, in that the band consisted of one accordion, two fiddles, a pianist, a drummer, and a vocalist who doubled on the penny whistle. To Logan's chagrin, the bagpiper had taken a sudden illness and was unable to be there.

A glorious day had dawned for the party. The autumn sun shone bravely, warming the frozen earth to almost 50 degrees by noon and melting the last remnants of the snow about the grounds. Though it would be dark by five o'clock, Logan made sure that the grounds would be well lit and hoped the warmth would linger long enough into the evening that their guests would be able to enjoy a walk outside or in the garden. The great hall opened out into an inner courtyard to one side and to the south lawn on the other.

At 4:30 Hilary drew herself a hot bath and slid into the soothing water with a contented sigh. It had been a hectic day, yet she anticipated the evening which lay ahead. Logan's idea had indeed been just what the situation called for. She had not seen Emil since leaving him bewildered on his yacht. And now that her emotions had had a chance to cool, she wasn't sure if she wanted to, or what she would say to him when she did. Of only one thing she was certain—he would be here tonight.

She had conspicuously avoided Ashley for the past two days, and he seemed to be likewise avoiding her. Why he had done what he had, she had not a clue. She would find out what he was up to, but not until after the party. He was too much a puzzle to be able to walk straight up and have it out with him. In the past two days her wrath had changed in character to a smoldering irritation that she did not quite know where to direct. Therefore, she kept to herself, watched his movements, her suspicions still in place, though she saw nothing more to increase her mistrust of his motives.

Once back in her room she laid out her new outfit and nodded her head with approval. Whatever the circumstances surrounding their madcap little drive to Fraserburgh, at least she had to admit that it had proved serendipitous for her. She had a new dress to wear to the party.

She dressed leisurely. It was not yet five and the guests were scheduled to arrive between six and seven. She spent more time than usual on her hair, then finally took up her dress and slipped it over her head. Its lines were simple, as she liked, but soft and feminine. The silky skirt flowed in gentle folds, its subdued colors entwining in a manner reminiscent of heather swaying casually in a mild September's breeze. She had purchased a strand of simulated pearls, but as she clasped them around her neck she could not help thinking how nicely the locket would have complemented this particular dress.

At 6:20 she left her room and made her way slowly down the corridor. At the top of the main stairway she paused. On the floor below, Logan stood among a half dozen guests who had just arrived. Hilary noted the contrast between them—a farmer and his wife, a single man wearing an expensive dinner jacket, a merchant she recognized from Port Strathy, the postmistress, Mr. Davies from the Bluster 'N Blow, and another couple, only that moment arrived, who had been brought to the door in a limousine and whose tuxedo and jewelry matched the extravagance of their ride to Stonewycke.

With each one Logan was at ease, and made them all comfortable with one another. *He really has a gift*, thought Hilary, *of putting people at ease and making them feel they are important to him*. The small group was laughing, and Logan had just slapped the farmer on the back. Now he proceeded to introduce the new arrivals, treating them all, despite their widely varying stations, as equals.

A moment more she paused, taking in the scene, reflecting how appropriately Logan's behavior at that moment epitomized what Lady Joanna would have said Stonewycke represented—its people and the ministry of the estate to the community of the surrounding region. She was proud of Logan, whether he turned out to be her father or not—just for the man he was. *He is a good man,* she thought, *a man of character, a man of depth, a man of compassion.* How little she had truly understood him when first they had spoken on the day of that London press conference!

Suddenly, as if with one accord some unseen force prompted them to glance up, Hilary became aware that the small knot of guests at the bottom of the stairway was looking at her. Flushing slightly, she began her descent, feeling strangely self-conscious. The amber tresses of her hair, which she had curled for the occasion, bounced as she went, giving colorful and correspondent motion to the graceful movement of her dress.

"You look lovely, Hilary!" exclaimed Logan, bounding up the stairs two at a time to meet her. He offered her his arm, which she took lightly and gracefully, and he continued the descent with her.

"Ladies and gentlemen," he said formally but jovially, "may I present our esteemed houseguest of the past week, Miss Hilary Edwards, of London and *The Berkshire Review.*"

"Bravo, Macintyre!" said the single gentleman, first with a glance in Logan's direction, then extending his hand to Hilary. "Where do you come up with such beauties?"

"A trait that runs in the family," said Logan, throwing Hilary a quick wink.

"Hello, Mr. Davies," said Hilary, moving from one to the other. "How nice to see you again."

Once introductions and pleasantries had been sufficiently exchanged, Logan said, "Hilary, I was just going to escort our guests to the ballroom. Would you care to join us?"

She smiled, took his arm again, and they turned and led the way down the corridor, Logan's face beaming with pride.

"Oh, Moryson," he called out to the factor, who was at that moment approaching from the far end of the hall. "Will you watch the door for a few minutes and greet our new arrivals? I'll be back shortly."

When they reached the ballroom, Hilary saw that most of the guests were already present, clustered in small groups about the hall, nibbling on the lavish spread of cold cuts, sliced cheeses and fruits, small sandwiches, smoked fish of many varieties, and of course at least a dozen platters each of oatcakes and shortbread, brought in by many of the local women who cherished each her own private recipe which she lost no opportunity to show off. Logan excused himself just as the accordionist and fiddler began with a rousing rendition of "Scots Wha Ha'e," and returned to the front door to play the part of host to the last-minute arrivals.

Slowly Hilary began making her way around the room, introducing herself, greeting the few people she knew, keeping an eye out for Karl and Frances Mackenzie, whom she had not yet seen. Neither had she seen Allison.

Jo was on the other side of the room, surrounded by several young men who were at that moment laughing at something she had apparently just said. Unconsciously Hilary began moving in the other direction, not wanting to encounter Jo without the protective cover of Logan's presence. Ever since arriving at Stonewycke she had had the feeling that Jo was too nice, too perfect. Now all at once, even though she could not see her face, Hilary felt a sense of foreboding as she looked in Jo's direction.

Even as she was reflecting on what might be the reason for the peculiar sensation, she heard a voice beside her.

"Miss Edwards?"

She turned around to see Flora the housekeeper.

"Ye hae a telephone call, mem."

"Now?"

"'Tis long distance, mem. The yoong gentleman didna want to leave a message."

"Thank you, Flora. Where shall I take it?"

"The parlor'd be the closest, mem."

Hilary followed her out of the hall. Who could it be but Murry? she thought, though it hardly seemed he'd had long enough to get the information she had requested already.

She opened the parlor door and walked to the phone. To her relief the place was empty. She picked up the receiver. It was Murry.

"Hi, Hilary," he said. "How ya doing? I hope I didn't catch you at a bad time."

"Oh no, Murry. We're just in the middle of the biggest social event of the year around here!"

"You're kidding!"

"Actually no," she laughed. It was refreshing to talk to someone from her old life, someone who represented the stability that had been so suddenly taken out from under her feet. "There are fifty or more people milling around here even as we speak. But go ahead. I want to know what you have for me."

"Well, I'm really onto something big. I wish you were here, because I can't go into it over the phone. I'll let you know specifics as soon as I can. Let's just say in one of our next issues we're going to take on a corporate giant that will make Goliath look like a gnat! But that's got nothing to do with what you asked me to look into. It's an outgrowth of that dull piece you asked me to work on last month. Man, you won't believe what's turned up!"

"Come on, Murry! What do you have for *me*?"

"Okay, I don't have all the stuff you wanted yet. But I do have the goods on the guy you first asked about, though I can't imagine why you'd want *him* run through the police computer. There are no goods on him. He's squeaky clean—"

"Who, Murry? Which name?"

"Jameson . . . Lord Deardon. If you'd only have told me about the Deardon business right off, I could have gotten this to you even quicker."

"Deardon? I don't understand. I don't know that name."

"Your Ashley Jameson is Lord Deardon. Inherited the title a couple of years ago. Aristocratic blood further back than you can see. Pretty low-key bunch, but nonetheless up to their ears in dough. Deardon . . . or Jameson—he keeps to his civilian name—sticks to his university pursuits. Thirty-six years old. He even relinquished his seat in the House of Lords to devote himself more fully to his Greeks. A real scholar, renowned in his field, I gather. More into his studies than playing the part of a nobleman. I'm surprised you hadn't heard of him—but then neither had I. I suppose Greek tragedy just isn't our bag."

"You're certain about all this? I would never have dreamed this guy would have a dossier so . . . I don't even know what to call it—impressive."

"It's all pretty much public record stuff. All I had to do is throw his name around Oxford. Didn't even have to trouble my pal at the Yard."

"I must say, I am astounded. This guy up here's been acting peculiar, doing strange things." She stopped for a moment, thinking. "Do you have a physical description?" she added.

"You think someone's impersonating him?"

"I doubt it. But I wish I had a photo."

"Well, here's what I got off his university files," Murry went on. "Six-one, about a hundred seventy pounds, or rather twelve and a half stone, light brown hair, gray-green eyes, drives a '69 BMW—"

"That's him. . . ."

"I'm surprised Logan Macintyre couldn't have supplied you with all this information," commented Murry.

"Why's that?"

"They are old chums, as I understand it."

"What!" exclaimed Hilary, incredulous at the unexpected revelation.

"Worked together on a couple government projects, and the professor's also worked with Macintyre's brother-in-law."

"How can that be?"

"Hilary . . . what is it?"

"The oddest thing! Those two have been dancing around here for days pretending they don't even know each other!"

"Why the charade?"

"I can't imagine! I knew there was something going on, but I would never have guessed it fell in *that* direction! I wonder where Jo fits into their little subterfuge," she added as if talking to herself.

"Jo?"

"Never mind, Murry. It's too complicated to explain. I'll fill you in on everything later. Anything else?"

"I'm sorry I've been dragging my feet on this. As I said, I've kind of gotten hooked into something else—but I'll get on von Burchardt right away."

"Okay. Thanks, Murry."

Hilary hung up the phone, her mind reeling. She could not even begin to assess the implications of what Murry had told her. Suddenly there were more doubts than ever with the revelation of his connection with Logan!

Why would they possibly keep that secret? And with all their talk about the nobility, why would he have kept back the significant fact that he was of aristocratic blood?

Of course none of this startling news in the least explained Ashley's bizarre behavior of spiriting her off Emil's yacht.

Beneath it all, Hilary's brain spun round and round with the question: *Why the ruse?*

Slowly she turned and walked from the room like one in a daze. For the moment she had completely forgotten the party. She exited the parlor and walked down the hall in the opposite direction from which she had come, aimless, with no destination in mind.

She had to think. Suddenly everything was upside-down. With Logan's candor now called into question, she no longer knew *whom* she could trust. If anyone!

For more minutes than she could keep track of, Hilary walked.

Paying little attention to her direction, she followed corridor after corridor, went up and down staircases she had never been on before, and met no one. All the family and guests were occupied in the other wing. Without even realizing she was retracing her steps toward more familiar regions, all at once she stopped before a door she recognized.

Quickly her mind came awake. This was the door to the gallery, which she had been wanting to see but had still never been inside.

For several moments she remained standing, merely contemplating the door. Then she slowly reached out, turned the latch, and swung the huge door open on its silent hinges. She stepped inside, fumbled about the wall nearby for a switch, found it, then flipped on the lights.

Immediately a subdued quiet overcame her, as if she had entered the cloistered chapel of a monastery. A great intimate hush permeated the very walls, intensified by the high vaulted ceiling. At first to Hilary it seemed the silence was due merely to the absence of sound. As she began to glance about her, however, she realized there was a more profound reason for it than what could be explained on the mere physical plane. Dozens of unmoving eyes filled the walls, pulsating with vibrant yet undisturbed motion, every face deepening the intense stillness, emphasizing the silence in the midst of their voiceless entreaties. If ever a "cloud of past witnesses" was visible, Hilary now found herself standing in the midst of it.

Holding her breath, she began to make her way slowly around the room. All about were family portraits, mingled with others of Scottish historical significance, with here and there selections that had obviously been acquired purely on the basis of pleasure and enjoyment. The owners of this hall were clearly collectors of art with a discriminating flair.

Gradually Hilary took in many paintings by masters—Raeburn, Wilkie, Gainsborough she recognized particularly. The far wall held but one painting, an enormous eight-by-fifteen foot exhibition of the battle of Culloden, surrounded by a one-foot wide gilded wood frame. To each side of it, enclosed in glass cases and sitting silently on brass pedestals, were two marble busts—one of Mary Queen of Scots, a replica of that which was housed in Edinburgh Castle, and one of the Bonnie Prince Charlie, whose full figure looked down upon the proceedings from his desperate perch in the painting above.

On the walls hung fierce Highland chieftains, delicate ladies in waiting, children in Eaton jackets and knickers or frilly crinoline. Hilary read each nameplate, finding many of the names familiar from her reading of the journal. Others were new; all held fascination. She paused at each, forgetful of time, lost in the solemn import of the moment.

Andrew de Ramsay, the original scion of the Stonewycke line, the builder of the castle, overlooked the descendants that had sprung from his stock from a portrait so old it was encased in glass to protect it from the air. His fiery red hair struggled, even while posing for the dignified painting, to break from the restraints of his plaid bonnet. Everything about her reminded Hilary that the Ramsays were of warrior stock, fierce Highlanders come down into the low-lying coastlands only lately in their genealogy to people the northern coast of their land, yet always but a violent breath or two removed from the savage Pict and Viking heritage which first spawned their energy and dynamism.

The independent nature of the family was clear on every face, whether it was Thomas Ramsey's insistence on changing the spelling of the family name, Colin's running off to die in Prince Charlie's ill-fated cause, or Anson Ramsey's attempt to deed the family property over to his tenants. Such a headstrong self-reliance seemed to have been the most prominent trait passed down through the years—either as a blessing or a curse, depending on how each recipient of new Ramsey blood chose to use it—right down to the carrying out of Anson's wish years later by two of the most remarkable of this breed, Lady Margaret and Lady Joanna.

Reading the journal could never alone give her the awe-inspiring sense of the flow of life through generation after generation as did gazing upon these portraits, though reading it had certainly prepared her for this moment. But as Hilary stood looking upon the faces of those who had come before—who could well be her own ancestors—she was caught up in the life that their faces conveyed. The room fairly exploded with silent vitality and power. As she gazed, there gradually emerged from each face a uniform consistency of expression—something in the eyes, the hair, the twist of the lips, the shape of the jaw . . . something which said, "I know what I am about, and I know from what roots I come. For I am a Ramsey. And my heart is proud of the Scottish blood that runs through my veins."

This look, this expression of defiance, boldness, and self-sufficiency had clearly been translated from the fierce males to the females who continued the direct line from Andrew down to the present. In the softer faces of the more delicate sex, the expressions of independence were more subdued and subtle, not quite as easy to identify amid the exterior trappings of outward feminine beauty. Stare as she might, Hilary could not exactly identify what she saw. But whether the portrait was four hundred years old or forty, something in each face made her very aware that these people were all of the same blood.

For several minutes she stood before the two most recent portraits to be added to the gallery—those of Logan and Allison Macintyre—scanning every detail. Both were appealing faces, full of life, full of love, full of zest. But there could be no doubt through which of the pair the blood of the Ramseys flowed. For while it was the hint of a roguish smile around the edges of Logan's mouth that drew a viewer's attention, when one's gaze fell upon Allison it could not be easily pulled away. It was not her mouth nor her beauty, however, that arrested further thought. In Logan the suggestion of mischief made you smile. In Allison the silent force of her eyes held your gaze, compelling you to look beyond, until you were drawn into the invisible vitality of the generations that had come before.

At length Hilary exhaled a long sigh and turned from the painting. She wandered back again through the room. She returned to the portrait of Lady Joanna she had already seen. The painting must have been done when she was in her mid-forties—from the style of clothing, probably some time during the depression. How lovely she was! mused Hilary, though no artist could ever capture the true beauty that was Joanna MacNeil's. Age and wrinkles and gray hair may have altered the exterior, but the lady who had visited her only a short time ago still felt life as she had when she had sat for this portrait.

"How I wish you were here now, Lady Joanna," Hilary murmured aloud to the lifeless figure. "I know somehow you would be able to help me with my confusion."

She found herself trying to compare this younger Joanna with the woman she had met so briefly in her office. So many similarities remained—the quiet refinement, the reserved dignity, that look in her eyes which she had obviously given Allison.

Hilary moved to the next painting immediately to her right. Central on the wall, in a place of honor, rested an early painting of young Maggie.

Hilary had already become quite familiar with two other paintings of the family matriarch. A picture of Maggie at nine or ten hung in the parlor. Another, which must have been commissioned after her return from exile, showed Lady Margaret at age seventy or so. It hung in the entryway to the castle, just to the left of the great stairway.

The one upon which she was now gazing, however, had been painted when the girl was about seventeen, no doubt just before events had conspired to force her to leave her homeland. Hilary stared at the portrait, probing every detail of the face, an inquisitive expression building on her own countenance. Something was there . . . something she couldn't quite identify. She had seen it before . . . somewhere.

She glanced quickly around. Was it in the portrait of Allison? No, she didn't think so. She looked over at Joanna's face again, then back to young Maggie's. What was it?

Suddenly the dress Maggie wore jumped off the canvas at Hilary, making her gasp audibly. Of course! That's why it looked so familiar! She's wearing a heather-colored dress . . . just like mine!

She laughed to herself. What a coincidence! She turned away and began to leave. But even as she walked in the opposite direction, Maggie's eyes seemed to bore holes in the back of her head, compelling her to turn back. *The dress isn't all*, Maggie seemed to say to her, though Hilary felt rather than heard the words. *There is more! Don't turn away until you have discovered it! Gaze upon my face, Hilary*, an inner voice seemed to say. *Gaze until you know . . . until you know!*

Hilary stopped, then slowly turned back to face the wall. Still silent, young Maggie returned her gaze, drawing Hilary closer, ever closer, by the eyes she had passed down, first to Eleanor, then to Joanna, and at last to Allison, whose eyes were even this moment looking at her from the adjacent wall next to Logan.

It *was* more than the dress! But it was more than the eyes as well. The familial similarities found in each of the women all were focused in this one youthful, commanding, unyielding, rugged, sensitive face—the vulnerability of the sensitive nose, the pale skin that subdued the other features and highlighted the shades of the hair, the strong cheekbones, the high forehead that allowed the robust eyebrows full expression, the eyes that always seemed looking into the distance, contemplating the depth and the grandness of life.

It was more than all these features. As Hilary continued to gaze at the portrait before her, suddenly it came into focus. The thing she recognized more than anything else was the chin!

She remembered the meeting with Lady Joanna. She had noticed it so clearly. It had looked strangely familiar in that first moment of their meeting, though subsequent developments caused her to forget. But now all at once, seeing it again in Maggie's face, offering a fitting foundation to the mouth, lips, eyes, and cheekbones that rose up from it, there again was that distinctive chin! Hundreds of people could possess such a combination of distinguishing physical traits. But only one person she knew!

No wonder they had jumped out at her all at once off the canvas! Those same eyes, those same cheekbones, those same eyebrows, and that same chin had been staring back at her for as long as she could remember, whenever she looked in a mirror!

And with the stunning realization came back into her mind the words of her reporter friend, the Irishman Bert: "If it weren't fer that chin, Eddie, me dear, I'd think you was the essence of naivete. But between the chin and those eyes, I know you're not one to tangle with!"

Unconsciously Hilary's hands went to her cheeks as she gasped again, this time audibly. For several moments she stood as one in a trance, unable to take her gaze away from the incredible face that had at last revealed the truth of its secret.

Behind her, she had not heard another enter at the door she had left ajar, nor was she aware of the presence which now stood beholding her, statuelike, as she stared upon the wall. But to the one observing, the scene as it spread out on the other side of the gallery could not have been more bitterly poignant, for to her too, more than resemblance of dress had been revealed.

"So . . . at last you know." Jo's voice echoed like a thunderclap through the silent gallery.

With a frightened start, Hilary spun around. Speechless, she opened her mouth, but no words would come.

All the effort in the world could not have wiped away the truth from Hilary's face. Their eyes met and locked together. For a long, uncomfortable moment they held one another's gaze in silence.

Then gradually a mask seemed to fall from Jo's innocent, well-controlled countenance. All shams abandoned, her eyes suddenly narrowed. Her mouth, which had always been so quick to trace a sweet smile, hardened with vehemence.

"It doesn't matter, you know." Her voice was as icy with harsh disdain as it had once been with musical simplicity. "They will never believe you. Allison loves me. She is so ill that a little shock could kill her. You had better watch what you say!"

"She is not that ill," said Hilary, finding her voice.

"She is *very* ill!" spat back Jo. "If I were you, I would be careful not to do anything to upset her. Anything, do you hear? I do believe she is quite suicidal."

"You don't mean to say—"

"I mean watch your step, Miss Edwards, so that no harm comes either to the woman you may think is your mother . . . or to yourself! Just remember—before you say anything to anyone, they will never believe you. I will make sure of that!"

Before Hilary could say anything further, Jo spun around and left the gallery.

47 / Outside the Ballroom

The gathering was in full swing when Hilary wandered back into the great hall, still in too much of a stupor to pay much attention to those about her. She must have been gone for more than an hour before Jo's untimely appearance. The band was in the middle of "The Flowers of Edinburgh" and the floor was filled with at least five highly animated sets of dancers. Yet even with forty persons dancing, the floor could easily have contained another five sets. Laughter and pleasant conversation echoed throughout the room in spite of the music, all of which fell almost discordantly on Hilary's keyed-up, flustered senses.

Logan stood at the far end of the room, chatting with friends, now and then clapping in time to the music and adding a rousing *whoop!* or yell to the accompaniment. Beside him stood Allison, looking drawn and strained, a mere shadow of the hardy woman of the portrait Hilary had just seen. Beside Allison stood Jo, showing her every attention, lavishing upon the ailing woman the care and tenderness she seemed to require.

Slowly Hilary began making her way toward them. She had no idea what she would say or do. Something inside her sensed danger. But whether she could avert it, and whether she had any who might be allies in this house, she did not know.

She had walked about halfway around the perimeter of the room, her brain gradually clearing as she considered what action to take. But her thoughts and her steps progressed no further.

Suddenly von Burchardt was at her side, and in a flurry of ebullient greetings had firmly taken her arm and half-led, half-propelled her into a St. Bernard's Waltz which had just begun.

"Emil, this is a surprise!" she said.

"So I would assume," he replied, smiling broadly, his white teeth flashing. "After your desertion the other day, I assumed you wanted to see me no more."

"That's not fair, Emil," said Hilary, attempting to turn on what charm she could muster. "You saw what happened. That horrid Professor Jameson grabbed me off your yacht."

"You appeared walking willingly under your own power," persisted the viscount, his smile unable to mask the cynicism in his tightly controlled voice.

"He lied to me, Emil. He told me I was needed urgently at the house."

Ruminating momentarily, von Burchardt nodded thoughtfully. "I see," he said. "Yet when I called only a short time later, neither of you were there. I could not help fancying myself the fool."

"I'm sorry, Emil. He kidnapped me. I had no choice. I was positively furious at the man."

For the next couple rounds of the waltz they danced in silence, though on neither part did there appear any desire toward a more intimate embrace. Stiffly they went through the motions, each lost in his own private thoughts regarding the other. Emil contemplated recent days, the interference of this busybody Jameson, and whether or not he could work his way back into the good graces of this little vixen in his arms. If he could, was there time for such a ploy to do any good, or were stronger measures called for? If he could not get her onto his yacht voluntarily, perhaps a forceful abduction would prove necessary after all, just as his accomplice had suggested in the first place.

He should have listened. Now there was going to be the devil to pay for letting her slip through his fingers right when he had been just minutes away from casting off and eliminating the source of their difficulties for good.

For her part, Hilary found herself struggling with remaining last-minute uncertainties about where loyalties lined up around here. The professor had been too easily absolved in one convenient stroke by Murry's call. What if his presence here was part of some evil scheme? What was more likely to follow than that he would have covered his tracks with a well-documented cover? She could not escape the fact that he had lied to her, and had been seen at least once alone with Jo, whose motives she now had reason to suspect as well.

Perhaps I should confide in Emil, she thought. *What harm can it do? If he is merely a disinterested visitor to Port Strathy, his knowing a few more of the family secrets would cause no trouble. He already knows as much as anyone else anyway!* She had to get it off her chest, and besides Logan—who was too close to the situation to be objective, she said to herself—there was no one else she could trust.

"Emil," she said as the dance ended, "perhaps we could talk somewhere. More seriously."

"Certainly!" responded the viscount, thinking to himself that getting Hilary away from this crowd was the obvious first step toward his yacht. If they cast off tonight, they could be standing outside Newcastle by morning.

"Shall we go to my yacht? We will have all the privacy there we could desire. I have an automobile, and we could be there within minutes."

"I'm not ready to leave the party just yet," replied Hilary. "How about a walk outside?"

Hiding his displeasure, von Burchardt nodded, then led the way with a wave of his hand. As they approached the door, out of the corner of her eye Hilary saw Ashley enter the ballroom from another door with a small group of locals. Unexpectedly her heart gave a little leap at seeing his relaxed, friendly countenance. Was it fear or relief that prompted the unsought flutter? She could not tell, but in spite of all logic, her instincts told her his motives had to be honest and that, all unexplained actions aside, he was a friend.

Before she had opportunity to reflect further, however, they were out the door and into the chilly evening air.

They walked some distance on the lawn in silence, Hilary pondering how to express the concerns on her heart. Without realizing it, she allowed the viscount to lead her inconspicuously toward the front of the house. As they went he commented innocently about the weather, the coming of winter, the conditions of the sea for sailing, asking here and there a harmless personal question, displaying all the charm which had endeared him to the inhabitants of the house after his first appearance. Hilary carried on her share of the conversation, while underneath her mind debated with itself, trying to sort out the new events this evening had revealed. Before she knew it, they had left the courtyard and were passing the gates.

"Hadn't we better turn back, Emil?" said Hilary with a shiver.

"Nonsense, my dear," he replied with a laugh. "Let's just enjoy a little walk among the trees along the drive."

"Please, I think——"

"These firs really are magnificent," he persisted, now clutching her arm more firmly and walking on. "You will see what I mean once we get beyond the glare of the lights from the castle."

"Emil, please! You're hurting my arm!"

"Come, my dear, let's walk a bit farther," he replied, not relaxing his hold.

Recognizing herself powerless to resist, but still not divining the extent of her peril, Hilary submitted, and they continued forward.

All of a sudden, from out of the dark in front of them, a figure stepped onto the road.

"Ah, my good man, Herr von Burchardt! Splendid evening for a saunter about the grounds."

It was Ashley!

Unable to believe her ears, for she had only moments ago seen him absorbed in conversation in the ballroom, Hilary felt a great surge of relief at the sound of his voice, rising above the viscount's muttered cursing of the blackguard meddler!

Still puffing from his dash through the trees, Ashley walked toward them, gave von Burchardt a rousing handshake, turned, and fell in on the other side of Hilary. He had seen them exit the hall, had followed them long enough to spy out the direction in which they were headed, and then had gone back through the house, out a door on the opposite side, run across the lawn, through a break in the hedge, through the grove of trees that extended out from the courtyard, finally winding up beyond the walkers at the point where he met them on the road.

"Where are you two headed?" he asked with cheerful innocence.

"Merely out for a walk, Jameson," replied the viscount with forced calm, "which I hope you'll allow us to continue by excusing us."

"I was just going to ask Miss Edwards to join me for a dance when I was in the hall a few minutes ago."

"As you can see," said Burchardt, "she is at present occupied."

"Indeed. But it really is rather cold out. What do you say, Miss Edwards—do you feel like warming up to a quick-stepping reel?"

"Why, yes, thank you," replied Hilary. "That sounds—"

"Now look here, Jameson," interrupted von Burchardt, his temper at last getting the better of him. "Do you make it a practice of going around interfering where you're not wanted?"

"I'm sorry, Burchardt. I only thought the lady might—"

"The lady is fine! And she is with me!"

"For the moment. But she says she would like to dance . . . with me."

The viscount stopped and turned to face Ashley. "If you are serious about your meddling, Jameson," he said with scorn. "Then perhaps we ought to have it out right here and now between the two of us!"

"I have no desire to fight you, Burchardt," said Ashley. "But I will not allow you to take Miss Edwards another step from the house."

"You will not *allow*!" yelled the viscount, laughing in derision. "You expect to stop me from doing as I please? Ha! ha! ha!"

"Hilary," said Ashley softly, turning toward her, "go back to the castle . . . please."

Hilary retreated a couple of steps, but was arrested by the viscount's voice. "Stay where you are, Miss Edwards! I want you to see your supposed hero's true valor after I have punished him as he deserves!"

"Go, Hilary," repeated Ashley.

Hilary walked farther back toward the gates. Von Burchardt stepped menacingly toward Ashley.

"If you so much as lay a hand on him, Emil," shouted Hilary from where she stood, "I swear to you I will bring every truth-loving man from inside that hall out with my cries. And then it will not go so well with you, I think!"

Von Burchardt stopped.

"Come, Ashley," said Hilary. "Will you please accompany me back inside?"

With one final glance in the direction of the esteemed Viscount von Burchardt, Ashley turned and rejoined Hilary, leaving Emil standing in the middle of the darkened roadway in a white fury.

Hilary slipped her hand through Ashley's arm and held tightly.

"I'm glad he didn't hurt you," she said.

"I don't think he would have."

"But he might have."

"That was a chance I had to take."

"Does this have anything to do with that hairbrained abduction you pulled at his boat the other day?" asked Hilary with a laugh.

"I suppose," he replied. "I was sure he was up to no good. I can't prove it, but I'm certain he has been trying to get you away from here . . . permanently. I couldn't let that happen. Not only for your safety's sake, but for the sake of Logan and Allison. That's why I've been watching you so close, both then and tonight."

"All this time I thought you were his ally . . . or Jo's!"

"Me . . . hooked up with von Burchardt?" said Ashley incredulously.

"I thought you must have lured me away from my room that night so he could come in and prowl around."

"That's a good one!" laughed Ashley; then his face turned somber. "Hmm, though perhaps you're onto something."

"What do you mean?"

"Just before I arrived at your door that night, I thought I caught a faint whiff of perfume lingering in the hallway. At first I dismissed it as yours. But then when you opened the door it was not there. If von Burchardt did indeed have an accomplice that night . . . ."

He let his thought trail away unstated.

"You're not Jo's ally either? You've been spending a lot of time with her."

"Not so much, really."

"I've seen you together."

"Just sorting out the evidence. I have to spend enough time with the both of you so that I know you. How else can I—"

He stopped, realizing he had gone too far.

"How else can you what?"

"I suppose not much harm can come from your knowing, now that we have come this far. Without spending time with the two of you, there's no way I can make an accurate report."

"A report? You make it sound so clinical. Whom do you have to report to?"

"It seems only fair that you have some explanation. I hope he'll forgive me." Ashley paused, took a breath, then said, "I am here at Logan's request. He wanted someone he could trust to act the part of a neutral party. He thought perhaps he and Allison were too deeply involved in the situation emotionally to judge accurately between you and Jo—if no concrete evidence presented itself. At the same time he felt the two of you would feel reticent around someone you knew was his friend. Thus the charade. He asked me to come incognito, as it were."

"Well, you certainly pulled it off! I was so suspicious of you that I even called an associate in London to have you run through the police computer."

Ashley chuckled, amused at the idea.

"You were completely exonerated, as far as it went. I should have known all along that your intentions were noble, or at least genuine."

"*Noblesse oblige* and all that, eh?"

"That is a subject we are going to have to deal with one day, Ashley," laughed Hilary. "But something tells me this is not the time."

They walked on a few more steps in silence. They were again nearing the house, and in the distance voices could now be heard of the merry-makers. Overhead the night sky was speckled with pulsating stars, appearing crisper, even closer, in the chilly air. Rising through the trees to the north of the castle, the moon was just now making its appearance felt. Both Hilary and Ashley inwardly found themselves wishing the circumstances surrounding this moonlight stroll had been different.

"I did not have the chance to see your new dress for long inside," said Ashley at length. "But now that we get nearer the light, I must say my first assessment was correct. It is beautiful. I should say *you* are beautiful in it!"

"Thank you." Hilary was glad for the cover of darkness, for she felt the red rising in her cheeks.

"Are you warm enough?" he asked, seeing her shiver.

"We'll be in soon. What about you? Or do those midnight walks of yours give you such a hardy constitution that you scoff at the cold?"

"My, you really have been suspicious of my actions!"

"Do you blame me?"

"Maybe not. But am I entitled to no secrets at all?"

"You owe me no explanations whatsoever . . . unless you want me to trust you."

"All right then," said Ashley. "Yes, I have been about at night a couple of times. On that particular night you saw me, I wanted to have a closer inspection of the bridge where Lady Allison had her fall. I have also been snooping around the place in search of both the missing locket and the missing pages of Lady Joanna's journal, but without success."

"Do you suspect—well, that the fall was not an accident?"

"I haven't known what to think. Logan told me to leave no stone unturned. And you know what Sherlock Holmes wisely instructed—'Once you have eliminated the impossible, what you have left, however improbable, must be the truth.' "

"You go in for that sort of cloak-and-dagger thing?"

"Another secret we unfortunately have no time for."

"I'm afraid something we must take time for," said Hilary, "is Allison's well-being. I'm worried about her."

"So have we all been."

"I don't mean from her illness." Hilary paused, running the brief conversation with Jo in the gallery back through her mind. At length she spoke again. "Ashley, how well do you know Allison? Do you think she could be suicidal?"

"What! Impossible! No truth whatever! Why would you ask that?"

Hilary recounted Jo's words of earlier.

"It was not the words themselves," she concluded, "but the *way* in which she spoke them that frightened me."

"Dear Lord!" breathed Ashley. "We've got to get back inside, and fast!"

"You actually think she could be capable of—"

"I don't know. But I shudder to think what might be afoot."

He turned, grabbed Hilary's hand, and walked quickly toward the door to the ballroom. "Whatever happens from now on," he said, "you keep near Allison if at all possible. I don't know what I may have to do."

Hilary stopped him. "Ashley, there's just one other thing I have to know. Did you meet Jo, out there near where we left Emil, in the trees, two nights before you arrived?"

Ashley looked earnestly into her eyes, still clutching her hand. "The only young lady I've been with under the stars since coming to Stonewycke is with me this very moment." He paused, still taking in the light reflected in her eyes. "Now, come," he went on, "we must go in. Things have begun to move quickly, and we must be vigilant."

While Hilary and Ashley had been occupied outside, Jo walked up to Logan and slipped her arm affectionately through his.

"Father," she said, "I am worried about Mother." Her soft voice almost quivered with its distress.

"We are all concerned," replied Logan.

"Something happened yesterday I must tell you about."

"What is it?"

"Mother was working on a particularly involved landscape—"

"She painted yesterday? I thought I told you no more painting until she was feeling better."

"She seemed a little more perky," said Jo demurely. "She asked me to let her paint."

"Go on," said Logan.

"All of a sudden she became frustrated and threw down her brush. I tried to encourage her. 'It's coming along fine,' I said. But she shook her head with such despair and then said, 'It's not just this. It's . . . it's everything! Life! I am miserable . . . I can't go on like this any longer!' "

Jo stopped, then glanced up into Logan's face with all the sincerity she could bring to her command, and said, "Oh, Father, I am so frightened for her!"

"Those were her exact words?"

She nodded. "I am hesitant to mention something like this, Father, but don't you think it might be time to consider some kind of therapy?"

"That's preposterous! Allison is strong. We will work this out."

At that moment, at the far end of the hall Jo spied Hilary and Ashley entering through the door. Whether or not the look on their faces told her the truth, her eyes flashed darkly. She quickly recovered, however, and went on. Logan had seen nothing of what transpired, and did not yet feel the urgency in her tone.

"This kind of depression is not uncommon after the death of a loved one," Jo said convincingly. "Perhaps the right psychiatrist could snap her right out of it. But if these feelings of hopelessness are allowed to deepen—"

She paused, but only momentarily. Out of the corner of her eye she saw Ashley approaching.

"—they can lead to self-destructive—" she continued, but Logan cut her off.

"Not Allison. She would do nothing of the kind."

"There have been cases of insanity in the family, have there not? I do not like to mention such a thing, but it is a fact that these tendencies are often inherited."

"Dorey's case was entirely different." Logan paused and appeared to ponder her words. But just then their conversation was brought to a close by Ashley's appearance.

"I say, Mr. Macintyre, might I have a word with you?" he said.

"Professor Jameson," replied Logan, shaking Ashley's hand. "Of course, of course. But I must tell you, I promised Allison you would have a dance with her, and she is quite tired. Perhaps you might oblige her that pleasure first, and then we'll have a little chat."

"With pleasure! Where is your wife?"

"Let me see . . ." said Logan glancing about. "Oh, there she is! Over there, talking with Hilary."

Ashley left Logan and walked in that direction. A few minutes later the Viscount von Burchardt entered the hall, though as he made his way toward where Jo stood he kept as much as possible to the shadows. Their brief tryst involved no more than a few whispered words and was unseen by anyone.

Meanwhile, Allison safely occupied with Ashley, Hilary approached Logan with a smile.

"You look radiant tonight, my dear," said Logan.

"I've just been outside," replied Hilary. "I suppose my cheeks are hot from the walk."

"They're just forming up sets for 'The Rakes o' Glasgow.' Won't you join me?"

"These Scottish country dances are mostly beyond me," laughed Hilary nervously, attempting to mask her internal agitation.

"Come on. I'll lead you through it!"

Logan offered his hand and they walked out onto the floor.

"Here . . . we'll just slip in with Mr. Jameson and Allison. They seem to need a fourth couple for this set."

As they settled into place, Logan waved down to the other two couples. "Creary . . . nice to see you!" he said. "Jones, you're looking fit tonight!" Then suddenly the music was underway.

"You are quite proficient with our dances, Mr. Jameson," said Allison when the dance was about halfway through.

"It is not the first time I have been to such a gathering, but I must admit they are rather complicated." Even as he spoke Ashley missed a step and had to skip and shuffle to get back in time.

"I've made you lose your concentration."

"It doesn't take much, Lady Allison," laughed Ashley. "I am glad to see that your ankle is recovered."

"Yes, it mostly is. I only wish I weren't always so tired."

Ashley found himself staring at the hand which was at that moment clasped in his. Even as they moved across the floor, his brain zeroed in on the fine lines of Allison's fingers. Then his attention was arrested by the paint stains on her hand, as if she had not cleaned up thoroughly from her last session. *Funny*, he thought to himself, *that she would leave herself so.* But now that he thought of it, she had had bits of colored pigment on her hands and fingers ever since he had come. He had just never consciously noted it before now.

In the midst of his reflections, the music stopped.

"Good show, Jameson!" shouted Logan. "Thank you. I'm sure my wife is very grateful!"

"I doubt that! You are talking to a man with two left feet!"

"You did yourself proud, Mr. Jameson," said Allison with a sigh, "but I really must sit down. I am positively exhausted."

Logan led her to a chair. "I'm sorry," she said, looking up into his face with almost a forlorn expression of sadness. "I'm just not myself. I don't know . . ." Tears began to well up in her eyes. "Logan, I just don't know what's wrong," she said.

Logan took her hand and gave her a reassuring smile. But she was right, and he knew it now. Something *was* wrong.

Ashley had to move quickly.

He glanced around. Allison was with Logan. Hilary was engaged in a lively conversation with one of the farmer couples not far away. He should be able to sneak away for a few minutes.

He inched toward the main door, then casually slipped unobtrusively into the corridor. Not a single one of the guests noticed his departure. His stealthy movements had been noted by only one member of the house, who now realized the curtain was coming down on her three-month engagement. Whether her performance achieved her final goal or ended in failure depended on how skillfully she played this final scene which was about to commence. She checked her pocket, then slid across the dance floor, forcing her mouth into a pretty smile.

Meanwhile, Ashley Jameson moved cautiously and quietly on his way through the house. The situation was serious. He knew that. In spite of this however, he could not prevent the excitement that rushed through him as he began to reason through the mystery now facing him. This was not a plot he would write. Actual lives were at stake!

In many ways, Ashley Jameson was a simple man, despite his intellect, his position, and his noble upbringing. He was a renown authority on Classical Greece, and was also beginning to gain a reputation in the study of the antiquities of his own country as well. Besides his translations of *Euripides* and *Aristophanes*, he had published several scholarly essays, and had lectured widely, most notably at Harvard and Berkeley. But he viewed his pursuits as natural extensions of himself, and not a few of his colleagues envied him the ability to handle it all with such ease and matter-of-factness.

The academic life particularly suited Ashley. At thirty-six years of age, he had found at Oxford the perfect environment to nurture his interests. He thoroughly enjoyed intellectual debates with fellow dons as well as his students, and was most content with a good book in hand in front of a crackling evening fire.

But there was another Ashley Jameson, one the public never had the chance to view—one unknown even to his colleagues. This was the man who reveled in the intricacies of unraveling a good mystery. Call it a closet interest, a hidden passion, a secondary vocation. Whatever term one applied to the phenomenon, Oxford professor Ashley Jameson had all his life been fascinated with criminology, as his friend, Chief Inspector Harry

Arnstein could well attest. They had put their heads together on more than a few knotty London crimes. And though Ashley allowed no credit to come his way, he had been highly instrumental in solving several cases in Arnstein's file. He was glad to let Harry take the bows, for the Chief Inspector threw plenty of material his way too, even if Ashley had to change the names and circumstances before any other eyes saw it. It was, after all, Harry himself who had first propelled Ashley in the direction of his secret obsession, his private endeavor that gave him such pleasure, but which must always be kept from the public eye.

He only hoped that his peculiar talent, when put to the test of real life, as it was tonight, would serve him as it had in other areas. He prayed that right here and now his senses would be sharpened and his eyes opened. Logan was his friend. Allison was Ian's sister. He had promised Logan he would help him, but thus far he felt as if his mind had been on a treadmill. No clues seemed to lead anywhere. Now he knew that his loyalties had extended beyond his friendships with Ian and Logan, but had come to involve Hilary as well. For all their sakes, he prayed he would find something which would uncover the truth.

Ashley was no romantic in the strictest sense. Perhaps it was unfair ever to expect a woman to compete with his scholarly pursuits and his criminological avocation. He had come to accept the single life as one of the necessary drawbacks to the hermit-like existence within the confines of Oxford, where his books, his typewriter, and his collection of Doyle, Christie, Gardner, Sayers, and Chesterton, were his sole companions. He had always considered that it would be asking too much for a woman to enter that world with him. But was it possible he had simply been waiting for the right moment to open the doors of that world to the right woman? Before he could allow himself to even think about such things, however, he had to solve this mystery at Stonewycke, which seemed to be growing more portentous by the minute.

He rounded a corner, walked up a flight of stairs, down another long corridor, up still another staircase, and at last arrived at his destination. From his pocket he pulled out a ring containing perhaps a dozen keys that Logan had given him. He had already used half of them, at odd moments in various places throughout the castle searching for the journal. But to date he had not been in this room.

He found the key, inserted it into the lock, turned the latch, stepped inside, and flipped on the lights.

Ashley took a quick look around, walked across the room, switched on a low-wattage bedside lamp, then returned to the door and turned off the overhead. He doubted the light would penetrate the heavy draperies even if there should by chance be someone outside to observe it, but he could not conduct a proper search without some light, though the less the better.

He paused to take in a general impression of the place. It certainly had a lived-in look, tidy, yet full, nicely decorated and arranged. It was obvious Jo planned to stay for a good long while!

The furnishings were all of antique walnut, rather dark, but Jo had apparently added touches of color to brighten the dreariness of the medieval decor—a frilly pink pillow on the bed, baskets of flowers, and several paintings on the walls. Ashley moved about slowly to take in a closer look at these last items. They were mostly all Jo's own work, and in spite of himself Ashley found he was impressed.

He halfway expected someone of her nature to create art of a shadowy, surrealistic variety, hinting at ominous intent, like the flash of her eyes that gave mixed signals of warmth as well as deceit. But what he met here was rather a Renoir-style adaptation, where children, gardens, country settings, and simple people predominated. He was particularly struck with a vivid scene of a local Scots woman milking a cow while her two barefoot children looked on. But then as Ashley examined it closer, he realized the signature on the corner of the canvas was Lady Allison's. She possessed clear talent too, though as he understood it, that ability had remained undiscovered until Jo's arrival.

"Perhaps some good will come of all this in the end," he murmured to himself as he moved on.

There were no suitcases to be seen. All Jo's belongings had long since been put away into the wardrobe or one of the dressers. Ashley pulled open the doors of the massive oak wardrobe and ran his hand randomly through the dresses and slacks, skirts, sweaters, and jackets hanging inside. Nothing of apparent interest presented itself, although toward the back of the closet sat a closed suitcase.

He removed the case, set it on the bed, and opened it. All that was inside was a rolled-up canvas. He took it out and spread it open. It was a painting of Jo's, of the same style as what he had already seen, except the setting was very different. Scotland was nowhere to be found in this scene of an old adobe building with a red tile roof. "Hmm," mused Ashley to himself, "looks like Mexico or Central America somewhere." A large dog was sprawled out on the porch, sound asleep.

He wondered why she hadn't put it with the rest. If he were himself ever inclined to purchase some of her work, he would have chosen this particular piece. The dog was uncannily lifelike, and even in sleep, rather endearing. Her work was good, he had to admit. He could not help hoping his worst doubts would prove wrong.

Replacing all as he had found it, he next moved to the dressing table. The top was dominated with the usual variety of women's accouterments. He picked up several items and looked them over. Most were American-made, though some had been purchased in Britain. To one side of the mirror sat two tubes of oil paint, one a cobalt blue, the other China white. They rested on a small tray along with two small plastic cups and a palette knife, apparently awaiting mixing. He began to turn away when it occurred to him that he had seen no other art supplies or equipment in the room—neither brushes nor spare canvas nor kits nor easel. He recalled someone saying that the solarium on the fourth floor had been converted into a studio. He glanced again at the small tray in puzzlement. *Why two tubes of paint, and nothing else?* he wondered. Aside from their apparent isolation, he could see nothing unusual about them.

Next he began a search of the drawers. This process was the most distasteful of his entire enforced burglary. As his hands rummaged through Jo's personal belongings, he felt more than ever the common sneak-thief. Just as he reached the bottom drawer, suddenly his hands stopped dead.

Had that been a noise in the hallway!

He cocked his ear toward the door. All was quiet.

Ashley tiptoed to the light, turned it off, then crept to the door and opened it a crack. The hallway was deserted.

He returned inside, sat down on the bed in the darkness, and waited. For five minutes he listened intently, but no other sound came. At length he switched the light back on and resumed his search by resolutely pulling out the top drawer of the second dresser.

It was filled merely with a few handkerchiefs and hair combs. He pulled it out as far as the drawer would come, but nothing else was revealed. It occurred to him that if Jo was clever enough to orchestrate such a cunning deception as had apparently been planned, she would not be so dull-witted as to leaving something incriminating out in the open where any visitor to her room might notice it. Surely she would have destroyed all ties to her true identity; even the initials on her luggage had been in keeping with the ruse: J.B.—though that might indeed be her real name.

If she had been so careful, what was he hoping to find, anyway? The room was bound to be clean.

Ashley was about to push the drawer back in when he suddenly recalled a ploy he had used himself a time or two. An amateurish trick, to be sure, certain to be discovered by any master detective. But it was worth a try—Jo was no doubt herself an amateur.

He smiled smugly to himself as he pulled the drawer out again, this time all the way out of its rails until he held the drawer in his hands. He examined the underside with one hand. Disappointed to find nothing, he stood a moment longer, then quickly turned and set the drawer down on the bed. Then he spun around, bent down, and scanned the vacant cavity of the dresser where the drawer had been.

Yes! There was something there, along the back side of the dresser.

He reached far back. His fingers felt a small white paper packet. He pried it loose and brought it out and set it in the palm of his hand. He opened the unsealed flap of the tiny envelope, sniffed, then peered inside to see about a teaspoonful of a white, crystalline powder. He moistened his finger and took up a few grains to taste, thought better of it, brushed them off, and sniffed it again. It smelled bitter, but even the most innocent of concoctions could be that.

More to the point, was this envelope Jo's? And why was it thus concealed?

Ashley examined the packet more closely, noticing for the first time a tiny bit of handwriting on one corner. He had missed it before because the words were few, written small, and in a light pencil. He had to hold it under the lamp to read it clearly. There were but two words: *Friar's cowl.*

Ashley rubbed his chin in contemplation. Where had he heard that name before?

He set the question aside for the moment as he realized he might now be able to determine ownership. If he could find a sample of Jo's handwriting, he could at least clear up that part of the mystery.

Going on hastily to the next drawer, he was rewarded in his quest as his eyes fell upon an appointment calendar. Thumbing through it quickly, the pages were oddly blank through August, the first notation being August 27: *Arrive Port Strathy.* Other engagements followed that: *Dinner at Smiths. . . . Market with Mother. . . . Lady Joanna to leave for London.*

It was clear this belonged to Jo. Ashley wasted no more time. He took the calendar and packet together, held them up to the lamp, and even in the poor light there could be no doubt the handwriting was the same. It did not answer every question, but at least he now knew that whoever the calendar belonged to was also the owner of the envelope of powder.

He removed his handkerchief from his pocket, poured out a small portion of the substance from the envelope into it, then carefully wrapped up the handkerchief. He wished he had something less porous to put it in, but this would have to do. He dropped it into his pocket, then carefully replaced the packet in its original hiding place, making sure the tape held it firm, then picked up the drawer off the bed and slid it back into the dresser.

Still puzzling over the words on the envelope, Ashley went on with his search. He examined the remainder of the bureau, drawer by drawer, though the contents were scant. In the bottom drawer, however, hidden inside a stocking and shoved far to the rear, his fingers felt something Logan had mentioned in a quick whisper to him the day he had arrived, and which he hàd later heard about from Hilary's own lips. Of course, in and of itself it would hardly be incriminating. Yet it was an interesting place to find it.

He closed the drawer, sat down again, still perplexed by the nagging uncertainty of the strange envelope. If only he could place that powder! He should know it. He had done extensive study of—

All at once Ashley jumped to his feet.

He spun around, his hand on his forehead.

Of course! he exclaimed half-aloud. *That's it! Dear God, I hope I'm not too late!*

He rushed out of the room, forgetful of the lamp still on and not even locking the door. In a full sprint he ran down the corridor, turned and flew down the stairs two at a bound.

In the ballroom, the moment "Scotland the Brave" had begun from the band, Logan interrupted Hilary's warm visit with the Mackenzies with the request for her favor on the dance floor, to which she assented with a smile and curtsy.

"I don't know very many of your northern dances," she confessed. "Though I'm having a good time trying."

" 'The Gay Gordons' is one of the easiest and most enjoyable of all," said Logan, "especially to the national anthem. I never tire of it."

"You'll show me what to do, then?"

"Just keep in step with me, and watch the other couples as we move in a large circle," said Logan, taking her left hand in his left, and her right hand as his arm came over her shoulders. "And when we need to turn, I'll give you a push or pull. Okay . . . here we go . . . right, left, right, *turn* . . . back, two, three, four. Change directions! . . . two, three, *turn* . . . back, two, three, four. Now I spin you slowly with my right hand . . . once, twice, three times . . . and now waltz position for a little quick-step around . . . perfect! You see, nothing to it!"

Hilary laughed.

"Now, here we go again!"

By the time the song was half over, they had gone through the dance four or five times and Hilary's feet were obeying her smoothly. But in the middle of the next two-step sequence, Ashley suddenly burst into the large room, glanced around hurriedly, then rushed toward them the moment he had found them among the many guests and dancers.

"Logan!" he called out, breathless, trying to keep his voice down so as not to arouse suspicion, yet obviously worked up. "Come with me."

"Why, Mr. Jameson—"

"No need for that any longer, Logan. She knows. But you must come . . . immediately! There's no time to lose!"

Leaving Hilary alone in the middle of the floor without even an explanation, Ashley led Logan back the way he had come, not even pausing to allow the latter to explain the hubbub to the astonished guests nearby.

Once in the hallway, Ashley began to grill Logan with questions as they made their way toward the stairway.

"I have been observing a great many things," he said as they hurried along, "not the least of which is your wife's deteriorating emotional state.

It has occurred to me that the problem may have other than an emotional cause. Tell me, has she been taking any medications lately?"

"None that I know of. An aspirin or two perhaps."

"Anything for her ankle?"

Logan paused in thought. "The doctor did give her a liniment."

"A liniment . . . hmm. That's interesting. I suppose it could . . ."

"But all this began long before she hurt her ankle."

"Can you say when, exactly?"

"It came on gradually. Perhaps around the time of Lady Joanna's death. Well, no—actually I recall some incidents even before that . . . nausea, depression. But I couldn't give an exact day."

"Perhaps two months ago?" asked Ashley, still walking rapidly along.

"That could be. Mid . . . late September. Yes, I suppose that's about right."

"What about von Burchardt? What do you know of him?"

"Only what he told us. Seems a nice enough chap."

"When was the first time you saw him?"

"Just the day before you got here, Ashley. Why?"

"I don't know, Logan. I don't know. I'm still trying to piece all this together. I'm grasping at anything."

"Why the urgency?"

"I may not have the full picture yet, but I have found some things that will interest you. For one thing, do you recognize this?"

Ashley pulled the locket from his coat pocket.

"Thank the Lord!" exclaimed Logan. "That's the locket . . . the one Allison gave little Joanna thirty years ago! Where did you find it?"

"It may or may not surprise you to learn that it was in a drawer in Jo's room."

"But I thought Hilary—"

"I did not say how it reached Jo's room," rejoined Ashley. "I just said that's where it was. We'll have to figure that out later. What about Lady Joanna. Just why did she go to London?"

Logan hesitated a long while before answering. When he at last spoke it was not without sadness in his tone. "She never said exactly. But though I've never wanted to admit it before, I think the reason was indeed just as Hilary's story implies, that she had doubts about Jo from the very first."

"You think your mother-in-law apprehended something deeper than you did?"

"I'm embarrassed to say it, but I think I blinded myself to what she saw because of how Allison took to Jo at first. She was so pleasant, made Allison feel happy and whole. I wanted to think everything was resolved. Joanna tried to tell me once. She got as far as suggesting that we ought to investigate Jo's credentials further, and I nearly blew up at her. It was the first time I can recall us having *words* with each other. After that, Joanna kept mostly to herself, probably thinking that if something was to be done about the situation, she would have to do it herself.''

"And what became of it?''

"Well, you know the rest. One way or another—I don't know how—Joanna located Hilary . . . their meeting . . . the journal. But Joanna's secrets died with her.''

"Then Hilary showed up here . . . and you called me?''

"Yes,'' said Logan with a sigh. "I think I always sensed something amiss, though I couldn't put my finger on it. That's probably why I insisted that Hilary stay.''

By this time they had arrived in the corridor that led to Jo's room. "Well, we're almost there,'' said Ashley. "I can guarantee what I have to show you will not be pleasant.''

Ashley opened the door. It was exactly as he had left it.

He walked straight to the bureau, pulled the top drawer out, again set it on the bed, then said to Logan, "Look in there.''

Logan obeyed.

"Take it out. I want you to find it just as I did a few moments ago.''

Following Ashley's example, Logan reached in, unfastened the small envelope, and brought it out into the light.

"What's inside?'' asked Logan.

"I'll tell you in a moment. But first I must ask you just a few more questions. First, is there *anything* Allison has been taking besides aspirin? Think, man—*anything!*''

Logan was silent, shaking his head slowly.

"All I can say is that *I* know of nothing.''

"Okay, then perhaps . . . I don't know. It could be the liniment,'' he said, speaking softly almost to himself. "But then there's the time problem. Still, it could absorb internally.''

"What's this all about, my friend?'' asked Logan.

Pondering but a second more, Ashley looked up, took a breath, then plunged ahead with his startling revelation.

"Logan,'' he said, "what you are holding in your hand is one of the most lethal poisons in existence. Just two milligrams of aconite internally is instantly fatal.''

"But Allison's fine! What does a deadly poison have to do with her?''

"I said *internally* that's how it works. The point here is that Allison is not fine! She has been more ill than we have had any idea—that is, if I am correct.''

"You think this white powder is responsible?''

"Yes, I do believe so. Aconite can also be absorbed through the skin. In past times they actually used the stuff in lotions and potions, in minuscule amounts of course, as a pain killer, for things like neuralgia—to deaden an area of muscle tissue.''

"But how would Allison—"

Before Logan could say a word further, suddenly Ashley's hand shot to his head as if remembering the missing piece to the puzzle.

"Logan!" he exclaimed. "When I was dancing with Allison just a while ago I couldn't help noticing that her hands had paint stains on them."

"She's been painting with Jo whenever she feels up to it."

"But why doesn't she clean it off her hands?"

"She always said it was the mark of a true artist to let some of the color remain behind."

"That's bunk! What artist have you ever heard of who only cleaned his hands halfway! What do Jo's hands look like?"

"Now that you mention it, they're always pure white."

"Precisely my point! That's got to be it, Logan!" He glanced almost frantically about the room, his eyes coming to rest on the top of the dressing table. The two tubes! . . . the palate! . . . the small cups! Of course! That had to be it! She mixed the poison right here!

"Logan!" he exclaimed. "It's the paints!"

"But how could—"

"In strong enough amounts, even a little on the skin, for a prolonged period of time . . . the cumulative effect!"

The swift rush of evidence bombarded Logan's consciousness, ripping the scales from his eyes. In another instant he was jolted into potent wakefulness.

With an outburst of righteous fury his hand slammed down upon the desk beside which he was standing. Without another word, he turned, flung wide the door, and—his hand still clutching the deadly packet, his eyes filled with fire, and his nostrils flared in indignation—strode from the room as a man possessed, prepared to do battle.

Ashley followed behind, not even pausing for a backward glance at the chamber from which such vile deception had secretly originated.

Had he looked in the opposite direction down the corridor, he might have seen a silent witness to their discovery, who had followed them, hiding in waiting, watching from a secluded shadow as Logan exited. The full effect of the revelation registered plainly upon his face; then he stealthily returned by another route to the room where his co-conspirator was at that moment attempting to consummate her wicked design.

51 / Flight

Logan stormed into the ballroom with such a fierce expression on his countenance that almost immediately the music ceased and all heads turned in his direction. As he strode purposefully into the room, he seemed to grow in stature, until the very resplendence of the ancient clan chieftainship came to dwell bodily upon him. With eyes aglow he quickly scanned the faces of his loyal people, searching for the tares among the wheat, that he might root them out and bring them to a righteous justice.

From where she stood, once again engaged with Frances Mackenzie, Hilary perceived at once—however calm and good-natured a man her father was—that the kettle of his wrath had boiled over. She rushed toward him.

"Where is Jo?" his voice thundered, not at Hilary, but to any who might care to listen.

All eyes scanned the hall. She was not to be seen.

"Has anyone seen the Viscount von Burchardt?" growled Logan. "I have evidence of a plot in my home, and I want to speak with him!" He gestured with his hand as he emphasized each word.

There was no sign of the Austrian.

As if in a single moment, Hilary, Logan, and Ashley each became aware that neither was Allison present. They glanced at one another, dawning dread in their eyes, then all three rushed toward the door into the main corridor of the house.

As he went, Logan shouted out orders.

"Hilary, you check the west wing—ground floor, then first floor. Ashley, go to the library."

Before he had well finished his words, they were gone.

"Jake" Logan went on, "I have no idea where they might be. Take a look outside . . . the stables . . . the barn. Moryson, run down to the kitchen and tell the cook that Mrs. Macintyre is missing. Tell her to enlist what help she can to look in that quarter of the house."

The two men went.

"Now, let's see . . . Creary, come with me. Mr. Davies, would you wait out by the main stairway, in front of the door? If anyone brings news, dispatch it about the house that the rest may be brought back. Let's go, Doug!"

They exited, leaving the ballroom in a storm of buzzing and bewildered anxious questioning.

Logan ran first to the drawing room, then the dining room, then the family parlor. Each was empty.

When he and Creary ran back along the corridor toward the front door, Hilary was just descending the staircase. In another moment Ashley ran up from the direction of the library.

"Moryson told me to say he went to look in the East Wing," said Davies.

"The East Wing?" repeated Logan. "There's nothing there but—"

At that very moment the sound of a revving car engine was heard, then the grinding of spinning tires across the graveled courtyard.

Logan spun around, as if debating whether to go after it.

"There is a little sitting room just where the East Wing connects with the inner courtyard," said Hilary. "I think I've seen Jo there a time or two."

"It's worth a try!" said Logan, leading the way. "We'll have to let the car go."

The small band followed him, but had difficulty keeping up. By the time they reached the spot and walked in the open door, Logan was already kneeling beside Allison where she lay on a sofa at the far end of the room.

"Jo brought me here to help me rest," Allison was saying in a weak voice. "She was just about to give me this"—she pointed to a glass sitting on a nearby end-table filled with some colorless liquid—"when that man rushed in. She said it would help me sleep."

"What man? Von Burchardt?"

"Yes . . . him."

"What did they do . . . where are they now?"

"I don't know. He said something to her about the game being up," she went on in a weak voice. "Then she tried to come back over and was going to give me the medicine. But he grabbed her hand and pulled her away. He said, 'We've got to get out of here!' "

Logan spun around. His eyes sought Ashley's, and in another moment the professor was on his way outside to check the car garage.

Slowly Logan took Allison in his arms. "Well, my dear," he said with a smile, "let's get those hands of yours cleaned up, and then put you to bed."

Just as they reached the hallway outside the room, Ashley returned.

"I don't know which car it was that drove away a minute ago," he said. "But there's only one missing from the garage . . . Jo's. Do you want me to go after them?"

Logan pondered for a moment.

"No," he said at length. "They're long gone by now. Once they're on Burchardt's yacht, we'd never be able to stop them. We'll have to find some other way."

In the late morning quiet of what had once been the proud command post of a high-placed generalissimo, now only one of a dozen such run-down villas stretching between the capital and Punta Norte, a man sat stirring his morning cup of coffee.

The weather here is downright fine, he thought to himself. Even after all this time he was still not tired of the sunshine and the 80-degree mornings, though he could not for the life of him acclimate himself to the inverted seasons. Summer in November and December—the thing was ridiculous! But he'd learned to live with everything else in this backward, rat-infested place—why not the seasons?

He paused in his reflections to sip the strong brew the servant had brought him.

"Fine weather," he muttered, "but these blasted provincials still can't make a decent cup of coffee! Crying shame, too—this close to where they grow the cursed beans, it ought to be better!"

He took another sip, grimaced, glanced at his watch, looked around, then added: "Where is that confounded idiot with the mail?" As if any of these foreigners could understand him anyway!

This sedentary life hardly suited him, though he had long ago managed to accustom himself to the inevitable. For one who had thrived on exercising his power over others, such a transition had not come easily. However, seated in the east garden of the villa, with servants at his beck and call— he would have been pleased to know that *they* at least still trembled at his command—he did manage to maintain a remote suggestion of the appearance of a retired country caballero surveying his range. But his expensive white linen suit was draped over an emaciated, almost wasted frame, and the rakish white straw hat shaded mottled, wrinkled skin from the searing sun. His mind these days was more occupied with reliving past glories, not to mention fomenting of past hatreds, than with the contentedness that should instead have come with old age.

With a bony hand, yet remarkably steady, he poured more cream into his cup, followed by one more cube of sugar, as if thinking to mask the bitterness of the concoction. It was a ritual he amused himself with every morning, realizing its futility all the while, yet choosing to play out the diversion as one of the few ruses left with which an old conniver could indulge himself.

His dark thoughts were interrupted by the approach of a servant, also attired from head to foot in white, but whose three-day growth of beard revealed that he was not a valet or house steward by profession. He, too, had once trained for what he regarded as better things. But in these days, with the Fatherland so Americanized, one had to go where one would be safe, and do what one could to get by. Such a strategy of pragmatism bound the inhabitants of Villa del Heimat together in an amalgamation of loose symbiotic relationships of convenience, seclusion, and survival.

"Die Post ist here," he said. "Shall I bring it to you, mein Herr?"

"Yes, of course, you fool!" exclaimed the other. "I'm expecting an important letter from—never mind from where! Just bring it here!"

Three minutes later he grabbed away from the hand that delivered it a single letter addressed in the handwriting he had been hoping to see, a flowing hand with which he was intimately familiar. Yet as he ripped open the envelope, the distinctive fire in his eyes reflected venom rather than love.

Hastily he scanned the two onionskin sheets. This was no time for dilly-dallying with familial pleasantries; he wanted news, even if the letter was dated a week earlier!

At length he put the letter down and gazed into the distance. The confounded new arrivals at the place had certainly thrown a kink into their plans. But it would all be over soon, and he would have what he had so long coveted. "So," he mused half articulately, "in the end it is I who remain." The hint of a smile crept over his aging lips. "And in the end it will be I who achieve this one final conquest. Not this time will you—"

His dark thoughts were interrupted by the crisp step of an approaching visitor. Glancing up, his face displayed immediate recognition.

"Ah, Herr Gunther."

"Mein lieber Kommandant!" replied the new arrival with a faint grin.

"I've told you not to call me that," croaked the other with as much visible anger as he could summon. "You know my title! Word must not leak out about my past identity."

Gunther laughed.

"You and your eccentric notions!" he said. "No one down here stands on protocol. No one cares about us. The world has forgotten, don't you know?"

"But I have not forgotten! I will never forget. And I will have my revenge!"

"Yes, yes, and I will do your bidding and help you keep fighting your private little war. But at least I suffer from no false delusions. Even your own company goes on without us."

"They do nothing without my consent!" squawked the old man, leaning forward in his chair as if he would wring the neck of his right-hand man for such an impertinent suggestion. "They will yet pay for humiliating me! I will make them pay!"

"Ah, General, look around," said Gunther in a highly uncharacteristic moment of philosophy. "This is a time to enjoy the fruits of our labors. It's not such a bad life. Better at least than that sardine can of a sub where—"

"You don't need to remind me of the past—I remember every bitter minute of this wretched existence I'm supposed to call life."

"You were glad enough for that existence thirty years ago when you stole the Reich's U-boat and made your escape."

"I well remember the incident!"

"Then you should know that you are fortunate to still be alive. Many of our comrades have not been so lucky. You know what happened to our friend—"

"I don't pay you to preach to me!"

With a sigh, which indicated that he knew how things were, and that he would continue to wield the General's gun and carry out his designs of treachery despite his words about pausing to enjoy life, Gunther pulled a yellow envelope out of his pocket. "I have been to the village," he said. "There was an important communique there for you—an urgent telegram."

"Give it to me!" demanded the old man, his shrieking voice cracking with the effort of the words.

The moment the paper was extended toward him, he snatched it away with a swiftness that contradicted the feebleness of his body, reminding the onlooker of the lightning-quick stroke of a frog's tongue snatching a fly out of midair. The old man ripped open the Western Union envelope and held its contents up before his rheumy eyes. Then he swore angrily, dropped the letter in his lap, and began groping on the table, knocking over the pitcher of cream in his exasperation.

"Where are those absurd spectacles?" he shouted.

The younger, albeit graying, man stepped forward and quickly located them on the table, then handed them to his employer.

The old man shoved them on his face, then grabbed up the telegram again. His lips moved, ruminating silently on the words his aged eyes beheld:

IGNORE PREVIOUS LETTER STOP PLAN EXPLODED STOP IDEN-
TITIES IN DANGER STOP HAVE FLOWN COOP STOP FULL RE-
PORT UPON ARRIVAL STOP.

His face flushed, his eyes bulged with incensed wrath.

"They cannot beat me again!" he screamed, his entire body now shaking with the culmination of his passion as he threw the telegram from him.

"Calm yourself, General," said Gunther, concern etched on his hardened sinister features.

"Shut up! I will never be calm! I will never rest! Not until they pay for this!"

He bent over in an attempt to retrieve the telegram, but lost his balance, and would have toppled from his chair had Gunther not been there to steady his emaciated frame.

For thanks the old man spat a barrage of profanity at the man—who now had been with him twenty years—and continued in a steady stream even as another paroxysm of coughing possessed him, his heated face growing red from mingled anger and exertion.

Gunther turned and walked into the house, leaving the once mighty leader gasping for breath. He sent the servant for the doctor, then left the villa, wondering how much longer the old man could cheat death out of its due.

Three people in Stonewycke's family sitting room enjoying tea together was not an unusual scene.

Two women shared the divan, while the acknowledged head of the family stood in front of the sideboard on which he had just placed the pot from which he had poured tea.

A familiar setting, an afternoon chat in the sitting room, it was indeed. But never before in the lives of these three had there been a gathering quite like this one. And never would there be again.

Allison had been in bed since the evening of the party, and had only a short time ago come down for the first time. She was still frail, but a smile had returned to her lips, a hint of the real Allison already beginning to re-emerge.

Since that fateful night, Logan had spoken to Hilary only briefly, and more casually than he would have liked. It was clear from the upbeat mood about the place that everything had suddenly changed at Stonewycke, and he had looked for an opportunity to bring it out into the open. However, he had driven to Aberdeen the following day in order to set investigations in motion. In addition, he felt it fitting that he await his wife's recovery for this emotion-filled moment.

Logan turned and cleared his throat.

"I don't really know what to say . . ." he began.

The two women chuckled and glanced at each other, a nervous release for all the feelings pent up inside.

"That's a switch, isn't it?" he added. "Logan Macintyre at a loss for words!"

Now they laughed outright, and Logan could not help joining them.

"I *don't* know what to say, Hilary," he went on more seriously. "I'm sorry I was away yesterday. But maybe it's better this way, since now that Allison is feeling better we can all have our first tea together."

"I couldn't help keeping to myself yesterday either," said Hilary, staring down into the cup she held in her lap. "I had a lot to think about, and I almost found myself avoiding this moment. It's all so new to me. I didn't know what to do at first. I felt like a shy schoolgirl on her first date."

"Well . . . here we are at last," said Logan. "And I've not been able to avoid the feeling that some sort of more formal—I don't know . . . apology, perhaps, was called for on the part of Allison and myself—"

"Please," interrupted Hilary, "you know that's not necessary."

"It is necessary," he repeated. "At least it's necessary for us. We did not behave to you when you came as we now wish we had."

"You couldn't have known," protested Hilary.

"Nevertheless, we are sorry it was difficult for you. Needless to say, we grieve over the years since you were . . . lost to us . . . that we did not do more—somehow . . ." He stopped, took a deep breath, and struggled to continue. His voice was gruff and uncertain.

" . . . that we did not do more . . . to confirm the reports . . . of your death—though we exhausted what resources we knew of."

Still Hilary gazed into her cup, her thoughts far away. Her eyes were clouding over with tears.

"Thankfully," said Logan, laboring to keep his voice intact, "those long years and these last uncertain months are now behind us. As frivolous as it may sound after all we have just been through, we mean it with all our hearts when we say we want to welcome you back into your family."

"Thank you," Hilary whispered. A lump rose in her throat. "I . . . I don't know what to say either," she half laughed.

Allison's hand reached toward her. Hilary clasped it and held tight. Even as she did so she lifted her eyes, and they met those of the man she now knew she loved, not merely as a statesman or a friend . . . but as a *father*.

Logan set down his cup of tea and slowly approached his wife and daughter. Suddenly, Hilary was out of her seat and in his arms. Without restraint, her tears of thirty years flowed out onto Logan's chest, while his strong arms wrapped around her shoulders and pulled her tightly to him.

For a moment they stood—silent . . . weeping. Allison rose and walked toward them. Without words, Logan gently loosened himself from Hilary's embrace so that mother and daughter might join their hearts as well.

Hilary turned. There stood Allison gazing upon her, her recently beleaguered countenance now overspread with a radiant smile, tracks of tears falling down her pale cheeks.

"Oh, Mother!" exclaimed Hilary, rushing forward to embrace her.

"I'm so sorry I doubted you!"

"It's over now, Mother," breathed Hilary softly.

"Oh, but I feel like such a fool," wept Allison, "being taken in like that when my own daughter . . . shouting at you like I did . . . I'm so sorry . . ."

She could not continue, but broke down, her shoulders convulsing with sobs.

Hilary held her close, while Logan now stretched his arms about the two women, his own tears flowing freely.

"We all have to live with the pain of our regrets," he said softly. "How deeply I wish I had been a better father when you were with us thirty years ago!"

"I weep in my heart to think that I nearly rejected what Lady Joanna told me," said Hilary. "I almost did . . . I didn't want to see my life turned upside-down."

"All our lives have certainly changed . . . and will change," said Logan. "And though perhaps all three of us will have to bear these pains yet a while longer, they will be healed. Our Father will use them to strengthen the bonds of our love which we are only beginning to discover."

Gradually the tears began to lessen and they resumed their seats around the fire.

"I want you to know," said Hilary after a moment, "that I no longer have any doubts. I'm . . . I'm *glad* you are my parents."

"We love you, Hilary," said Allison.

"Thank you . . . Mother," replied Hilary, tears rising in her eyes afresh. But she brushed them back and tried to laugh.

"I don't even know what to call you," she said to Logan.

"Call me whatever you are comfortable with . . . Logan suits me fine."

"Then I'll call you Logan," said Hilary with a smile, "until the word *Father* comes a little more naturally."

"And what do *we* call you?" asked Allison. "I must admit it's going to be difficult to think of you as Jo or Joanna now. But I love the name Hilary too; that's why we chose it for you."

Hilary laughed. "It's served me well for many years!"

"I think our daughter will always be Hilary to me from now on," said Logan. "Hilary—one who brings joy! I can't think of anything more suitable. It was as Hilary we came to know you. But tell me . . . *Hilary*," he went on, "when did you first know? I mean really *know* . . . that is, after you arrived here?"

"In the gallery. But I haven't yet told you what happened the night of the party, have I?"

"No. Tell us, please," insisted Allison.

"Oh, but we've got to be there! It can't really be told at all. What I experienced that night has to be seen!"

"By all means then," said Logan enthusiastically. "Let's go to the gallery!"

"We'll have to go by way of my room," said Hilary, "so that I can slip into another dress."

"Whatever you say!"

Logan led the way to the door, opened it for the two ladies, then, with his wife on one arm and his daughter on the other, escorted them down the corridor and to the stairway.

Only the daughter was prepared for what awaited them. Indeed, had the husband and wife been aware of the astounding revelation which was shortly to greet their eyes, they would much earlier have realized in whom the legacy of young Maggie Duncan had flowered.

"The local doctor has kindly given me permission to use the small laboratory in his surgery," Ashley said to Hilary when he knocked at her door the following morning. "Would you care to join me for a drive into Port Strathy?"

"Sure," answered Hilary. "What do you need a lab for?"

"The packet. Thus far I have only speculated on the contents of what I found in Jo's room. It's imperative not only for the police investigation but also for Allison's continued treatment that we identify it precisely. I want to run some tests."

Hilary grabbed up her coat and a hat, then joined Ashley in the corridor.

"Can't the police do all that?" she asked as they made their way downstairs.

"Logan is still uncertain how far to bring the authorities into this. He's made some discreet inquiries of his own, but he wants to know more before it turns into a full-blown public investigation."

"And you're his sleuth, eh?"

"No comment," said Ashley, a boyish grin tugging at the corners of his mouth. "Let's just call it my little hobby."

Hilary threw him a sidelong glance as they walked down the stairs, finding it difficult to keep her curiosity in check.

Once out in the open air by a side door, they walked around to the front of the house where Ashley's car awaited them. Ashley opened the passenger door of the BMW for Hilary and saw her comfortably seated, then went around to the driver's side and slid in.

A few moments later Dr. Connally emerged from the house, climbed into his own car, and followed them into town. In ten minutes the two automobiles pulled up in front of the doctor's office on Port Strathy's main street next to the mercantile. Dr. Connally ushered them in, led them down a narrow hallway to the back of the building, then, switching on a light, welcomed them to his laboratory.

"It isn't much," he said, "but it does save me having to send out many of my samples and specimens. It takes at least forty-eight hours to use the Aberdeen facilities."

He began to clear a place on one of the counters. "Here you go, Mr. Jameson. I hope we have everything you need. I'm not exactly equipped for this sort of thing. I'm not even certain I could make such a test without using a reference book."

279

"I'm sure we'll manage fine," said Ashley.

"I'm still rather curious where a Greek historian comes by a knowledge of forensic medicine."

"So am I," added Hilary with a raised eyebrow.

"Just picked it up here and there," said Ashley, coughing nervously. "Now, let's see," he went on, changing the subject, "what will we need?"

With the help of the doctor, he gathered a petri dish, a vial of phosphoric acid syrup, sodium molybdate solution, and a Bunsen burner. He poured a portion of each of the chemicals into the dish, then sprinkled in some of the powdered solution from the envelope. He gave the concoction a stir, then, clamping the dish with a handle, held it out over the flame, moving the dish gently back and forth. Before long the substance in the dish began to turn color, eventually becoming a brilliant violet. The three observers exchanged meaningful glances.

"Just as I suspected," said Ashley. "This confirms aconite. Now to see if my further speculation is true. By itself, perhaps, the mere presence of poison would not be considered incriminating by a court of law, but . . ."

He did not finish the sentence, but instead took from his pocket a small container of the blue paint he had removed from Allison's own palette in the solarium. He had taken two other colors also, but had particularly chosen the blue because of the tube he had found in Jo's room, which he assumed was sitting on her dressing table awaiting its fatal addition.

He repeated the procedure he had used on the powder.

Because the paint was a diluted concentration, the change when it came was not so startling, but there could be no mistaking the change to violet when the mixture was held over the flame.

"I can hardly believe it!" said the doctor.

Ashley had spent too much time prowling about Scotland Yard not to believe it; long ago his naivete about human nature had been abandoned.

"The tests will be finalized," said Connally, "when I have completed the analysis of Lady Allison's blood sample. That will take somewhat longer. I will also send a sample to Aberdeen to confirm the testing."

"Will she recover from all this?" asked Hilary with concern.

"Yes," replied the doctor, "but it will take time for all the effects to work their way out of her body."

"We are fortunate in one respect," said Ashley. "Had Jo been in a hurry and administered this substance orally, Allison would have died almost instantly—especially in that she possessed the crystalline variety, which is ten to fifteen times more poisonous than other forms. I only wonder where she could have gotten it. Aconite is obsolete these days, extremely difficult to come by."

"I have a colleague," offered Connally, "who served as a medical missionary in Central America. He was appalled at the outmoded drugs still to be had there."

"Central America, you say?" pondered Ashley. "Hmm . . . that is interesting."

"What is it?" asked Hilary.

"Oh, I don't know . . . maybe nothing. But when we were having a look about von Burchardt's yacht, I took a good look at the registration sticker."

"And?"

"I can tell you it wasn't registered in Austria or Germany. Nowhere in Europe at all. That was when I began to have extreme doubts that our friend Emil was telling the truth."

"Where was the boat from?"

"It was carrying an Argentine registration."

Hilary let out a long, low whistle.

"Argentina," thought the doctor aloud. "Yes, I suppose it's possible. In fact, it wouldn't surprise me a bit if you could still come by such compounds there."

"Let's get home," said Hilary, turning to Ashley. "I don't want to be away too long."

"Are you coming back to the house, Doctor?" asked Ashley.

"I have another patient to see in a few minutes. Then I want to prepare some medication for Lady Allison. I'll return in about an hour."

"Thank you again for the use of your facilities."

Back in the car, Hilary turned to Ashley as he started up the engine. "It continues to amaze me—the wide range of your knowledge," she said. "You're a regular Renaissance Man! How do you fit everything in?"

"All in a day's work, you know."

"Something tells me there's more to it than that."

"You're not a mystery buff, are you, Hilary?"

"On the contrary, I love mysteries. Unraveling them is one of my jobs as a reporter."

"It's my job too."

"The mysteries of the past?"

"Yes . . . of course." He paused, carefully considering his words. "But I am highly interested in present-day mysteries too."

"The clues . . . the poison . . . going about the house at night looking for manuscripts and lockets and evidence?"

"Have I really been so obvious as a prying would-be Sherlock Holmes about the place?"

Hilary laughed.

Suddenly Ashley seemed to grow very serious, as if pondering some weighty matter. He drove up the hill out of town very slowly, his mind far from the actions of his hand. At length he spoke again.

"So, Hilary," he said, "you like journalistic mysteries."

Hilary nodded.

"Do you like to *read* mysteries?"

"You mean stories?"

"Yes. Mystery novels."

"Conan Doyle . . . Ellery Queen? Yes, in fact, I do."

"Would you think it peculiar if I told you I do too?"

"No, I don't think so." She paused, then laughed. "Is that what this is all about? Renown Greek scholar secretly a devotee of pulp mystery novels! It's my scoop of the decade!"

"I'm afraid it's more serious than that."

"They're not going to defrock you because you enjoy a good story. Everyone needs a diversion."

"But as I said, it's a more serious compulsion for me than that."

All at once he pulled the car to the side of the road and ground to a stop. "Come with me," he said. "Let's go for a walk."

They got out of the car, crossed the road, and continued walking in the direction they had been headed. They were only a hundred yards or so from the crest of the hill, toward which they now made their way, the vast blue North Sea spreading out below them. For a long time Ashley was silent, and Hilary did not press him.

At last he drew in a deep sigh, exhaled, and then spoke.

"What I'm about to tell you only one other person in the world knows. It's one of the best kept secrets in the modern publishing world, and you've got to promise me you'll never tell a soul."

"Is it all really so serious, Ashley?"

"For me . . . yes, it is. My private life is important. Sacrificing it is not something I am willing to do."

"Then I promise. But you don't have to tell me this. I promise, I won't press if you'd rather—"

"I *want* to tell you," he interrupted, emotion obviously building within him. "I have known I would have to tell you for some time . . . ever since that day I wasn't exactly truthful with you."

"You had to keep the truth from me, Ashley. I hold none of what happened against you."

"I don't mean about Allison or my knowing Logan or what I was doing here or the ruse about meeting Ian. I wasn't altogether comfortable with that, but I accepted that I would have to play such a 'role' so to speak in order to get at the deeper truth of what was going on. But there were other times, when we were talking more personally, when I could not escape the feeling that I was lying to you."

"Oh, Ashley, don't torture yourself with guilt over such little things."

"But don't you see? Everything I said that day about truth mattering— it really does matter a great deal to me. Living by truth is my whole life. I've not had the chance to share with you as much as I would like. But I am a Christian—"

"I knew that."

"How?"

"It's obvious. By the way you live, the way you care. You're a very compassionate individual, Ashley Jameson."

"Then maybe it won't come as such a surprise for me to say that the little things are important to me. And I haven't been able to get out of my mind that day when we were walking out in the snow. Do you remember?"

"How could I forget?"

"You asked me if I ever wrote anything but history."

"I remember."

"I said no. I lied to you—point blank. It had nothing to do with Jo or Logan or my so-called investigation at the house. I just lied. And I've been uncomfortable with it ever since. Your question caught me off guard. I fumbled around for words, and before I knew it, I'd allowed myself to tell you something that wasn't true. So now I have to try to make it right."

"I understand," said Hilary. "Just so long as you know that you have in no way injured or offended me."

"Understood," said Ashley. "Besides," he added, stopping and looking into her face, "now I want to tell you. I want you to know me, because . . . well, the revealing of a close secret to a friend is a rather personal thing to do."

"Ashley, is this your rather Victorian way of saying that you care for me?"

"I suppose it is." He cleared his throat and chuckled awkwardly. "Of all my varied areas of knowledge, affairs of the heart is one arena in which I am an unskilled and inexperienced participant."

Hilary chuckled softly, then slipped her hand through his arm. He smiled, seemed to gather strength from her simple yet heartfelt gesture, then plunged ahead.

"Like I said, I like mysteries."

"As do I," added Hilary, her heart bounding as she walked by Ashley's side.

"Not only do I like to read mysteries, I like to try to solve them. I have a friend in Scotland Yard. Sometimes he lets me in on his cases. That's how it all started, in fact, years ago, when we were both students in the university. But that caper is another story altogether!"

"Promise you'll tell me someday," said Hilary.

"Promise. But not only do I like to get involved in real cases, I then . . ." He paused. This was more difficult than he had anticipated. He took another breath. ". . . I then write down my experiences."

"A mystery journal. What a great idea!" exclaimed Hilary.

"Not exactly a journal. I . . . I change the facts around from the way they really happened . . . add color here and there . . . change the setting . . . change the names."

"Ashley! Are you trying to tell me you're a closet mystery writer, with a drawer full of short stories taken from the police files?"

"In a manner of speaking . . . yes."

"That's exciting! I love it! Why would you be embarrassed to tell people that?"

"Because I've even had some of my work published."

"You have? That's great! But I've never seen your—Of course!" she exclaimed. "You use a pen name!"

Ashley nodded sheepishly.

"Ashley Jameson the historian turns out to be none other than a whodunit mystery writer! No wonder you wanted to keep this under wraps! So, what magazines have your stories been in? I'd like to see them."

"They haven't been in magazines, actually."

"What then . . . a book . . . an anthology of short stories?"

"I didn't say I wrote short stories."

"Long stories then . . . what?"

All at once a portion of the truth broke in upon Hilary.

"Ashley . . . you don't mean you write mystery books . . . novels?"

"I'm afraid so."

"That's fantastic! Please, stop beating around the bush. What's your pen name?"

Ashley sighed. "I've come this far, I guess you might as well have the whole enchilada, as they say on the streets of New York. Well . . . here it is—but I'm afraid you might recognize her name. And then what will you think of me?"

"I'll think none the less of you!" pleaded an exasperated Hilary. "Just be out with it before I—" Suddenly she paused. "Did you say *her*?" she asked.

Ashley nodded.

"She! Your pseudonym is a woman!"

"Rather a well-known one I must confess. The name was first given me by my friend at the Yard. I've since thought of having him drawn and quartered."

"Ashley, you don't mean. . . ?"

Again Ashley nodded modestly.

"But, Ashley, she's one of the best-selling mystery writers in the country. Over a dozen books! You can't be . . . but, you are serious!"

"Now you see why I've got to keep it quiet."

Hilary's mouth hung open in dumfounded amazement.

"I can't believe it!" she said. "I just can't believe it! Ashley Jameson, my toe-in-the-sand, tweed suit, soft-spoken Ashley Jameson, stuffy old Greek scholar, is none other than—Lady Hargreave herself!"

Ashley did not reply. His mind was too full of the revelation he had just made, and his heart was too full of the woman at his side, for words to be possible just now.

Hilary clung to Ashley even more tightly, then slowly rested her head upon his arm, a quiet smile of contentment on her lips.

Together they continued walking, in silence, long beyond the gates of Stonewycke, eventually discovering a long disused path down the bluff to the sea. They talked about many things, not the least of which was their future together.

It was well over an hour before they returned to the car.

"Well, I'll tell you when I first knew something was up," said Logan. "During that very first luncheon with our old friend von Burchardt. I had a nervous feeling about him all along. Do you remember how he slipped around all my attempts to pin him down?"

He and Ashley were seated across the table from Allison and Hilary in the inner courtyard where they had just finished a light lunch. The sun was shining and the air, protected as it was from any breath of wind, was unseasonably warm. Ashley and Hilary had arrived back at the house just as Flora was setting the table.

"I was confused all along," said Hilary. "Just when the viscount would flash that smile of his, making me sure he was up to no good, I'd see Ashley walking off across the lawn with Jo, and grow so suspicious and infuriated with him that I'd begin to succumb to Emil's oily charms."

"I've explained that," laughed Ashley. "That time we were talking in your room, just after the incident with the music box when you were so distraught—"

"When I berated you for all your truth and integrity talk—"

"That's the time! You were so upset, passion written all over your face, your eyes aglow. . . . Suddenly it dawned on me whose face I was seeing in yours. It was Logan's! In that moment I knew beyond any doubt that you were his daughter."

"So why then did you rush right out and take up with Jo again?" asked Hilary with a twinkle in her eye.

"Because before I said anything I had to be positively sure. I had to look at her face again. I even tried to bait her with some leading questions, seeing if I could get a rise out of her, seeing if I could detect anything whatsoever that reminded me of either Allison or Logan. I had seen such confirmation from the flash in your eye that I had to gather my final bit of evidence from Jo's face."

"What did you find?" asked Allison, clearly feeling much better.

"Nothing. Not a trace. She was a cool one. She could almost have fooled me if I hadn't gotten to know Hilary so well."

"Of course I had to keep my distance from you," Logan said to Ashley, "when anyone was around. It wasn't easy getting you off by yourself so we could compare notes. And von Burchardt was a complication I'd never counted on when I called you."

"Speaking of von Burchardt," said Hilary thoughtfully, "do you remember, Ashley, that I told you I asked my friend at the *Review* to check up on you? At the same time I gave him Emil's name."

"And?"

"He hadn't found anything out when we last talked. I ought to give him a call."

"Why don't you, right now?" suggested Logan. "We need to know who we're up against in this plot against us. And what are their motives."

"I will," said Hilary, rising. "I'll go call him right now."

She left and walked to the library. Fifteen minutes later she returned.

"I have some most interesting news!" she announced.

"You got through?"

"Did I ever! I'm not sure where this leaves us, but one thing is certain—we're up against something bigger than merely Jo and Emil."

"Out with it, Hilary," chided Ashley. "We're on pins and needles!"

"Okay. My associate on the *Review*, Murry Fitts, did an investigation on our friend the viscount. He hadn't called me yet, he said, because there were some other names he was trying to get that he thought might tie in. In any case, here's what he has so far."

She paused, flipped through the small notebook she had been holding, and then began. "Emil's story, as far as it went, is true. A titled Austrian family whose wealth goes back many generations. However, they lost everything during the depression and were quick to espouse Nazi propaganda. The elder viscount was made a minister in the Nazi regime formed in Austria in 1938 when Hitler annexed that country. This von Burchardt was eventually promoted to Hitler's own inner circle in Berlin. At the end of the war he escaped with many other war criminals and disappeared. He was thought to have wound up in South America."

A whistle escaped Ashley's lips.

"What is it?" asked Logan.

"I was just telling Hilary this morning that von Burchardt's yacht was not from the Continent at all, but bore an Argentine registration. It had a Buenos Aires port of entry emblem just below the registration."

"Most observant of you," said Logan, impressed.

"He is rather remarkable, isn't he?" added Hilary coyly. "I think I shall have Murry put his name in the police computer after all."

"The results will be quite boring, I assure you!" rejoined Ashley.

"I doubt that!" said Hilary. "But I wouldn't doubt that the implication of your discovery regarding the yacht is correct. Emil has indeed spent a great deal of time in South America. But—and I can't imagine how Murry got this; I'm afraid to ask—the Israeli Mossad has tried to trace Emil to possible war criminals, but have come up consistently empty. Nevertheless, it does make one wonder."

"War criminals," mused Logan. "Will it never end?"

"The old Nazis are dying off," said Hilary. "But I suppose their progeny must be accounted for."

"The sins of the fathers, and all that," said Ashley. "But it would be blind on our part to fall into such a trap."

"I fully agree," said Hilary. "On the other hand, it would be unwise to become lethargic as long as even a remote possibility exists. In Emil's case, however, there is no such direct evidence. He is doubtless a liar and a deceiver, apparently even an accomplice to an attempted murder. But that does not make him a Nazi, too."

"What *does* it make him?" asked Logan pointedly.

"That is the substance of my chat with Murry," answered Hilary. "Murry has been involved in his own investigation of a seemingly unrelated matter. Now all of a sudden the paths of these two sets of circumstances have intersected in a most interesting fashion—intersected at the common point of our friend the viscount."

"What is Fitts's story about?" asked Ashley.

"A contact of his—a man, I might add, who is running for his life, supposedly because of this very information he possesses—came to him with an incredible story that connects one of Europe's most influential international companies, Trans Global Enterprises, with syndicated crime."

"Logan, that's the company you told me about after Ringersfeld's call," said Allison, who had been paying closer attention to the course of the conversation than her scant contributions would have indicated.

"Yes . . . I know," said Logan soberly. He gave a thoughtful nod, still pondering the implications of what he had just heard. "It appears perhaps there are more intersecting paths here than any of us realized. My staff has recently begun its own investigation of that company. But go on, Hilary."

"Have you heard of an underworld figure known as 'The General'?"

"Seems to ring a faint bell," said Logan. "Like something I heard when I was talking to a chap from Interpol."

Ashley shook his head. "I probably should know the name. But I'm sadly out of touch with things—you know, the cloistered Oxford lifestyle."

"Not as much as you think, Ashley," said Hilary. "Murry's contact is an ex-Oxford don himself, an art expert who now deals extensively on the black market, high-stakes stuff. Murry didn't take the time to tell me how all this relates, if he even knows yet himself. But this General is an enigmatic figure whom Interpol and other intelligence agencies have been after for years. No one knows who he really is, where he operates from, or exactly what he's into. But he's suspected of racketeering in everything from drugs to weapons to diamond smuggling—you name it. So then all of a sudden this Oxford fellow of Murry's quite by accident stumbled upon a connection between the General and Trans Global—a connection which, if true, is front-page stuff that would have a thunderous impact on the stock market, government contracts, and all kinds of economic implications."

Logan sat as one transfixed. As recent Minister of Economics, he was intimately familiar with the effect news such as this could have, and could not believe what he was hearing.

"So Murry has been burrowing his way into the maze of that company," Hilary went on, "as quietly as possible, to say the least. And in so doing he chanced upon the piece of news that concerns us—our very own Emil von Burchardt, it seems, is a product consultant for that organization, actually a vice-president in charge of international marketing, or some such title. Of course, that could mean just about anything."

"An impressive, though shady, dossier to have come up with in such a short time. Your man Murry must be quite a guy."

"He's a workhorse. I couldn't run the magazine without him," said Hilary.

"Considering von Burchardt's record," suggested Logan, "it's entirely possible that his so-called position could be little more than a front that allows him free movement all over the world."

"Exactly!" said Hilary.

"And that yacht of his is the perfect cover," added Ashley. "Who knows what he might be carrying in that thing?"

"He could easily be a liaison between the General and the more legitimate side of the operation," said Logan, thinking aloud.

"Which, as farfetched as it sounds, could be Trans Global," said Ashley.

"A big assumption, I realize," admitted Hilary. "But what a journalistic coup if it is true. Can you imagine the story?" Her eyes glistened with the thought.

"And you'd like to be there with Murry when it comes off the presses?" laughed Logan.

"I have a feeling my thirst for adventure will be sufficiently fulfilled right here."

"Where does Jo fit into all this?" asked Ashley.

"Unfortunately, that's all Murry has at the moment—just this connection between Emil and Trans Global. He's trying to find some other names that tie in. Whether we'll get a line on Jo and who she is and what part she plays, I don't know. He promised to call back the minute he has something more."

The small group fell silent.

"I don't know how all these fragments of information are going to tie together," said Logan at last. "But I have the strong sense that we are only beginning to unravel them. Where they will lead us in the end, only the Lord knows at present."

"Well, I need some air," announced Ashley. "Hilary . . . how about a stroll outside?"

"I have an even better idea," she replied.

"Why won't you tell me where we're going?" asked Ashley.

"You'll find out, all in good time! It's a mystery—you should enjoy being kept in the dark!"

At Hilary's insistence, she and Ashley had taken two horses out and were now crossing the desolate heath south of the castle. Jake had carefully saddled the two animals, checking their blankets twice for any foreign materials.

"I dinna want to see nae runaway creatures for the twa o' ye, Leddy Hilary," he said.

"The last time I took out one of the horses," she explained to Ashley, "I nearly broke my neck. Someone had put a thorn under my saddle when I left the horse for a few minutes. At least I do owe that much to Emil. He saved me from a horrible spill."

"Do you think they planned the whole thing?"

"Who knows? I'm now convinced she knew he was coming. It had to be the two of them I saw together in the woods. Then the next day he showed up just in time to rescue me and begin trying to charm me. Whether the thorn and the rescue were part of the scheme, or just a spur-of-the moment nicety on Jo's part, I don't know."

"They sure didn't let on they were acquainted. I'd never have guessed it at first, though as time went on and I watched them both more closely, I began to wonder about some things."

"Almost as secretive as you and my . . . father."

Ashley looked over at her. "It has a nice ring to it, Hilary," he said. "I truly am happy for you."

She reached across, took his outstretched hand, gave it a squeeze, then smiled. "Thank you."

"You know, what Jake said a while ago is true—you are a 'lady' now. How does it feel?"

Hilary did not respond for some time. The only sound to be heard was the rhythmic clip-clop of their horses' hooves over the damp earth.

"It's scary," she said at length. "Everything I resisted for so long is suddenly a part of me . . . who I am. It's not just the nobility itself, it's everything this family is, all it stands for—there's such a spiritual heritage. Scary . . . but I have to admit there's an excitement to it, too! What might God have in store for me as . . . as a Macintyre, a Duncan, a member of the Ramsey clan! Oh, that reminds me—I have to call Suzanne! She won't believe all this!"

"Suzanne?"

"Suzanne Heywood—a friend of mine. Daughter of a lord. You might have known him. She lives down in Brighton. But to answer your question, I don't really *feel* a lot different. But this will take a lot of sinking in. It's going to alter the way I view my job, my writing, my perspective on the country—everything!"

"You have time to get used to it," said Ashley comfortingly. "You've been through a great emotional upheaval."

Again they fell silent.

"You know," said Hilary at length, "you sit that horse pretty well. If I didn't know better, I would think you've spent some time in the saddle."

"Us renaissance men, who double as mystery writers, like to indulge in a wide range of experiences—grist for the mill, I believe it's called. Like riding horses and attending fashion shows."

"Will you ever cease amazing me? Well, I'm no horsewoman, I can tell you that. But I had such a good time the other day—before the thorn, that is. And the horses were always such an intrinsic part of Stonewycke. I thought it fitting that we go out for a ride."

"Then how about a little canter!" As he spoke Ashley urged his mare forward into a gentle trot. Hilary's mount followed.

"Ohhhhh!" she yelled, hanging on to the horn as if for dear life.

Within another thirty minutes, with some perceptive pointers from Ashley, Hilary was becoming comfortable with the old-fashioned mode of transportation. They had traversed through the outlying farmlands southeast of the castle and were now circling south onto the bluff where only sparse vegetation was visible.

"Your question about my adaptation to life as a *lady* has other implications than just my life at Stonewycke," said Hilary as they rode along. "It also adds to my puzzlement of what I am to do with you in my thinking."

"Because you are a *lady*?"

"No. Because *you* are a lord."

"What has that to do with anything?"

"I don't like the aristocracy, remember?"

"Rather a difficult position to maintain now, I would think."

"Just because I have to accept myself as of noble birth doesn't mean I have to automatically change all my associations."

"I see. So you are going to continue holding my birth against me, even though I had no hand in planning it, but as for your case, you will allow yourself to be absolved completely?"

"I see nothing so unreasonable about that."

"Spoken with the logic of a woman," said Ashley, who then broke into a good-natured laugh.

"Ashley Jameson, you are determined to infuriate me!"

"Hilary, be reasonable. Jesus went about with the poor, with the middle class, and with the wealthy. Just as He did not hold poverty against a man, neither did He hold riches. How can we do any differently? God looks at every man's and every woman's heart, be they poor or rich. To discriminate against the nobility in attitude is as unacceptable to God as the rich keeping the poor downtrodden under their feet. Both are errors of extreme."

Hilary thought for several moments.

"I should know better than to expose my quirks to you, Ashley. How can you be so reasonable . . . and so right?"

"I've thought about these things."

"Do you think everything through?"

"I suppose I do."

"Why? Don't you ever just react spontaneously?"

"Of course I do. But even then, I think about my actions, even after the fact. It's part of my stewardship as a Christian. To me, every detail of life is to be submitted to Christ's lordship. Therefore, I have to think through the details of life so I can be aware of those areas where I need to focus my prayers more intently."

"I would not have known that about you just by looking."

"You once said you could tell I was a Christian by seeing how I did things. I'm glad of that. But at the same time, my faith is something I don't go spreading about all the time."

"Is that why you said nothing to me about it for so long?"

"I've always felt that matters of belief, heart attitudes, are an intensely personal thing. I'm not comfortable sharing on that level until I genuinely know someone, and they know me. Very few of my colleagues at Oxford know that I pray for them as I walk in their midst across campus, or that I start every day with prayer, or that my tiniest actions I hold up to scrutiny against the commands of the Bible. Those are personal things. It's not that I think any of them would laugh or consider me a kook. That hardly concerns me. It's simply that my priority in life is to *live* by what Jesus taught, to model my life after His, rather than to talk about spiritual truths. In other words, I want to live my faith first, talk about it second."

Again Hilary was silent. It was some time before she spoke again.

"Being with you is showing me many things about myself," she said quietly. "I've been a Christian for years. I take my faith seriously too. But I think I have never really weighed the necessity for taking my belief into the tiniest details of life, as you said. There has always been within me a— I don't know . . . a feeling, I guess, that God was in complete control of my life and everything in it."

"That's faith too. A wonderful, strong sense of His hand undergirding all of life. There's nothing wrong with that."

"Yet perhaps God does want more from me. More of that daily, moment-by-moment, detailed sort of awareness of what really comprises godly behavior—in *every* interaction, *every* attitude, *every* decision."

"I think He wants that from us all. That's why I do think through my actions and attitudes—as unspontaneous as it may seem! Because I think God is worthy of my dedication to Him at the deepest levels of everything I say and do and think."

"Ashley, you are something!" sighed Hilary. "I think I could very easily become attached to you!"

"I'm not sure how to take that," replied Ashley. "As I recall, you were rather taken with von Burchardt, and look at what he turned out to be."

"That's not fair! I wasn't taken by him for a minute! I couldn't stand the fellow. I was only trying to see what you would do."

Ashley threw his head back and laughed. "There's that woman's memory to go along with your woman's logic! Think now, Hilary. You couldn't stand me!"

"Well . . . maybe just for a while there I was a bit confused." She threw him a coy grin. "Oh, but look!" she exclaimed. "We're here!"

"Where are we?"

"This is where I wanted to bring you."

"All I see is a deserted hillside with nothing visible for miles."

"But that's the beauty of this place. Come this way. There's something I want to show you. As a historian, I'm sure you'll appreciate it."

"I still see nothing."

"The stones are obscure from this distance. They blend right in with the rest. But when we get closer, you'll be able to pick the ruins out easily."

"Ruins? I'm intrigued already!"

"Just wait till I tell you the story!"

Logan had been watching impatiently for the return of the two riders. While they were still in the stable turning over their steeds to Jake, he rushed out to them.

"We have found the missing pages to the journal!" he said as he ran up. "I could hardly wait until you got here to read them!"

"Where . . . what do they say?" said Hilary all in a rush.

"I don't yet know what they say," answered Logan. "We decided to wait until we could all be together. Come . . . I'll answer your other questions on the way inside."

He led the way as the three crossed the lawn, entered at the kitchen door, and proceeded upstairs to the drawing room.

"It was Allison who unraveled this particular mystery," he said. "She was lying in bed, her mind idly wandering about over all the family stories. She wasn't even thinking about the journal at the time. She had been reflecting on her mother's coming to Scotland and the difficulties she had faced. Suddenly it came to her: Both Atlanta and Maggie had hidden very important items in the framing and backing of a favorite picture, actually a stitchery Maggie had done as a girl. Where else would Joanna have hidden something special in her life?"

"In Maggie's stitchery of the family tree!" exclaimed Hilary. "Of course! But where is it? I don't remember ever seeing it . . . though come to think of it there were some stitcheries in the heirloom room."

"Those are different ones. The family tree was hanging in Joanna's own room."

Logan chuckled. "Dear Joanna was a sly one!" he said. "A place so obvious, yet it was the last place we thought to look. I even had Ashley right there hunting in her secretary when what we sought was hanging on the wall just a few feet away all the while."

"So did you get it?" asked Hilary excitedly.

"Yes, yes! But not without having to pry apart Maggie's poor stitchery once again!"

By this time they had reached the drawing room. Entering, they saw Allison sitting on the divan, manuscript pages on her lap, tears streaming down her face.

"I couldn't help myself, Logan," she said. "I had to read Mother's words. Oh, it's so hard to have to live through it all again! But I suppose

it's good for me too, for the Lord is working healing in my heart in so
many ways already. I want you to read it to them . . . aloud."

Logan nodded, then walked to his wife, kissed her tenderly, and took
the pages from her hand.

"Hilary, come . . . please," said Allison. "Won't you sit beside me
for this?"

Hilary walked forward, sat down, and Allison took her hand. "Now
then," said Allison, "we are ready."

Ashley found a seat. Then Logan took up the pages written in Joanna's
fine script and began to read.

*. . . whatever truth He chooses to reveal to me. What I am to do, He
will make clear in His time. One thing I do know, that the Lord our God
surrounds and protects and delivers them that are His people.*

"That section makes little sense," said Logan. "It was apparently a
continuation of something that came before."

"I am sure it continues just as it is from the end of the last page that I
have," interjected Hilary. "Shall I go get it from my room?"

"Not now," answered Logan. "We can compare them later. The most
important section—indeed, the reason I believe Joanna hid this portion of
her journal—is still to come. I think she was fearful of the result should
this have chanced to fall into the wrong hands."

"But she knew we would find it eventually," said Allison. "I know she
knew, dear Mother! But go on, Logan. I want them to hear it."

"The next entry is dated September 16," said Logan. "But after that
there are no more dates and the story flows together." He paused, took a
deep breath, and began to read.

*I could not have anticipated that the small act of opening a door could
so alter the lives of so many. But when, on the evening of August 27, a
young woman stepped out of the past and into our home, many unforeseen
changes were immediately thrust upon us. Logan and Allison's daughter,
as we had been told a week before, was suddenly come to life in the person
calling herself Joanna Braithwaite. Our dear, lost Jo was suddenly restored
to us after almost thirty years!*

*Oh, what a day of joy it should have been. And I cannot say I was not
swept up in the exuberance at first. The atmosphere about Stonewycke was
positively buoyant for days. I scarcely think I had seen Allison so happy
in memory, especially when she and young Jo began to do things together—
ride, paint, walk in the garden. I was happy for them, yet something began
to eat away in my spirit, something I was reluctant to identify at first. The
change came over me gradually. I might not have even noticed, or might
have brushed it aside as irrelevant, except for that day—that single moment—in which a single unguarded look escaped from Jo's well-schooled
demeanor.*

Allison had pressed me to recount for Jo some of my experiences when

I arrived in Port Strathy, also a stranger, after a long absence. I had been reluctant. In fact, since Jo's very coming I had been hesitant to share with her about our family history. I didn't know why; it was such a peculiar reaction for me to have. I never did mention my journal to her. But on that particular day Allison was persuasive, and I gave in and began to tell Jo about the events of that summer when I arrived at Stonewycke.

She listened attentively until I arrived at last to that fateful day of the town meeting in the meadow when Dorey came miraculously through the crowd to my side, and Alec galloped to our rescue a heroic knight, and how I gathered my courage to walk forward and denounce Jason Channing to his face, while Palmer Sercombe slunk away unnoticed. At that moment in the tale, I chanced to glance up at Jo, and the look on her face nearly struck me speechless. In her dark eyes flashed the venom of hatred. And as often as I recall the incident, I have not been able to account for it. Allison was seated so that she could not have seen it, and even had I attempted to describe it, I doubt Allison would have believed it possible. I might not have myself had I not been witness to it. Somehow I managed to finish the story, and by that time Jo was, to all appearances, back to normal.

After that it seemed my eyes were opened. I began to see so clearly through the facade that Jo presented so expertly. I began to wonder if those odd forebodings only hours before her arrival had been God's way of warning me, or at least preparing me for this terrible intrusion into our lives at Stonewycke.

But what could I do? Allison had completely accepted Jo as the daughter lost to her for thirty years. I could not blame her for that. All the documents had been verified. I hated myself at times for my suspicions. But just as I would be on the verge of thinking I had made up the reasons for my doubts, then I would see that flash from Jo's eyes again, as if warning me against causing a stir. There was something in her look I seemed almost to recognize, but I could never put my finger on it. Sometimes I even wondered if for some twisted reason, Jo purposefully revealed her true nature to me in these subtle ways, perhaps to encourage discord between myself and Allison and Logan, which it did in fact accomplish before long.

Finally, I could live with my doubts no longer. I approached Logan. I hoped I could reason with him. And I could not blame him for becoming upset. I had no facts, only the vague feelings of an old woman. Everyone—the maids, the neighbors, the village children—was taken with Jo. I stood alone with my doubts. But I knew as long as they plagued me, I could not live with them. I knew at last that I must find proof of some kind, either that she was or she was not who she claimed to be. I had to know.

That was when it occurred to me that the best proof—if indeed Jo was not their daughter—was to find the real daughter. If Jo had documentation stating that she had lived through the crash, then perhaps the real daughter was *alive. I knew that the whole charade could have been made up and that it could turn out that my granddaughter really had died as we had long thought. Yet Jo had so many facts correct that cast no small amount of truth upon her tale. It certainly seemed to bear investigating.*

Where was I to begin? I had no knowledge in such matters. Therefore I spoke one day, using only generalities, to our local constable—a man whose discretion I could trust, especially after I swore him to secrecy.

"How does one go about finding a missing person?" I asked him.

"Weel, m'lady," he said, "they ought to be missin' for twenty-four hoors afore the police can do anythin'. But in yer case, perhaps—"

"It has been much longer than that."

"That bein' the case, I can fill oot a report."

"I'm afraid it has been many years," I said. "I doubt a report would be of much help." I could not help feeling rather sorry for him trying to make anything of my cryptic explanations. "I'm not even sure the person is alive," I added.

"Hmmmm . . . 'tis a puzzler, to be sure, m'lady." He paused and scratched his stubby beard. "Noo, on the television," he went on, "they're always hirin' them private investigators—private eyes, ye ken."

I smiled. "I hardly watch much television these days." The mere thought of me, at eighty-one, traipsing all over who knows where with someone dressed like Humphrey Bogart was too bizarre. Especially when I was looking for a needle in a haystack—a needle that might not even exist.

But in the end I found myself asking for his advice in securing such a man, as silly as I felt to do so. He put me in touch with a friend of his from Glasgow, a good man who had been a policeman but retired early because of an injury to his foot, taking up the less demanding occupation of private detecting. We arranged our first meeting in Culden. I had Logan drive me there to visit a friend, and at my friend's house, I first met Caleb.

Logan paused to smile at the memory. "Why, the cagy old fox!" he said to himself. "She put that over on me but good!" He then went on.

If ever God directed my steps in this old-age adventure of mine, it was in the finding of Caleb Boyle, a faithful and trustworthy friend. He could instantly upon hearing my story have written me off as a senile old woman. Sometimes I even had doubts about my sanity myself! But Caleb took me seriously, believed in me, and worked like a stout horse on my behalf.

It was his suggestion that we forget for the time being trying to discredit Jo, and concentrate instead on discovering whether another daughter—the true daughter—was indeed still alive. To do this I had to take us back thirty years and relive that awful nightmare of the day our little Joanna was lost. It was not easy for me to keep making excuses about my unexplained absences, and the travel was taxing, but I felt I had to go back in time myself, and lay my eyes again on the places involved, hoping something—

miraculously—would present itself that we had overlooked before.

The incredible story told by Jo's solicitors contained so many details which rang true, I could only conclude that they had truly made contact with Hannah Whitley at some time after her call to Logan in London. Whether she actually changed her mind about talking to him, or else spoke to someone perhaps she shouldn't have in an unguarded moment, I don't know. The fact remained that poor Hannah was never heard from again, and then Jo appeared at Stonewycke with a story based entirely on Hannah's testimony. Therefore, we began with the assumption that much of Jo's story was true, and then went back to attempt a reconstruction of events ourselves to see if we might get on a track Jo's people had not taken into account.

What was always curious about Jo's story was the lack of detail. I sat in a couple of times on discussions Logan had with the solicitors, prior to her coming. And though I said nothing, it struck me that none of the people involved knew exactly where the events following the crash had taken place.

Thus, as Caleb and I began looking into the matter, I knew we had one fact no one else did—I had been there during the crash. If only, I thought, I could remember something that had not surfaced before!

We went to the site of the accident. Many changes had taken place in the ensuing years. The railway now bypassed that area, running five miles to the south. I have strong doubts that Jo's people ever located the crash site, because it took us days to do so ourselves. Over and over we rode as I scanned the surroundings. But nothing seemed familiar. All at once, Caleb thought to check with the railroad. That is when we discovered about the line being changed. We hadn't seen anything because we were on an altogether different track! Caleb managed to uncover a thirty-year-old map of the area, and finally we drove to the site of the old ammunition dump. It was of course no longer there, but the moment we were in the vicinity, I knew we had come to the right place. What a thrill it was when we stepped out of Caleb's automobile and walked over to the old track bed where once the train had gone, now grown over with weeds and brush.

Two days we spent close by the crash site. Caleb applied no pressure, but drove me about, walked with me, let me look and think and remember. And gradually images of that fateful day began to come back to me. I recalled certain farmhouses I had seen from the train window just before the bombing, and then when at last Caleb and I came upon the pretty little stone bridge with the stream beneath it, and a matching stone cottage just beyond, I knew we had found the exact spot. "This is it, Caleb!" I shouted. "I remember! We passed this bridge just before the explosion!"

It was a long shot, Caleb said (his colorful language is so intriguing!). But he began to canvas the entire area, walking to every farmhouse within sight. Most of the residents had come since the bombing. Others remembered but had seen nothing. Some had been little children at the time and *their memories were garbled and dreamlike and of little use. The lady in the stone cottage with thatched roof, however, remembered the day clearly and had heard rumors from the direction of the village to the north about survivors who had been seen wandering about.*

The time came when I had to return to Stonewycke. But Caleb diligently continued his painstaking survey of the area. I did what I discreetly could to inquire how much Jo's lawyer's had actually learned from Hannah and whether she was still in contact with them. But in neither attempt did I find out anything new. I am, I fear, worried about Hannah.

One day Caleb telephoned me. I will never forget his words. "I have news," he said. "Big news. Go down to the town and call me back when you can talk." If I hadn't been so anxious to hear what he had to say, and had the situation not been so tense, I probably would have enjoyed all Caleb's cloak-and-dagger precautions. But I was too nervous to have fun.

"I found them!" he said excitedly the moment I had him back on the line from the phone at the Bluster 'N Blow. "An older couple. They knew nothing about a train wreck or a bombing. Their little farm is miles away! There is no way anyone else could have found these people! They are in the exact opposite direction from the new train line, and two miles from the town."

"If they know nothing about the crash," I said, "then what have you found out from them?"

"Just this," said Caleb; "they woke up one morning thirty years ago to find a lost, bewildered little girl sleeping in a pile of straw just inside their barn door. They took her in, but had no idea where she'd come from. The child talked about a nurse bringing her there, but the old couple saw no evidence of anyone else, could make out nothing more of the child's story, and eventually took her to a shelter in the town."

"My granddaughter is alive!" I exclaimed, hardly able to breathe. "Oh, Caleb, how will I ever be able to thank you?"

"You can save your thanks until I find her for you," the dear man replied.

"And what now?" I asked, hardly able to contain my joy.

"I'm off right now to the shelter. I'm going to go through their records and follow every lead until I find your granddaughter, Lady MacNeil. I can smell it. I know we're getting close!"

As I hung up the phone I'm afraid I felt too much like screaming for happiness to be able to go back to the estate. Instead, I went for a walk down along the shore to collect my thoughts. It was then that I decided that I should continue to keep my quest secret, even from Logan and Allison, until I knew for certain where it would end. In due time they must be told, but not until I had the full story. In the meantime I determined to be more faithful than ever to my journal and to write down what we were learning. Whether my decision will prove to be a wise one, only time will tell.

Logan paused in his reading to take a deep breath and glance around the room. On the divan Hilary's head rested on her mother's shoulder and Allison wept softly. In a voice which seemed to indicate that had he not had to continue reading, he too would likely have given way to tears, Logan continued with Joanna's words.

The records Caleb found were scanty, but they did speak of the child that had been found, and then documented her later placement in a London orphanage. He followed the trail to London, where the course of events became difficult to trace in that there were several orphanages involved, one of which had been closed down in 1946. Why more was not done to locate the parents of these children lost during the war, I do not know. But there was much confusion, many records had been destroyed, shelters and orphanages set up during the war were temporary at best, and in our case, because of the reports following the crash, we never even considered that our young Joanna Hilary could be alive.

How thankful I am for dear Caleb for disproving that error once and for all! After many weeks in London, he gained the following information. First, he had surprisingly run across some scanty news of Hannah again. She had apparently been hospitalized in a delirious state in the same town to which the child had been taken. She was sent to London for more thorough care, lay in a hospital for some time, and when she was finally released was suffering from amnesia. Caleb could find out no more about her, and everything else we know has come from the direction of Jo's solicitors.

Secondly, in London Caleb eventually isolated five possible candidates from the records of the final placement papers for children during the time period in question, of the right age. I interviewed two of these before the fateful moment, just three days ago, when I walked into the offices of The Berkshire Review.

The moment I laid eyes on Hilary, I knew she was my granddaughter. I'm sure God was causing the truth to leap within my mother's heart, yet one look in her face sent the truth shouting at me as well. There, in a glance, I could see my dear grandmother, Lady Margaret, and so vividly the features of my own daughter Allison. And yes, not a little of my own face as well! Such a beautiful young woman she was, reflecting the very heritage of which she was a part, yet which she did not know.

If only Allison and Logan could lay eyes upon Hilary, I thought, then they would know beyond any doubts. Yet then I realized that Jo's face, too, contains many similarities to Hilary's—uncannily so. It causes me to wonder how long this deception has been planned.

I want so desperately to tell of my discovery to Logan and Allison. But Hilary has asked me to wait and I will honor her wish. In the meantime, I am not sure what to do about Jo. Is she an impostor? Or is she but the victim of a regrettable error?

I do not want to push, yet I am anxious for this affair to end and for truth to prevail. I feel more fatigued than I have in a long while. Inside there is a glorious contentment in my heart. I am joyful, exhilarated. Part of me feels young again, just in the memory of those moments of reunion with Hilary. Yet another part of me is very tired. That part of me wants only to embrace my dear granddaughter again, and then have a long rest.

As he read the final words, Logan could contain himself no longer. Tears overflowed his eyes and he wept without shame.

After a moment he laid the papers aside, then walked softly toward his wife and daughter. He fell to his knees on the floor before them, clasped each of their hands, and—gazing first deeply into Allison's face, then into Hilary's, with a huge tear-stained smile on his own—said, "Thank God! . . . Thank you, Lord, for preserving our precious heritage . . . in spite of our own weakness!"

"How I wish I hadn't been so reluctant to accept grandmother's revelation," said Hilary, "so that I would have been able to embrace her again."

Logan had taken a chair opposite the divan, and Ashley had left the room, thinking the family should share this time alone.

"We all had our reluctance and our blindness," said Logan. "I as much as anyone."

"That is all past," said Allison. "Now we can rejoice that half of Mother's final wish was fulfilled—for she has indeed now found eternal rest with her Lord."

A brief silence followed; then Allison spoke again, voicing a thought that had only just then occurred to her.

"Mother's journal is complete," she said. "I feel as if an era has ended. I cannot help but be saddened. Yet I see now that this journal was Mother's life's work. It truly counted for something important, perhaps more than we will ever know."

"I have no doubt," said Logan, "that it will reach into the future and deeply touch yet unborn members of this clan."

"Might Lady Joanna have even wanted it to continue beyond her lifetime in a more tangible way?" suggested Hilary. "This journal is so rich, not only in family history, but in a documentation of events to do with this land, with Stonewycke, with the Strathy Valley, and especially in capturing the spiritual perspectives that have been woven in and through the lives of such a diverse range of individuals. Might it not be a legacy, in its own way, to be passed on to the two of you, in order to continue the keeping of the family record—an ongoing tribute to Grandmother's dream?"

"I hadn't thought of that," Allison replied.

"It's a great idea!" said Logan. "Hilary, you are the writer. I think Joanna's journal would be best left in your hands. She passed it on to you for a reason. A good one, I think. Who knows how many lives might be blessed by the events recorded by Joanna through the years if you were able to chronicle the story in a more organized way."

"Do you really think so?" asked Hilary, thrilled at the very prospect. "But I have been so removed from events for so long. I wonder if I am qualified?"

Allison again took Hilary's hand in hers. "For years," she said, "an unusual phenomenon has operated in this family. I have thought about it often and have wondered why it has been so. When I question the Lord concerning it, He repeatedly drives me back to the principle in Scripture of the desert as symbolizing the purifying time of preparation. Moses was exiled in the desert to ready him to lead his people out of bondage. Then the children of Israel spent forty years in the desert to prepare and humble them for the taking of the promised land. After his conversion, Paul spent years in the desert as the Lord prepared and strengthened him for his ministry. And before His public preaching and teaching began, Jesus spent forty days in the wilderness."

As she spoke, Allison's countenance took on a distant look, as if she were gazing down the long span of history. "All this may seem far removed from Stonewycke," she continued, bringing her attention back to the present, "but the principle still applies. I am the only woman since Atlanta who has lived here at Stonewycke, or even in Scotland, continuously since birth. And even I was emotionally separated from my heritage for several years. Maggie and Joanna were in America for large parts of their lives. You spent thirty years in London, separated even from the knowledge of your roots. But I believe God uses those times of exile to strengthen the legacy of what this family has come to represent, to deepen within us our love for the land, and especially to cement our faith in a mighty and loving God."

Allison paused, gazing deep into her daughter's eyes with a look of love that had not before now passed between them, the love not only of a mother but also of sisterhood. "Hilary," she concluded, "I think you will find that your separation makes you as much one with us as anything possibly could. However, it is a family characteristic that I pray will be passed on no further."

"Thank you, Mother," said Hilary, tears forming in her eyes again. She leaned over and put her arms around Allison, and both women wept together.

A soft knock on the door temporarily interrupted the family gathering. Logan immediately stood and answered it.

"I'm sorry to disturb ye, sir," said Flora, "but Miss Hilary's got another telephone call."

Reluctantly Hilary rose and followed the housekeeper out. By the time she reached the library, her equilibrium was restored and she was able to present a normal voice to Murry on the other end.

She returned about ten minutes later to the drawing room. Ashley was now with Logan and Allison.

"Your associate on the magazine again?" asked Logan when she entered.

Hilary nodded. "With some additional information. Although none of it makes much sense to me."

"Don't keep us in suspense," said Logan eagerly.

"Basically all Murry had for me this time was a list of names." She turned back a few pages in her notebook. "These are other prominent figures in Trans Global's hierarchy. If Emil is tied in to TGE, then perhaps other of Jo's accomplices are as well."

"The only accomplices I could think of would be the lawyers," said Logan. "I had them checked and rechecked, and everything appeared on the up-and-up. But I did not know at the time to investigate whether there might be ties to TGE. That is something we should do immediately. But let me see your list, Hilary. Perhaps something will ring a bell."

He reached over, and Hilary handed him the open notebook. Logan sat back and scanned the list of about ten names.

Suddenly Logan froze, his eyes fastened to the seventh name on the list. After a moment's hesitation, he shook his head in disbelief, took his reading glasses from his pocket, put them on, and read the name again.

He stared at the sheet of paper. How could it be? But there the name was in the middle of the list, like a ghost from the past!

It couldn't be! No one could possibly know!

Slowly he looked up and glanced around at the others.

"This is incredible!" he said slowly. "A mere coincidence, perhaps . . . yet something tells me . . ."

Still shaking his head, he held the notebook up for them to see, pointing to the seventh entry.

"This is a name I have not heard or seen for thirty years!"

"Who is it?" asked Hilary.

"It is no one," he replied. "A fictitious nonentity."

"Then what did the name mean when you knew of it back then?" asked Ashley.

Logan drew in a deep breath, then exhaled as he answered, "It was *me!*" he said incredulously. "Monsieur Dansette, merchant from Casablanca, a man without even a first name, a supposed Nazi sympathizer. The man never existed. It was a cover I used during the war while I was in France . . . a cover conferred upon me by an officer in the SS . . . a *general!*"

"Logan, what are you saying?"

"Perhaps I am making a quantum leap here, based on mere speculation. But instinct tells me differently. The name is just as we used it back then! Yet, why would he resurrect that name? You would think he would make every attempt to erase all possible links to the past."

"Who, Logan?" asked Hilary.

"His name was—or is?—Martin von Graff. SS officer and escaped war criminal. If he is still alive, he'd have to be in his late seventies, early eighties . . ." He stopped and thought for a moment. "But now that I recall," he went on, "I remember reading a report from the Israclis several years ago listing him as dead. I thought then that that segment of my life was officially behind me completely."

"Could he be alive . . . could he have masterminded Jo's deception?"

"He certainly would have had motive," answered Logan. "Motive against me, at least. I'm afraid my activities put quite a black mark on his SS record. I heard that following my escape from France, von Graff was suddenly transferred to the Russian front. He would have had plenty of motive to seek revenge."

"There was also the matter of my rescuing you from his firing squad," put in Allison.

"And no small caper it was, my dear!" laughed Logan. "Yet I just can't see von Graff coming against us after all this time. As insidious and subtle as he could be, he was still from the old school. A man of some honor, I always felt, lurked beneath that Nazi skin. Had circumstances been different, I could even have imagined us friends. Had he wanted revenge, I would have thought him the type to choose a more direct approach— pistols at dawn, that sort of thing. After what we did to him, he had every reason to hate us, that is true, but . . ."

He shook his head. Something still didn't fit. When he continued, his voice sounded like one debating within himself.

"The Mossad are pretty thorough about their war criminals. If they say he is dead, then I would think it must be true."

"Yet here is a name," reasoned Ashley, "a major executive in a company with links to a criminal called 'The General.' It makes one wonder."

"And," added Hilary, "Emil von Burchardt, Jo's own accomplice, sits right in the middle of it, with known ties to the Nazis. It would appear von Graff could be behind it. But we must not forget whom we are really after."

"I wonder . . ." Logan rubbed his chin, his mind racing with the staggering possibilities. "It is entirely conceivable that Jo is only a soldier, dispatched to perform a task in the cause of the General. If that is the case, then it truly is *The General*, whoever he is, whom we are after."

"I think you may be right, Logan," said Hilary. "But I cannot forget that look I saw in Jo's eyes when she discovered me in the gallery. It was just as Lady Joanna described. It was not the look of a mere underling. For some reason, I am sure Jo has a personal stake in all this."

Later that afternoon Logan walked alone into the library.

He had made several phone calls, one of which had confirmed that his information about von Graff was correct—the Nazi general was dead.

Where does that leave me? Logan wondered. *Where could the name Dansette possibly have come from? What is the connection to this modern-day general? Might von Graff have used the name Dansette before his death, which reports confirmed to have occurred in 1959? Why, then, did the name remain on the company roster? Why had von Graff used the pseudonym at all, if he had indeed used it?*

Logan leaned back in his chair at the library desk, laced his fingers together behind his head, and allowed his mind to wander once more over the discussion of earlier with Hilary, Ashley, and Allison.

The General . . . Nazis in hiding after the war . . . von Graff . . . Trans Global Enterprises . . . an attempt to infiltrate the estate, their very lives, with an impostor . . . revenge . . .

How were all these factors related?

More importantly, how were they connected to Stonewycke, especially with von Graff dead? He seemed the only link tying Dansette and the General to Stonewycke. Yet he had been gone twelve years, and the plot against them hatched only recently.

Logan's mind drifted further back. . . .

SS Headquarters, Paris. . . . There came into his memory the scene of von Graff entertaining his protege Lawrence MacVey. The suave, urbane aristocrat staking his entire reputation as a Nazi on an ex-con man. Yes, von Graff had reason to be bitter . . . but he was dead.

All at once the panorama of Logan's thoughts widened.

They were not alone in that elegant SS office. Another man was there, not dressed in a uniform at all, whose chilly presence Logan began to feel even before he moved out of the shadows of Logan's memory into view. But as he stepped forward, he seemed to emerge from further out of the distant past than Logan's thoughts could take him.

Jason Channing!

Logan snapped upright in his chair. Could it be possible?

The notion was unthinkable! Yet Channing always seemed to turn up in the life of Stonewycke, his malicious figure perpetually lurking in the shadows like a tiger stalking its prey.

Without a shred of proof, without a scrap of evidence, in that moment Logan knew beyond any doubt who was his adversary. It *had* to be Channing who had leveled this latest attack against his old nemesis. But the man would have to be a hundred years old! Logan would never forget the fire in Channing's eyes that day he had been foiled in the guardhouse of Fort Montrouge. As love and honor sustain Godly men, so do malice and vengeance possess and sustain men who give themselves over to evil.

Yes, the whole twisted masquerade of Jo's deception and attempted poisoning of Allison reeked with the malevolent aroma of Jason Channing! There could be no doubt . . . the man was alive!

He had not forgotten that hideous day which had tormented him for sixty years, when a shy, untried girl had thwarted his greedy scheme and denounced him boldly in front of hundreds of witnesses.

Channing would *never* forget! And the memory would goad him until he tasted revenge.

59 / Parental Vile

She had almost forgotten what the heat in Buenos Aires could be like at this time of the year. Leaving the winter of northern Scotland to find herself suddenly in the middle of a southern hemispheric heat wave was shock enough. Dread for the reaction awaiting her, however, was an even worse torment.

Jo dabbed her damp forehead for the third time as Emil wheeled the Jaguar around the final curve of the drive up to the villa. Ahead she could see the tile-roofed main house of the villa's sprawling complex. Well, she thought with a sigh, home at last.

The flight from London had been ghastly enough, exhausting after their hurried departure from Scotland, though she should have been grateful to have gotten out of the country at all. Then they had been delayed at the airport due to some mix-up with what little luggage they had. Finally, the ride to the villa had been hot and uncomfortable, no matter that they had picked up Emil's Jaguar in the city and driven in some elegance. But however she looked at it, home was not a welcome sight. After all, her mission had not been successful. She looked over at Emil, who was now braking in front of the empty fountain that stood before the house.

"You will go in with me, won't you?" she asked with uncharacteristic nervousness in her tone.

He glanced over as if the request surprised him, then gave his moustache a careless pat. He is looking rather superior and smug, she thought, especially for one who has failed no less than I.

"Well?" said Jo crossly.

"My dear, you are more than capable of handling this yourself." He paused to turn off the ignition. "Besides, he will only think less of you if you display weakness now."

"And what about you! No last-minute heroics?"

Von Burchardt smiled. "I do not have as much at stake, now do I, my dear Jo?"

"I do not want to hear that name again—ever!"

Angrily she pushed the door open and jerked herself from the car. "Don't think you will get off scot-free, my dear!" She slammed the door and stalked away toward the house.

Kicking the dust up toward one of the dry cactus plants that bordered either side of the walk, she approached the door. The servants had seen the

Jaguar approach, and now a houseboy opened the door to welcome her deferentially.

She inquired about *El Patron*. The boy's face turned solemn.

"El señor has taken to his bed, señorita," he said.

Jo's brow creased—whether with concern or disguised relief, it would have been difficult to determine.

"How long ago?" she asked, increasing her pace.

"Two days, señorita."

"How bad?"

"Not bad. Only weak. The doctor, he come twice a day."

"Send someone out to get my things from the car and then take them to my room. I will want to be alone with El Patron for a while. Comprendes?"

"Sí, señorita, yo comprendo!" replied the servant, who then hurried off to be about his assigned tasks.

She continued on her way, traversed a long corridor, arriving at last to a closed door. She paused, took in one last deep breath as if preparing for her fate, then raised her hand to rap briskly on the door.

"Who is it?" came a weak but still gruff voice from inside.

Instead of answering, she turned the latch and entered.

The room was dark, the drawn shades allowing in only tiny splinters of the sunlight from outside. Even though a ceiling fan was churning overhead, the air was stifling—both hot and too well used. Without waiting for her eyes to accustom themselves to the subdued light, she walked straight but calmly to the bed and bent down near the figure lying there with covers pulled up about his chin.

"I'm back," she said.

The notion crossed her mind briefly of giving the wrinkled cheek a kiss, but she thought better of it.

Jason Channing's eyes flew open and glared wrathfully at her.

"How dare you!" he cried, though his fury lost a great deal of its intended menace as it passed through his debilitated, ancient vocal chords. "How dare you come and show your face!" fumed the old man.

"I'm sorry I failed," she replied, with attempted contriteness.

"Don't put on that sweet vulnerability! I know it is a mere act! Remember, I am the one who paid to give you the best lessons money could buy."

"Then, what would you have me do?" she said, a hard edge now in her voice. "Shall I slit my throat for you right here?"

"For all you have given me, it might be a good start!" Channing's tone was cold, giving no evidence that his words were anything but what he intended.

She turned and walked a couple paces from the bed.

"I should have made my getaway the moment that woman showed up," she said petulantly. "Everything was going so well until then. But I knew how important this was to you, so I stuck it out—"

"You ran at the first sign of trouble!"

"I stayed well beyond the limits of safety!" she countered, spinning around to face the bed again.

"I thought you had more guts than that!"

"To the very last instant I even tried to pour the poison down her throat, but Emil—"

"Bah! You flew like a frightened rabbit!" shouted Channing, rising shakily from his pillow. "You ran like the cowardly swine you are!"

She sucked in a ragged breath. She had known this was coming, but was still not quite prepared for it.

"I did the best I could," she said.

"Well, it wasn't good enough!" he shrieked.

"It never is!" she hissed bitterly.

Channing shifted in his bed and tried to hitch himself up on the pillows, swearing angrily when the activity exhausted him.

"Curse those fool doctors!" he muttered, "coming in here with their antiquated remedies to do nothing but weaken me and keep me in this absurd bed! Blast them all!"

She reached her hand around his shoulder to help him. The action seemed to mitigate his anger momentarily. He shook his head mournfully.

"All that work," he moaned. "Two years! Plastic surgeons and theatrical coaching for you . . . buying off those muddleheaded lawyers . . . setting the plan up in such detail—all wasted! What a poetic victory it would have been!"

"It may not be too late, Father."

But Channing waved an impatient hand. "Does it matter anymore?" he lamented. "I thought we had them when I learned about that old crazy woman—what was her name? Whitley . . . something Whitley—the loony old woman trying to get up her nerve to tell the Macintyres about their daughter. It was my moment!" He sank back, his voice losing its force. "Now it looks like I had the old goose put away for nothing. But what does it matter? She's beaten me again!"

"It was a beautiful plan, Father," she said, sitting down on the edge of the bed.

"A coup!" he rejoined, half rising again. "The coup of the century! Installing my own daughter as the unknown heiress to their precious Stonewycke! I could have gone to my grave a contented man. But that snip of a Joanna Matheson did it to me again!"

"Perhaps we can yet undo what she has done."

But Channing was no longer listening. Hearing the name from his own lips that he had hundreds of times vowed should never pass from his mouth again seemed to send him into a trance. Suddenly he was many miles and many years removed from the Villa del Heimat.

"Oh, Joanna," he moaned. "Why do you hate me so?"

"I do not hate you, Father."

"I don't mean you, you fool!" spat Channing, lurching back to the present only long enough to denounce his own daughter for her stupidity. "I mean *Joanna* . . . the only woman I ever loved!"

"What about my mother?" Jo shot back. "And what about me?"

"Your *mother*"—Channing's lips twisted cruelly around the word—"was a mere convenience. I did, after all, need to be respectable among my peers. You were the result of that union—my only joy, my only hope for—"

"For what?" Jo spat the words at him. "For revenge against Stonewycke? How can you speak of *love*? You have never loved me—you have only used me. I doubt that you ever for a moment really loved your precious Joanna Matheson! You only wanted to possess her, to use her the way you use—"

"Shut up! Why else do you think I gave you her name? It's *her*, I tell you! *She's* the cause of all the grief that has ever come to me!"

Again his eyes glassed over. He continued to gaze at his daughter, but his voice had again passed backward in time, erasing six decades in an instant of his own dementia.

"I could have given you everything, Joanna," he said, his voice rising with passion. "The world was mine! Together we could have reigned over it. But no! Your damnable pride would not be broken! You and your stiff-necked notions of honor! You and that oaf of a ridiculous manure-tromping lout you called a man! Hah! Oh, Joanna, how could you have been so blind! What possessed you to say those things about me to the town? I hated you that day! But in that very act you showed what you were made of. Ironic, isn't it, my dear? The day I swore eternal vengeance against you was the very day my heart was forever spoiled for another. That day I despised you, yet I also knew I could have no other woman. How I hated you, but could not live without you. Joanna . . . Joanna—"

"Father," broke in Jo sharply. "You mustn't go on like this!"

Jolted as if slapped in the face, Channing stared at her blankly, trying to focus his bewildered eyes.

"And stop looking at me like that! I am not that Joanna. It's enough that I have to bear her name. Don't speak to me as if I were her! She is dead. And I wish to heaven all the rest of her brood were dead too!"

"Dead?" repeated Channing, still stupefied.

"Dead! Do you hear me?"

"She will never die," he said softly, his face contorting in the macabre agony of his self-inflicted insanity. "You will not die before . . . before . . . I—"

Jo watched with horrified fascination, aware that Channing was losing all grip on reality.

"I can see you . . . Joanna, you will not go away . . . before you and I . . ."

His voice trailed away and he glanced toward the door as if looking for someone.

"Perhaps you are right," mused Jo icily, almost to herself. "She lives on in that daughter of hers—Allison Macintyre—still sitting on that hill, mistress of all she surveys! Gloating over their victory! Sitting where *I* should be sitting! I have borne that hateful name, cursing it every day of my life! Stonewycke should have been mine!"

Without warning Channing's dulled eyes suddenly came into focus and he was himself again.

"They do not know I was behind the masquerade?"

"Of course not," replied Jo. "But they still hold Stonewycke."

"Yes . . . yes." Channing's eyes narrowed, his head rolling from side to side, agitated. "They still hold Stonewycke, but perhaps they have not won yet. I hate them . . . I hate *her* more than them all! I will yet vanquish them! I will not rest! Oh, what a pleasure it would be to break her proud spirit . . . and then watch her die!"

"For me the moment of triumph would be to grind that pompous Hilary under my foot in the dirt!"

"There might yet be time . . ."

Channing closed his eyes as his features grew taut, while evil machinations consumed his thoughts. His aging brain was once more sharp and in control.

"I want her!" he cried passionately at last, rising from the pillow. "Bring her to me! Ha, ha! I will find a way to crush them yet!"

"*We* will find a way," said Jo. "We will have our revenge or die. Neither will I rest until it is done."

"Get back up there immediately! But be on your guard. This time they will be alert for trouble."

"I will be wary. Don't worry. I know every inch of the place."

"I *am* lucky to have a daughter such as you," said Channing, in a voice not of love but rather shared cunning. His pinched lips twisted briefly into what might have been interpreted as the semblance of a smile. He grasped her hand in his and closed his eyes, for the moment assuaged in the delicious taste of anticipated revenge.

60 / Father and Daughter_____

Even as Channing and his daughter were planning the final act in a diabolic and empty vendetta, their chief adversary puzzled over his own role in this unsought drama of hate and retribution.

Logan sat alone in the loft above the stables.

He still could not believe it was Channing! The man's malice against the Duncan clan had spanned six decades, growing each year like an unchecked cancer, never healing, becoming more and more destructive with age, leaving only misery, perhaps even death, in its evil wake.

It had to stop!

Not only for the sake of Logan's family, but for the future of Stonewycke, Port Strathy, his own posterity . . . and perhaps most of all for the sake of Channing himself. He had to be rotting inside—both physically and spiritually—from the effects of his own pernicious hate.

No longer, Logan now realized, could he sit passively and allow it to continue. Channing was a dangerous man who had wrought much havoc in the world through his greed. Unless it were stopped, his organization would continue to plunder and destroy lives long after the General's death. The entire network had to be broken.

Whether there was hope for Channing himself, only God could know. In himself, Logan doubted it. But that could not alter his course. What God put in his hand to do, he must do, however unlikely results might appear. There was always the possibility God intended him to be the instrument of the man's repentance.

Notwithstanding spiritual concerns, however, Channing had to be stopped. There was no question about what had to be done. The problem was *how* to go about it without being ensnared by the vicious workings of Channing's machinery, which appeared to have arms and eyes and ears everywhere.

Logan spoke to the Chief Inspector of the London branch of Interpol. They wanted the General and would do whatever it took to get him, but they had already been futilely on his cold track for twenty years.

"These things take time," said the CI regretfully. "He works entirely through blind intermediaries. Probably no more than a handful of men have ever *seen* him, and these are so bloody loyal that even if we managed to get our hands on one, we'd have him dropping on the floor with half a cyanide tablet falling out of his mouth before we got a word out of him."

"You need something—or someone—to bring him out in the open," suggested Logan.

"And I need a secluded little spot on the Riviera and a fifty-foot yacht!" scoffed the detective. "But I doubt I'll live long enough to get them."

"I have a plan."

"You, Mr. Macintyre? Sleuthing about in our bailiwick, that's hardly in the province of Members of Parliament, is it?"

"Do you want the General or not, Mr. Rollins?"

"I want him!"

"Enough to give me carte blanche?"

"I don't know . . . there are dangers—"

"I can get him for you. The man and his methods are not entirely unknown to me—"

"You know the identity of the General!"

"Let me put it this way: I have a strong and educated speculation."

"Then you must tell us!"

"Not yet. I have an idea, but I must work alone—one whiff of the law, as it were, and his inner circle will bolt so fast it will take another twenty years to ferret him out again."

"This is highly irregular."

"*Regular* methods have yet to be successful."

"That is true." Rollins paused in thought. "I'll bring the matter before my superiors. One more question: are we to be absolutely uninvolved, or may we arrange for discreet backup?"

"I will not turn down a safety net, but it must be *very* discreet, and utterly invisible. One more thing—there may be some problems with extradition. That is something you could look into and help me on."

"Consider it done."

"Good," Logan replied briskly. "I'll get back to you tomorrow," he added, hanging up the telephone before the man could protest further.

That had been two hours ago, and Logan now wondered about his assumed confidence on the phone.

A plan indeed!

He didn't even know where to find Channing! He could be anywhere from Siberia to Monte Carlo for all he knew, although Logan had been giving the location of the man's hiding place a great deal of thought.

Of one thing he was confident. He *would* have a plan. He *would* come up with something, and somehow he *would* put a stop to this sixty-year war Channing seemed intent on waging.

He leaned back in Digory's old chair and closed his eyes.

Dear God, Logan prayed silently, *keep my heart pure. Don't let me fall prey to the very malignancy I am trying to halt. Give me wisdom, O Lord. Guide my path. Open my eyes to subtleties and details I might otherwise overlook. And somehow, Lord, as difficult as it is to say, I pray too for Jason Channing. Infiltrate his twisted heart with your Spirit that the man may see the futility of his bitterness. And make me willing to be your instrument in the answering of that prayer.*

Logan heard a soft rap on the rough wooden door, and opened his eyes.

"Come in," he said, looking up. He smiled when he saw Hilary.

"Allison said you might be here," she said. "I hope you don't mind my intruding."

"Not at all."

"I have never seen this place, and I thought it might be a good spot to talk, though it could have waited."

"I'm glad you came. I am happy to share my great-great uncle's little home with you. But then Digory is your uncle too—let's see, how many greats would that be? I tend to lose track." He laughed.

"What was he to us exactly?"

"He was my mother's great uncle. Brother to her great-grandfather MacNab. He never married. His possessions went to my mother's grandfather when he died, and later to her, where they remained buried for years in an old trunk."

"Until you came along?"

"Almost," laughed Logan. "But that's another story!"

"You'll tell me someday?" said Hilary with an affectionate smile. "That is one area where Lady Joanna's journal is a bit scant on detail."

"No doubt!" rejoined Logan. "Yes, perhaps one day I shall tell you all about my discoveries and my coming to Stonewycke. There's Digory's Bible," he added, pointing to a small table. "I keep it here—sentimental reasons, you know."

Slowly Hilary walked over and picked up the ancient black volume. She held it silently for a few moments.

"This isn't such a remarkable place, really," Logan said at length. "But then, I believe it is that very thing which makes it so special to me. A haven of simplicity in a world that can at times seem overwhelmingly complicated."

"I can't picture you as one easily overwhelmed," replied Hilary, setting the Bible down and rejoining Logan, taking a seat in a plain wooden chair opposite him.

"Is that a daughter or a journalist speaking?"

"A little of both, perhaps."

"Well," said Logan with a thoughtful sigh, "all my life I have been too adept at putting on fronts, even when I don't intend to. That's how I made a living, that's how I managed to stay alive during the war—donning one facade after another. And now for the last thirty years I've been trying to break the habit. It is an aspect of my character God deals with constantly. But early patterns die hard, and I still have to work to be just myself. Every once in a while I find myself slipping unconsciously into one of my old characters whom I've missed."

"Don't you ever find it, I don't know—fun?"

"Sure. I'm not one who necessarily despises my old life. God gave me a fun-loving personality, and yes, I enjoy who I am." He paused, smiled, a twinkle in his eye, then chuckled lightly. "I still laugh when I think of some of the crazy things I pulled. At the same time, I know God intended more for me. That's why I am thankful to Him for bringing me out of the *need* to wear a facade in order to more deeply develop my true personality in Him. Yet still, after all this time, I am often overwhelmed, or would be without God's steadying hand."

"It sounds as though you are thinking about this on more than merely an abstract plane."

Logan sighed. "I hadn't really stopped to consider why this is so heavily on my mind today. You're right. It's no doubt because I have a feeling I'm going to have to slip into a disguise of some sort in order to get to the bottom of this thing with Channing. But I want to do it under the direction of the Lord, not in the power of my old nature. I guess what I'm battling with is whether that's possible."

"Why wouldn't it be? Surely God is able to use us as He made us to accomplish His purposes."

"I think you're right. But where the flesh is involved, it always pays to walk warily. The battle I'm waging within myself could too easily requite malice with malice. I mustn't let that happen." Logan stopped and rubbed his hands across his face as dark memories from the past intruded into his thoughts. "Jason Channing has brought much pain into my life, and he has haunted those I love like a demon wraith. My human desire is to lash back at him. But, thank God, I am being purged of that desire."

"What will you do, then?"

"I must confront Channing and make him stop. He is an evil man, a politically and morally and socially dangerous man. He must be stopped before he hurts and destroys further. I know he will not quit until he sees us destroyed. But the confrontation I speak of must grow out of the power of God to work righteousness, not the power of the flesh to seek revenge."

"The thought that his own people were *here* among us is enough to make my skin crawl when I'm lying in bed at night."

"We have to be aware of the fact that your presence is now an added irritation to Channing, making you a target as well."

Hilary shuddered. "Murry called again this morning," she said. "Do you remember his man in Oxford—the fellow who first put him onto Trans Global?"

Logan nodded.

"He was found murdered yesterday. A suspect has been arrested, an Argentine national, a man named Raul Galvez. The police have tied him to the General, but Galvez knows nothing. He was merely hired to do the job."

"The guy in Oxford got too close and Channing had him killed," said Logan flatly.

"And now Murry is more than a little concerned about his own safety. I told him to back off the story."

"This is just one more reason, is it not?" asked Logan.

"Reason for what?"

"For me to find and stop Channing."

"You mean for the police to stop him."

"No, Hilary, I mean *me*. Channing as the General has eluded the police agencies of the world for many years. He will be even more cautious now as he senses the walls beginning to close in on him. Only one thing will force him out of whatever hole he is hiding in, and that is the hope of retaliation against the clan he so despises, the family that has once again foiled his designs. He must be lured out into the open."

"If I didn't know better, the journalist in me would think you were hatching a plan using yourself as bait."

"Do you know anything else more likely to draw him out than the thought of turning his defeat around and gaining control of Stonewycke? I am the perfect decoy."

"But he's already tried to kill you once!"

"Twice, actually," corrected Logan. "A few years ago I learned that Channing was involved in my capture by Chase Morgan's blokes during the depression."

"You nearly died because of that!"

"But I didn't. The firing squad failed, too. The Lord will protect me again." A faint smile flickered across Logan's face. "I only hope the saying *Third time's a charm* has no basis in fact."

"How can you joke about such a thing?"

"Sorry. I suppose once I felt the Lord saying I had to confront Channing, a bit of the old con man in me began to surface. As long as I keep my motives straight, I might as well enjoy it, wouldn't you say?"

"One last big sting?"

"Not exactly how I might have phrased it . . . but that's the idea."

Hilary did not say anything for a few moments, clearly in thought.

"It's not just you Channing is after," she said at length.

"True enough. His wrath is leveled at all of us."

"Then let's take no chances," Hilary went on. "We must make the hook absolutely irresistible."

"What do you mean by that? Who is this *we*?"

"I am doing this thing with you."

"You are most certainly not," declared Logan.

"I read in Grandmother's journal," said Hilary, "that when Channing and von Graff had you before that firing squad, Channing was not looking at you or anticipating your death as much as he was watching Mother—gloating over her distress, relishing her anguish as she watched you die—as if through her he was really getting to Grandmother."

"That's right."

"It will be a Stonewycke *woman*, then, that will be the true *piece de resistance* in whatever scenario you are cooking up. A woman from Stonewycke will be the one inducement he will not be able to resist."

"I ought to feel offended," smiled Logan. "Reverse chauvinism, you know! But I am proud. I do not know how I could ever have doubted that you are our daughter. But I still have strong reservations about letting you in on this one. This is no light undertaking. I cannot overemphasize the danger. Channing means deadly business."

Hilary rose and walked toward Logan. "Please," she purred, placing her arm around his shoulder. "I won't be in any danger with you there to protect me."

She was conning *him* now. And Logan knew it!

"I have just found you, Hilary. I do not want to risk losing you again."

"And I have just found this family. I have wondered about my place in it. Now I believe it is this—fighting for those I love, and for the land, as so many generations of women have done before me. I am not a little girl. I am a grown woman able to take care of myself. Please . . . Father. I want to be with you!"

Logan hesitated, pondering her words.

"Father and daughter side by side, eh? One last fling together for the good guys!" He glanced up at Hilary, the old twinkle lighting up his eyes.

"That's it!" she said, reflecting the same sparkle.

"I know that look! You got those eyes from me! Unless I miss my guess, what they're saying is that I might do my best to stop you, but I'd never succeed. You'd follow me anyway!"

"You're absolutely right!"

"My eyes and the Duncan feistiness!"

"Can't help myself. It's in my blood!"

Logan laughed. "Then who am I to refuse?"

"So what is your plan?" asked Hilary eagerly, sitting down again.

"Plan? Whoever said I had a plan? We'll have to wait for the Lord to show us one."

"I still don't like the idea of you being bait," said Hilary. "Channing might decide to have done with you right then and there."

"That's a possibility," Logan replied. "But if I were still a betting man, I'd lay odds against it. That is not Channing's way. He prefers a slow death so he can watch the suffering. Look at the elaborate ruse with Jo. She could have killed any of us at any time, but that would not have suited Channing. Besides, he won't kill me as long as he thinks he can further extend his power over us. That's exactly what we'll use against him. We'll make him think he can still gain the ultimate victory. But now we have to get down to thinking through the details. I have a feeling we might be able to use Ashley. At this point our only real connection with Channing is through his Oxford so-called 'colleague.' It's a place to start.''

"I hope you're right about Channing playing along,'' said Hilary, trying to match Logan's smile with a courageous bravado.

"He will. I know him. But before we do anything further, we must commit our way to the Lord. Let's pray, not only for boldness, but that His will may be accomplished through our actions.''

Gunther's austere features were particularly grim as he strode purposefully through the portico. The heat wave of last week had given way to several days of rain, and now, though the temperature had dropped eight degrees, the air was muggy and humid. The General was seated at the far end of the open veranda in a high-backed wicker chair, a blanket laid over his legs in spite of the warm, sticky air, and a young boy was seated on the floor at his feet slowly waving a large leafy fan back and forth.

Still entertaining his delusions of grandeur, thought Gunther sourly, as if he were Caesar or—God forbid!—Hitler himself. Well, maybe he is a neo-führer, after all, he thought. He had set them all up after the war—with his money, his power, his worldwide connections, keeping them all safe and hidden from prying eyes.

But Gunther shook his head as he glanced at the newspaper he held in his hand. It could not last much longer. *He* would not last much longer. By all normal standards he should have died long ago.

"Mein Herr," said Gunther as he approached.

Channing's eyes opened. Gunther noted that they were still sharp, clear, and incisive no matter how debilitated his body appeared.

"What do you want?"

"You are looking particularly well today," answered Gunther.

"Forget the banalities!" rejoined Channing. "I want news, not flattery. What do you hear from my daughter?"

"Nothing yet, mein Herr. But no news is good news, eh?"

"It better be!" snapped Channing.

"Speaking of news," Gunther went on, "this came today." He stretched out the newspaper toward Channing. "Look at the lower left-hand corner."

Channing grabbed the paper in his gnarled hand, laid it in his lap while he dug out his eyeglasses from his pocket, then quickly scanned the columns until he finally focused on the specified place. The headline glared unpleasantly at him.

GUNSHOT VICTIM: POSSIBLE LINKS TO UNDERWORLD

Oxford, England—Ex-Oxford Professor, Mitchell Dodds, is in critical condition following a shooting Friday not far from his residence on Windham Street. Dodds remains comatose, but informed sources believe Dodds had dealings with a notorious underworld organization, headed by the enigmatic international criminal known only by the cryptic title "The General." The

General has eluded Interpol and other national and local police and investigative agencies for two decades, but Interpol's London chief Rollins is confident that if Dodds survives, he will be able to lead police closer than ever before to the infamous crime lord. Queens Hospital sources, however, remain guarded about Dodd's recovery.

When Channing finished the article, he lifted the paper in his hand and flung it away from him.

"Fools!" he screeched. "Those two bumbling idiots! I hope they rot in jail!"

"Only one has been captured," corrected Gunther. "Mallory got away. At least Galvez knows nothing."

"Everyone knows *something*, you fool!" shouted Channing. "Why did you hire such imbeciles in the first place?"

"Galvez will not talk."

"I want him taken care of anyway! Where is the fool of a Texan?"

"I don't know. Probably in some cantina in Galveston."

"At least he was smart enough not to show his miserable face around here."

"I will see to it that he remains away," said Gunther coldly.

"Yes. You know how I hate loose ends. Find him and dispose of him. I do not want Scotland Yard getting on his trail."

"And the Professor?"

"The same, of course. But this time, no bungling! Take care of it personally!"

"They will no doubt have him under tight security."

"That newspaper is almost a week old. He might be out of the hospital by now."

"I doubt it. The paper said he was comatose and in critical condition. By now he may have died and saved us the trouble."

"Or lived and talked!" Channing ran a hand through his white hair. But before he could utter any further imprecations, Gunther cut him off.

"I will attend to it immediately, mein Herr!" Gunther turned to go, but Channing's failing voice stopped him.

"And, Gunther—" Channing croaked with menace, "do not fail!"

Gunther nodded, then continued out, while in his chair a fit of coughing overtook his aging chief. The exertion from the heated conversation had overtaxed his weakened system. The boy ran for the nurse, and within ten minutes Channing lay again in his bed, silently cursing all the fools around him, and himself for being at their mercy.

Ashley Jameson had dreamed up many an eccentric scenario as Lady Hargreave. But this real-life drama was the most incredible of all.

No doubt it struck him as incredulous because he happened to be, for the moment, right in the middle of the plot. It was one thing to set characters of a book into motion doing crazy things. But when it was your own life on the line, all romantic notions suddenly fled, and all that was left was pure, undiluted fear.

Yes, here he was. Ashley Jameson, dull university professor, closet mystery writer . . . but certainly *not* a detective—here he was, sitting in a stranger's flat—a dead stranger's, no less!—waiting to be discovered by a ruthless killer. And here he would remain. For he had, in a moment of insanity he now thought, actually asked for this particular role in Logan's scheme.

With the assistance of Interpol, Professor Dodds had been resurrected from the dead via a bogus newspaper article planted in *The London Times*. In the role of Dodds, Ashley hoped to throw a curve to whomever the General sent to finish the job someone else had botched. If it worked, Logan would find himself with an invitation to meet personally with his old nemesis, Jason Channing himself.

The entire scheme, with all its twists and subplots, was a long shot, as Logan would say. But Dodds was the only possible link to Channing's location. Thus Ashley had stepped into Dodds' now vacant shoes, spent a few days at the hospital, and then, after an astounding recovery, was released. For three days now he had been living in Dodds' Windham Street flat. He only hoped that when Channing's assassin came for him, he would be ready. The police had men staked out around the place at a safe enough distance so as not to scare off their prey. Ashley himself remained indoors as much as possible.

Ashley glanced at the clock. It was ten P.M., Dodds' usual bedtime, or so Ashley had established over the last several days. He laid aside the book he had been reading and rose from the leather easy chair.

Nights were the worst. Although it had been arranged for a policewoman in a nurse's uniform to come in daily while he caught a few hours' sleep, he could not keep from becoming extremely drowsy at night. How much longer such an upside-down schedule could go he wasn't sure.

He turned out the lights, then walked toward the window, careful not to make an easy target in front of it. Pulling back the shade a crack, he glanced outside. A light rain fell. The streets glistened with moisture, but were otherwise dark except for the occasional passing of an automobile with its bright headlamps.

I don't know what I expect to see, Ashley mused to himself. Surely no professional killer was going to hang about under a streetlamp with his trenchcoat collar pulled up over his neck, waiting for the whole world to see him.

Sighing, Ashley turned back into the room and sat down again in the chair in the darkened room. The hands of the clock on the wall loudly ticked off the minutes. Logan warned him the waiting would be the worst part. He had been right.

Ashley tried to divert his mind into more pleasant channels. He recalled the last time he had seen Hilary several days ago. They both had been a bit too eager to point out that their parting was not a *real* goodbye, and that they would be parted for only a brief time. They each realized, of course, that they would have to stay clear of one another while he was "undercover," though Hilary had smiled when he had used that oddly out-of-place term.

"I think you are rather enjoying all this, Ashley," she had said.

"An exciting change of pace from the grind, you know."

"You will be careful?" she said as she wove her arm around his while they walked under a full winter moon over the snow-covered university paths.

"Of that you may be certain!" He took a small package from his coat pocket, simply wrapped in brown paper. "Perhaps this will help the hours pass more quickly," he said.

"Ashley, a present! You are a romantic, after all!"

"The well of the scholar runs deep, my dear."

"I am only beginning to discover just how deep!" Hilary tore off the paper and found her hands clutching a clothbound book. She smiled as she read the title: "*The Mystery of the Designing Debutante:* A Lady Hargreave Mystery."

"Hot off the presses, as you journalists say," said Ashley. "Perhaps it may serve in some small measure to explain my interest in the fashion industry. And you are the first person in all of Britain to possess a copy."

"Autographed, I hope?"

"Certainly not! Lady Hargreave never signs her books—a quirky sort of lady, you see. My publisher seems to think that the mystery surrounding the lady sells as many books as her stories themselves. I myself prefer to think it is pure creative and artistic excellence, but I see no reason to burst the old fellow's bubble."

"I shall simply devour it."

"I hope it won't entirely keep you from thinking of me."

Hilary drew closer to him. "It could never do that, Ashley, don't you know?"

Even sitting alone in the black apartment, Ashley could not restrain a pleased grin as he recalled her words. A year ago he would have thought that at such a seasoned age in his life, it would have been impossible to fit a woman into his staid and ordered bachelor routine. Yet now he found himself wondering if it would be possible to imagine his life *without* the daughter and niece of his two old friends, Logan and Ian.

The university tower clock striking the quarter hour pulled his thoughts back to the present.

Ten-fifteen. Still no intruders.

Ashley began to wonder if they had made it *too* easy for Channing's man. Logan said there was always a fine line between a good piece of bait and a tip-off.

Ashley began to reflect on everything else Logan had told him before he set out on this madcap task—a crash course in the confidence game! Logan would have been so much better in this part, to be sure. Or an undercover detective, if things got too rough. But Channing, and possibly his men, knew Logan. And those kinds of men had an uncanny knack for smelling the law no matter what the disguise. Or so Ashley had argued when he had wanted the assignment, even though Galvez insisted he was the only one to have had face-to-face contact with Dodds.

Logan had pointed out one other factor, too, probably trying to convince himself of the rationale of letting an untried scholar confront a hit man:

"After all, Ashley," he had said, "you already know all the professorial lingo. Your very inexperience and authenticity will give us an edge against Channing, who will be on the alert for a setup."

They both knew there were many risks. The plan could unravel at any number of points. But it was all they had. Logan was counting on its one most important feature. Channing would *want* Logan now more than ever, and in his blind obsession he was liable to overlook practicality. "His wanting me will be our foot in the door," Logan said. "The dodge can only work when the mark desperately desires what you're offering him. Remember, Channing doesn't know what *we* know. That's our ace."

Suddenly a noise out of the night met Ashley's ear.

He listened intently. Had it been his own overwrought imagination, on edge, waiting for something . . . *anything* to happen?

There it was again! A faint creak on the third step outside. He noticed it himself every time he entered the flat.

He swallowed hard. His whole body tensed as an inner sense told him this was it. He opened a drawer in the table next to the chair where he'd placed the automatic pistol Inspector Rollins had issued him. He'd done a good deal of hunting on his estate in Cornwall, and was a fair shot. But he'd never be able to use a weapon against a human being.

Logan had assured him he wouldn't have to. They wouldn't expect him as the scholarly type to be a killer. But they'd have no way of knowing for sure. His very unpredictability would throw them off guard. Ashley wrapped his fingers around the hard cold steel handle of the revolver, withdrew it, and pointed the weapon at the closed door.

He swallowed again. His throat was suddenly very dry. The only thought his brain could focus on was the possibility that both Lady Hargreave *and* Ashley Jameson had at last bitten off more than they could chew.

63 / The Professor and the Assassin _____

Whoever stood outside the door was good. Ashley hardly detected another sound. Had he been asleep in his bed, as was supposed, he would have been an easy target. But Ashley would not be a victim tonight, not if he could help it.

A faint scraping could now be heard. The intruder was picking the lock. In another minute the door inched open.

Ashley sat like a statue, daring not even to breathe. When he acted, it had to be fast and unexpected, and perfectly timed. His left hand was poised by the switch to the lamp that would send its blinding light toward the door. His right still held the gun.

A moment more and a dark figure, tall and rather trim, slowly shouldered its way into the room. It turned to close the door. For a brief moment its back was to Ashley.

Now!

He flipped on the switch, bathing the man in light and momentarily disorienting him.

"Don't move a muscle!" said Ashley, in the shaky voice of one unaccustomed to such scenes. "Don't even think of turning around. I am holding a gun on your back."

"You are insane if you think you will get away with this," said the intruder in a menacing Germanic accent.

"Nearly getting killed sometimes does that to a man," replied Ashley. "I may be insane, as you say. But that does not lessen the potency of this gun in my hand. Now please, drop your weapon."

"So you can kill me?"

"Good heavens, no!" exclaimed Ashley. "Unless of course . . . but you wouldn't do that, would you? I do so hate the sight of blood."

Gunther hesitated another moment, then dropped the pistol he held onto the floor with a thud.

"Now, you may turn around," said Ashley.

"What do you want?" asked Gunther impatiently as he turned and did his best to take in his surroundings while squinting against the light. He did not like being on this end of an attack.

"Come in and have a seat. We may as well be comfortable as we talk."

"And I suppose you'll want tea too?" scoffed Gunther.

"That might be nice, but I suppose we'd best get down to business first." Ashley motioned with the gun toward a chair directly opposite him.

Gunther sat down, looking cold and superior despite the fact that an inept professor had so easily gotten the drop on him. As he did so, Ashley rose, moved toward the door while still keeping his visitor in the sights of his gun, retrieved Gunther's pistol from the floor, then resumed his seat.

"What is this business you want to discuss?" Gunther asked in a blunt, irritated tone.

"Well, I expect you have come here to finish the job those other two chaps started." Ashley paused as if expecting a response from Gunther. But the German remained impassive. "I suppose you want to kill me," he continued, "before I tell anything to Scotland Yard. Was that your thinking?"

Still Gunther did not reply.

"As you can see," Ashley went on, "I have been out of the hospital for several days, and though I am still weak, I have said nothing."

"Why should I believe you?"

Ashley thought for a moment. "I see what you mean. That does make it a bit sticky, doesn't it?" He paused. "Well, for argument's sake," he went on, "let us just accept that for now, what do you say?"

Gunther did not protest, when Ashley went on.

"Good! Now . . . I haven't talked because, to be perfectly honest, I have my own business interests to protect."

"What interests?"

"All in good time."

"And what about the story in the *Times* saying you had connections to the General? He was very angry to read that!" As he spoke Gunther shifted threateningly in his chair.

"Sit back please," said Ashley, gesturing with his gun.

"He wants you dead, Dodds! He does not like his name appearing in the newspaper!"

"I do apologize for that. I rather lost my head when I first realized I might be dealing with the General. But you can't really blame me, can you? I'm afraid I mentioned something to a reporter before I slipped into the coma. Later, when they released me, I denied everything. And as it was the word of a respected Oxford professor—well, actually an ex-professor—against an overzealous reporter . . . well, the poor newspaper fellow was left with a bit of egg on his face."

"We try to kill you, and then you turn around and *protect* us?" said Gunther skeptically. "Why should I believe you? I *don't* believe you!" Again he half rose, as if the weapon in Ashley's hand were a mere toy that concerned him not at all.

"You really must relax. I'm not at all used to guns, and I wouldn't want you to frighten me into using this before I have had my say."

Again Gunther sat back. His face wore the expression of a caged tiger awaiting the merest momentary lapse that he might spring upon this nincompoop of a dim-witted professor.

"As I said, I was protecting myself every bit as much as I had any noble notions regarding your employer," said Ashley. "I saw no reason to jeopardize any of our positions when we could all benefit so handsomely from an alliance that keeps us all healthy."

"Just what do you mean by *benefit*?"

"Quite simple, actually." Ashley relaxed, lowering the gun slightly. "I think I have something the General wants. Besides my silence, of course."

"What might that be?"

"The reason he contacted me in the first place was to analyze and possibly dispose of some rare and ancient artifacts."

Several days earlier a careful search of Dodds' flat had turned up a file containing descriptions of several items delivered to the Professor for inspection by two men named Mallory and Galvez. It was easy to assume that this had been the reason for the initial contact between the General and Dodds. But the moment Hilary had read Dodds' descriptions of the few sample relics, she knew she had seen something of the same sort before.

Lady Margaret Duncan was one of the few persons in recent times to have ever seen inside the ancient Pict box which had lain undisturbed under the great stones on Braenock Ridge for a millennium. Later in life, after the box had long been lost track of, she described some of the pieces, as best her aging memory could recall, to her granddaughter. These found their way into the journal, and the descriptions were still fresh in Hilary's mind. When the search of Dodds' flat turned up the list, Hilary immediately noted distinct similarities. The fact that Channing, the last known possessor of the box, was now mixed up with Dodds seemed to corroborate the correlation. Ashley now planned to use this knowledge as his trump card.

"Before my unfortunate *accident*," Ashley went on in a carefully measured tone, keeping a mistrustful eye on Gunther's every move, while continuing to nurture the image of an absent-minded buffoon, "I was able to conduct a little research, along with my preliminary tests. I concluded that what your General possesses is extremely valuable indeed, very rare, very ancient. I also discovered an interesting fact that I did not put in my original report."

"And what is that fact!" spat Gunther, growing weary of this simpleton.

"Just this. That it is also—how shall I put it?—very *hot*. The relics appear part of a collection belonging to the Stonewycke estate in northern Scotland. They were stolen some forty years ago, and besides still being an open case, that theft is connected to an unsolved murder."

"What does that have to do with me?"

"Perhaps nothing . . . perhaps a great deal. I understand that items of this kind pass through many hands over the years. In my business it does not usually pay to look too closely at the histories of the items which I am paid to deal with. But I assume the General came to me because he hoped to unload this cache of his, which no doubt has been a rather difficult undertaking for him due to the circumstances of the theft and the antiquity of the items.''

"As you said, such things pass through many hands.''

"And as I have been *trying* to say, I have a client who is interested in purchasing this collection of relics, and will ask no questions regarding how your employer came by them. He happens to know that the original— what should I call him—*guardian* of the goods following the theft is now dead. He is only interested in retrieving them.''

"You have been quite busy for a man only just risen from his deathbed.''

"I daresay, Mr.—by the way, I don't think you mentioned your name.''

"I didn't. It is unimportant.''

"Ah, yes. Of course. Well, as I said, I do have a party interested in the sale, and had already begun initiating these arrangements before the—ah, the shooting. That has, I'm sure you can appreciate, slowed me up somewhat.''

"Bah! You are a fool!'' said Gunther. "There was never any talk of a *sale*.''

"Isn't that what all this was about? I naturally assumed—''

"The General is not a man to make careless assumptions about! He was merely having the items valued and authenticated. I doubt he would sell them at any price! He is sentimentally attached to the ridiculous things.''

Gunther paused a moment to reflect on Channing's obsession. "He lets no one near them,'' he went on. "I've never even seen them.''

"Surely he must keep such priceless objects displayed in some fashion?'' Ashley lowered the gun unconsciously as he became more absorbed in the interchange.

Gunther threw his head back and roared, in part hoping to make Ashley drop his guard even further, but also amused at the humor of his last remark.

"On display! They are so locked away, or buried, no one knows what he's done with them! Occasionally a peculiar mood comes over him and he goes off in private, sometimes for hours on end—once he was gone all night—muttering all the while about his treasure. But no one goes with him. It's . . . but never mind all that! No one knows where they are, and wherever they are, they're not for sale!''

"Then why contact me in the first place?''

"I only follow orders—and right now my orders are to kill you!''

With a sudden movement, Gunther jumped to his feet. He had been watching his captor with the eye of an eagle, and the moment he perceived he had relaxed and grown overconfident, he wasted no time in attempting to seize the advantage.

He had not counted on Ashley's quick reaction, however. Nor had he believed this droll professor would have the gumption to use the weapon he had held so inexpertly in his hand. Ashley, on the other hand, had been waiting for a counter-attack. His only surprise was that it had taken so long to come. The moment Gunther lunged forward, Ashley fired the automatic. The slug missed Gunther, as Ashley intended, but it was close enough to make him wonder.

At the unexpected blast from the pistol, the German fell back. He gaped at Ashley, momentarily stunned that this unassertive professor had the guts to pull the trigger.

"Dash it all!" yelled Ashley. "Don't force me to do something nasty! Can't we approach these negotiations like gentlemen?"

A dry, hard sound, somewhat resembling laughter that had grown rusty from disuse, escaped Gunther's lips. "Gentlemen? An interesting idea." He scratched his head thoughtfully, then eased back into the chair. "Well then, what is on your mind, Professor?"

"I have a proposition that could make your employer a wealthy man."

"Ha!" mocked Gunther. "He will be warmed to hear of your offer! Ha! ha! It will prove to him that you do not know his true identity. For he is too rich ever to see a fraction of his wealth."

"Be that as it may, my prospective buyer would be willing to part with a tidy sum to make the acquisition."

"I tell you, he will never sell. He will go to his grave with the treasure still in his possession and its location unknown."

"Just tell him my buyer is anxious."

"How tidy is the sum we are discussing?"

"In the millions, if the other pieces are of the same quality as those I examined."

"What do *you* want out of this?"

"I should think my life would not be too much to ask—that, and my usual ten percent, of course."

"You *are* audacious! That is one thing I can say for you."

"I am also holding the gun." Ashley waved it for effect.

"You cannot sit up nights indefinitely," replied Gunther. "Your guard will have to relax eventually. When it does, nothing will prevent me from doing what I came here to do—some dark night, long after your business with the General is concluded."

"I am fully aware of that possibility," said Ashley, "and thus I have taken the precaution to invest in a bit of insurance—in the form of a safe-deposit box and a letter containing its key which has been entrusted with a friend. In the box are documents revealing everything I know. Whether or not you and your employer had anything to do with the events that occurred in Scotland forty years ago hardly concerns me. But I think Scotland Yard will find highly interesting the General's connection to Trans Global, various other crimes and murders that have taken place over the years, the transporting of certain stolen items of great value, as well as your possession of the Stonewycke treasure itself and your part in my own murder. All this will make fascinating reading, and will be made public upon my demise."

"You *know* the General will not be toyed with!"

"I do indeed, from personal experience." Ashley patted his stomach as if to indicate his wound. "Believe me, I am not toying. I live, and the General and I benefit mutually. I die and . . . well, we both lose. Simple logic, actually."

Gunther leaned back, folded his arms together, and appraised Ashley carefully.

"All right, Professor," he said at length, "for the sake of argument—as you would say—let us just assume my employer *was* interested in selling his precious relics. Who is this buyer of yours?"

Ashley paused. If the bait was to be dangled, he had to give it just the right touch.

At last he opened his mouth to speak.

"Logan Macintyre," he said matter-of-factly.

Gunther jerked forward again, but this time in stunned shock.

"What are you trying to pull, Dodds?" he roared.

"Logan Macintyre, Member of Parliament," Ashley repeated. "I see nothing so irregular about a man, if he is willing to pay, attempting to purchase back something of which he was the original owner."

Gunther hesitated, thoughts running rapidly through his mind. If Macintyre was involved, questions could not help being raised. . . . Why now, all of a sudden, was he interested in retrieving what had once belonged to the estate which he had inherited by marriage?

"You had better understand, Mr. Dodds," Gunther warned, "that if this is any kind of a ruse, you are a dead man—whatever your threats of exposure!"

"Why would I risk my life unless I am telling you the truth? Really, must we be so barbaric?"

"It's a shame my old general is not still around," mused Gunther. "*He* would have appreciated your pluck." A look almost of sentimentality momentarily disturbed Gunther's iron-like visage. Quickly his features hardened again. "Unfortunately he is no longer here, and you have five minutes to convince me you are on the level. How did you make contact with Macintyre?"

"*On the level* is a rather inapplicable phrase for men in our business it seems," replied Ashley. "But to answer you—this is how he contacted me. Before my accident, I had already put the word out—discreetly, of course—for persons interested in rare artifacts of this kind. I have certain clients who are particularly loyal customers in various categories of merchandise. Thus it got around—nothing that could be traced, you understand—that certain old relics of possible Pictish connection might soon be available.

Macintyre is not one of my clients. But apparently he has had his own word out for years now in hopes of relocating his goods. So by way of the underground grapevine he has found me."

"Was anything said to him about the General?"

"Good heavens no! I already learned my lesson on speaking that name too freely."

"Did Macintyre mention any names?"

"None. He wants the family heirlooms back where they belong and is willing to pay. That's all he said. He is unconcerned with ownership or specifics of where they have been through the years."

Gunther rubbed his forehead, his brow deeply creased. He had not expected this. It would seem Macintyre would have enough on his mind these days, what with phony daughters and attempted poisonings, to concern himself with that treasure.

But if the Professor's story was true . . . then all this had been in the works long before Jo and Emil had been forced to flee. It might even be that Macintyre had intensified his search *because* of the daughter, wanting the restoration of the family wealth to pass on, soon after Jo's original appearance.

Dodds would have no reason to lie. For all his stuffy ways, he was a shrewd businessman, with his own profit his major interest. This could be the very thing Channing had desired for years—a prime opportunity to get to Macintyre. The beauty of it would be that Macintyre would walk right into it not even realizing he was stepping into Channing's stronghold.

Still, there was the possibility Channing might think otherwise. Gunther had his orders, and Channing did not like his orders disregarded.

Could he afford to take the chance of not informing him of this new development in the scenario? He didn't think so. Gunther well knew of Channing's consuming passion in life—not that he cared anything about it himself; he thought the ancient vendetta was ridiculous.

But he knew Channing would want to be told of *anything* regarding the Stonewycke clan. He would not be happy if Gunther acted independently in this matter.

Gunther looked up at Ashley.

"All right, Professor, it looks as though you have talked yourself into staying alive for yet a while longer," said Gunther. "I will relay your proposition to my employer."

British Airways flight 829 touched down at Ezeiza Airport on schedule. The fine skyline of Buenos Aires, the largest and most cosmopolitan city in South America, was bathed in a luxurious warmth of a humid 72°. Not bad for early December, thought Logan as he collected his suitcase from the conveyer. Allison and he would have to try it sometime for a vacation. But thoughts of pleasant times would have to wait.

As Allison came to mind, not for the first time in the last days, a knot tightened in his stomach. She was going to be all right, and had already thrown off most of the effects of the poison. But he had to struggle to prevent a bitter anger from rising within him when he thought of Channing's attempt to snuff out her life. He had to continually remind himself what his true motives were in this attempt—to destroy the cancerous feud, not be drawn into it himself.

He strode across the tiled airport baggage dock to customs, where his government position allowed him to pass through quickly. Outside, the heat was even more noticeable, but not unpleasant after Britain's chill. He hailed a cab.

His instructions from Channing's man, with Ashley acting as intermediary, were simple: Fly to Buenos Aires, register at the Grand Hotel Royal, and await further instructions. Though the man's absolute insistence that the Professor's interested buyer come himself, in person and alone, was an unusual request, they had expected it. Ashley had feigned hesitation when the requirement was made part of the deal. He had taken enough time to fake a call to Logan, and in the end had reluctantly agreed.

Channing had taken the bait, they had played the little game of being indecisive over his terms, and in the end—once Gunther had relayed his employer's final message: "You tell him if he wants to buy those relics, he comes to me in person!"—had consented. The deal was set.

At least half of Logan's mission—finding the General's whereabouts—would soon bear fruit. They now knew Channing was in Argentina, probably near Buenos Aires. But this was a metropolis of several million. Even Interpol had come this close. Channing could be anywhere within a fifty- or hundred-mile radius. They still had to get to his door.

The taxi dropped Logan at the hotel. A bellhop took his luggage at the curb, no doubt expecting a generous tip, which he got. He was escorted to the front desk, where he registered.

"I'd like a room toward the front," said Logan, "with a window facing Florida Avenue." He didn't know if such precautions would be necessary, but he wanted everything covered.

He went straight to his room, made two phone calls, then kicked off his shoes and stretched out on the bed. It felt good to relax after the tiring flight and he knew he'd better take advantage of these moments while he was able. He hoped Channing gave him the chance to have a good long sleep before contacting him. But no, Channing would not be so considerate. He would want Logan as frayed and out of sorts as possible. Logan closed his eyes and was soon dozing soundly.

An hour later he awoke to the sound of a sharp knock at his door. He tensed momentarily, then recalled he had ordered a meal through room service when he registered. The waiter brought in a tray; Logan paid him, then sat down in one of the simulated leather chairs to eat. Hungry, he consumed what had been delivered, despite the fact that the food was poor and he was restless. When he finished he soon found himself pacing the floor of the small room.

He glanced at his watch. He had been here two hours already. No doubt the hotel concierge was under orders to notify Channing or his intermediary the moment a registration was made under the name Logan Macintyre. How long would he wait before he made contact? No doubt he'll make me sweat first, thought Logan. But that wouldn't take long in this heat; the air conditioning in the Grand Royal did not seem to be working.

Logan paused in his pacing in front of the window. It was midafternoon. In the outlying villages, no doubt, siesta time would have quieted down the pace. But in the heart of Buenos Aires, the streets full of tourists and traffic, one would never guess this to be other than the international center of over five million it had become. He noted the hotel directly across Florida, the Richmond. The view of the street was better from there, but that detail might not matter should Channing's man decide to come upon Logan unawares. He had to consider that possibility, for he would definitely be taking counter precautions to prevent being followed.

Logan turned back into the room and continued pacing.

At half past five, the summons finally came.

The soft knock on Logan's door was in itself unportentious, but Logan answered it not without some trepidation, and with a silent prayer on his lips. When he swung the door open, he found himself face-to-face with an unexpected ghost from the past.

"Gunther!" he exclaimed in true amazement.

"We meet again, Herr Macintyre." Gunther's mouth twisted in a half smile, his delight in Logan's discomfiture obvious.

"Where . . . how in the world do you fit into all this?" asked Logan, now remembering that Ashley had mentioned that his late-night caller had spoken with a German accent. Logan had never even guessed that Ashley had been face-to-face with the old double agent with whom he had worked in the war. Had he realized Ashley was going to confront Gunther, he would never have let him pose as the Professor! His estimation of Ashley's bravery suddenly increased tenfold.

One look told him that Gunther had not changed much over the years, except for gray hair and a few more wrinkles. His features were still hard, and his countenance as lethal as a steel saber.

"We can talk over old times later," said Gunther. "We have a small journey before we reach my employer."

"Then it is not you I am to deal with?"

"I am still only a hatchet man."

"For whom?"

"All in good time, Macintyre."

"Von Graff?"

"He's dead."

"So I heard. Who then?"

"I do what I must do."

"Still working both sides of the fence, eh?"

Gunther's eyebrow arched. "Expediency was and is my motto, Macintyre. It has kept me alive, healthy, and financially well off for many years."

"I, too, am alive, healthy, and well off, my friend," said Logan pointedly, "but from following a different creed."

"Will you preach to me, Macintyre?"

"As you said, we have a journey ahead of us. Surely there will be much to talk about."

Gunther grunted sullenly.

"So . . . you cannot tell me who your employer is?" continued Logan.

"I think he would prefer to remain anonymous a while longer." Gunther paused. "Get your things. It is time to go."

"I will not be returning here?"

"Not in the near future," Gunther replied cryptically.

Logan gathered up the few items he had unpacked, dropped them in his suitcase, latched it, grabbed the handle, and followed Gunther out the door. As they stepped into the corridor however, he stopped.

"Wait!" he said. "I forgot my razor."

"You can get another."

"This was a good one. It will only take a moment."

Logan ducked back inside, closing the door behind him. He hurried to the bathroom and retrieved the cheap single-blade razor he had put on the sink counter. Walking back through the larger room, he paused long enough to pull the curtains almost shut, leaving a one foot gap of open space, then rejoined Gunther in the hallway. He opened his suitcase and tucked the razor inside.

The two men continued down the corridor to the elevator. As Logan feared, they followed a surreptitious route out of the hotel, keeping to rear hallways, finally exiting through a service door. They continued on foot down an alley, Gunther glancing about.

"Still the cautious one, eh, Gunther?" chuckled Logan lightly.

"It has not harmed us yet, Macintyre," replied Gunther. "Besides, in dealing with a *swindler*, would you not be cautious too?"

"I see what you mean. But many years have passed since those days. I am now a respectable politician!"

"A contradiction in terms!"

Gunther nudged Logan forward. They turned left from the short alley at the rear of the hotel into a semi-deserted street that appeared used mostly for deliveries. Logan glanced about, as if trying to get his bearings. A black Lincoln Continental was parked about half a block away. They walked to it. Gunther paused, took a ring of keys from his pocket, then unlocked the passenger door for Logan. Without pausing to open it, or to help Logan with his luggage, he walked around to the driver's side.

As Logan swung his suitcase inside, out of the corner of his eye he noted a young Indian boy, a street waif by the look of him, who had been standing at the farther end of the block eyeing them, dash off and out of sight. Getting his luggage situated, Logan seated himself and closed the door. Gunther started the ignition and pulled away.

Logan rolled down his window just as Gunther stopped at the first intersection. Then the huge automobile pulled out quickly through traffic, as Gunther wheeled his way east onto a large boulevard.

"What's this street called?" asked Logan.

"Avenue Corrientes, but what does it matter?" snapped Gunther. "Roll up that window!"

Slowly Logan complied, but not before he had taken a good look up and down the street, spotting the avenue called Florida as they sped across it

Around the corner, only moments before, a woman exited the Richmond Hotel. Though not tall enough to attract attention by it, she was lanky, and her movements were made awkward by the bulky camera bag strung over her shoulder and the bulging Indian-weave tote bag in her hand. Her pink-rimmed sunglasses, in combination with her brightly embroidered peasant outfit, such as were at that moment being offered in any of three dozen bazaars within a mile, marked her as the consummate tourist, probably an American by her ostentatious display of purchasing power.

She shambled down the hotel steps, paused a moment to speak with a breathless young street beggar, then jogged south along Florida. Her paraphernalia bobbing about, she reached a rented Volkswagen sedan, threw in her gear, then jumped in with surprising ease behind the wheel. As Gunther's Lincoln cruised by, she started her engine. The VW eased its way into traffic, turned onto Corrientes, and settled into the late-afternoon rush, four cars behind the Lincoln.

Within two hours she had returned to the Richmond. Leaving her cumbersome baggage in the car, she hurried up the hotel steps, purposefully crossed the hotel lobby to where a bank of pay telephones stood. She inserted two coins into one, then dialed the operator.

After a moment she spoke into the handset:

"Overseas assistance, por favor."

65 / In the Spider's Lair

Fifty minutes after departing Buenos Aires, the black Lincoln pulled through the gates of the villa.

Logan was quick to note the armed guards posted at the gate. He wondered how many such sentries there were about the place. But his attention was soon diverted to the villa itself. By the look of it, Channing had not made much of a point to showcase his wealth. Men in his position were better off keeping a low profile; perhaps that extended to the security too. Still, armed sentries were probably not an uncommon sight about the homes of wealthy patrons in these third-world republics.

Gunther braked to a stop. They had not even stepped out of the car before a servant appeared from the house. He took Logan's suitcase, while respectfully keeping his distance from Gunther. Inside, the entryway to the villa was spacious and well kept, though sparsely furnished.

Logan found himself wondering what had filled Channing's years since they had last met—what besides the obvious obsession with vengeance and hate. During the drive Logan had continued to attempt conversation, but Gunther had proved his usual taciturn self.

"Would you care to go to your room, Herr Macintyre?" Gunther asked formally.

"My room? I assumed we would make arrangements for our transaction and then you would take me back to the city."

Gunther smiled. "I have a feeling your business may take somewhat longer than you anticipated, and that you will be spending the night."

Logan eyed him carefully. This could be more dangerous than he planned on.

"Well then," said Logan, "let's do get on with it. I am rather anxious to be about our business—and not a little curious besides."

"I thought so," said Gunther. "My employer is anxious also, and if you were up to it, wanted you taken directly to him. Come this way."

Toward the end of a long corridor they came upon closed double doors. Gunther paused and knocked.

"¿Quien es?" The voice that came from inside was scored with age, but contained no less self-important arrogance than it had thirty years ago when Logan had last heard it.

"It is I . . . Gunther. I have our guest."

"Ah, very good! Come in!"

337

Logan entered behind Gunther, and beheld a man standing with his back to the door in front of a marbled hearth. No doubt wanting to make the most of the surprise revelation of his identity, he remained several moments after the door clicked shut exactly where he was. He wore a tan-colored smoking jacket, and was supporting himself with a cane. The back of his head still contained probably half its original quantity of hair, but it was pure white, as was his skin, giving himself away as clearly not at home amid the dark-skinned natives in this climate where the sun shone hot.

Slowly the lean, wasted figure turned. On his face was plastered a smile of insidious delight, which, notwithstanding his physical impotence, yet emanated a malevolent power.

"Channing!" exclaimed Logan in disbelief, his stunned tone, now that his eyes actually beheld his adversary, only half an act.

"Who else do you think would possess the legendary Stonewycke treasure?" returned Channing wryly, hardly able to contain his delight to find Logan Macintyre at last within his resourceful grasp.

"But . . . but . . . I thought you were dead! I thought . . . I assumed . . ."

"You thought I had unloaded it, eh? Ha, ha, ha!" croaked Channing, his elation curbed only by the evil in his soul. His laugh did not ring with joy, but rather struck the dissonant chord of wicked vindication. "Ha, ha! That's a good one, Macintyre!" he went on, savoring the moment. "Surely you didn't think me such a fool?"

"So . . . you have kept it all these years?"

"I once fancied the notion of selling it," replied Channing, wiping his eyes and still chuckling. "But then I realized the only interested buyers would be one of *you* fools from that backwater northern province. Besides you cursed sentimentalists, only legitimate historians would take a second look at it. And I certainly couldn't have pawned it off on any reputable historical buyer without having to answer too many questions. Besides, what could I have gotten for it? Worthless bits of scraps, nothing more." He sighed purposefully. "But I have over the years grown rather fond of it."

"And now . . . what has changed your mind? Why sell it now?"

Again Channing began to laugh—at first softly, then rising in volume.

"Excuse me, Macintyre," he said through his laughter, "but this really is too humorous! You are more of a fool than I took you for!"

"I merely asked why all of a sudden you want to—"

"Ha, ha!" roared Channing. "Oh . . . that's a good one, eh, Gunther? Ha, ha, ha! Sell it! Ha, ha! I have no intention of selling it, Macintyre!"

"But I thought . . . then why this elaborate ruse to get me here? I thought I was coming here on a legitimate business deal."

"Oh, Macintyre! You really must stop! Ha, ha! All this exertion is going to be the death of me! Ha, ha! Don't you yet get it, Macintyre?"

"Get it? What are you driving at?"

"The treasure is not for sale, Macintyre," replied Channing, calming.

"Then why am I here?"

"Don't you know, Logan? May I call you Logan? Why, you are my friend. I merely wanted to see you again! Come . . . sit down."

Channing waved Logan toward one of the expensive chintz-covered chairs situated before the hearth. "I will have some refreshments brought."

Logan sat down, as one recovering from a great shock. Channing took the adjacent chair, then glanced up at Gunther. All humor was gone from his countenance, and his eyes were again empty of life. "See to the refreshments, Gunther," he ordered in a deprecating tone.

Gunther made no response, either silent or verbal; he merely turned and exited the room.

Channing turned fully toward Logan. "I'm certain this change in your plans will be somewhat disconcerting," he said benevolently. "But we will do our best to make it up to you. Dinner will be served soon. You have been traveling the better part of the day and must be fatigued. So I am having our finest guest accommodations prepared for you."

"I assure you that's unnecessary," said Logan.

"It's not the least trouble."

"If you'll simply have Gunther drive me back to town after dinner, I'd be most—"

"Please, Mr. Macintyre. I wouldn't think of it! You are my guest!"

"I've never known you to be so hospitable, Channing," said Logan.

"I've never before entertained a Member of Parliament in my home."

"I see," said Logan, pausing thoughtfully. "I seem to recall an old proverb to that effect. Something to the effect of, 'Visit the spider in his own lair before you judge his character.' "

"Exactly! But you misquote, Macintyre. The saying is in regard to a wolf, not a spider."

"I didn't know you were a literary man, Channing."

"I am full of surprises, Macintyre, even at my age. But the point of the saying is well taken. One never knows when one will find the wolf, so to speak, a congenial sort. You've read your Kipling, I assume."

"Yes, of course. Well, I hope you're right, Channing."

At that moment a servant entered with a tray containing coffee service. He set it on a table and served each man submissively. Logan did not see Gunther again until dinner.

"So, what became of you after the war?" Logan asked, sipping his coffee.

"I kept busy. I aided a few of my German friends."

"You mean Nazi friends?"

"Yes, that too. I helped some relocate. I found myself quite out of favor with several Western governments, and it became beneficial to all of us to find a place far from the madding crowd, as it were."

"Here?"

"And other places. We are quite diversified, you know."

"So I had heard."

Channing cast Logan a quick glance, but let the remark pass.

"I reorganized my company under a new name, set up a figurehead chairman and major stockholders, while I continued to exercise control. I gave my expatriate friends new identities and positions within the company hierarchy. I even took a couple of new identities myself."

"What about von Graff?"

"Oh yes, him too. He didn't fancy a firing squad, and he was perfectly suited to operate the U-boat I stole from the German Navy just before the end of the war. He died twelve years ago—a massive heart attack. Never knew what hit him."

"At least he deserved that much," commented Logan. "Von Graff would not have been the type to put up with a long enfeebling illness."

"We *all* get what we deserve, Macintyre." Channing's emphasis of the word had a sinister edge.

"What about you, Channing?"

"Prosperity and long life . . . just like a saint." He chuckled dryly. "I wager you never expected me to last so long!"

"And happiness?" said Logan, ignoring his final comment.

"Thank God I was never sentimental about such tripe."

"Have you known peace, Channing?"

"Bah! Don't preach to me, Macintyre!" Channing challenged sharply. "I've heard of your grating religiosity and moralism. No doubt you think I've been a bad sort and will burn in hell. You have probably even prayed for my soul! Well, you are a fool! I don't care what happens to my soul— I don't believe in such rubbish. I've had everything I wanted out of life."

"Everything?"

Suddenly Channing's cup rattled in its saucer while his face turned red. His eyes glared, flashing like sparks from hot metal. The muscles in his wrinkled face twitched violently. All at once he looked old and on the verge of collapse, and his voice weakened into a hoarse gasp from the rage that had seized him.

"I will have everything before I die!" he spat with choking venom.

"I hope so, Channing. I truly do." But as Logan spoke the words, he knew full well that he and Channing were speaking of things as different as black and white, as far removed from one another as heaven and hell.

Logan and Gunther dined alone. Channing did not appear. The word was that he had taken to his bed.

The meal was quiet and uneventful. Logan could not help wondering if he had been wise in allowing himself to be brought here. Channing was unpredictable. He could fly into a rage at any moment and order Logan hanged or shot. He could also die without warning. There were too many variables for Logan to feel entirely at ease.

After dinner he was escorted to his room.

Bidding him a cool good night, Gunther closed the door behind him and walked away. Immediately Logan placed his hand on the latch and turned. It was locked tight.

He walked across to the only window in the room and pulled aside the faded shade. The window was firmly encased in steel bars.

Even if he had planned on getting back to the city, now there was little chance left. He had known this might happen, while still praying against it. The reality of the situation was that he was a prisoner in Channing's home.

He only hoped he got out of here alive, and hadn't indeed, of his own volition, entrapped himself right in the middle of the spider's web.

The following morning Logan was let out of his prison-like room by a servant. He breakfasted alone, deprived even of Gunther's chilly company. Another man, however, maintained a somber vigil over him the entire time. Logan decided the time might be right for some reconnaissance.

"Do you speak English?" he asked as the man poured out his coffee.

"Un pocito, señor."

"Tell me, where is—uh—the master of the house? He is feeling well, I assume?"

"Sí. He well, but he want no veesitors."

"I will see him today, perhaps?"

"It is not for me to say, señor."

"Yes, of course." Logan paused, buttered his bread, and wondered if Channing had his people too well trained for him to expect them to talk freely. "What about Mr. Gunther?"

"Zee tall German, he come and he go."

"He is gone now, I presume."

"Sí."

"How long will he be gone?"

"I do not know his business. I am criado—servant. Nada mas." He snapped his mouth shut and Logan knew he'd get nothing more out of him.

He had learned one thing from the conversation. Gunther could present a problem. Not knowing where and how people moved around this place had created a number of loose ends. Gunther's presence in the villa was perhaps the worst of the batch. He could show up at any time, and they would have no control over what he might do.

Logan quickly offered up the problem in prayer. No plan was foolproof, but he was thankful at least that he had a God who *was* in control no matter what. In control of their very lives, if it came to that.

Immediately after the meal another servant came and escorted Logan to a patio garden where Logan encountered Channing once more.

"I trust you passed a comfortable night, Macintyre?" he asked from where he sat in a wicker chair, basking feebly in the morning sun. His voice was soft, though he put on a bold front. He did not look as though *he* had slept well, but he would never admit that Logan's presence in the compound unnerved him.

"As comfortable as one can in a *locked* room," returned Logan.

342

"An unpleasant but necessary precaution."

Logan drew up a chair opposite Channing's. "I came here thinking to conclude a business deal," he said. "Then you tell me you never had any such thing in mind, but merely wanted a visit with me. An odd arrangement, I must say, keeping a guest under lock and key."

"You insist on humoring me, don't you? These trivial little jokes. Surely you get the picture now, Macintyre. I have *plans* for you! As you correctly surmised, I did not have you brought here for no reason."

"I have wondered what you were going to do with me."

"You are worried for your life? How nice!"

"The last time we met," said Logan, "you made a nearly successful attempt in that direction. But I would not say I was worried. Merely curious."

"If you give me what I want, I may even let you live."

"Luckily the last time my wife was there to foil you."

"Your wife . . ." Channing's voice shivered over the words. Logan could only glimpse the raw edge of his hatred, kept scarcely at bay beneath his show of mock cordiality. "She will come to your rescue no more, Logan Macintyre. This time it will be *I* who emerge victorious!"

"That's what it's been about all these years, isn't it? Defeating us. That's really all you want. Most men would have given up long ago."

"That has always been your foolish error, Macintyre! Thinking that I was like most men. But I do not give up! Oh, you may think you have defeated me. But those past battles were mere insignificant skirmishes. Soon the war will culminate, however, and I will be the conqueror! Do you realize, Macintyre, that with you in my power I now possess the leverage to force that arrogant wife of yours to give me whatever I ask, even to signing over Stonewycke?"

"So that's your game, Channing! Lure me down here, and then hold me as ransom for the estate?"

"A brilliant maneuver, wouldn't you say?" Channing leaped shakily to his feet.

"It will never work!"

"It will work!" shrieked Channing in an unexpected outburst. "You don't know the half of what I will bring to bear against you! I will win, I tell you!"

"My wife would never do such a thing."

"Not even for her precious husband?"

"Perhaps you've overestimated even *our* sentimentality."

Regaining his control, though his lower lip still quivered, Channing gazed down his nose with a superior sneer. "I think not. But this is more than a simple case of blackmail. As I said, I have something a little more certain in the works."

"Haven't you tormented us enough?"

"Oh no! Not by a long sight!" Channing's voice broke with wrath. "Don't you understand? I plan to have it all—each and every one of you at my mercy, and all that is yours in my possession! It's so simple! Ha! You're a sentimental fool, Macintyre. The game is over! I have *you* . . . I have it all!"

"Why, Channing? I will never understand why you are so obsessed with us and with Stonewycke. What could it possibly mean to you?"

"It's *her* . . . she's the cause of it all!" Channing was raving now. "Tormented *you*? What about the torment she's caused *me*! My money was dirty . . . not good enough for her—the haughty little vixen! But I will show her! I have the treasure where she will never lay eyes on it! I have her arrogant politician of a son-in-law! And soon I will have—"

He stopped, his eyes aglow with the fire of cunning, and rubbed his hands together in warped anticipation. "Oh yes, the war is finally over. I've waited sixty years for this moment . . . and my victory is at hand!"

He fell back into his chair as one expended.

Logan shuddered at the man's diseased passion. He attempted to divert the tone of the conversation.

"I thought the so-called treasure was worthless," he said, with as much control as his own voice could manage.

"Worthless on the black market," replied Channing, his tone calming. "But in the esoteric world where people care about such absurdity, I suppose it is priceless—my man in Oxford verified that. When I can bring it out into the open *legally*, who knows what price I will be able to command for it? You yourself were willing to part with a sizable sum for it." Channing rubbed his wrinkled chin. "I still can't figure where you would have been able to produce that kind of money."

"We were willing to do anything to get it back where it belongs."

"Ha, ha! It will not return to Scotland until I am master of Stonewycke!" he laughed wickedly. "Ruminate on that a moment, my high-and-mighty Mr. Macintyre!"

At that moment a servant appeared at the patio door. He walked across the flagstones to where Channing sat.

"Excuse my interruption, sir," he said, "but a message has arrived." He handed Channing a Western Union envelope.

Channing tore into the paper like a starving beast, his bony fingers trembling as he put on his glasses and then held the paper up close to them. His eyes devoured the words with elation; then slowly his twitching lips began to part, his yellowed teeth glinting through the wide smile of delirium that spread across his face.

Finally he looked up and leveled the ludicrous expression of wild-eyed ecstasy upon Logan.

"There . . . you see!" he cried. "Just as I said—I *have* won! You snivelling simpleton . . . you imbecile! Did you really think you could keep me from my due? I have won, I tell you! You and your idiotic family, and your precious worthless treasure, and your ridiculous valley full of bovine dimwits! Mooncalves, all of you! Fools! To think you could stop Jason Channing! I've won! At last . . . at last I've beaten you all! *It's all mine!*"

With the last cry of triumph still ringing in the air, he flung the telegram at Logan.

Logan picked the paper off the floor where it landed. The brief message was simple:

EVERYTHING HAS GONE AS PLANNED STOP WE'VE DONE IT STOP ALLISON MACINTYRE IN CUSTODY STOP ARRIVE B.A. TO-MORROW STOP STONEWYCKE WILL SOON BE OURS STOP

Logan's hand dropped limply to his side. Propping his forehead in his other hand, he slowly shook his head.

"You can't do this . . . you can't do this, Channing," he murmured, all strength draining from his voice.

"I have done it, Macintyre!" gloated Channing. "I can hardly believe they pulled it off," he added almost as an aside to himself. "They sneaked back in there and made off with her right under their noses! I didn't think that fool Burchardt had it in him!"

Becoming aware of Logan again, Channing addressed him once more, as if he had only just then thought of the idea. "There is, of course, always the possibility of a trade. What do you think, Mr. Proud-faced Politician?"

"What do you want?"

"You *know* what I want!"

"Then you should also know I cannot give it to you."

"You have no choice now, you fool! I have your wife!"

"It is my wife, not myself, who controls the Stonewycke property. She will never give it to you, even to save her own life," said Logan, looking at Channing with a forlorn expression as tears rose up in his eyes.

"Perhaps not! But when she sees the rope around your neck and me standing ready to give the order, she will relent!"

Logan said nothing in reply.

"Ha, ha! I've done my homework. I know Stonewycke has no cash. All your bleeding-heart notions of doing good. You give away half your income! You're a sucker for every sad-storied beggar who comes along! You gave away the land to those moronic peasants you have such ridiculously fond notions about! Where has it left you? Fools! Now I have your treasure *and* your wife, and your own life in my power! You have nothing to bargain with, nothing to trade to get her back. You have nothing! She has nothing! Nothing but . . ."

As he spoke a sickening leer spread across his face, again revealing his remaining yellowed teeth: ". . . nothing but the deed to Stonewycke! And if either of you want to leave here alive, that is my price!"

Logan slumped back in his chair, rubbing his face in agony.

After a long and painful moment, he finally looked up and stared Channing full in the face.

"You *have* won, Channing. You can have anything. I will talk to Allison. Just *please . . . please* don't hurt her."

Channing threw back his head and laughed mercilessly. Unfortunately the exhilaration brought on by his moment of supreme triumph was too much for his frail body. After only a few seconds of uncontrollable laughter, his voice broke like an ancient hinge, and his mirth ended in a paroxysm of fitful coughing.

Logan glanced around, spotted a pitcher of water, hastened to it, poured some into a glass, and brought it to Channing. He took it, struggled to sip the liquid, but could only swallow with difficulty. When the seizure had subsided after a few moments, he attempted once more to speak, but by now his voice came out in a mere whisper.

"You call your solicitors, do you hear?" he croaked. "Begin having the arrangements made."

Again he began to cough and sent out his thin, wasted hand toward the glass of water.

"Can't you give me a few minutes to take all this in? In the name of all that's true, Channing, even you must have *that* much humanity left."

"I have nothing left for you but impatience! You have made me wait for years . . . for decades . . . for what has always been rightfully mine! You talk of patience! I am out of patience . . . and you are out of time. You will make that call!"

"Not until I have seen Allison and am sure she is safe and that no harm will come to her."

Logan eyed Channing steadily, as if to say, *On this point I will not back down.*

At length Channing glanced away. "I suppose that is how these things are done," he conceded.

"Now please, let me go," said Logan. "I just want to return to my room and be alone."

Channing waved him off. "Try nothing foolish, Macintyre, or it will go badly for your wife."

Logan turned and walked defeatedly toward the door. As he went he sighed raggedly. "I don't know what . . ." he began to mumble to himself, just loud enough for Channing to hear. His voice was disjointed and he rubbed his face and eyes as he spoke.

". . . I don't know what this news will do to my mother-in-law," he went on. "I doubt she'll be able to hold up when I tell her. It will probably kill her. . . ."

Channing's head jerked forward.

The impact of Logan's words caused what little color was left in his withered cheeks to vanish instantly.

"What?" he cried, though his voice was pale and worn. Leaning forward, his thin fingers clutched at the arms of the wicker chair until the bones seemed about to pierce through the skin.

Logan turned back toward him with a confused look. "My mother-in-law . . . she's not well, you know."

"What are you saying?" demanded Channing. His face was ghostly white, his red eyes bulging out of his head.

"She will be devastated."

"Who?"

"My mother-in-law . . . Lady Joanna MacNeil."

"Why . . . why that's impossible! What are you talking about?" Channing laughed, but it was a hollow, desperate attempt. "You've finally snapped, Macintyre! She's dead—died four or five weeks ago. I read it in the paper." As he spoke, Channing began to breathe heavily, and his eyes seemed unable to focus on Logan.

"She was very ill," said Logan. "Even failed to register a pulse rate at one point. The news hounds grabbed the story prematurely. But in the end she pulled through."

"Impossible! I don't believe a word of it!" Channing continued to suck in deep draughts of air as if his lungs were suddenly too small to contain what they needed.

"She was always a strong woman. I suppose they don't keep abreast of our local news down here," Logan went on.

"This is madness!" raved Channing. "I read it in the *Times*! She cannot be alive!" His voice shook with passion and disbelief.

Slowly Logan reached into his pocket and took out a folded newspaper clipping. "I keep this as a reminder of my many blessings."

He handed it to Channing.

The headline over the two-column article read: LADY JOANNA MAC-NEIL RECOVERS MIRACULOUSLY FROM NEAR-FATAL HEMOR-RHAGE.

Channing crumpled the paper into a wad in his fist and threw it on the floor. He glanced around wildly, attempting to make the worn-out circuits in his brain focus this bewildering new information. "But why didn't . . ." he muttered to himself. ". . . how could she . . . but, no . . . then why didn't she notify . . . unless . . . but it could be a fake. . . ."

Again Logan turned to go.

"Wait a minute, Macintyre!" yelled Channing after him. "You can't go now! You've got to . . . got to tell me whether it's true! I don't believe it for a second . . . the article's a sham!"

Once more Logan paused and looked back. "Look, Channing," he said weakly, "the last thing I would want is for you to know Joanna is alive." He stopped for a moment and sighed. "But now it is all changed. Suddenly we are on the brink of losing everything. Under the circumstances, I know she would want to see you one last time, talk to you—"

"*See* me . . . she would want to see *me*—how . . . ?" he stammered incredulously.

"She is here."

"What . . . I don't . . . how . . . ?" As he struggled to find any coherent words, Channing's tottering body trembled with involuntary emotion.

"She came to Argentina with me. She had to be here to verify the authenticity of the treasure."

"But we had you under surveillance!"

"I had no idea what kind of people I was about to deal with—we all know the Professor did not gain his reputation by singing in choir. You don't think I would let her near any danger, do you? I insisted we travel separately, so if it turned rough, she would be well in the clear."

"She . . . she . . . is *here*?" Channing's words were labored as he continued, trying to cope with disbelief and a fierce eagerness.

Logan nodded.

"I must see her! The swine! . . . I will make her pay!"

Logan closed his eyes.

"I must! Do you hear me!"

"I was afraid it would come to this," Logan whispered in a voice filled with distress.

But Channing was hardly heeding him. His fiery eyes rolled about in his head while he muttered gleefully to himself, rubbing his hands together in sick anticipation, "The impudent hussy . . . she will be the best prize of all! Grovel—that's what she'll do! I'll make her beg . . . beg for her precious Stonewycke! And it will still be mine!"

He laughed cruelly. "The fool . . . to think she could keep it from me! I told her I get what I want. Curse her for not believing me! Curse them all! I will destroy her . . . topple her from that proud perch where she sits with that lout of a farmer looking down on me! I'll show the little jade what real men are made of! I'll show—"

"Please," interrupted Logan, "don't make her come here. Keep Joanna out of it. I'll do anything you ask. I'll sign the deed."

"Silence, you fool!" screamed Channing. "You think any of that is important now? Only one thing is left . . . the only thing that ever mattered! Oh, you'll sign the deed! But first I will see her beg in the dust before me! Get her here—now!"

"I will need a vehicle—"

"Not you! I can't send you!"

He heaved himself up from his chair and began hobbling forward, but his thin cane could hardly support his agitated frame, and his shaking hand did little to steady it.

"I have to think," he mumbled, "—Joanna . . . here! Unbelievable, yet—yes, it is fitting . . . this is how it should be!"

He turned toward the door. "Mario!" he shouted. "Mario!—where is that fool?" he added to himself. "Order a car immediately!" he yelled again.

That same evening a black limousine wheeled easily through the villa gates.

The dark glass of the windows obscured sight of any passengers, but when the automobile stopped at the guardhouse, it was waved quickly on. It proceeded down the drive, finally coming to a stop before the house.

The driver jumped out, hurried around to the passenger door. He opened it and reached in. A slender gloved hand emerged from the darkened recesses of the limousine, lightly took the offered assistance, and in another moment an elegant woman stepped out.

As she stepped onto the brick pavement, it was clear in an instant that she was graceful and shapely, dressed in a tailored gray linen skirt and pale rose silk blouse with long sleeves and a demure purple bow at the neck. A wide-brimmed, pale pink hat shaded her delicate skin from the late yet still hot Argentine sun, but it could not hide her rich auburn hair, streaked with gray and pulled back from her face. At first glance the woman gave the appearance of youthfulness, but closer inspection revealed lines about the eyes and forehead. She might have been forty or sixty, maybe even seventy. The subtlety of her movements made it impossible to tell.

The driver escorted her to the door, her hand on his arm. When another servant appeared at the door, the driver bowed slightly before departing in deference. The house servant then led her through several corridors, finally stopping at the double doors of the room where Logan had first met the master of the house.

A voice from inside instructed them to enter. It sounded anxious, cold, with almost a disguised hint of nervousness.

Two men stood inside to receive her: Jason Channing and Logan Macintyre. The eyes of both were fixed on the door as it slowly opened.

The woman entered and stood. Exhaled breaths from both men indicated their reactions upon at last laying their eyes upon her.

Channing's stunned response was a gasp he struggled to mask. In speechless shock he gazed upon the object of his combined attachment and bitterness. For sixty years his depraved mind had misguidedly told himself that he loved this woman. His warped emotions had desired her, yearned for her, lain awake nights dreaming of this moment when he might behold her once more, if only to convince himself she had not all along been some phantasm out of a youthful nightmare. He had never loved her, though even now, as he stood there, his failing heart beat wildly—too wildly to last much longer. He had never loved at all; his was a self incapable of truly loving. He could only possess . . . take . . . control. What he could not possess and control, he desired—desired all the more that he could not have it! This desire, he tried to convince himself, was love.

Now suddenly before him stood the one thing, the one person, in all his life, he had not been able to control, not been able to possess, not been able to buy. If he felt anything beneficial toward her—he was not a man absent of emotion; he was well-endowed with an abundance of keenly-cultivated hate—it might have been something akin to a respect for her determined strength of will, an inner power of character he did not meet in the circles with which he was associated. Certainly he did not meet it within himself.

Meeting such an unknown—a strength that stood up to him, resisted him, denounced him!—was too great a threat to the inner world of a man like Jason Channing. His heart, his mind, his very soul could not cope with being rejected . . . defeated. He was familiar with inner power. Corrupted, Joanna's strength could have almost offered an equal to his own. Uncorrupted as it was, pure, guileless, determined to turn her back on him, she had become a fixed obsession in his twisted brain, blinding him to all reality.

Silence hung in the room for several moments. The sounds of the ticking clock, a buzzing fly, even the breathing of the three persons standing there quietly, were magnified unbearably as time itself stood still. At last the woman's voice broke into the hushed stillness, more like the gentle tap of a wave against the shore than a hammer against rock.

"Jason Channing," she said. "It has been many years."

Channing licked his parched lips. She should be older, he thought. But he wasn't surprised. She was still beautiful! In his mind's eye she would forever remain the lovely young woman who had boldly stood up to him that day in the meadow at Port Strathy. Incredibly she was even wearing the same outfit!

"You are alive!" he murmured at last.

"I doubt your eyes would deceive you," she answered.

"You look . . . wonderful," said Channing, his breath coming in short spurts. "You have hardly aged!" His eyes began to fill with tears.

"Thank you. You're very kind to say so."

"Oh, Joanna! Why did you do it? We could have been so happy—could have had so much together. The world lay at our feet! It is still not too late! You may still share it with me! Joanna, come back with me. We will together have what we should have had long ago."

"It was impossible then, Jason, and it is equally impossible now. I did what I felt I had to do."

Channing looked deeply into her face. Suddenly his eyes narrowed.

"You have not changed," he said. "Still proud . . . still impudent . . . I can see it in your eyes."

She sighed. "But all my pride will not help me now, will it, Jason?"

His mouth twitched, violently fighting against conflicting passions—rage, what seed of love might be attempting to sprout within the stone he would have called his heart, triumph, revenge, bitterness. From somewhere deeper than them all, the most distressing thought he had ever had was knocking on the door of his consciousness—the dawning awareness that even now, in the moment of his supreme and final triumph, he had still not really won over these people; the sense that they were from another world, and that he could do nothing to conquer them, that even in death they would defeat him.

He blocked the hideous notion from his mind, forcing instead a sneer upon his face.

"You admit it, then!" he cried, barking a hard laugh. "You *are* defeated, and at my mercy!"

"Yes, Jason. After all these years, you at last have your victory. All the life is gone out of Stonewycke and it is now ultimately in your power. The granddaughter I thought I had found has suddenly disappeared. My son-in-law is your prisoner—"

"I have your daughter too! I have everything, Joanna!"

The woman's hand clasped her mouth in shock, and she staggered back. Logan caught her and gently led her to a couch. Channing remained where he was, as if the very act of standing before her emphasized his triumph.

"Yes . . . I suppose you do, Jason," she said quietly. "Even the treasure. It is still in your possession?"

"Of course! Your fool of a son-in-law thought he could buy it from me!"

"We should have known it was too good to be true."

Channing's eyes again grew blurry as the awareness of time vanished from them. "Joanna," he said softly, approaching the couch and reaching out to take her hand, "don't you see? It is not too good to be true. We can still be happy together. It can be *ours*, Joanna! Yours and mine—Stonewycke . . . the treasure . . . all we wanted . . . we can share it."

He struggled to pull her up from where she sat, but was in danger of toppling over himself. "Come, Joanna . . . come with me . . . we will get the treasure; we will take it with us back to Stonewycke! We will be happy there . . . together!"

She rose. "Thank you, Jason," she said. "That will be nice. I would so like to see the treasure."

"Come . . . come with me," he said, leading her toward the door.

Just as they reached it, he glanced back at Logan, who had followed them. "Stay where you are, MacNeil! This does not concern you. She is mine now!"

Logan hesitated. Channing continued to eye him carefully.

"Why do you look at me like that, MacNeil? But wait—" As he stared the fog began again to clear from his befuddled brain.

"—you're not . . . no, of course! You're not the clodhopper!"

He spun his head around for a moment toward the door, as if to insure himself that Joanna was still there, then back into the room.

"Macintyre! What are you doing here? But . . . I see it now . . . it's a trick—you're trying to make me think you're that fool who passes himself off as her husband! Well, it won't work, Macintyre!"

"No, Jason. This *is* my son-in-law, Logan Macintyre. You have known him for many years."

"Of course . . . I know that! What do you take me for, a dottering old fool?"

"Might we go now, Jason? Grant me the one last pleasure of allowing my eyes to look upon the treasure that has for so long been yours."

"No! I am not such a fool as to fall for your chicanery. I know you, Macintyre! Bring your wife's mother in here to beguile me into revealing where I have that worthless parcel of relics! Well, you will not find me such an easy mark! Your lost granddaughter, indeed! You fools! You don't even yet know the truth: your precious Jo, that you took into your hearts, was my *own* daughter! Ha, ha, ha! What do you think of that, Joanna! And now she and I will rule Stonewycke! My daughter, Joanna Channing—named after you, my sweet—how do you fancy that? Joanna Channing, mistress and heiress of Stonewycke! Ha! ha!"

Logan caught his breath at Channing's stunning revelation. Joanna staggered back away from the door and again sought the couch.

"It is true," she said feebly. "My days are over. I have nothing else to live for." She cast sorrowful eyes toward Logan. "I am sorry for bringing this upon you, my dear son. So very sorry." Then she turned back toward Channing. "Where is my daughter?"

"She will be here soon."

"What will you do with us, Jason?" she said in a pleading tone.

"I don't know," he said with superiority, folding his arms. "Perhaps if I yet see the proper compliant attitude, I *might* show mercy." He spat out the words with the contempt he felt for the very idea of clemency.

"I will go to my grave destroyed. Will you not grant me the dying wish of seeing the treasure that has been our undoing?"

"Never! No eyes but mine shall ever see it again! The thought of you all going to your deaths wondering where I've stashed it away warms my aging heart!"

"Perhaps this is but a ruse," suggested Logan, "and you don't have it at all."

"Oh, you would like to believe that, wouldn't you, Macintyre? But you are wrong. I fished it from the bottom of the ocean in 1936—*your* ocean! You never even knew what was going on just a mile from your blessed coast!"

"What would it hurt for me to see it now?"

"Hurt! You dare speak to me of *hurt*! Well, suffer, Joanna! It is *your* moment to feel the hurt you have inflicted upon me all these years! Suffer . . . as I have suffered!"

He tightened his grip on his cane, turned away, and hobbled from the room.

Logan and the woman exchanged quick, questioning glances. But before either had the chance to speak, two servants entered and bade them follow.

They were taken to separate rooms, and the doors locked behind them.

In the dark of the night Jason Channing paced like a caged lion back and forth across his bedroom floor.

His old bones seemed suddenly enlivened, as if from some fiendish fire burning from deep within. Notwithstanding his apparent energy, the glow came from the dying embers of life. The very lust of his victory was consuming the last remaining vitality from his spirit. In the core of his being sat a cold stone, and thus the peace that should belong to a man who has gained his heart's desire was instead to him mere emptiness. The passion of his hate fed upon itself, leaving only death in its wake.

His agitation intensified through the night.

She had returned from the dead, but still she would not bend her proud neck before him! Even in defeat, she haunted him! Why could he not, even now, erase from his memory that picture of the proud, majestic, despicable girl in that confounded meadow? Why could he not see her on her knees? Even in his mind he could not make her bow in front of him!

She *had* been vanquished today! He had defeated her. She had even admitted as much! Yet still that look remained in her eyes—that smugness, that lovely, irritating, beautiful tilt to her chin! Even as she said the words, "You have your victory, Jason," inside she had still not been broken. She was still—she would always remain—her *own* woman!

Would the memory of her face *never* leave him in peace?

Just before dawn, he collapsed in an exhausted heap upon his bed. He slept like a cranky child, who only gives grudgingly over to fatigue.

Channing did not awaken until about nine.

When he appeared for breakfast, he looked wasted and feeble. He had nothing to eat, only drank black coffee and ordered trays sent to his guests' rooms.

He still did not know what to do about them. Though he could hardly admit it to himself, he could not bear just yet to see *her* again. Soon his victory would be complete. Then he would stand before her to mete out his wrath.

At 10:30 the phone rang.

He listened a moment. "Bring her immediately!" he barked into the receiver. "Gunther . . . what do you need him for?"

He paused and listened. "Well, he's not here. How much help do you need with a woman? Get her here now—I want no more delays!" He slammed down the receiver with a crash.

Some time after lunch had been brought to his room, Logan heard the key once more in his door. He was wanted by El Patron.

He followed the servant who delivered the message. Halfway along the corridor he met another servant escorting the Lady of Stonewycke. He cast her a heartening smile, but they dared exchange nothing beyond the commonest of pleasantries in front of Channing's people. Soon they were back in the salon where Channing had the habit of receiving his visitors.

"I thought you would want to be present with me as I greet my new guests," he said.

"I tell you, Channing," Logan said hotly, "if my wife has been harmed in any way!"

"You will see for yourself in a few moments." He waved a tired hand toward the chairs. "Make yourselves comfortable in the meantime."

Joanna took a seat on the couch, Logan remained standing, too tense to relax. Channing sat in a chair opposite Joanna, his eyes leaving her only when the knock came to the double doors.

"Enter!" he called out, turning his head from her with effort.

Allison stepped in first, her arm in the firm grasp of the Austrian viscount, von Burchardt. He held a .38 revolver in his other hand.

Channing grinned lecherously. "Welcome to my house, Allison Macintyre." Then he looked sharply at Emil. "Well, von Burchardt, I see you managed *this* job without bungling it!"

He scrutinized him for a long moment, taking in the viscount's eyes, pencil-thin moustache, and expensive, fashionable white linen suit. "You've lost weight," he mumbled off-handedly.

Emil snapped his heels together smartly and bowed in that grandiose fashion for which he was known. "My labors for you, Mein Herr," he said in his oily German accent, "take precedence over all else—even eating!"

Channing grunted, unimpressed.

"Where is Jo?" he asked.

"There was an important matter in the city she had to attend to. She does not anticipate being detained long."

"There is nothing more important than this!" fumed Channing. "She should be here!"

"She sends her regrets, and will be here shortly."

"Well, I won't wait!" Channing bellowed. He turned his attention to his guests.

"So, here you all are—all of you . . . together!" He flashed a lopsided grin. "Touching, is it not, Emil? And kind of me to arrange this little family reunion."

"Allison, have they harmed you?" asked Logan, hurrying toward her.

"Not so fast, Macintyre!" said Emil, pointing the gun toward Logan.

"I am fine. We can be thankful at least for that. And you, Mother?" she asked.

The older woman nodded but said nothing.

"I should have hired a photographer!" gloated Channing, filled with the moment he had so long desired. "Ah yes, a photograph would be perfect—to capture this momentous occasion for our progeny to remember—especially since my daughter could not be here!"

"Your daughter!" exclaimed Allison.

"Oh yes! You did not know? Ha, ha! Had my original plan succeeded, it would have been the tour de force of my life. My own daughter installed as heiress of Stonewycke, while all the time you were taking her to your hearts as if she was one of your own! The poetic beauty of it!"

"Jo is . . . your daughter?" said Allison in disbelief, glancing toward Logan. He merely nodded sadly.

"Oh, no doubt she would have told you eventually—perhaps when you were on your deathbeds, helpless to do anything about it. Ha, ha! But I begin to think it better that she failed. Had our design worked, only she would have been able to exult in our triumph. This way, I too am able to see your faces in defeat! Ha, ha, ha! I must admit, it makes every one of the past sixty years almost worth it to see your despair on this glorious day!"

"And what now, Channing?" said Logan.

"What now, you ask! What do you think? You will give me Stonewycke, and in my compassion I will allow you to live. If you refuse me, I will have you all killed, here and now, while Jo flies back to Stonewycke to claim the inheritance as *your* daughter!''

A soft voice came from the couch, speaking to him for the first time. "Jason," it said quietly.

Channing stopped and turned his head. His gaze was arrested by a penetrating stare from the eyes he had dreamed of so long. Deeply they probed his mind, unflinching, commanding his own eyes to remain and not look away. Gradually an involuntary twitch of mental distress began to flit about the edges of his mouth.

"Jason," the voice beckoned again. "It is I you want. Is that not true?" Still her eyes held his.

"You are all I have ever wanted," he replied, the tenacity of his will losing its grip.

"Now you have me, Jason. I am here . . ." As she spoke he was helpless to resist the magnetism of her eyes. "Let my family go, Jason."

"I—I cannot . . . he will—"

"No harm will come to you, Jason, I assure you. None of us would hurt you. We care about you, Jason."

"*Care* about me? Why, that's—but . . . but of course you do! You must! I am the new master of Stonewycke!" His voice contained none of its former power. His eyes fought to look away, but could not. She had gained mastery over him, and now held him fast.

"We *do* care about you, Jason," she said, her voice still hushed, "in a way you perhaps cannot grasp. All of us in this room—"

But at last he succeeded in looking away, and the spell was broken.

"And care you shall! For I will soon be in Stonewycke . . . I am preparing for our journey even now! Come, Joanna," he said, rising and grabbing his cane, "we are going by ship, just as we did last year from New York . . . only this time without that busybody, Mrs. Cupples!"

He made for the door. "Come, Joanna . . . come! The steamer is sailing this afternoon . . . We must gather our things!"

"You will take the treasure with you?"

"What's that, my sweet?"

"The treasure, Jason . . . the treasure of Stonewycke."

"Yes, yes . . . of course. I shan't forget *that*! It must go back with us! I'll go retrieve it now. Come! You must help me . . . it is heavy!"

She rose. He half-grabbed her arm and led her with what force he could manage out the door. Once they were outside, the others rose also, exited the room, and followed slowly down the corridor. Emil trailed behind, still carrying the gun.

Channing led the way through several corridors, toward the back of the elongated L-shaped house, through servants' quarters, past the kitchen, and finally out into the hot, humid air. The small entourage crossed an open dirt quadrangle, and arrived at length at a run-down adobe structure that looked like little more than an unused shed.

Still Channing hobbled gamely along, though once inside, in the darkness, he found the footing more treacherous. Immediately after closing the huge oak door behind them, he turned sharply to the right, traversed a narrow corridor, then arrived at another heavy, iron-studded door that faced left.

Channing stopped, pulled out a large ring of keys from his pocket, selected an old-fashioned one, well rusted, inserted it into the door, and shoved it open. With his free hand he pulled the chain on a dim lightbulb that hung from the ceiling, illuminating a narrow stone stairway which descended under the earth. Led by Channing's faltering step, which every moment appeared ready to collapse beneath the weight of his body, they made their way down in single file.

At the bottom, a maze of underground passages spread out before them. Though they passed several locked doors, and others with bars across them that appeared to be cells of some ancient dungeon, it was obvious the more recent use of the place had been as a wine cellar. On either side of the corridor, which gradually opened wider and wider, revealing long narrow, low-ceilinged rooms, sat rows upon rows of barrels and casks and crates of bottles filled with wine.

"It won't be long now," said Channing. "There is one special room here . . . of my very own. No one else has a key. And no one knows what a special wine I keep in storage," he added with a gleam in his eye. "Come, Joanna . . . we will be there shortly!"

The echo of his voice seemed to disturb him. He looked about and, though he had been aware of their presence as they descended the steps into the cellar, he seemed now all at once to see the others for the first time.

"What? But, Joanna, I thought we were alone . . . we have to—"

He paused, focusing on Logan. Gradually the dawn of recognition spread over his face, and with it came back to his eyes the demon of hatred.

"Macintyre, what are you doing here!" he demanded. "This is private business between Miss Matheson and myself!"

"I keep no secrets from my family, Jason."

"But, Joanna, who . . . who are these? I don't understand." His eyes narrowed and he squinted at her, then glanced at Logan, then back at her.

"—I see it now!" he shouted. "It's a trick! You were only trying to trick me into showing you the treasure! Well, I've spoiled your little game! What do you pack of fools take me for?"

"We take you for nothing more than what you are," said Logan, who had had his fill of the trick they were perpetrating. "That is a man in need of healing, in need of what can give life. Believe me, Channing, we want nothing but life for you. This life of yours, this enmity and hatred, is no life. It is a living death."

"How dare you preach to me, you pathetic fool! Let me out of here! You will never see your blessed treasure! I will take it with me to my grave!"

"The treasure is meaningless, Channing, alongside your life."

"Good . . . good! Meaningless it might as well be, for you'll never lay eyes on it!"

"You may scorn my words, Channing. Though you hate me, I cannot bear to see this cancerous bitterness destroy you." Logan took a deep, sorrowful breath. "Yet there must be hope for you. Will nothing make you listen?"

"Hope! Ha! You *are* a fool!" he cackled vilely. "Well, I have had enough of you—all of you!" He tried to push Logan out of the way with his cane, then, failing that, went around him and began hobbling off in the direction from which they had come. "Von Burchardt," he cried, "shoot them! Each one of them, right here—now! I'm finished with them!"

He took two more paces, stopped, turned back, and saw the viscount standing, making no move to carry out his order.

"Shoot them, I tell you!" he shrieked. "Or I will shoot you!"

"I'm afraid I cannot do that, Mr. Channing," the man replied.

"Cannot . . . what? How dare you disobey me!"

"I *must* disobey you." He let out a prolonged sigh, glanced toward Logan, then lowered his gun and let go of Allison. With the hand that was now free, he reached up to finger his moustache. Then to Channing's horror, he peeled it off.

"What! . . . von Burchardt, what are you . . . oh, God . . . no!" cried Channing as the truth broke in upon his benumbed consciousness.

"May I present my friend, Ashley Jameson," said Logan calmly. "I'm afraid he was the one who helped me apprehend your friend the viscount in the attempted kidnapping of my wife. The real von Burchardt, as well as your daughter, are at this moment in the custody of the police in Aberdeen."

"What have you done? It is an evil trick . . . Joanna!"

"And this—"

Logan held out his hand to the older woman, who now had a handkerchief in her hand and was proceeding to wipe away the cosmetic wrinkles on her face. "—this is my daughter, Joanna Hilary Macintyre—my *real* daughter, as even you can see by her resemblance to my mother-in-law, who has indeed gone to be with her Lord."

"No . . . it cannot be true!" Channing stammered as he staggered back against the dirty stone wall.

"It is true," said Logan with feeling in his voice. "It is over, Channing."

Channing looked away, walked a few steps, then turned back to face the two men and two women. His skin was ashen. His eyes stared in disbelief. For several moments all was silent. Slowly he slumped to the floor.

"It cannot be true," he repeated. "The victory *must* be mine! I cannot let you defeat me again!" But even as he spoke, the vitality of life slowly drained from him.

Logan sighed, then approached him. When he spoke again, his voice was full of compassion for the broken man who would have killed him.

"*We* do not defeat you, Channing," said Logan. "It is the devil of hatred, the demon of bitterness who would defeat you. *They* are the enemy, not us."

"But who set them on me?" he whimpered. "It was her! *She* forced them on me!"

"We bring them upon ourselves. Hatred comes from within, Channing. No one can force it upon another."

"Well, she did her best of it!"

"I'm sure she did do her best. She tried to turn you to the truth."

"What! By turning the whole town against me? By making me look the fool?" he cried, struggling to his feet. Then grabbing his cane, he began to pace around.

"By keeping you from cheating the townspeople, which was the best thing she could have done for your soul, if only you had allowed it to start you down the road of truth."

"My soul! It's precious little she ever cared for my soul! Tormenting me day and night for sixty years."

"I happen to know that she prayed for your soul, Channing, during all of those same sixty years."

"Prayed for me! What rubbish! That's just the sort of thing she would do! Prayed that I'd repent, no doubt. It's rubbish, I tell you!"

"It's truth. Repentance is the door into life."

"Telling God you're sorry, I suppose," Channing spat.

"And that you want Him to remake you in the image of His Son."

"Well, I'm not sorry! I've lived my life and I had my way with it. And it's low I'd sink before I'd ever ask to be made like that fool they call his

Son! Going around preaching that nonsense they call the gospel, and then letting them kill Him without trying to get away. If God had a Son He would have more power than that! Nonsense, I tell you."

"It's truth."

"It's humbug!"

"His Son's power was of another kind than can be seen by the eyes of this world. You've probably heard the story of how He conquered death, and walked away from the grave?"

"A fairy tale!"

"A historical fact," asserted Logan.

"I suppose you believe it?" asked Channing.

"Not only do I believe it, I base my entire life upon the fact of Jesus' resurrection. By His victory over death are we given power to live."

"*I've* lived, I tell you—and no doubt much better than if I had spent my years trying to be religious and worrying about my conscience pricking me every time I turned around!"

"Have you lived, Channing? Really lived?"

"I have, more than you, Macintyre! I'm a rich man!"

"And powerful too, from what I hear."

"Yes, powerful! A formidable opponent they find Jason Channing when anyone tries to cross me!

"Rich and powerful," mused Logan. "And happy?"

"As happy as any man can be! We've all got to go sooner or later. In the meantime we might as well get what we can!"

"Which is what you did?"

"Certainly!"

"And now?"

"What do you mean *now*?"

"What will you do with all that you have? Your greed has gained you wealth and might. Can you take it with you?"

"Of course not! I'm no fool! Neither can you take your precious Stonewycke with you! I'm not a religious man, mind you, but I know my Scriptures. Dust to dust, ashes to ashes. I know we go the way we came!"

"Ah, but there *is* something we can take with us into the next life, Channing."

"Poppycock! Where'd you get an idiotic notion like that?"

"From the Scriptures."

"And just *what* can we take with us?"

"Our soul."

"Oh, well . . . if you believe in that moonshine!"

"Whether you believe in it or not, Channing, your soul *does* live on. And it takes with it the character it has become during life on this earth."

"The soul has a personality? That's absurd!"

Logan's heart leaped within him at the mere suggestion that, even in his anger and pain, Channing had dared to ask a question about the eternal being of man.

"What is the soul, Channing, but the essential *you*—that innermost part of your personhood which is left when everything to do with this world suddenly vanishes. You have been fashioning the essential personality of your soul all your life long, by every word you have spoken, by every choice you have made, by every action you have taken toward another fellow human being."

"And now my soul is damned to hell, I suppose!"

"God only knows, Channing. All I know is that it is never too late to begin making marks of selflessness and goodness upon your soul. You cannot make yourself pleasing to God only by doing good. But every kind deed, every gracious word, every repentant attitude—they all reflect the state of your soul—whether or not you are genuinely seeking to discover and live by the truth God has revealed."

"Even if I believed what you say—which I don't for a moment!—there's no time. It's too late for me!"

"It's never too late. As long as there is one gasp left in a dying man's heart, it is not too late for him to begin."

Channing stifled a cry of mingled anger and despair. "I *am* a dying man, Macintyre. I can feel death stalking me. God help me, I hate it!" he cried. "And I hate Him for bringing me to this. I'm not ready to die!"

"You may hate Him, but He loves you. He's the only one who can help you face what is ahead. It's true, Channing; it's never too late to begin."

"A poor beginning that would be—ten thousand black marks on the soul, and one deathbed mark on the other side. Foxhole religion, Macintyre—what good is it?"

"When you face Him, God will not tally up a scoresheet. He will only want to know in which direction you were trying to move. It is never too late to change directions. That's what repentance is, turning around and going the other way."

Channing was silent a moment and seemed to be thinking. Again he slumped to the ground and sat, breathing heavily. His face was pale, his skin cold. In his eyes could be seen the exhaustion from the inner struggle.

"You think I'll see Him then . . . face-to-face?"

"We all will."

"And he'll condemn me to hell, no doubt! I thought He was supposed to be forgiving. Sins white as snow and all that claptrap."

"*He* does not condemn us. We condemn ourselves. *He* offers us life. It is up to us to receive it."

"When did He ever offer *me* life?"

"Every day you lived, He was trying to speak to you. Did your conscience never bother you?"

"Oh, a time or two, I daresay, but I put a stop to that early enough. A man with a touchy conscience will never get far in this world."

"There you see—He was speaking to you, but you refused to listen. The world is upside-down from true reality, Channing. Getting on, as you call it, in the *real* world—the world of spiritual reality, the world we will all suddenly become part of the moment we die—getting on in that world means denying this world around us now. It's all backward. The more we strive to get ahead here, the further behind we will be then. The last shall be first, you know."

"Leaves a man like me in a bit of a pickle, I daresay, who was told nothing about all this!"

"We've all been told, Channing. Jesus came two thousand years ago to tell the world. His followers have been telling us ever since."

"No one told me! If they had, maybe I'd have been different."

"We all know the truth in our hearts. Even if no one tells us, the truth of reality—the truth of God's character—is all about us and inside us. The world He created, and the conscience He put inside us, they are there to tell us about Him all day and night, every moment of our lives. No man can say he has not been exposed to God's truth. No man will *dare* say it when he faces Him. In that moment we will know that we knew the truth all along, but we chose to turn our backs on it. Every man, every woman— we all make the choice, whether consciously aware of it or not."

"Rather an infernal mess that leaves me in, if what you say is true."

"There are consequences to what we do with our lives."

"So how is a poor fool like me to get out of such a predicament?"

"By doing what He has been telling you all your life."

"Being good, I suppose!"

"That's a good thing, but not the starting point."

"Don't toy with me! What am I to do?"

"Lay it all down. Your bitterness, your hate, your unforgiveness. Lay it down that He might heal your soul."

"And then keep the Commandments and be a good boy, is that it? There's no time for all that! Look at me, Macintyre! I'm a dying man!"

"There's only one command you need worry about, and there's always time for that."

"And what is that?"

"To believe in the Lord Jesus Christ."

"Poppycock! That's nothing you can *do*!"

"You can *do* nothing *until* you've done that."

"My life's behind me, I tell you!"

"A life of greed, of thirsting for power, of hurting others, a life of bitterness and unforgiveness."

"How dare you speak to me like that!"

"The day will come when you *must* face what you are, Channing. Better you hear it from my lips, while there is still time, than from His."

"Curse you, Macintyre! To speak so to a dying man! If I could just stand—this wretched cane!" he exclaimed, struggling to rise, but falling back as the cane slipped under him. "If I could only—by heaven, if I were a younger man, I'd kill you myself!"

"Channing," pleaded Logan, "do you ever want to see *her* again—face-to-face?"

The question sobered him and he fell back.

"Of course I do! But it's too late for that too. She's dead."

"Her soul is not dead. And I'm sure she wants to see you again. What do you think she would say to you? Will she forgive you for the misery you've brought her family?"

The unexpected question bit deep into what was left of Channing's blunted conscience.

"She will, when I explain how I loved her."

"Did you love her, Channing?"

"Of course I did! Why else would I offer her the world? Why else—"

"Why else would you scheme and kill in order to destroy all she held dear? What kind of love is that?"

"How dare you!" he shrieked.

"I dare speak the truth to you because you will soon face your Maker, and He will speak the truth to you . . . and more! He will not be put off, Channing! You must face reality. The only path left you, the only *life* left you, is to lay down the demons of hate and vengeance and greed and selfishness that have ruled in your heart."

"She will forgive me, I tell you!" he screamed.

"Indeed, she will. She does forgive you! And so do I, so does my wife, so does my daughter. We harbor you no malice, Channing. For what you have done, our hearts are open with forgiveness toward you."

"Then God will forgive me too! Can His forgiveness be any less?"

"Infinitely greater in every way. But neither our forgiveness nor the forgiveness of God can enter your heart while it is yet full, blocked by the hate that has kept you in bondage and misery all these years. Until the bitterness is gone, there is no room for the forgiveness to enter."

Channing thought for a moment. His body was still, his mental and physical energy nearly spent. His breathing came in short, weak pulses, and when he again spoke, Logan had to strain to make out the words.

"So what you're telling me is that I have to lay down everything I've lived for—"

"Only your *self*, and the bitterness and unforgiveness you've carried with it all these years."

"And then believe, you say, in Jesus Christ? What am I to believe about Him?"

"You need believe nothing *about* Him. We must believe *in* Him."

"How do you do that?"

"By laying down your self, your past, your *own* desires, that you might trust Him to give you life. Give yourself into God's care, Channing. The moment you open the door of your heart to let *out* the sin and evil you have harbored there, in that moment His forgiveness enters and all is changed. In that moment, your soul becomes forever His."

Channing did not reply. His eyes were wide open and clear, but his thoughts were far away, reliving the many years that had led up to that moment he was about to face. The damp, darkened wine cellar was hushed like an underground cathedral as each person present was aware of the internal and eternal struggle then being waged within the mind and heart of the old sinner.

Gradually Logan felt the grip of Channing's hand tighten.

"I . . . I see," he struggled to say, but his voice was a mere whisper and he was having difficulty gasping for air. "They are coming . . . I see them . . . but—where did that bright light come from? Macintyre . . . Logan—are you still there? I'm . . . I'm going . . ."

Logan felt the withered hand slowly relax. A long final breath of air escaped Channing's lips. Logan looked long upon the face. The eyes were closed. The twitch was gone from the lips. He was dead.

Silent tears fell from Logan's eyes as he released the lifeless hand and sat back upon the floor.

Slowly Allison walked toward him, knelt down, and laid a hand on his shoulder.

"You did all you could, Logan," she whispered.

"I will always wonder," he replied. "There is always so much one *wants* to say."

Hilary and Ashley drew near and knelt down also.

"Dear Father in heaven," Logan prayed aloud. "For this man's soul we now offer our prayers. Whether or not he made his peace with you, only you know. We just ask that you cleanse *us* of any remaining bitterness or unforgiveness. Let us truly know your forgiveness, O God! Jason Channing made his life a grave filled with dead men's bones. I pray, Father, that Channing's hate will stop here, that the chain of his corruption and evil will be broken, and that the hold he must surely have on his own daughter be undone. For Jo we pray too, that your healing forgiveness might pour itself out on her. Dear God, your love still prevails, and has the power to heal—let each one of us experience that healing now."

"Is it over, Logan?" asked Allison. "For us, as well as Channing?"

"I don't know, dear," he replied. "I think so. Though the Lord will never be through with our lives, nor with the work He wants to do in our family."

"What are we going to do . . . now?"

"We are going to trust God . . . and believe He will deliver us."

Logan and Allison still sat with Hilary and Ashley in the corridor where Channing's body lay slumped on the ground. They had been praying together for some minutes.

"We have committed our way to Him," said Logan, "and He will guide our steps."

"I do not think Channing's men will simply let us walk out of here, Logan," said Ashley.

"But I am so sick of the guile we are using," replied Logan. "while speaking to Channing about truth."

"You mustn't forget that we prayed before undertaking this venture, and asked God to guide us," said Hilary. "You knew you had to face Channing, stop the evil and let it go no further, and talk to him, as a man, as a brother, about his soul. How else could you have done that but to get him alone, in a state that he would listen? I don't see how it could have been achieved any other way."

"It simply seems that there might have been a more straightforward way . . . I don't know."

"*If* God had opened the doors in that direction. But He gave you *this* idea . . . and it worked."

"Did it? Channing is dead."

"He died hearing of God's love, and with four Christians with him praying for his eternal destiny," replied Hilary. "Under what other circumstances could such a thing have occurred? You did not misread the signals from God, Logan. Even though this was, in a sense, a con on the unsuspecting man, I think God knew it was the only way to break in upon the hardened crust of his heart. You prayed for guidance, and I think He gave it to you."

Logan sighed. "Perhaps you're right."

"Besides," added Allison, "look at it practically. Had you tried to stop Channing any other way, more out in the open, there would surely have been bloodshed. He was a wicked man. Confronting him could have meant death for innocent people, even for yourself or any of us. You had to protect your family, too. The legacy of this family is not over. I, for one, want time to spend with my daughter!" As she spoke, she smiled at Hilary. "God used you, Logan, in His way, which might at the moment seem a little peculiar, to confront Channing and to protect your family. I thank God for what you did."

"It's not over yet," reminded Ashley. "We may still have to con our way out of here."

"Wise as serpents, eh, Ashley?" said Logan.

"And innocent as doves."

"I only wish we'd have found the treasure," sighed Hilary. "It is part of the legacy too."

"Not so important, however, as how Channing spends the *rest* of his life," said Logan. "It will not seem such a great loss in the light of eternity."

"Who said it must be a loss?" asked Ashley. "We have to be close. I think we can spare a few minutes before we plan our escape."

"Of course!" said Hilary. "It must be in one of these rooms nearby!" She jumped to her feet and continued through the cellar, pausing before every door and opening each to look for clues.

"What exactly are we looking for?" asked Ashley, rising also and following.

"Who knows?" answered Logan. "None of us have ever seen it."

"Mother's journal spoke of a large box. That's all Maggie said."

"Channing spoke of historical relics," said Logan. "That could mean just about anything."

Hilary had run on ahead, excitedly probing every corner of the corridor.

"Here . . . come here!" she called out. "There's another large room!"

The other three followed, reaching the end of the passageway they had been in, off which two doors opened. One led only into a small room filled with empty barrels. The other led into a large, open room which was nearly empty.

"There's nothing here," said Allison.

"But look, Mother," said Hilary. "At the far end—another door! I tried the handle, but it's locked."

"It's hard to believe they would have installed electricity down here unless they had an important reason."

"Didn't Channing mention something about another room . . . a key?" said Logan.

"Yes, he did!" exclaimed Hilary. "A special room, he said. And no one had a key but him!"

They glanced around at one another.

"A bit quirky, perhaps," said Ashley. "But do you suppose it might be in order for me to borrow Channing's keys for a minute?"

Without awaiting an answer, he turned and ran out of the room and back along the corridor. When he returned he carried Channing's ring of keys.

It took several attempts to find the correct one, but at length his patience was rewarded when one of the keys slid in. He turned the latch and gave the door a shove. Its rusty hinge scraped from the friction; it had not been oiled in years, and was apparently not often used.

All four heads peered into the black opening.

"Stand back," said Logan. "Let me."

He took a step inside, nearly falling as he did so. "It's another set of stairs," he said, recovering, then gradually disappearing downward. "I'm feeling the walls," he called back, "but there appears to be no light switch."

The others continued watching, but in another moment or two he had disappeared into the dark cavity. All they could hear was the sound of his feet probing their way downward through the blackness.

"Ah, here it is. I think—yes, that's it!"

Suddenly a light flipped on, revealing the treacherous narrow passage. Logan stood at the bottom.

"A rather ingenious way of discouraging visitors, wouldn't you say?" he called up. "Placing the switch at the bottom! Well . . . what are you waiting for? This has got to be the place!"

Eagerly Hilary skipped down the stairs to join him, followed by Allison, then Ashley.

The passage in which they now found themselves was extremely narrow, allowing but one to pass at a time. To either side were occasional doors, unlocked, in which were housed various vintages of wine, undoubtedly rare, presumably from Channing's private stock. The fourth door they reached was again locked.

"Ashley . . . the keys!" Logan called back.

Ashley handed the ring forward.

Logan fumbled with them a while. At last the door yielded. He walked inside, found the light easily, and switched it on.

The room was perhaps ten feet by twelve feet, with a low ceiling. Against one wall were stacked three or four cases of wine. Three large wine barrels lay on their sides at the far end. The four detectives spread out in silence to examine the contents.

"Curious," said Hilary, picking up a bottle from one of the chests. "Every bottle here, though from different vineyards from all over the world, is labeled 1911. There's probably a small fortune here, just in the wines!"

Logan was thumping at the three barrels.

"Do that again, Logan," said Ashley, approaching.

Again Logan knocked against the casks.

"Do you hear that," said Ashley. "This one has an altogether different tone. I'll wager you there's no wine in that cask. It's as empty as a hollow log!"

Quickly Logan glanced about. "There must be a crowbar, or something we can use to pry off that lid!"

As he looked around in the darkened light, meanwhile, Ashley was examining the label on the barrel. He stood before it stumped. This was certainly no wine, and no vineyard he was familiar with.

"*Steenbuaic—1936,*" he murmured aloud.

"What is it, Ashley?" asked Hilary, coming up beside him.

"This label . . . it's most unusual. If I didn't know better, I'd think it was—"

"Ah ha!" exclaimed Logan, interrupting his thought. "Just what we need. Probably left here for this express purpose!"

Ashley and Hilary stood aside as Logan approached. He plied the crowbar to the questionable barrel of curious vintage. The lid fell away, and all four gasped simultaneously at what they beheld.

It was not wine.

The heirs to Digory's and Maggie's legacy stood on the cold earthen floor of a dungeon-like room. Before them sat the ancient box that had been the object of such greed, such hopes, such mystery, and such speculation, where Logan and Ashley had placed it after lifting it out of the barrel.

For several moments each of the four was too awed to speak. Gradually they began to examine it more closely.

The metallic box was no larger than a small steamer trunk, perhaps one foot by two feet, and some eighteen inches high at the peak. Most of the exterior was of some kind of enameled metal—certain iron rivets and other fasteners were rusted, parts displayed the green corrosion of copper, but most seemed made of bronze. It had held up well through its wanderings over many hundreds of years.

A pyramidic lid of four slabs—two isosceles triangles and two isosceles trapazoids—were hinged to the box itself, joining at a peak where an ornate bar fastened each of the lid pieces to one another, apparently serving as a handle for two men to use in carrying the box, which Ashley judged to weigh some seventy or eighty pounds. The surface was richly engraved, and within moments, unable to restrain his historian's curiosity an instant longer, Ashley was on his knees examining it all over in minute detail. He ran his hand over the rough surface of the once smooth and shiny metal.

"This outer layer appears not an original engraving at all," he said, "but rather taken from a mold of some sort."

"Let's open it up!" said Hilary, her eyes glowing with anticipation.

Logan turned to Allison. "This should be your honor, my dear."

She smiled, but quickly became solemn. "After witnessing Channing's lust for this thing, I almost don't care what is inside. Yet it is such a part of my heritage, at the same time I feel compelled to know once and for all what it contains."

Encircling the outside of the box were several lengths of heavy chain, obviously a new addition, probably Channing's fitting legacy. A padlock held the chain links together and it required another search of Channing's ring to locate the proper key. Ashley handed it to Allison, who inserted it easily into the lock. It must have been kept in good repair, for it snapped open readily. They pulled away the chain; then Allison took hold of the bar, unlatched the hooks binding the portions of the lid to each other, slid out the bar, and slowly spread back the sides of the lid and opened the box.

Inside, it was lined with the same thin enameled metal. Two large woolen blankets took up a good amount of the space, though they were mostly decayed with age. They had apparently been used to pad the other items. They seemed newer than the relics they had been used to protect, but by the look of the plaids they were probably not put there by Channing. Perhaps Digory had added them, suggested Logan.

Carefully Allison unfolded the blankets. There were a dozen or so items of some size, as well as miscellaneous small trinkets, a few coins, spoons, knives, two penannular brooches, some scraps of silver, and several smooth polished round stones almost resembling marbles. Of the larger items, several were of obvious value, and others appeared purely commonplace. Most were of ornamented silver alloy, including four bowls, a gilt pommel, one chape, three silver chalices, a pair of heavy candlesticks, two sword hilts, and an odd looking piece of fine silverwork that resembled a sword hilt but was at the same time quite distinct. This last caught Ashley's attention and he lifted it out.

"This is marvelous!" he breathed in awe. "Positively unbelievable! At last the pieces of this ancient mystery begin to fit together!"

"I could see the gears of your brain turning furiously as you eyed the outside of the box," chuckled Logan. "Can you regale us with your expertise? But please, we are mere laymen. Keep it simple."

"Look at these engravings," he said, pointing to the exterior of the box and tracing his finger along the lines of the filigree. "I had a suspicion when I first saw it, but the reproduction is not of the best. You see here"—he pointed with his finger—"you can tell that the box itself has been plated with what we see. If we could see the original underneath, I'm certain the engravings would be much more detailed. Nevertheless, you can see here what looks like a *chi-rho* monogram. The greek letters *chi* and *rho* are known as the Chrisma, a symbol used by early Christians in the period of about the fourth to the sixth centuries. This box is very similar, almost a replica, of one I've seen at the Scottish Museum of Antiquities. It would not surprise me to learn they had the same origin. That one is the Monymusk Reliquary in which King Kenneth MacAlpin carried the personal belongings—perhaps even the remains—of St. Columba from Iona to Dunkeld."

"The patron saint of Scotland," said Hilary.

"I believe that title more officially belongs to St. Andrew," said Ashley. "But Columba was one of the major forces in bringing Christianity to Scotland and is certainly revered to this day."

"Ashley," said Logan, "are you saying this box is somehow linked to the spread of Christianity through early Scotland?"

"An old wine cellar in an Argentine villa is hardly the place to make such pronouncements," said Ashley. "But I would stake a heavy possibility on it. The items inside are quite indicative. This"—he held out the odd-looking item—"looks like the top from a pastoral staff. And some of this other silverwork could be vestments from some early church. I don't know about the sword hilts. They look of Pictish make. The rest, these smaller items, could be nothing more than some family's belongings, even a child's treasures. I don't know. It will take a great deal of time for someone more knowledgeable in these matters than I to go through and analyze each one. But I cannot help but be reminded of the discovery beneath the floor of the little church on St. Ninian's Isle in, let's see, when was it?"

"In 1958, I believe," said Logan.

"That's right. Well, some of this bears a striking resemblance to that find at St. Ninian's. So I would assume Pictish origins for much of it, probably in connection with some early monastery or Christian hermitage, perhaps along the northern coast there, or even upon what were once Stonewycke lands."

"What you said about the engravings . . . and the connection to the Picts—" Hilary's voice was breathless with excitement. "Do you mean it's possible this box could date from as early as the fifth or sixth century?"

Ashley nodded. "I would say no later than the eighth. Perhaps earlier."

"It's older than any of us ever thought," said Allison.

"Were there any old churches, monasteries, or the like, along the coast, say between Lossiemouth and Fraserburgh?'' asked Ashley.

"There are stories of a St. Aiden," replied Allison, "who traveled in northern Scotland, a disciple of Columba who was sent out from Iona to establish churches. Nothing much is known of him. But as a child I remember hearing tales of ruins someplace. Whether it was a monastery or church of some kind, I don't know. Nothing had ever been seen. But even Ramsey Head and the Old Rossachs Kyle were mentioned in connection with it."

"Hmm," reflected Ashley. "Churches in those days were often repositories for treasures of many kinds. But then that made them all the more subject to Viking raids. That could explain how the box found its way inland—to escape, perhaps, an impending Viking attack that would have come from the sea, and for which there would have been at least some advance warning. It will take a great deal more research, not to mention excavation, to get to the bottom of the history of this reliquary."

"If the casket in the museum," Hilary asked, "once held the remains of Columba, could this have been put to a similar use? Perhaps for a different saint?"

"It's very possible," answered Ashley. "That could explain the sword hilts. In days long ago such relics as these, especially relics with any religious significance, were held in great esteem. There were those who even attributed supernatural powers to them. Often they were carried into battle as a talisman. If it contained a possession of a particularly favored saint, all the better. Some were indeed reported to carry bones or ashes of saints long after their death. I can't wait to get home. There I'll be able to compare both the box and the contents with known museum pieces, and perhaps even to ancient descriptions we have of relics that have been lost."

"Isn't it wonderful," said Allison, "that this box, this so-called 'treasure,' should be linked to the very roots of Christianity in Scotland? A box full of gold and jewels could hardly be so meaningful!"

As they spoke, Ashley had been slowly rubbing his hand over the engraved exterior of the reliquary.

"Hullo!" he exclaimed all of a sudden, "what's this!"

He bent down, then lifted up one end of the box.

"Logan," he said, "hold that up there for a minute, would you?"

Logan complied.

With his finger Ashley continued to probe at one of the corners. "There seems to be a small edge of the plating material peeling away," he said; "just a tiny little piece. The corners seemed to have borne the worst of the wear and tear, although I'm simply amazed at how well the thing has weathered."

He continued to pick at the bit of torn metal, then bent close and squinted in the dim light. Finally he stood back up and let out a long sigh.

"You can set it down now, Logan," he said. "Well, Allison," he went on, a broad smile spreading across his face, "you may have spoken more prophetically than you realized just now."

"Why . . . what did I say?"

"Bend down there . . . look at that corner."

Allison did so. Hilary and Logan bent down as well.

"Why, it looks like—!" exclaimed Logan.

Allison was still looking intently. "It's a different color underneath," she said slowly. "Bright, yellowish."

Suddenly the truth dawned on her. She spun around. "Ashley! You don't mean—?"

He nodded. "That's right," he said. "Gold!"

They all looked at one another, stunned.

"The whole box!" asked Hilary in disbelief.

"I would guess," Ashley replied, "that would account for the weight."

"What would it be worth?" asked Allison.

"Oh, not much, really—as pure gold, that is. Let's see, sixty, maybe seventy pounds . . . perhaps a thousand ounces . . . that's—I don't know, three, maybe three-hundred-fifty thousand pounds. A lot of money, to be sure, but nothing alongside the priceless historical value of a find such as this. One of the original owners of the box no doubt had it plated in order to cover the gold and hide its wealth."

"I wonder if Channing knew?"

"I doubt it," said Logan. "He would have melted it down long ago."

"I wonder who made it . . . and why?" sighed Hilary, "and how it came to rest under the Braenock stones?"

"There is probably much we will never know about the history of this remarkable container," sighed Ashley. "But it makes one hungry to travel back in time . . . to explore that early era, and try to discover where things like this had their roots."

"We always thought," said Allison, "that the treasure belonged to the Pict village that had been wiped out in the eighth or ninth century—or at least so the old stories go."

"It probably was hidden at that time."

"It is possible the beginnings of its history go back much further, even two or three hundred years earlier than that! Oh, the journeys it must have taken in that time, the hands that must have held it, the stories it could tell about our country's beginnings, maybe even Stonewycke's beginnings! All before it came to be buried for its long rest under the stones of Braenock Ridge. My mind simply reels!" exclaimed Allison. "Look at all its travels in the mere speck of time since Maggie's days!"

"George Falkirk, wasn't it," said Logan, "who first dug it up?"

"With his henchman Martin Forbes," Allison replied. "But both men were cut out of the same cloth as Channing, became greedy, and that was their undoing. I wonder if either of them discovered about the gold underneath the thin layer of plating? In the end, Forbes killed Falkirk, and then he himself met his end falling from the rocky cliffs of Ramsey Head."

"All the intrigue surrounding that murder nearly destroyed Lady Margaret and Lord Ian," said Hilary, remembering clearly what she had read in Joanna's journal.

"Then dear old Digory, after he and young Maggie somehow were able to lug this thing out of the ground and load it on the back of a horse and bring it to the garden at the estate—"

"Maggie told me once," broke in Allison, "in one of her rare moments of talking about the treasure—I'd completely forgotten this until now!— that they took out all the contents and put them in two bags, thinking to more evenly distribute the weight. But then the box weighed just as much empty as it did full."

"It's a wonder they managed it!" remarked Ashley. "What were you saying, Logan?"

"I had just been thinking of Digory's loyalty to the family he loved, how, thinking to spare them, he dug it up from the garden where he and Maggie had hidden it and then buried it again in a place no one knew."

"Where was that?" asked Ashley.

"At the top of Ramsey Head," answered Logan. "I'll not soon forget that! I too was afflicted with the disease—the desire for the kind of fulfillment I mistakenly thought riches would bring."

"There were no riches of that kind here anyway!"

"But your quest, however misguided, did bring you to God," said Allison. Then she added with a smile. "And to me." She paused, recalling the special time when she and Logan had met. "All this makes me think that perhaps our concept of this treasure has been incomplete all along. Digory meant well when he tried to hide it. But I think we're mistaken when we attribute intrinsic evil to the treasure itself.

"From its very beginnings it was intended for some good—no doubt to glorify God, and even draw a heathen nation closer to His Son. What a wonderful heritage that is! No wonder it refused to stay hidden—from its burial on Braenock, to the garden, to Ramsey Head, even to the bottom of the sea where Channing somehow located it, and finally to an old unused dungeon of a wine cellar in Argentina! But always it comes back to light, just like the light of God's truth! Though it has been connected with violence, corruption, and greed, it has also acted as a catalyst to lead people to the Lord."

They all stood silent for some time, reflecting on Allison's words. Each one, in his or her own way, felt as if he had personally traveled with the box over its many miles and centuries of journeys. Within each of the four hearts beat the elation of fulfillment and completion, as if the quest of the treasure for a peaceful and final resting place was nearly at hand.

But they could tarry no more, at least for the moment, reflecting on the still-to-be-revealed mysteries of the antiquities before them or the current implications of their find. They were trapped in an armed villa, whose master was now dead, but who still wielded power over his servants.

It was time to think about getting out.

Logan and Ashley re-secured the lid and bar to the box.

"I think we should put it back into the barrel," suggested Logan. "As heavy and bulky as that will be, it's our only chance of getting it out of here."

"You're probably right. You and I ought to be able to handle it."

"But I'm afraid, once we get out there in the vicinity of the guards," answered Logan, "we're going to have to have Hilary's assistance with the barrel, even though the weight could be a problem."

"I don't mind," said Hilary.

"And me?" Ashley shot a puzzled glance at Logan.

"I have something else in mind for you, my friend."

"How will we get it past the guards?" asked Allison.

"That's the plan," said Logan. "Ashley, you will have to use your pistol again and once more don the role you earlier pulled off with such finesse."

Ashley took the .38 from his pocket and looked down at it distastefully. "I will be glad to return this to the Inspector," he said.

"Soon enough," said Logan sympathetically. "In the meantime, we will become your prisoners again. Oh yes, and you'll need that charming moustache too."

Ashley pasted the thin moustache back in place.

"You make a better viscount than Emil!" laughed Hilary.

"Ah, Fraulein! At your service!" Ashley clicked his heels and flashed a toothy grin.

"Are we ready then?" asked Logan.

The underground passages seemed much quieter. Perhaps it was from the knowledge that Channing's body now lay in its temporary repose—or the awareness that unexpected danger might lie around any corner. Logan had always known that getting into Channing's fortress would be far easier than getting out again.

In ten minutes they had reached the narrow flight of stairs which would take them back out into the sunlight. Here Logan paused.

"As soon as we get it to the top," he said, "you and I are going to have to manage the wine cask, Hilary. Ashley, you cover us from the rear. Remember, the secret to a good con is confidence. That's what the word means. So walk steadily, and you especially, Ashley, have to look as if you know what you're about. Don't let any of the servants or guards cow you. You're about Channing's business, which is to take us out the main gate, and you're unconcerned about any of them.''

"Got it.''

"I suggest that instead of going back into the house itself, we just move through the compound, around the house, and to the gate. The way will be more direct, and from what I've seen, we'll run into fewer people. I'll lead, but, Ashley, you've got to make it look as though you're calling the shots.''

Logan and Ashley carried the bulky wine cask up the stairs and set it down at the door.

"Okay . . . places, everyone," said Logan. "Here we go!''

He and Hilary hoisted up the barrel. Logan shoved the door with his foot, and into the compound they slowly walked. At first the sun was blinding, but not a soul was to be seen as they made their way slowly along. Outside the kitchen a few servants came and went, but beyond an initial glance or two, seemed to pay little attention to the unusual entourage. No cars were to be seen within the precincts of the house itself, thus their most likely means of escape would be Ashley's rented automobile, which still sat where he had parked it at the front gate.

At the door to the servants' quarters, Logan spotted one of the Argentines who had been with Channing a time or two. The man eyed them carefully as they passed, said nothing, but seemed to stare with particular interest at Ashley's gun. As they approached, Ashley gave Allison an irritated shove with his left hand for good measure. She winced in apparent pain, carrying out her share of the ruse to annoyed perfection, and stumbled forward.

As they went, something began to nag at the back of Logan's brain, a feeling he couldn't pinpoint as if something important had been forgotten, overlooked. But as often as he replayed the events of the last two hours over in his mind, he could fix upon nothing.

They were by now approaching the outside corner where the two wings of the villa's L-shape joined. Once around it, they would be only some seventy-five feet from the gate, and in plain view of Ashley's car. Hilary's arms were tiring, but she bravely held on, the only sign of her fatigue being large beads of perspiration on her forehead.

Logan was fixing in his mind what to say to the guards at the gate when, just as they rounded the corner, a figure came striding briskly toward them. His appearance was so unexpected that the four escapees were brought up short. All of a sudden Logan was brought face-to-face with the unknown loose end he had forgotten to reckon with in his escape plan.

"Well, Gunther," said Logan calmly, "I've been wondering where you had gone to.''

Taken just as much by surprise as they, Gunther was quick to size up the situation. Logan, of course, he knew immediately. The women he didn't recognize, though the older one appeared vaguely familiar from long ago in his past. But it was Ashley who garnered his longest scrutiny. He was familiar . . . but there was something out of place . . . the moustache—of course! It was none other than the Oxford professor in some ridiculous disguise. Why would he be holding a gun on these people?

"It looks as if I've returned none too soon," replied Gunther. "What are you up to, Macintyre?"

"He's up to nothing!" barked Ashley, feigning the best German accent he could muster. "Now out of the way, mein Herr. I've orders from Herr Channing to get these people out of here!"

"What are you talking about?" replied Gunther, unimpressed. "You're no more German than I am English!"

"I am the Viscount von Burchardt!" replied Ashley. "No doubt you've heard Herr Channing speak—"

"You are no such thing!" growled Gunther. "I know perfectly well who you are! Do you think my memory's that short? What kind of idiot do you take me for?"

"Nevertheless, I *do* have the gun," said Ashley, now in his own voice.

"Channing is dead, Gunther," said Logan. "My companions and I feel it would not be appropriate for us to continue our visit any longer. We are leaving, and I hope you will—if not for old times' sake, then for prudence on your own part—stand aside and let us go calmly."

"What do you mean, Channing is dead? Did you kill him? I didn't think you had it—"

"He died because his time had come, Gunther. His own hate had weakened him beyond recovery. Whether he died still clutching it, or having released it to his Maker, I do not know. You will find his body in the wine cellar. Now, if you will step aside—"

"You are jesting!" scoffed Gunther. "You do not think I will let you walk right out of here!"

"Ashley," said Logan, "if you will be so kind."

Ashley waved his gun in Gunther's direction.

"You are fools if you think you can get out of here alive! This place is surrounded by a dozen armed guards. Their orders are to protect Channing. If they believe he has been compromised, even if I tried to help you, nothing would stop them from doing their duty. You're a dead man, Macintyre!"

"We will take our chances," replied Logan. "We'll worry about them when the time comes. But remember, for now we have the gun on *you*."

Gunther laughed, in that dry, hard sound which contained no hint of joy or humor at all, only mockery.

"You will never shoot me, Professor—or whatever you are!" he said, eyeing Ashley disdainfully. "I let you get away with it before because I was curious about what you had to say. But I read it in your eyes then, and I see it now—you haven't got what it takes to shoot a man!"

As Gunther spoke, Logan and Hilary set down the cask. Logan stepped up near Ashley and relieved him of his weapon. Though everything Gunther had just said of Ashley was equally true of Logan, perhaps *L'Escroc* might call upon one more supreme bluff, for old times' sake, to gain freedom for his family.

Logan took the pistol firmly in his hand. Unlike Ashley, he knew well enough how to handle such a weapon. Moreover, the .38 *looked* secure in his grip, and Logan possessed half a lifetime's practice in making his eyes convey a steady and unblinking confidence. Now he would have to call upon that old experience once again.

"You are right, Gunther," he said. "Ashley is too intelligent and sensitive to harm another human being. But I am an old street punk who grew up with crime. I may have reformed in my latter days. But down inside that impertinent swindler is still part of me. Look into *my* eyes, Gunther, and you will know that I am not bluffing now. Do not forget, my old wartime colleague, that I killed back then and am no stranger to danger."

He paused and stared deeply into Gunther's eyes, holding them in his grip. His words had been measured and forceful. At length he went on, in a low tone that contained not a thread of detectable pretense.

"I *will* use this if it comes to that," he said. "I hope it does not. I could never live with having to kill again. But here are my wife and my daughter and my friend. And make no mistake, Gunther . . . *I will not see them harmed*!"

Several agonizing seconds passed. Logan knew Gunther was mentally assessing all the possibilities, not the least of which concerned the likelihood that, for all his bravado, Logan was indeed bluffing. But this had to be balanced against thoughts for his own safety. Gunther well knew all von Graff's illuminating stories about Logan's stint in Paris. The General used to laugh and say his friend Trinity, or MacVey, or whoever he was, could talk a charging rhinoceros into lying down for a nap.

But in matters of familial loyalty and protection, you could never tell what a man might be driven to do. He continued unflinchingly to hold Logan's steady gaze. There was an edge to the man's voice that hinted at the truth. These women *were* his wife and daughter, as he said, and even the mildest man was known to be able to kill to protect those he loved. Even if it had been thirty years, Logan still knew his business, still knew how to survive.

At last Gunther spoke. "This was Channing's battle anyway," he said. "I certainly have no intention of getting myself killed for it."

"Then if you will be so kind as to accompany us," said Logan, taking Gunther's arm, "we will be on our way."

With Allison now free to assist Hilary with one end, Ashley lifted the other end of the cask, and they continued slowly on toward the gate.

"I am curious about one thing," said Gunther as they walked. "You obviously planned this thing from the beginning. Planting the phony newspaper article, and the phony professor—"

"I'm actually quite a real professor," interjected Ashley.

"I thought you played the part too well," said Gunther. "But, Macintyre, did you know Channing would be here?"

"Yes," answered Logan. "We discovered his daughter's masquerade, and also learned of his identity as the General, and the connection to Trans Global Enterprises."

"So you came to Buenos Aires knowing full well what you were walking into?"

"In a manner of speaking. But I was not without people keeping an eye on me. My daughter here"—Logan indicated Hilary with his free hand "—planted herself in the hotel across the street. I signaled her with the curtains in my room before leaving with you—"

"And I had the back of your hotel being watched," put in Hilary, "and my own car parked so I could keep an eye on both hotels and the alley."

"So you followed us here, and that's how you all learned the whereabouts of the villa," said Gunther, with reluctant admiration. "I've got to hand it to you, Macintyre. You covered yourself rather well!"

"From you, Gunther, I take that as high praise."

"Just one more question. How did you connect it all in the first place? The General's identity has been safe for all these years. How did *you* find out it was Channing?"

"Elementary, Gunther," smiled Logan. "A mutual friend of ours left me a thirty-year-old clue."

"I don't follow you."

"A name, Gunther. A single name, still listed on the roster of TGE corporate executives—a name known to no one but von Graff and myself, a name I had used as a cover in France—one Monsieur Dansette. Once I saw that name, I knew there had to be some connection with von Graff. But there is one thing that still puzzles *me*. And that is—why would von Graff resurrect that name when there was always a remote possibility I might one day stumble upon it?"

"That cagey old rascal!" said Gunther, not without the hint of genuine affection in his voice. Then he glanced up at Logan. "You really have no idea, Macintyre?" he asked.

"None at all."

Gunther did not speak for a moment, obviously caught in his memories of his old mentor. When at last he opened his mouth, his words were nonetheless forceful that they fell so unexpectedly on Logan's ears.

"It was *you*, Macintyre," he finally said. "You always were to von Graff . . . almost like a son. He respected you . . . never forgot you."

"But . . ." said Logan incredulously, "but I was the enemy!"

"One thing you have to understand about von Graff," Gunther went on, "is that a part of him was never cut out for the military life. He could be ruthless, but there remained another side to him."

"Whatever became of him?"

"After the war, the General lost everything, including his own self-respect. Channing gave him a new identity and a position in the company. Eventually he even put him in the figurehead top position. But in the underground operation he was always known simply as *The General*. But von Graff was a man of some refinement. He prized his honor above all else. Though involved with Channing, his ways of doing business were foreign to von Graff, who always, I think, felt a bit guilty about what he did. The General even took to reading a Bible before he died. You were one of the few men he truly respected, Macintyre. He followed your career and many times swore he would go see you one day. Channing would probably have had him killed if he had tried. But when it became necessary to assume a new identity, which it did for all Germans in his position who hoped to get away clean, it's hardly surprising that he would have clung to a reminder of an honorable man he had once known."

Logan sighed deeply, remembering with fondness his old adversary.

"Then why is the name still on the roster?" asked Logan. "Didn't von Graff die in 1959?"

Gunther nodded. "By then the company was enormous—worldwide. It was worth millions. All the while Channing himself had remained completely hidden from public view, pulling strings behind the scenes. It made it easy for him to achieve his purposes when his name and background were nowhere to be found. Von Graff was an executive in the company, going by the name Dansette. But everyone in the shadow organization still just called him *The General*. It was a comfortable disguise, and by the late fifties all traces of any connection to Nazism were gone. When von Graff died, Channing slipped into this already-existing identity. The facade was so neatly in place, so Channing took on von Graff's identity as 'The General,' in his continued underground activities, thus keeping his own personality still obscured."

Gunther shook his head. "I imagine he kept the name Dansette on the TGE's roster, too, just for convenience, having no idea what it signified. Neither did I. Neither did anyone. A clue out of the past that perhaps helped von Graff recall those days before the war when he had been a man of honor, but which no one else knew anything about. I wouldn't doubt if he secretly hoped someday you would discover the name and destroy Channing's corrupt organization."

Gunther's uncharacteristic soliloquy stirred Logan deeply. He found it increasingly difficult to hold the gun on Gunther in light of such startling and personal revelations.

They were now entering the courtyard. Ashley's car was not far now.

"What will it be, Gunther?" said Logan. "Can I trust you to help us get through the gates?"

"Channing may be dead, but I have my own survival to think of. I can't let you get to Interpol with my name."

"You won't even help us for the sake of the memory of our mutual friend?"

"My own skin means more to me than sentimentalities, Macintyre!"

"I thought as much. I guess we'll have to take you along." Logan nudged Gunther forward. "I'm going to put this gun in my pocket. But it will still be aimed at your midsection. Let's go!"

They crossed the courtyard and reached Ashley's car without incident. The guards standing outside the main door nodded to Gunther but apparently saw nothing so unusual about the strange procession, led, as it appeared, by their well-known comrade.

Anxiously Ashley and the two women removed the box from the wine cask, careful to keep out of view as much as possible, and then loaded the reliquary into the trunk, while Logan prodded Gunther into the back seat, following after him immediately. Ashley climbed in behind the wheel, with Hilary and Allison crowding in next to him. He started the ignition and wheeled into motion.

Ashley drove the remainder of the way across the courtyard, pulling up at the main gate where one of the two guards present waved him to a stop.

"Buenos dias, señor Gunther," he said, peering in. "You are off again so soon?"

Gunther hesitated momentarily, then felt an unseen jab into his ribs.

"Sí . . . sí, Miguel," he replied. "I am escorting some guests into the village. I will be back soon."

Miguel waved Ashley on, and the car passed through the open gates. The instant they had rounded a slight curve in the road and were out of sight, Ashley pressed down the accelerator. Audible sighs could be heard throughout the cramped automobile.

Some two or three miles from the villa, Logan asked Ashley to stop.

"What now?" asked Gunther with some concern in his voice.

"It is time for you to get out," answered Logan. "You have cooperated with us, but I want no further danger to my wife and daughter. I think it is time for us to part ways."

"You are letting me go?"

"Yes," said Logan. "But I know the location of the villa, and enough about Channing's organization to bring it down. I doubt you will be able to remain free for long."

"I will do my best!" said Gunther, with a look that might have been interpreted as a faint smile. Whether a smile of camaraderie or one which merely indicated pleasure that this chump of a do-gooder still had too much heart left for his own good, Logan could not tell. The German climbed out of the car and began walking along the dirt road. Then suddenly he turned back.

"Macintyre," he said, his cold, impassive voice not softening, but his words revealing more than his eyes would let on, "you will see to it that Channing gets a proper burial?"

"Yes, Gunther, I will do that."

"And his personal effects taken to his daughter?"

Logan nodded. "Gunther, I do believe you have a heart, after all!"

Gunther laughed dryly. "A moment of weakness. The first and last you will ever see!" Then he strode away.

Again Ashley pressed on the accelerator and they sped away toward Buenos Aires, where both Interpol and the local authorities were immediately notified.

Hilary drank in the lovely sounds around her—clicking typewriters, ringing phones, the buzz of many voices in a half-dozen impromptu conversations around the room. It did indeed feel good to be back in her office at the hub of the activity she so loved.

But Hilary knew she was not the same person she had been when she left this place so many weeks ago. Much had changed . . . *everything* had changed! Her horizons, both internal and external, had broadened considerably. She had grown to love another world outside the bustle of London.

"I am different," she said to herself. "But I am the same person, just as Ashley said it would be."

She looked down at her IBM and, suddenly inspired, began working the keys. She had been wondering all day what she would write for this editorial. It had to be special, for it would be somewhat of a farewell. For a while, at least.

Something about values . . . change . . . the deeper meaning of life. That's what she wanted to write about. A bit ambitious, perhaps. But after what she had been through, she had to try touching a meaningful chord. She must just focus it down, concentrate on one particular element in all that had come her way.

Yes, it was time for a leave of absence. As much as she loved the magazine, she was looking forward to the opportunity of returning to Scotland to get better acquainted with her new family and their beloved Port Strathy—and Stonewycke. It would be a time to begin a new phase in her life. She smiled when she thought of all that would be happening in the next few months. As much as the rest of it, she was eagerly anticipating beginning to organize the material in the *Stonewycke Journal* in hopes of writing a more orderly chronicle of her family's history. Would six months' leave be enough?

Six months . . . eight months . . . even a year. She would stay in touch. The magazine was still very much a part of her life. And it would be in Murry's capable hands during her sabbatical. As interim editor, he would blossom from a good journalist into a fine manager and administrator, directions she had been wanting to take him for some time. And the new staff writer and columnist-at-large she had hired to fill in Murry's vacancy would no doubt make life at the *Review* interesting. It had taken some smooth salesmanship on Hilary's part, but she was delighted when Suzanne had finally agreed to try journalism as a change from poetry.

"It's only temporary," she had insisted.

"Agreed," consented Hilary with a laugh. "But you'll love it—believe me! Now you'll have an audience to try out those outlandish ideas of yours on!"

"Who knows?" Suzanne said. "A taste of the hard-boiled world might inject new life into my prose *and* my poetry."

The romantic in Hilary could hardly refrain from smiling inside when she noted the special energy flowing between her two friends from the start. "Hmm," Hilary said to herself, "you never can tell what's going to happen!"

She came to the end of the page, removed it from the carriage, and was just slipping in a fresh sheet of white paper when Betty knocked on her door.

"This package just came," she said as she entered. She laid it on Hilary's desk, then left.

Hilary remembered the last time a strange package had come to the office. It had changed her life.

She wondered what this one could contain. The return address was unfamiliar, but it had originated in London. It was not large, perhaps about the size of a small shoe box. She tore off the brown paper and lifted the lid, then pulled out the brief note that lay inside.

"These were among the items confiscated from the Villa del Heimat. The police have no further use for them, and we were told to forward them to you."

It was signed, Chief Inspector Rollins.

Hilary examined the items in the box—a few assorted mementos, some photos. Not much really, when you considered they represented nearly a century of a man's life. A man worth millions, who had controlled financial empires, yet this was the only heritage to be left behind from that life of greed and ambition.

Jason Channing had not built his life with the bricks that lasted beyond death. No gold nor silver nor precious stones here—only wood, hay, and stubble. A business crumbling beneath the revelation of its sordid foundation, a criminal organization now breaking to pieces from the onslaught of the law. The only guests to attend his funeral beyond Logan, Allison, and Hilary—his lifetime adversaries—were a few locals, and a handful of men who had worked for him. Not a single person he could have called a friend.

In the end, he had lived for nothing. And now he had nothing but this small box to pass on to his daughter, who was herself facing a prison sentence. She probably did not even have the memory of his fatherly love. *Not much of a legacy,* Hilary thought.

She sighed sadly, glancing at her watch. She would just have time to stop by Holloway Prison, where Jo was awaiting trial. Then she had to pick up her mother in Whitechapel and catch her train.

Hilary recalled her adoptive mother's reaction to the astounding news of the location of Hilary's parents. The dear woman was simply marvelous, thrilled that the once-orphaned child could now enjoy *two* families!

"But, dear me!" Mrs. Edwards had exclaimed, "what a family! I'll want a new dress to meet them!"

Hilary laughed. "I think we'll *both* need new dresses, Mum!"

Yes . . . her life was changing. But the things that mattered most were still constant, and would always be so. When *she* died, she knew that the sum total of her life would mean more than this handful of mementos left behind by a wealthy man. God had blessed her beyond all the earthly riches a person could imagine—blessed her with love, with family and friends, and with a future of eternal meaning.

With these thoughts fresh in her mind, her fingers began again sailing over the keys. In fifteen minutes the editorial was finished. She re-read it, satisfied, then slipped the first page back into the typewriter and typed in the title she had omitted earlier: "A Lonely Shoe Box."

Hilary rose, gathered up her things, and walked to the door. There she paused and took one last look behind her.

"I'll be back soon," she murmured, then opened the door.

The morning would dawn bright and fair.

It was too much to expect, in this land of contrasts with its inclement and unpredictable weather, that on *this* special day the sun would shine.

But spring had come to Stonewycke, and this day in early May looked as though it would display all its glory. The song of the wren in the budding trees could be heard in the valley. The heather on the hills was green with new life, preparing itself for the burst of purple glory four months distant. The gentle breeze was clean, with just a touch of the tangy salt from the sea and the chill from across the waters to give assurance that this was, indeed, the far north of Scotland.

Hilary had risen early. It was only natural that she would be flooded with a sea of sleep-inhibiting emotions and thoughts. On the contrary, however, she had slept soundly, and when at five she suddenly found herself wide awake, it was with the peculiar sense of having been roused for some purpose. She dressed quickly and slipped quietly out; for whatever compulsion was upon her, she knew it was calling her outside, into the freshness of the northern morning, to be alone.

Notwithstanding that in two or three hours the sun would be bright and high, the clean air was bitingly cold and Hilary bundled herself well. She walked first to the old garden and sat awhile on the stone bench in mingled reflection and prayer.

The treasure once was here, she thought. Buried in this very spot by Maggie and Digory, though no one ever knew it. Hidden, yet alive, not decaying, nurturing the essential life within, like a seed under the ground, awaiting the moment when its life would again blossom with the coming of dawn.

How could any of the hands that had possessed, or buried, or sought, or dreamed about, or moved, or thirsted after the treasure know the fullness of what it represented, both to the history of this land and to the heritage of this region?

Slowly Hilary rose. She walked out of the garden and toward the footbridge that led across the stream and south onto the moorland which gave way in the distance to Braenock Ridge. The dawn was advancing now, and she could see her way clearly.

The treasure was on her mind. She was full of the very essence of it, her keen mind probing, as if to discover some hidden significance they had all overlooked in the five months since its discovery.

Slowly she walked, in no particular direction, pausing every now and then to note the progress of the rising sun behind Strathy summit to the east. Mingled in her reflections were images and faces and scenes from Joanna's journal. She had set up a temporary office on the fourth floor of the castle, where on a clear day she might look out over the treetops to behold the valley and even the sea in the distance. There she had been working assiduously on . . . she didn't even know what to call it! Since first reading it, some inner compulsion had said to her that the story of this family—*her* family now!—had to be told. Not in dry, statistical numbers and dates, births and deaths, but as a "story"—a living, breathing tale of *real* people, whose lives, all taken together, left a *living* and vital legacy—not only to their own descendants but to God's people everywhere.

But there was so much to tell! So *many* people were an intrinsic part of the legacy, some for good, others for ill: James, Anson, Atlanta, Talmud, Andrew, Thomas, Robert . . . so many stories . . . so many lives. And then of course Maggie, Ian, and Joanna, and even Eleanor's part, unknown to her . . . Alec . . . her own parents, Allison and Logan.

Oh, thought Hilary, *it is so huge! It's a legacy that* cannot *be told!* In despair she had risen dozens of times from her typewriter in the last few months, vowing to cease her futile effort of attempting to put the story down on paper.

Yet something always brought her back, just as something had called her out on this chilly morning. *He* would not let her rest. It was, after all, not *her* story, not Joanna's story, not Maggie's story. It was *His* story! It was a legacy He had been building into the lives of men and women since the creation of His world, a legacy He had built into the very nature of the ongoing family structure—father passing his heritage on to his son, who passed it on to his own son, and on, and on throughout time; mother giving life to daughter, who in turn gave life to granddaughter, and down through the years, from generation to generation . . . the life of God passing from parent to child, spreading out, deepening, extending itself in wider and wider circles, transforming the world with the news and the impact of God's love and mighty character.

What a heritage! thought Hilary. *The people of God passing on His life throughout the world! And what a family I am part of . . . a family in which that life can be witnessed again and again, blossoming in fullness in one generation, spreading out, influencing many lives, perhaps being lost sight of for a season, then re-surfacing to grow and deepen again. Thank you, Lord, for the faithfulness of my own forebears whose lives and whose prayers for their posterity are so responsible for implanting the seeds of your life into me. Thank you, Lord, for those seeds of faith that never die!*

"It's just like the treasure," Hilary pondered. "Hidden . . . yet always alive, waiting to be rediscovered by every successive generation. The life of God hidden within the human heart—implanted in many cases by prayers and faithful obedience of a righteous ancestry—awaiting in every new generation the discovery by each individual soul whom God, in His timing and in His own unique way, calls into relationship with Him."

Hilary sighed. The treasure . . . the individuals she was coming to know out of her own descent. God had indeed bestowed upon her a rich legacy!

She had been so deep in thought that she had been paying little attention to the direction of her steps. She glanced up. In the distance a figure was approaching.

Allison, too, had risen a great while before day. The same compulsion had fallen upon her, driving her from her bed. She, too, had needed on this day to be alone with her Lord, the God of her ancestors.

She had long ago made peace with God in the quietness of her heart. And she had made peace with the circumstances, painful though they were, of her life. Out of necessity she had neither thought nor prayed much during the years of her middle age about the passing of life on to future generations. She had grown to accept her lot as a mother without a child to build her life into.

Now suddenly all was changed. Now she found herself standing, as had those who preceded her, as representative of the elder generation of Stonewycke women, to whom had been entrusted the passage of the legacy left to her by the likes of Atlanta, Maggie, and her own mother. Now it was *hers* to transmit to *her* daughter—that it might continue beyond her present life.

A formidable responsibility . . . an awe-inspiring blessing!

Like her daughter, Allison had found herself mingling thoughts and prayers concerning the recently discovered treasure with those about her ancestry. She, too, had been walking now for about an hour, though she had left through the front gate and wandered in a large circle to the point where she saw Hilary walking in her direction. She waved, and picked up her pace. How fitting, she thought, that we should meet out here on this, Hilary's wedding day—alone, just the two of us. This is, after all, the traditional day when the hearts of mothers and daughters are often drawn closer than at any other time.

As she walked toward her daughter, she looked upon the face that was smiling back to her in greeting. The sun had just risen, and from behind Hilary now sent its bright morning rays radiating through her amber hair. Around her head a glow encircled her face, as if the light were coming from the auburn locks themselves.

"What a beauty!" murmured Allison to herself. "My own daughter—and so lovely! What a blessing she is, Lord. Thank you! She is more to me than any treasure could ever be! *She* is a treasure!"

With the revelation, suddenly Allison caught her breath in a short, involuntary gasp. "Of course!" she exclaimed inaudibly. "That's it! That's why you wanted me out here, isn't it, Lord? You wanted to show me what it all meant!"

As her mother came forward, Hilary beheld anew the face she had so grown to love, radiant now, both with the morning sun and with a beaming smile of love. Hilary thought she would never tire of gazing upon that face, not only because there were so many years of loving it to be regained, but also because in that face seemed to be embodied the very essence of all the faces she could only imagine in the eye of her mind when reading the journal. But this—her mother's—was a living, dynamic, loving face, a countenance that reflected both the heart of a mother and the glory of God. All the others, whose faces she had not been able to know, lived on in this wondrous face she did know. And she even hoped, in some small measure, the face of her mother would live on . . . in her.

Now upon Allison's face she saw a great smile. Her mother was running toward her with open arms.

Suddenly into Hilary's heart broke a stunning truth which in an instant, in the single flash of a moment, unified all the thoughts she had had since arising on this most special of all days.

"Now I see, Lord!" she cried in her heart. "*This* is the treasure—not the box, not even the abstract heritage of Stonewycke! This is the legacy, the heritage of life passed on through the generations in this family. The box is only a symbol. The *true* gift, the *real* treasure is the life you have passed on—through Maggie to Joanna, and to my own dear mother Allison! And now you are passing on the treasure to me! The treasure is in that beautiful face of my mother!"

With tears streaming down her face, Hilary began to run forward, arms outstretched.

Thirty minutes later the two women approached the footbridge arm in arm. Their tears of joy and mutual discovery had by now mostly dried. The conversation just past, though unheard by any other, was one both mother and daughter would treasure the rest of their lives.

Now what promised to be a long and memorable day was upon them. There was much to be done.

Allison glanced around at the guests seated on folding chairs in Dorey's lovely rose garden.

In certain ways this gathering reminded her of Lady Joanna's funeral seven months ago. Many of the faces were the same. But today there was the crisp brightness of a warming spring day instead of the drizzle of late autumn. And today the eyes contained smiles which looked forward with anticipation, rather than tears which lamented the passing of an era. The past was behind, the future lay ahead—as it always would. The life which was in Stonewycke and its people continued to move forward.

Allison smiled at her friends and neighbors. They were here to celebrate with the family a grand and wondrous occasion. A lump rose in her throat when she thought that not so very long ago she had no hope of being in such an enviable position. Yet here she was today, the mother of the bride!

The very thought still sent a thrill through her body. Then she remembered that this bride had *two* mothers. Allison turned and smiled at Mrs. Edwards, and patted her hand affectionately.

Yes, it was a grand day—the day her new daughter would be married to a man of God's choosing. What a pair they made—the imperturbable, traditionalist professor, and the progressive, firebrand journalist. Yet their very differences complemented one another.

Just three days ago the two of them had ridden on horseback to Braenock Ridge. Allison and Logan had driven the car out as far as possible and then had hiked the rest of the way in to meet the young couple. They had come upon them unannounced and had paused a short distance off, unable to resist a few moments silently observing their daughter and her husband-to-be as they poked about the ancient stones. Both were alive with curiosity, talking furiously—not only about the original site of the treasure they were exploring, but about all kinds of things.

It was obvious from watching them—in their blue jeans, boots, and loose-fitting shirts and jackets—that they were going to have fun together. Neither was satisfied to accept superficialities, either in relationships or—as they now displayed as they scrambled about the rocks and earth—in matters of science or history or knowledge. Where Ashley literally dug in the earth to discover the roots of man's historical being, Hilary dug into the motives of human hearts with her literary investigations. They were, in that sense, very much alike after all. Together they would have quite an impact on the world around them.

But at that moment the violins began the wedding march, and Allison's attention was diverted to the front of the colorful gathering. There stood an oaken altar, bordered by large wicker vases full of roses and lilies. Rev. Macaulay appeared from the door at the side of the house and took his place at the altar. Then followed Ashley's best man, a Chief Inspector from Scotland Yard by the name of Harry Arnstein. "Now *there* is a mismatched pair," mused Allison with a silent chuckle. Arnstein appeared the perfect stereotype of the policeman—thick, muscular, with a broad homely face and small drooping eyes. How he and the lanky scholar had ever become such close friends, Allison could not guess. And to her every inquiry they had been very evasive. But again Allison's musings were interrupted as a third man stepped from the side door.

Ashley Jameson, styled Lord Dearden, appeared every inch the noble gentleman now, no matter how much he might choose to downplay it. The black pin-striped tuxedo suited him well; he looked even taller than usual. Even on so momentous an occasion as his own wedding, he walked with more than a trace of his usual casual manner. Yet Allison could note at the same time a purposefulness in his step which revealed immediately there was more to this man than could readily be discerned on the surface. Hilary would have a lifetime to discover all the fine nuances of the personality and character of this man of God who would soon be her husband and the latest of Stonewycke's line of noble family heads.

Allison reflected on the men God had integrated into the family heritage over the past hundred years. In a birthright where women had dominated the line of descent, the husbands of their choosing had in recent times been men of great inner strength and stature. Each added new facets to the vitality of life that passed from generation to generation. Ashley, too, would make his mark upon this posterity, infusing his own genes and character and perspectives into the family bloodstream.

Suzanne Heywood, Hilary's maid of honor, then appeared, her long blond hair set off by a gown of pale blue silk, the wide neckline accented with frilly lace in tones of cream and blue.

All at once the violins struck the chord announcing the approach of the bride. A chill of pride coursed through Allison's heart as she stood. In the seats behind her, in addition to the many neighbors and townspeople, her sister May and brother Ian were on their feet too. Behind them were Hilary's friends from the magazine, Murry and Betty and several others. On the opposite side of the aisle, Ashley's colleagues from Oxford were rising now. Allison could not stop the tears streaming down her face, nor did she want to. Mrs. Edwards quietly slipped a hand through her arm. When Allison glanced toward her with a smile, she saw that the dear woman was weeping too.

At last came the processional. Many moist eyes turned to see father and daughter, arm linked through arm, begin down the aisle under the smiling blue sky.

How handsome Logan looked! Never on the floor of Parliament, thought Allison, could he have been so distinguished! Joy and fatherly pride beamed from his face; the twinkling eyes and broad smile inevitably reminded Allison of the Logan in his younger days. His smiling eyes had always been full of life. But today they were filled to overflowing with the exhilaration of having his daughter's arm through his, and knowing that their love, long lost, was now marvelously and mutually shared to the fullest. His grip on Hilary as they slowly moved forward with the music gave evidence that he might have difficulty giving her away when the moment came.

Logan turned his head slightly and smiled down at her, as if he could still not believe his good fortune in discovering his daughter. At last the tracks appeared down his cheeks. But no one thought the less of him, for his tears were caused by the joy and thanksgiving only a father can know on the day of his daughter's marriage.

Hilary herself came down the grassy walkway the perfect vision of the bride. Though her white gown was simple and understated, the overall effect was nonetheless elegant. The dress was silk, overlayed with lace. The flounced, over-the-shoulder peasant neckline beautifully set off Lady Margaret's gold locket. A ring of spring flowers, all gathered from Dorey's greenhouse or upon the hills themselves, adorned her amber hair, and a short veil hung down to her shoulders. In her hands she carried a matching bouquet.

Allison's lip trembled. Here indeed was the true treasure of Stonewycke! The box they had retrieved could never compare with the wealth that now graced Dorey's garden. It had been with them all along, in the heritage of God's presence abiding within this family, and this land, through the centuries, a pearl of great price now visible for the world to see. No doubt Maggie and Joanna were watching, sharing the fulfillment Allison felt.

Who could tell how far into the future this eternal treasure would extend? God's very life was waiting to be instilled within those yet unborn. The heritage would continue, as His Word promised, even to a thousand generations of those who loved Him and kept His commands.

Logan and Hilary reached the end of the aisle. The violins stopped, and Rev. Macauley stepped forward.

"Who giveth this woman to be married to this man?"

Logan cast a wistful yet loving glance down at his daughter, then smiled through the tears he was not ashamed to show.

In that moment Hilary realized anew that she had become part of something much larger than her limited vision could grasp. She had been swept into an ongoing stream of generations, every one of which had to "choose this day whom they would serve." None who had gone before had been perfect, yet each had left his or her own special mark upon the family. She could not help but wonder what would be *her* stamp of individuality, and Ashley's.

Hilary smiled up at Logan. Perhaps the minister's question was a more difficult one than for most fathers. After all, they had just found each other, and now he was being asked to give her away all over again! But Logan knew he would never lose the companionship which had begun to grow between them.

"Her mother and I!" came his buoyant answer. Then he leaned over and tenderly kissed her cheek.

"I love you, Father," Hilary whispered.

Logan gave her arm a final squeeze, then took her hand and offered it to Ashley.

Hilary and Ashley now moved side by side in front of the altar, and proceeded to pledge their lifelong commitment to one other, before family and friends, and the great cloud of witnesses watching from above.

The village down the hill was quiet and nearly empty. The shoreline stretching west and east was calm; the many vessels tied to their moorings in the harbor sat idle and unconcerned. Little work was being done today in the valley called Strathy. A great hush seemed to have descended upon the land. No soul was present on the foothills to the south, upon whose heather-covered slopes had ridden the progenitors of the heritage that was at this moment being rediscovered anew. In the distance, great silent white clouds hung over the Highlands. All life seemed to have paused in the region and come to rest upon the couple now dedicating themselves to each other before family, friends, and God.

The sun glowed upon Hilary and Ashley, and a gentle sea breeze wafted in from offshore, as if offering a loving benediction from their dear Father in heaven who had unfailingly led them on these converging paths where their lives and love were now joining as one. Also as a reminder that His Spirit would continue with them always.

Epilogue

Slowly the line of visitors wound its way along the corridor toward the East Wing of the great house.

"As I mentioned," the guide was saying, "this portion of the castle was for many years in disrepair. Only last spring were the renovations at last completed. Mr. Macintyre oversaw most of the repairs."

"I'm from America," said one of the visitors, "and I've toured quite a number of castles. It seems as if you never see anyone, even in these that are listed as still being family homes. *Does* somebody actually live here?"

"Oh yes," the guide replied, "both the Macintyres and the Jamesons make this their home, but only for part of the year."

"Macintyre—isn't he the politician?"

"That's right. Mr. Macintyre just began his twenty-fifth year as a Member of Parliament. However, his schedule does not permit him to be here more than two or three months out of the year. There has been some talk lately about his retirement, and if that does indeed come to pass, he has made it clear that he and Lady Macintyre will spend the remainder of their lives at Stonewycke. In the meantime, the details of administering the estate fall to Lord Ashley and Lady Hilary."

"It was my understanding that Lord and Lady Deardon also live in England?" asked a woman near the guide, her greater knowledge of the family betrayed by her Scottish accent.

"That is partially true. They too split their time between the north and south. Mrs. Jameson still functions as the chief editor of *The Berkshire Review*, of which she is now co-owner. And Lord Deardon remains a professor at Oxford. However, both of them have so arranged their duties and responsibilities that they are able to divide their time between their home in Watlington, the Deardon estate in Cornwall, and here at Stonewycke."

"How do they manage it?" asked an Englishman with a laugh.

"For one thing, they're both very efficient and productive," answered the guide. "But also they have greatly scaled back their commitment of time to the magazine and the university. As some of you may know, Hilary Jameson carries on a rather heavy writing schedule outside the magazine itself, and her husband is involved in several notable archaeological explorations, on some of which his wife accompanies him."

"When are they here?"

"They manage to be at Stonewycke usually about five or six months out of the year, administering the affairs of the estate, as well as coordinating their other projects. Most of their writing takes place here as well. Lord Deardon is a noted historical scholar whose research he documents completely after every project or expedition. For the two or three months out of the year when neither family can be here, usually falling between March and June, they graciously allow the National Trust of Scotland to conduct these tours of the Stonewycke castle. During this time, the grounds and castle itself are maintained by their factor and excellent staff. Now, if you'll all just step through this door here, we have arrived at the Heirloom Room, which is, I'm sure, what most of you have come to Stonewycke today to see."

The guide led the way, followed by the fifteen to twenty people in attendance. The moment they entered, an awed hush fell upon them.

In the center of the room, encased in glass and sitting on a massive bronze pedestal, stood the Stonewycke Reliquary, the most significant ancient historical find in Britain in twenty years, which had, three years earlier, dominated the historical journals, *The National Geographic*, and Hilary's *Review*, as well as gracing the cover of *Time* and being found worthy of a four-page story inside. Once its contents and the box itself had been thoroughly examined by a staff of experts, certain of the items had been given to the British Museum, others to the Scotland Museum of Antiquities, while others had been chosen to remain with the box.

The thin plating that had sheathed the box had been meticulously removed and kept intact as almost a shadow replica of the Reliquary; it was now on display in the Museum of Antiquities along with its sister, the Monymusk Reliquary. The removing of this sheathing had revealed a stunning and minutely complex engraved box, approximately one-eighth inch thick of solid gold, reinforced at all the corners with stronger metals. The box was concluded to be between twelve and fifteen hundred years old. Further research was even at that moment being conducted, a portion of it led by Ashley himself, into a more precise determination of the box's origins and early history.

The guide then began a brief history of what was known about the priceless gold Reliquary and how it had come to be discovered, as well as describing those items that had been found in it, which were displayed to the side. Slowly and quietly the visitors made their way up close to the box to view it while she spoke, then gradually spread out through the room to see the other Stonewycke mementos the family had chosen to let remain for public view.

Since the discovery of the Reliquary and the attendant publicity, both the Macintyre and Jameson families had been the object of far more notoriety than any of the four was comfortable with. Yet they recognized a certain amount of it as their civic and historical duty as persons in the public spotlight, realizing that time would ultimately diminish interest in the recently publicized find. They did, however, take the precaution to make sure that during their months at Stonewycke, no public tours or visits were allowed, thus preserving what privacy was possible to this nationally-known family.

By now Logan was recognized wherever he went, and even on the streets of Aberdeen or Edinburgh was constantly hounded for his autograph. His eyes still sparkled, his step still bounced, and he still bought his papers from the newsboys on the sidewalks of London.

Every day when she was at Stonewycke, Allison managed either to visit one of the women from the valley or have several up to the castle for tea. The stories told in fond tones by some of the farmers' wives began to sound very much like those told of Joanna twenty years earlier.

Suzanne still editorialized for the *Review*, though she had begun to give politics more serious consideration than when Hilary first mentioned it to her. She and Murry had hit it off immediately. Neither had seen anyone else socially for over two years.

Hilary had retold about two-thirds of Stonewycke's story from Joanna's journal and was trying to interest a publisher. She had been trying to talk Ashley into an excavation of the Braenock Ridge area as part of his research.

Logan and Donald Creary had together gone into the business of raising long-haired Highland bulls for export to Germany, and the venture had turned rather lucrative for both.

Ashley's closet obsession with mystery writing remained solely the family's secret. He managed to continue to write one new novel about every twelve to eighteen months, and the diverted royalties helped keep Stonewycke in the black for many years to come.

Let this be written for a future generation . . .

. . . He established the law in Israel, which he commanded our forefathers to teach their children, so the next generation would know them, even the children yet to be born, and they in turn would tell their children . . .

. . . Then would they put their trust in God and would not forget his deeds, but would keep his commands . . . through the generations to come of those who love him and keep his commands.

—Psalms 78:4–7